SAIGON EXPRESS

SAIGON EXPRESS

John Templeton Smith

POCKET
BOOKS

LONDON · SYDNEY · NEW YORK · TOKYO · SINGAPORE · TORONTO

First published by Pocket Books, 2000
An imprint of Simon & Schuster UK Ltd
A Viacom Company

Words by John Lennon and Paul McCartney taken from the song
'I'll Follow the Sun', by kind permission Sony/ATV Music Publishing.
And with the author's special thanks to Lee Hubner in Nashville,
and Eleonor Pitt, London.

1 3 5 7 9 10 8 6 4 2

Simon & Schuster UK Ltd
Africa House
64-78 Kingsway
London WC2B 6AH

Simon & Schuster Australia
Sydney

A CIP catalogue record for this book is available
from the British Library

ISBN 0-671-01604-0

Typeset in Melior by SX Composing DTP, Rayleigh, Essex
Printed and bound in Great Britain by
Omnia Books Ltd, Glasgow

For Michael & Mandy Collett

ACKNOWLEDGEMENTS

My grateful thanks to the following:

In the USA: Ray Carter for the specialized computer background. Dennis Hester for the technical gen on military tanker aircraft and systems. Doctors Gerald Walker, Terry Phelps, Peter Denman, and Viscount Tonypandy, who gave much encouragement and support during my tenure at Oklahoma City University.

In Russia: Captain Vladimir 'Sasha' Gritsouk for sharing a flight deck with me over the former Soviet Bloc, and for the tales of the real Russia.

In Ho Chi Minh City (Saigon), Vietnam: Steve Smith (British Consulate) for the 'local colour' over afternoon tea. Father Peter and Dr Francois Maurice for the invitation to the Maurice family mass at Notre Dame Cathedral and the stimulating afternoon conversation that further helped to set the scenes in this historic city. The management and staff of the Continental Hotel for taking care of me so very well.

And for those I cannot name: the 'banker' in Nassau – because, as he puts it, he sails too close to the Federal Reserve wind. The very charming, once-upon-a-time French spy – whom I have named 'Valerie Boulanger' in this story – for sharing his long-ago memories. The 'soldiers' in Vietnam, who gave me a behind-the-scenes look at the military bases – a deed that, in a still-repressive society, is enough to warrant the informants' disappearance one warm Saigon evening.

'There should be such days in every life.'
John Winter, a.k.a. 'Sibelius'

'He's two parts charlatan, one part black magician, and the rest unknown . . . the last part is what you should be worrying about, boyo.'
Edeyrn Owens, SIS

'Stolichnaya writes the script . . .'
Yuri the Yid

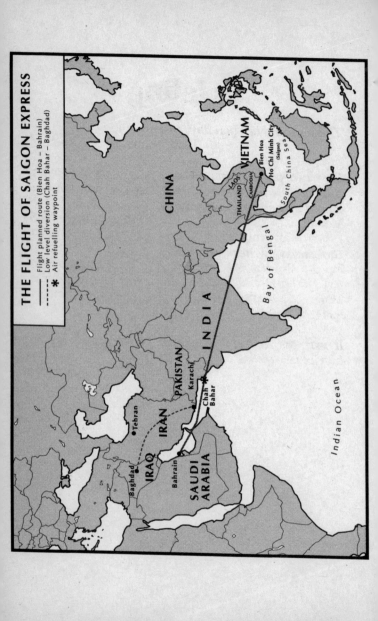

THE FLIGHT OF SAIGON EXPRESS

—— Flight planned route (Bien Hoa – Bahrain)
----- Low level diversion (Chah Bahar – Baghdad)
 * Air refuelling waypoint

CHINA

VIETNAM
Bien Hoa
Ho Chi Minh City
(Saigon)

LAOS
THAILAND
CAMBODIA

South China Sea

INDIA

Bay of Bengal

PAKISTAN
Karachi

Chah Bahar

Tehran

IRAN

Baghdad

IRAQ

Bahrain

SAUDI ARABIA

Indian Ocean

Briefing

Accidents follow a sequence of events. Sometimes the accident itself sets off a further chain reaction, much as it did following an aircraft crash in the Gulf of Mexico earlier that year.

The man (mistakenly) reported as killed in that accident might have remained 'dead' if it had not been for the Frenchman from Martinique and the eight million US dollars he was seeking to launder – and, more importantly perhaps, his meeting with a merchant banker in Nassau.

It was the first day of June, the beginning of the hurricane season . . .

PART ONE
Meeting Places

1

Mehdizadeh was a Lithuanian-born gypsy, or so he liked to tell the ladies over cocktails. It gave him an air of mystery. He was, in fact, only one-quarter gypsy, on his father's side. A big, olive-skinned man with thick black hair and a beard, he wore bespoke white suits every day of his life. He looked like an operatic lead. He wasn't. He was a banker, the president of the Ainsworth-Thorne Merchant Bank in Nassau. That he laundered black money on the side was something known only to a select few.

He was sitting at his desk, staring out of the window at the scarlet poinciana tree. Listening to the traffic sounds from the Nassau street, much as he did most days of the week. And today, for the first time in months, the distant rumbling of thunder. The smell of rain on the late afternoon air. Finally, having given a calculated number of seconds to the question put to him by the husky-voiced Frenchman, he leaned over

5

his notepad and wrote the number '25' on a sheet of paper that he slid across the desk.

Patrick van Fleteren glanced down at the note. 'You think I have not suffered enough already? All these years we have done business.' A disbelieving shake of the head.

'Risks, you understand.'

'More today than they were yesterday.'

'Quite.'

Van Fleteren lifted both hands, palms upward. Resignation. 'Agreed,' he sighed. 'Agreed.'

'And the amount was eight million dollars?' Mehdizadeh asked.

'Give or take the odd thousand.'

'And you wish to move it to the British Channel Islands . . . to Jersey?'

'Oui . . . yes.'

'And it would be originating from?'

'Ah . . .' Van Fleteren paused to take a cigarette from an engraved silver case. A small man, happy by nature. Slightly prominent eyes – exophthalmos caused by hyperthyroidism. Crumpled lightweight suit, beige in colour. Silk primrose-yellow shirt. Open-necked. A copper band visible on his right wrist. Talking hands. He offered the open cigarette case to Mehdizadeh, who shook his head but slid an onyx table lighter across the desk. 'The Caribbean . . . shall we say.' A few puffs on the cigarette. A thin strata-form smokescreen.

'Not a problem,' the banker said.

'I will need a bank mandate paper.'

Mehdizadeh opened his desk drawer and produced a buff-coloured form. 'How many signatories?' he asked, selecting a pencil from a leather-bound pen box.

'One . . . myself.'

The banker nodded and pencilled a cross by the first 'signatory' line. 'And the name of the company?'

'A new company yet to be formed: perhaps you could take care of this. The name would be Z-International Limited. "Zee" as in "zebra". If that name is not available then "X-International" or "Y-International" would be acceptable. A British Virgin Islands company, or similar.'

Offshore. Tax Free. Invisible.

The banker nodded and pencilled in the name of the company. 'What address would you like?'

'Perhaps care of your bank for the time being, if that is acceptable. And if you could write to me personally to confirm when the company has been officially formed.'

'Of course.' The banker filled in the bank address, checked over the document, and passed it across the desk for signature.

'What would be the route of the money to Jersey?'

'It is important?'

The cigarette prescribed complex smoke trails. 'Perhaps . . . perhaps not. My client, he may wish this information.'

'The Irish route.'

A reference to a little-known IRA funding operation set up with the help of the CIA. 'That is good . . . I think they are expert in these matters.'

'Better than the English,' Mehdizadeh observed. 'A long way behind the Swiss.'

'Everyone, I think, is a long way behind the Swiss.

Old money, new money, in that place it is all invisible, *n'est-ce pas?*' The accountant stubbed out the half-smoked cigarette in the crystal ashtray the banker had discreetly placed on the corner of the desk and rose from his chair.

'When do you wish to begin?'

'As soon as you have formed the new company.'

'And the money is presently with an individual or a company?' Mehdizadeh asked, escorting his visitor to the door of his office.

Van Fleteren took a business card from the breast pocket of his suit and passed it to the banker. 'This is the company: you will ignore the name of the director – one of my clerks, you understand . . . nominee shareholder.'

Mehdizadeh let out a low, rumbling belly laugh. 'They are good for something, at least, eh! Once again, thanks for the business, Patrick; I'll be in touch . . . *au'voir.*'

The banker looked down at the business card in his hand as he closed the door. The name Sibelius (Holdings) Limited jumped out at him.

Sibelius.

A name he had never heard before. And now twice in a matter of days! Coincidence? Possibly. Something to be disregarded? No, that was not Mehdizadeh's way of doing things. He was analytical about everything. A very boring man who possessed no conversational skills outside the topic of money (some said) – the reason he had never found a woman to share his life on a permanent basis (others inferred).

It was that boring and analytical mind that now

slipped smoothly into gear. Disregarding the increased 'investment rate' (up from 15% to 25% in line with current *market* trends) that had shocked the Frenchman, and promised to make a 'small' profit for the bank. Focusing instead on a client in Freeport – Sam Yeo.

The man who had first brought 'Sibelius' to his attention.

Sam Yeo: a Cajun from Bayou Cane, Louisiana. The son of a preacher who always swore that if he hadn't found bad women and good sippin' whiskey first, he would have followed his Daddy in the ways of the Lord.

As it was, he had found his vocation with the other side: the Devil.

Or, as most ordinary people knew it, the Central Intelligence Agency.

Allied to Satan or the Central Intelligence Agency both, it made little difference. Sam Yeo was a veteran of the CIA's clandestine services division, and a major investor in Mehdizadeh's bank. It was more than enough to influence the banker's decision-making.

2

Tbilisi, Georgia

It was three months and eighteen days later that a black Chaika saloon was pulled off the Georgian Military Highway, twenty kilometres north of Tbilisi, by a militia car. It was early on a Saturday morning.

The rear-seat passenger, a forty-year-old Englishman with sandy-coloured hair and green eyes, had been reading classified documents from MINATOM (Russia's Atomic Energy Ministry) when the car had suddenly slowed and pulled off the highway on to a bumpy dirt track. He looked up sharply. 'What seems to be the problem?'

The driver, an overweight man with shoulder-length grey hair, shrugged his broad shoulders and jerked a thumb over his shoulder. 'Police,' he wheezed.

The Englishman, William Mather, turned his head. Through the rear window he saw a grey police car a matter of feet away. Flashing blue light on the roof.

'Were we speeding?' he asked nervously, shovelling the papers back into his briefcase.

'No. Perhaps the highway is blocked ahead . . . a friendly warning,' the driver said, lowering his window.

The stone-faced policeman walked slowly up the side of the Chaika, eyes inspecting the car. 'Your destination?' he asked. Sharp, unfriendly voice. Old-soldier type.

The driver smiled. 'Ordzhonikidze.'

'Your documents.'

'The road through the mountains is blocked, perhaps!'

The policeman snapped his fingers. 'Your documents.'

The driver sighed and opened the glove compartment. He pulled out a bundle of papers. Adjusted his glasses on the end of his nose. Ranging the papers into focus to enable him to find the correct ones. He called back to his passenger, almost as an afterthought. 'You have your passport, Mr Mather?'

Mather, who spoke fluent Russian, had followed the brief conversation and passed his ID forward. 'Perhaps you should tell him who I am . . . that I am working with your government at the nuclear plant.'

The driver, a technician at the Tbilisi Nuclear Plant who was doubling as a driver this weekend, heaved his shoulders again. Foreigners did not understand that the old Soyuz mentality was still alive and well. You could be Christ reincarnated and they still wouldn't give a shit. He held the documents out of the window.

The policeman ignored them. He was looking down

at the nearside front wheel of the car. 'You have a flat tyre, I think.'

The driver swore and got out of the car. Went back to the passenger door and opened it. 'Perhaps you would like to stretch your legs . . . a flat. I need to change it.'

'Oh dear,' the Englishman muttered under his breath. This was all he needed. He would be late for his meeting with a senior MINATOM director in Ordzhonikidze. An unexpected phone call two hours earlier something of an emergency, the director had said; the luck at finding his driver sleeping in a chair in the hotel lobby – even though the driver explained it was his job to remain on call twenty-four hours a day. The driver didn't add that the hotel lobby was more comfortable than his tiny apartment, where screaming babies competed with blaring radios through paper-thin walls, day and night.

Mather eased his slim six-foot frame out of the car and went forward. There was nothing wrong with the tyre! He even prodded it with the toe of his shoe, just to make sure. It was as he was turning back towards the policeman and the driver, a question forming on his lips, that he saw the gun in the policeman's hand.

The sound of a nine-millimetre semi-automatic weapon being fired in an enclosed wooded area is unbelievably loud to the untrained ear. The driver fell back in shock against the side of his car as the Englishman toppled over.

There was a second of silence, of unawareness almost, and the smell of acrid smoke in the cold September air.

Then the policeman was yelling. 'Don't just fucking

stand there, Yuri . . . Grab his hands.'

The driver, Yuri Alexandr Becker, did as was told. They half-carried, half-dragged the man back a few metres into the trees. To a shallow grave, freshly dug. The body was dropped into the hole. 'You think it's deep enough, Skulov?'

The policeman snorted. 'Fuck that, start shovelling.'

Yuri grabbed at the spade that was lying by the side of the makeshift grave and began moving the soft damp earth as fast as he could. His breath, coming in short, sharp gasps, made a whistling sound through his teeth.

William Mather was numb. His face had turned grey and was clammy with sweat, but there was no pain. He opened his eyes and found he was looking up at the sky, through the branches of spruce trees. He was opening his mouth to cry out when soil rained down on his face. Some went into his mouth, choking him. He coughed and spat and reached a hand upward. 'Please,' he cried out. 'Please . . . For God's sake . . . Help me.'

The soil cascaded down even faster. Mather tried to scream but his mouth filled with the dirt. Somehow he dragged a hand to his lips, making a space to breathe. He lasted three minutes longer. By that time he had sucked soil into his lungs and soon choked to death. His last desperate thought on this earth was: *Why?*

3

London, England

Rain clouds had pressed down on London all night and were still persisting into the early dawn hours as the newspaper vans delivered their damp newsprint throughout the capital.

One of the stories to appear that morning – Tuesday, 22nd September – stated that Mr Blair had struck a secret deal with President Clinton concerning five kilograms of weapons-grade nuclear fuel being transferred from the former Soviet republic of Georgia to Dounreay, Scotland for immediate reprocessing.

But as one newspaper put it:

> To find that the Prime Minister is making major strategic decisions on nuclear shipments without informing the House in advance is an outrage.
>
> Especially when it is to offer President Clinton a way to avoid

14

confrontation with his own green lobby in America by shipping the uranium clandestinely to Britain. And more especially as Dounreay's ageing plants are closed for repairs which must be approved by the Nuclear Installations Inspectorate.

Did ministers seek advice from their own Radioactive Waste Management Advisory Committee (RWMAC) before taking in Georgia's dirty washing?

The article went on to say that the secret deal had come adrift when the story had appeared in the *New York Times* the previous day. It concluded by suggesting that government spin doctors had been caught on the hop and that they of all people should have known that when you operate in secrecy, leaks are not just occupational hazards, they are the most likely outcomes. But for once the highly professional and oft-times cynical press corps had got it wrong. It was the government spin-meisters themselves who had leaked the story.

Or, at least, part of the story.

4

Puerto Carreno, Colombia

It was the day after the London newspaper story that
an ex-CIA man, Tanner Williams, boarded an early-
morning Satena flight at Bogota's El Dorado Airport.
The service (by the commercial carrier of the
Colombian Air Force) to Puerto Carreno was in an
ageing Fokker F-27 turboprop, which carried a
mixture of cargo and passengers. It was a bumpy ride
that morning, the rainy season being responsible for
the thick cloud that persisted over the route. Even so,
Williams was aware that he had been lucky: he knew
from past experience that domestic flights in this part
of the world ran to a loose – and sometimes non-
existent – timetable. Today's flight to the capital of the
department of Vichada had, by some quirk of fate,
actually departed on schedule.

Even so, and for what seemed like the hundredth
time, Williams questioned his own motives for being
here. At fifty-five years of age, he was too old for these

games. He had realized that months earlier when he had attended a Navy Reunion. All of a sudden, Vietnam had become another old war fought by parents whose kids watched MTV and hadn't a clue who Walter Cronkite was.

An African-American Yale graduate and Navy hero, William's early life had been full of spectacular achievements. It was in his later years with the CIA that he had fared less well. He had worked for a man named Oscar Porteous, the CEO of a CIA proprietary company known as Lafayette Antiques – a commercial cover for a 'Black Ops' unit that effectively monitored the South American continent. He had had ideas of taking over Porteous's job eventually. Then, nine months earlier, his team had become embroiled in a political scandal with the Colombian government over the extradition of the top members of the Cali Cartel. It had been serious enough to have driven his boss Porteous to suicide.

Williams, under pressure from his wife to take early retirement, suddenly saw an opening, a chance to shine. Now was the time to take over Porteous's job. Except the Director of the CIA – J.J. Eberhart – had been pressured by Congress to close the Lafayette operation down. Of course, Williams was offered alternative employment – one of the jobs being at the basic training facility at Fort Peary known in the Agency as 'the farm'. He had declined. It would have been, at least in his book, a retrograde step.

Which left retirement.

He took Sophie, his wife, on a world cruise. Memorable. Especially the side trip to Cairo and the journey up the Nile to Luxor. Visiting the Valley of the

Kings. Spending two nights at the magnificent Winter Palace Hotel. It wasn't until he got back to his home in Virginia that he realized how bad his finances were. Especially with two children still in college. He began to look for a job.

A few weeks later fortune smiled. The Director of the CIA appeared on William's doorstep. They needed him to do a little freelance work, something that was irrevocably linked to the 'Colombian *guayabo*', as it had become known. Appropriate. *Guayabo* was a colloquialism for hangover. Williams listened and thought of his financial situation, mentally adding up the bills, adding a ten per cent contingency factor, doubling the total. He never had the opportunity to mention the amount; J.J. Eberhart offered him three times as much – tax-free.

Motives for being here!

Nothing more than money. It worried him, all the same. He had the feeling that he was changing into the man he was seeking. A mercenary. A chilling thought.

It was ninety minutes after take-off that the paint-peeled Fokker dropped out of the ragged cloud base over the west bank of the Rio Orinoco near its confluence with the Rio Meta. Across the river – Venezuela.

Williams glanced out of his window as the aircraft banked steeply towards its final approach. A brief but intense peckling on aluminium as they slipped through a squally shower. A jarring bump that dislodged something in the galley, sending it crashing to the floor. The old woman – with a cross of ashes on her forehead – seated next to him and shrouded in a black shawl crossed herself for the twentieth time since the start of the journey and began mouthing silent prayers.

Williams, who had never rated flying as one of life's greatest thrills, tugged his lap strap tighter and braced himself. The plane thumped down on the end of the runway. A ripple of applause from a number of grateful passengers. Not from the old woman though. She kept praying and fingering her rosary beads right up to the moment that the plane came to a standstill and the engines were shut down.

Williams left the airliner, carrying his suit jacket over his arm. A black leather briefcase was his only baggage. He was met on the ramp by a lean, fit-looking man of medium height. Pale skin, blond crew-cut. Protruding ears. Unsmiling thin lips. Frank Murchek. Quantico-trained, ex-Marine.

'Pity P.T. Barnum never found this place, Tanner. The greatest tourist attraction ever!'

Williams took in the ramshackle single-storey terminal building; the potholed tarmac ramp that led down to a solitary rusting hangar. Beyond the broken-down wire fence, a line of rain dripping ceiba trees under which locals had set up makeshift stalls. The smells of grass and oily machinery and woodsmoke and river silt. The wasting heat and humidity of the tropics rotting all it came in contact with. Barefoot children, faces pressed to the rusted wire, watching the disembarking passengers with wide, unblinking eyes. A shabby town with a population of a few thousand, little more than a village. *The greatest tourist attraction ever!* 'Convince me.'

'The end of the world,' Murchek explained.

Williams smiled. 'Very amusing, Frank . . . He's still here, I take it?'

'Yeah. Down in that hangar, working on a single-engine Cessna . . . I assume I now get to find out what is going on?'

'Any place I can have a quick wash and brush-up?'

'Sure. Hotel Safari. This way.' He led Williams through the dusty unlit terminal shack, littered with boxes and sweating dark-skinned men – immune to the heat and dust – arguing over weights of cargo to be loaded on to the aircraft. Murchek sidestepped a group of dirty children holding their hands out. 'It's just over there,' he said, pointing a little way down the street. 'The wharf is two kliks further on. Nothing else. Welcome to Metropolis.'

The two men crossed the street, chased all the way to the hotel by the ragged street urchins and the local joropo music that pulsed on the humid morning air.

Twenty-five minutes later they were sitting in the Bonde Mery restaurant near the plaza, sipping iced cokes. A lethargic ceiling fan stirred the clammy tropical air.

'Bill Rice told me about your retirement,' Murchek began. 'So how did they persuade you to come back to this godforsaken corner of Paradise?'

Williams had taken a slim gold Dunhill cigarette lighter from his pocket and was twirling it through his fingers. 'Money, Frank. Government pensions don't go too far these days.'

Murchek looked sympathetic. Waited for Williams to continue.

'You remember that guy Winter earlier this year . . . in Los Llanos?'

'How could I forget? Bombed the shit out of the Cali Cartel's stronghold in the mountains, then joined the KIAs by flying his plane into the Gulf of Mexico.'

'Except it seems he's still alive.'

Raised eyebrows. 'I thought they pulled bits of his plane out of the water.'

Williams reached to his jacket, draped over the chair back. He took a folded sheet of paper from the inside pocket. 'Read that.'

Murchek took it. Unfolded it. It was a photocopy of a letter. The final lines had been highlighted with a yellow marker.

```
'Your 300 kg uranium shipment
in exchange for return of my
$8m. Failure to comply will
result in its sale. Acceptance,
in principle, of this
transaction should be made by a
message in the Personal column
of the International Herald
Tribune. The message should
read:
BENINAJI, PLEASE WRITE SOONEST,
WASDOC.
You have ten days to respond.

                John Paul Winter'
```

Murchek looked round the restaurant. It was only ten in the morning, too early for the lunchtime crowd.

Even so, he dropped his voice. 'What uranium shipment?'

'We lost three hundred kilos of Uranium-235 from a nuclear reactor plant in Tbilisi, Georgia, a week or so ago.'

'Jesus. And this guy Winter.' Murchek looked down at the paper in his hands. 'What does he mean by the return of his eight mill?'

'Long story, but one of our people in the Bahamas accidentally uncovered an account in his name. The account was in the hands of a French accountant from Martinique . . . Black money, of course. Anyway, it was seized. Some weeks after that, the letter you're holding arrived at Langley. Addressed to the Director.'

Murchek folded the paper and passed it back across the table. 'What time-frame we talking?'

'The money was seized at the beginning of June. The letter came in at the end of July.'

'And nobody took it seriously, eh.'

'Why would they? As far as our intel went, Winter was dead. And, quite simply, no one had misplaced three hundred kilos of uranium.'

Murchek muttered something about 'Unreliable HUMINT' to himself. Then said, 'Didn't somebody realize how devious this guy is? Why the fuck didn't they contact you?'

'I was on a cruise ship with my wife. Out of the loop. However, one of our analysts finally came up with something. She decided that WASDOC was an acronym for Washington, District of Colombia. She then spent a number of fruitless weeks trying to tie down the meaning of BENINAJI. As the letter had a postmark, Vientiane, Laos, she naturally concentrated her efforts in South-East Asia. Eventually she gave up, but mentioned it to a colleague in the Mid-East Division. They had an answer within an hour.'

'Which was?'

'On the streets of Baghdad the British are referred to as Benin Naji. Apparently dates back to the days of Empire when a holy man of that name used to entertain young British officers, even though they were Christian. Infidel.'

A light slowly dawned in the ex-Marine's eyes. 'And you figure Winter is planning to do a deal with Iraq? With *Saddam*?'

'The kind of games he plays. Similar MO to the Cali business.'

'Shit.' Murchek rubbed his jaw. Thinking. 'Might have been easier to set up a sting operation with the eight mill.'

'Too late for that, Frank. By the time Langley had arrived at their conclusions the ten-day deadline had passed.'

'And this guy Neil Campbell that you asked me to locate – where does he fit into the equation?'

'His real name is Red Stevens. Australian. Lives in Caracas. He's a used-airplane dealer. Other than that, he used to work for Winter in the mercenary game.'

'Did he now.'

'We even think he might have been involved in the Cali business at the beginning of the year.'

'And you figure he'll lead you to Winter, right?'

'Worth a try.'

Murchek looked at his watch. 'The plane back to Bogota leaves in an hour, by the way. Miss that and we're here till Sunday . . . Only two flights a week.'

'Not a problem. Meet me over at the terminal in thirty minutes. If you can pick up some sandwiches, I'd appreciate it. No in-flight meals.'

'Tell me about it.'

Williams finished his coke. 'One last thing. How did you track Campbell to here of all places?'

'Simple. I called his office in Caracas, at the number you gave me. They said he was out of town. I told them I needed to speak with him urgently about buying a plane. The guy told me his boss had picked up a Cessna in Bogota and was ferrying it back to Caracas when he'd had engine problems and diverted to Puerto Carreno. I arrived last Sunday. He'd been here two days then. Some spares arrived from Caracas yesterday, by road and boat.'

'That it?'

'He's been staying at the Hotel Orinoco. He settled his account this morning. He then filed a flight plan at the tower. Destination: Caracas. ETD 1500 hours alpha.'

The rain showers had cleared and the cloud was breaking up. Sunshine peeped through the holes, lifting tendrils of vapour from the potholed asphalt ramp as Williams made his way towards the hangar and the half-opened judas gate at the south end. He carried his suit jacket over his arm. His shirt was soaked with sweat.

The inside of the hangar was dark and carried the smells of aero-engine oil and dope and fabric and metal. A few birds flapped noisily in the rafters. At the far end, a door had been partially opened and a blue and white Cessna Centurion pulled into a shaft of

24

daylight. The engine cowlings were off and a man, stripped to the waist, was tinkering with a magneto. An unlit cigar was clenched between his teeth.

'*Buenos dias*,' Williams said, walking towards him. 'Red Stevens?'

The man stopped what he was doing and turned to face him. Overweight. Thinning grey hair plastered to his skull. Sweat dripping from his chin, running in rivulets down his chest. Suspicious eyes. 'Gidday . . . Nah, I'm afraid you've got the wrong bloke. Name's Campbell.' Heavy Australian accent.

Williams ducked under the Cessna's high wing and placed his briefcase by the left main wheel. 'Mr Stevens,' he continued, 'I have a proposition for you. It appears that a good friend of yours, John Winter, has something of ours – a small but expensive package, shall we say. Something we would like back. It seems very likely that he's in Vientiane, Laos.'

The Australian studied the man before him. The creased black face, shiny with sweat. The closely cut black hair, greying at the temples. Jacket draped over his arm. Shirt and tie. *A Fed, what else!* He took the cigar from his mouth. 'You're wasting your time. I don't know anyone named Winter.'

Williams produced a limp business card from his shirt pocket. He handed it to the Australian. 'My name and contact numbers Stateside and in Colombia. Messages to either of those numbers will be forwarded to me any time of the day or night. On the back of the card is a phone number for a Miss Maria Espinosa in Miami. We understand she is very close to Mr Winter. Perhaps you could enrol her services. All we need is information on the whereabouts of Mr Winter. If this is forthcoming there will be no repercussions. We guarantee that . . . you have my word. On the other hand, should Mr Winter sell, or otherwise dispose of, our "package", I am very much afraid that he and his associates will be made accountable.'

The Australian glanced down at the card in his hand. 'There's a police station over by the plaza, Mr Williams. I suggest you try there. They might be able to help you locate this guy Stevens.'

'Not only associates,' Williams went on. 'We are aware that you have two grown-up children in Australia from your first marriage. And a grandson . . . Noah, isn't it? Not my decision, you understand, but there are people in my organization who will undoubtedly pay them a visit.'

The Australian eyed a wrench by his feet. A moment's thought that he might reach down, pick it up and beat the man's head in. He didn't. He counted slowly to ten under his breath. 'If I knew what you were bloody talking about it might help. As it is, the name's Campbell and I'm trying to get my plane fixed so I can get out of this hell-hole . . . End of story.'

Williams smiled. 'Thank you for your time, Mr Stevens.' He turned on his heel and began walking back through the darkened hangar.

'You've forgotten your briefcase.'

Williams kept on walking. Leather-soled shoes ringing out a military pace on the oil-stained concrete floor. 'You're mistaken – it must be yours. *Adios.*'

The Australian watched him go. Seething quietly. 'What the fuck was all that about?' he asked himself. 'What the fuck is Wint up to now!'

He jabbed the cigar back between his teeth, dropped

down on one knee and clicked open the briefcase. A large brown envelope: nothing else. He opened it and removed a number of papers held together by a paper clip. Sweat dripped off the end of his nose on to the clearly typed words. *The names, ages, and addresses, of every member of his family in Australia. And his second family in Caracas.* He almost missed the last item. A bank cashier's cheque drawn against Citibank, New York. The amount was $250,000. It was made out to 'Cash'.

He hurled the papers back into the briefcase. Slammed the lid shut. 'You think you can buy me, Mr fucking Williams?' The shouted voice echoed through the hangar. There was no reply.

Just the copper buzz of cicadas.

And the suffocating heat.

5

Canterbury, England

'Say Brito, de Tracy, de Moreville and FitzUrze to the
majority of Englishmen and they wouldn't have a clue
what you were talking about. Mention Thomas
Beckett, and you'll instantly get the response: "Oh, yes
. . . Wasn't he the priest chappie who was bumped off
by King-somebody-or-other? . . . Long time ago, of
course". Now, invoke the name Lee Harvey Oswald
and most of the world will tell you he was the shooter
who assassinated John F. Kennedy.' The speaker was
a pale man with longish dark hair, deep brown hooded
eyes and a gaunt face. The mouth turned down in a
permanent sneer was the result of a mechanism he had
employed in his prep-school days, when even his
above-average height did not save him from the
bullies. With the help of the school groundsman, an
old soldier who had parachuted into Arnhem in World
War II, he had been secretly coached in boxing. The
ex-para had also taught him the fighting man's

psychology: 'When face to face with the enemy, look bloody menacing: this will give you one or two seconds' advantage while the other man is trying to get a hold on his fear.'

The defence mechanism of the boy had unfortunately become a habit of the man, resulting in a chilling aura that kept people at a distance (and that worked rather well in the higher echelons of the British Civil Service). Something he did not really mind since he did not suffer fools gladly. His name was Timothy Jaggers, and he was listed as a civil servant with the Foreign and Commonwealth Office – the FCO. The reality was somewhat different: Jaggers was the Assistant Chief – Operations of the SIS (Secret Intelligence Service). At only thirty-five years of age he was generally considered at Century House – the London headquarters of the SIS – to be a man who would go far. The gossips in the 'Firm' said he would brown-nose his way to the very top. Few listened. Fewer cared. He paused and peered out between the pillars of the enclosed walkway of Canterbury cathedral's Great Cloister. Rain was beating down from a dark morning sky. Damp. Cold. Depressing. The smell of stone. The ages. 'Bloody awful day,' he added.

His companion, Edeyrn Owens, an old man with thinning silver hair and a Welsh-valley accent he had taken up to Oxford more than forty years earlier and had maintained – some inferred – as a weapon against certain elements of the establishment ever since, said, 'Power of the media, Timothy. If the BBC had had their cameras and microphones here at the time, Brito and his pals would have become household names like Oswald.'

'Quite, quite,' Jaggers replied. Cultured voice.

Both men started walking again. Measured footsteps ringing up through the fan-vaulting arches.

'And the problem is the media?' Owens enquired.

Three more paces.

'Problem?' Implied innocence. As if to indicate their meeting that first morning of October was nothing more than coincidence due to the Welshman being in Canterbury visiting his sister-in-law, while Jaggers was on his way to Dover to catch the car ferry to the continent. 'No, nothing like that . . . well, not yet, at least. You read about the uranium deal leaked to the press last week? Blair and Clinton and secret contracts: weapons-grade uranium being shipped from Tbilisi to Dounreay?'

'Nine pounds of enriched uranium and two pounds of spent fuel, and a bit of flack from the SNP.'

'And *The Times* headlines yesterday?'

'I take the *Telegraph*,' Owens said.

'Jack Giles's suicide,' Jaggers prompted.

'Ah, yes. Back-bench Labour MP throws himself under train on London Underground . . . What was it, hookers or little boys?'

A narrow-eyed look from the dark hooded eyes. No amusement. 'I fear it's a little more serious than that. Giles was a director of a company called Prometheus Limited . . . a company that deals with hazardous materials. They had the government contract to ship the Uranium-235 from Tbilisi to Dounreay.'

'Thought that sort of thing was handled by the military?'

'Before privatization and cost-cutting in the public sector, yes – much like the FCO had to cut positions for our staffers in most of their overseas embassies.' A reference to the fact that the great majority of intelligence officers serving abroad do so under the cover of an embassy. With the collapse of the Soviet Bloc in recent years, the diplomatic corps had expanded their activities across Central Europe and elsewhere, reducing in the process the availability of cover jobs for SIS officers.

Owens waited for more, but there was nothing. Just one of Jaggers's long silences. Another brooding look in the dark eyes. Enough for the old Welshman to ask himself: *Is what I have been presented with here properly thought of as history with the names changed?* He knew, from a lifetime of practice, that intelligence work was anti-historical. That by its stratagems it sought to frustrate the truth as well as find it. Facts were steered towards some distant, unwritten goal. An incriminating message might be forged. But was it created to reveal a truth that otherwise would have remained obscure? Or was not only the evidence contrived but also the proposition it was put forward to prove? Intelligence was anti-historical because it fed into history through falsehood. The highest purpose to leave complicity hidden and ambiguous. The Dounreay story had first appeared as a few column inches tucked discreetly away in the majority of newspapers and, even with the virulent attack by the Scottish National Party – among others – that Scotland was being turned into a toxic dumping ground, the story had quickly disappeared. Replaced by? The death of a back-bench Labour MP! A marginal seat. Up for grabs now.

The two men began another circuit of the Great

Cloister. They passed a knot of tourists – American students by the sound of their voices – wide-eyed at so many years of history. Comparing notes on a murder that had happened more than eight centuries earlier. Owens felt like stopping to talk with them, to tell them how, on a late-December day with the light failing, de Tracy had injured the Archbishop and Brito had finished the job by hacking off his head . . . breaking his sword in the process. Nothing like the quick and clean bullets of modern-day America. Cold steel slicing through flesh and bone. Timothy would have frowned at that. Familiarity was an American thing. England bore and raised her sons a different way. At least, Timothy's England did.

'We, er, wondered,' Jaggers began, 'if you'd like a trip to South-East Asia . . . Few days, nothing more.'

'I'm retired, Timothy.'

A little laugh. 'Oh, nothing official, Edeyrn. Merely a long weekend in the sun, you know the sort of thing.'

'Where, specifically?'

'Laos . . . Vientiane.'

'Not exactly a tourist trap, is it, boyo?'

'According to my travel agent, those are just the sort of places the discerning traveller is choosing these days.'

The distant music of windless afternoons. Beautiful women catering to your every whim. Exotic food. The smells of spices, sandalwood, flowers with magical names. You'll never want to go home again! The sort of thing Timothy avoided. He kept religiously to Europe, and then only the select English-friendly parts. He was a man to whom moral precepts such as honesty, courage, fair play and cleanliness had an exclusively English emphasis. They went hand in hand with middle-class schoolboy shibboleths about not wearing the collar of one's cricket shirt outside one's blazer, avoiding words like 'nice' and being the sons of gentlemen. More importantly, never sucking up to those from whom you could benefit, and giving the hand of friendship to avowed enemies. *Timothy's England. Gone. But not forgotten.*

'Reason?'

'William Mather is the managing director of Prometheus. He was one of a small and select team who went to Tbilisi to oversee the loading of the uranium. He and the shipment disappeared. My information indicates that he arrived in Bangkok four days ago, and from there was booked on a flight to Vientiane. Part of your old stomping ground.'

A frame of reference. Something like the Matrix Churchill affair (the company that had been involved in supplying the Iraqi supergun project), or the Astra and Jonathan Aitken arms-to-Iran scandal. In both of those, the previous (Conservative) government had used gagging orders known as 'Public Interest Immunity Certificates' to seek convictions of the directors. 'How did this fall in to your lap? Vientiane is hardly Western Hemisphere, is it?'

The little laugh again. 'Sanctioned from on high, you know the sort of thing.' Jaggers's eyes lifted, possibly towards heaven. Which was where he doubtless placed the Chief – Sir Peter Wishart. Or 'C' as he was known to those at Century. C, not standing for 'Chief' as one would naturally suppose, but rather 'Cummings'. The first SIS Chief: Admiral Sir Mansfield Cummings.

'Often wondered what it would be like to operate in the rarefied atmosphere of the Van Allen Belt!'

'What was that?'

'Nothing . . . Thinking aloud, that's all.'

'My father does that.'

'Prerogative of the old.'

'And says exactly the same thing when I pick him up on it.'

'Your turn will come, Timothy; have no doubt of it.'

Jaggers chose not to hear. 'We've got you booked on a flight out of Heathrow in the morning.'

'Via Bangkok?'

'I imagine so.'

'All for a few kilos of uranium. Hardly seems worth the effort. I mean, how much would a shipment of that size be worth on the black market?'

'It's enough to make a few small warheads . . . so I'm reliably informed.'

'Still not worth throwing everything away, though, is it?'

They left the Great Cloister and went out into the rain. Gaunt trees. Institutional-green park benches. Patches of sodden autumn leaves – an unlovely mosaic on lawns and pathways. Jaggers raised his umbrella without offering to share it. Peeped up at the dark sky. 'Hope it's better in Brussels,' he murmured.

'Holiday, is it?'

A tug at the upturned collar of the dark blue Burberry raincoat. 'Good God, Edeyrn, holidays? Haven't time for such luxuries. Problem with the country, I shouldn't wonder . . . Workers have too much time to sit and twiddle their thumbs.'

'I'm sure you're right,' Owens said solicitously.

'They should try a few of my eighteen-hour days.'

'Indeed.'

Jaggers took a last glance at the sky. 'How I envy you
. . . All that sunshine.'

'You should join me.'

'Ah, if only . . . If it's any consolation, Edeyrn, you
had the best of it: all that travel, all those memories.
Me, I spend the majority of my days surrounded by
mountains of paperwork, trying to decide what is best
for my chaps, and my nights not sleeping a wink
worrying over the decisions made hours earlier.' A
brief pause as he surveyed the pathway he was about
to take. 'Well, must be off. Back from Europe in a
couple of days . . . Keep me posted.'

A parting shot. 'The BBC news this morning
reported a rather large lorry arriving at Dounreay with
the uranium shipment we've been talking about . . .
Empty, was it?'

Jaggers stopped and turned. Dark eyes challenging.
'Ah, yes. Well, we can't have the great unwashed
getting upset over such trivial matters, can we?'

The fellowship of Orpheus without the love or
music. No looking back. Timothy's England again.
'Quite.'

'We are . . . shall we say, acting in the national
interest and in line with our wider obligations as a
nuclear power.' A martyr's smile.

Owens watched him go. A tallish figure,
prematurely stooped about the shoulders. *The weight
of the world. Real or imagined.*

And thought of the diplomatic phrasing . . . *You had
the best of it.* Owens had been a field agent for most of
his years, an 'Illegal' – one of those agents not under

the cover of an embassy. A man who had always enjoyed bending the rules, disappearing and reappearing at will, and who took pleasure in being a thorn in the side of the Establishment. An ex-grammar school boy, who had gone up to Oxford and taken a first in Greats, a good degree that had granted him entrance to the club but little else. Independent wealth would have helped, but then, there hadn't been much of that going around the small mining town he had sprung from.

Owens set off through the rain. Smiling. His annual fortnight's holiday with his sister-in-law Rebecca cut short after only three days, thank God. The widow and the widower glowering at each other over the breakfast table. Her idea. Retribution. Still blaming him for all the years that Eleanor – her sister – had been left alone and childless while he traipsed around the Far East. Of course, he needed to soften the blow. Take her some flowers, perhaps. A box of chocolates. *So very sorry. Call from on high, you see. I'll make it up to you, I promise.*

Chorus Benedictus.

6

Tan Son Nhat International Airport, Vietnam

Yellow sunlight was filtering through grimy window-panes, framing trapezoids of dust particles, in and out of which ten orderly lines of disembarked airline passengers shuffled towards Customs desks.

Any airport! Any country! Until the disturbance at the head of the far-left line caught everyone's attention. A young man being dragged away by two soldiers. His shouts beaten into whimpers with riot sticks. And even the cries faded as he was bundled through an exit door above which a sign proclaimed: 'WELCOME TO THE SOCIALIST REPUBLIC OF VIETNAM' – in four languages.

A thin trail of blood in the dust.

John Winter watched silently from one of the Customs lines. Recognized the old Soviet training. The communist regime that still ruled with a rod of iron in one hand and held out a begging bowl to the IMF with the other. He wondered what you had to do to warrant such a welcome. Or perhaps it had been staged for his benefit! Something the hierarchy would do to warn a newly acquired joint-venture partner exactly where he stood in the pecking order. Winter was fifty-four years old. A slim six-footer with military-cut blond hair, greying slightly, and blue eyes that matched the sky. A former British soldier turned mercenary fighter pilot. In the shadowy world of soldiers-for-hire he was known as 'Sibelius'. He had been listed, on occasions, as one of the world's most wanted men.

He took the British passport (in the name of William Durack) – duly stamped with the red circular seal of entry – from the unsmiling Customs official and moved on beyond the desk.

The little colonel, dressed in a lightweight grey suit, white shirt and red silk tie, came to meet him. The same prosthetic limp – the result of losing his flesh-and-blood left foot to a landmine in the final days of the American war. The same youthful appearance, even though it had been more than ten years since the two men had last met. A slight figure, slender enough to be that of a woman. Black silken hair and sad dark eyes. The brown teeth – a result of chewing betel nut – the only concession to age. Even so, at fifty-plus, with his mouth closed, he still looked twenty-some-thing. One day, soon perhaps, he would change into a withered old man. *Secrets of the East.* No middle age.

The colonel bowed formally before offering a hand. 'I am pleased you came, John Win-ta,' he said.

'Your troubles are my troubles also, Colonel Vin.' Winter had a soft voice, a southern English accent mixed on occasion with the tones of the American

Midwest. So much so that people were unsure whether he was an American who had lived in England for a long while or an Englishman who had spent many years in the States. One truth – his own – lay elsewhere. He had been born in Prague and raised in Odessa. That he had served with the British SAS as a young man was something rarely discussed.

The colonel said, 'But not for much longer . . . One week only.' Confidence in every word.

He sounded like a Chinese merchant dealing in anything that carried a price, Winter thought. A soldier turned trader who had business with both sides, where loyalty was a matter of rates of exchange.

The two men walked the short distance to the exit door. Passed through it into the oppressive heat and humidity of early afternoon.

'The French told me you were dead,' the colonel said.

'Retired.'

'So did the Americans!'

'Ah, but you know the Americans, colonel.'

'They said you had been killed in an airplane crash.'

'And what did you say?'

'Nothing. But I thought.' A small smile. 'I thought: John Win-ta might *make* airplanes crash, but he would never be in them.'

Pushing through throngs of locals the two men climbed into the back of a Toyota staff car. A nondescript white saloon but for the red number plates. That much also remained the same. Civilians had white number plates, and were summarily stopped and fined by the police for the slightest infringement of traffic laws. Civil servants had green plates and fared slightly better. The army had red. You stopped one of *those* cars at risk of your life.

The colonel said, 'And your reasons for coming out of retirement? Offering us your services?'

'My wife died,' Winter said simply. Well, that had been the beginning. It was enough for now. The car pulled away from the passenger terminal at Tan Son Nhat airport. 'The American kid you arrested,' Winter enquired. 'Can I ask why?'

The colonel waved a hand dismissively. 'He is Viet Kieu . . . Overseas Vietnamese. His father worked for the American CIA on Operation Phoenix. A traitor, you understand.'

And you have a blacklist for dissidents! And in the fullness of time the sons and daughters, and their children, will pay the penalty. *Gestalt* – no restrictions on what is permissible. Classical misinterpretation. 'I travelled with him from Taipei. He's a computer programmer. Lives in Los Angeles.'

'We know.'

'What will happen to him?'

'I am a colonel in the Ministry of Defence, John Winta. I know as much as you of such matters. Perhaps he will be asked a few questions and then deported.' He didn't sound very convincing.

Winter said nothing. He had liked the young man. That was all. So he ends up being fished out of the Saigon River one rainy morning. An accident. A statistic for the under-worked corrupt police force. Except he had only returned to Vietnam to bring the ashes of his late mother to the Buddhist temple of her youth, to be blessed and interred there. The sort of young man you rarely found any more. One with a sense of duty. Welcome to the sick world . . . what was his name? . . . Tran Van Can. Family name – middle name – and given name; in that order. But the Americans had never really come to terms with that. So he was now known as T.C. Except soon he would be spoken of in the past tense.

The staff car swung unexpectedly through a gate and up to the side of a small military hangar. A Huey helicopter was waiting. Sun-faded drab-green.

Waiting soldiers opened the car doors. Winter got out and glanced up at the early October sky. Towering cumulus. Scattered afternoon rain showers, weak in intensity – the last days of the south-west monsoon. Hot. Sticky. Uncomfortable. The smells of rotting vegetation blending with the sharp tang of jet fuel. Body odour through sweat-stained shirts.

The colonel steered his guest towards the helo, which was spooling up. The 48-foot two-blade main rotor beginning a slow scything movement, shush-pause-shush-pause-shush-pause-shush . . .

'A small surprise for you, John Win-ta,' he shouted.

Thirty minutes later they were standing outside a former American Air Force hangar at Bien Hoa. A military base twenty-five kilometres north-east of Ho Chi Minh City or, as it was still known by southerners, Saigon.

'She is sleek, no?' the little colonel asked in the Vietnamese way of phrasing questions in the negative.

Winter looked up at the F-4 Phantom, newly painted in battleship grey. No markings. Covered a lot of sins, new paint. 'But too old to be a virgin, I think.'

'Still, you will take me for a flight, no?'

'A ride around the patch, you mean?'

The colonel smiled. 'I have never flown above the speed of sound. My mechanics tell me she can exceed twice that.'

Winter let his eyes run over the McDonnell Douglas hardware, which had doubtless flown numerous missions up north all those years ago. His old instructor, Charlie Riker, would have had a few words to say about that. He had been the consummate professional. Had forgotten more about flight than most aviators would ever know. More than that, he knew how dangerous old military aircraft really were. Like living in the past . . . No future in it. Except Charlie Riker had died doing more or less what the little colonel was now asking of Winter.

'When do you want to go?'

The little colonel beamed.

'Warning flags down . . . Seat pins pulled . . . Handle down . . . Visor down . . . Seat locked . . . Ready to go, in the back?'

'Ready,' the little colonel replied.

Winter confirmed the trim setting and fuel. Checked frequencies and squawk code. The BLTs screeched as he rammed the throttles to the stops, and the F-4 Phantom accelerated down the runway. Temps and pressures checked . . . Throttles outboard and forward to the afterburner stops . . . Kidney punch . . . And . . . Airborne. Even in the leaden air the lightly loaded fighter was off the ground in 2,000 feet. At the instant the shaking stopped he rotated the gear handle up and lowered the nose to maintain an altitude of twenty feet. They were a little over halfway down the runway, abeam the maintenance hangar, speed passing 320 knots when he pulled up into a 2.5g left-climbing arc, laying the aeroplane on its back forty-five degrees through the vertical. Speed approaching 400 knots as the F-4 rocketed through 2,000 feet, directly above the flight line.

Rolling to the upright at 6,000 feet, Winter lowered the nose to let the airspeed build to 550 knots . . . Quick glance at instrument readouts . . . Looking for abnormalities . . . Clear . . . Thank you, God . . . And at 550 he rotated the nose thirty degrees back towards the vertical . . . The altimeter going berserk trying to match the climb rate of 40,000 feet per minute. By 18,000 feet they were supersonic . . . And on their way to their target speed of Mach 2.1 . . . Both men silent except for their breathing over the ICS . . . The little colonel still trying to catch up with what was happening . . . Winter running on pure adrenalin, looking for the first inkling of a problem that he knew had to come . . . Natural when flying an American military aeroplane that had sat in a hangar for more than twenty-five years and had recently been rebuilt by a bunch of non-English speaking Soviet-trained Vietnamese mechanics.

They were approaching Mach 2 when the master caution flickered on like a lightning flash. Winter's hand moved instinctively to the throttles. The windshield high-temp telelight had come on. *Thermal thicket.* On aluminium-skinned aircraft, the range between the speed of sound and the speed at which aerodynamic heating began to weaken the aircraft's skin. A limited range. The danger lay in the high temperature weakening the bulletproof portion of glass in the forward windscreen, causing it to lose temper. Following which, any sharp blow – from, say, a bird strike – might shatter it, showering the pilot with a load of glass. At high speed like a faceful of lead shot from a double-barrelled shotgun. *Extremely lethal.* Winter checked the Machmeter.

Half a needle-width off Mach 2. He removed his hand from the throttles.

'I have a light that has come on,' the little colonel said from the back seat.

'Windshield overheat,' Winter replied. Little more than a whisper.

'Is that dangerous?'

'Very.'

A small nervous laugh. Nothing else.

Winter, adrenalin-spiked, watched the Machmeter. Waited . . . Sweated . . . Prayed . . . The needle flickered . . . Once . . . Twice . . . And . . . 'Mach 2.1, colonel. Satisfied?'

'Very good, John Win-ta. Now we go home, no?'

Winter eased the throttles out of burner. Exhaled a sigh as the high-temp telelight went out as silently as it had come on. Then knifed the F-4 down the late-afternoon skies. Coming off the South China Sea at Nha Trang. Turquoise waters lapping a deserted seven-kilometre beach. The thousand-year-old east-facing Cham Towers of Po Nagar. Pewter sunlight washing through dissipating puffs of cumulus clouds. A magical day for flying.

Quite magical.

Except Winter was thinking of the young man being beaten to a bloody pulp somewhere in Saigon. Or if he got real unlucky by pissing off one of his interrogators he would be handed to the death squad. A team of executioners modelled on Joe Stalin's secret police. They shot their victims in the back of the head. A method so intimate it splattered the killer with gore. The NKVD executioners were provided with two buckets, one of vodka to steady the nerves and one of eau de cologne to disguise the smell of blood.

The sad part was, Tran Van Can had been born in the US. Had never before been to South-East Asia.

Had never witnessed its gentle face.

PART TWO
Ritual Whispers

7

Winter's Friday-afternoon flight had been consigned to a cryptic shorthand line in a logbook. Memory would record something altogether different. The altimeter rolling past 12,000 feet as the F-4 scratched through the ragged cloud tops into clear air. The upper deck pewter-coloured, textured with lines of ribs, and far out over the South China Sea a swathe of blue. Climbing towards the emptiness, which had known American airmen and, before them, French. A once-upon-a-time refuge from the less friendly skies to the north.

Forty adrenalin-filled minutes of pushing the isentropic-flow envelope for the benefit of his military passenger, waiting for the problems that he knew would come but that, when they did, proved small enough to be inconsequential. And, later, leaving the ghosts to their ruined beauty and magical history. Linked only by displacement and exile.

He knew they had been there, had felt their presence as surely as if they had drifted up alongside and raised a gloved hand. *Surreal images.* Things you never mentioned to civilians.

And returning to Bien Hoa for a visual recovery.

Exploding over the field at 1,000 feet doing 500 knots. Reefing the F-4 into a 90-degree bank. At high speed and high g-loading, some of the air over the top of the wings going supersonic. Creating a roll of dry thunder. Speed brakes biting the wind, adding to the din. Near-silence as the plane slowed on the down-wind – coasting until power was added. Boundary-layer controls coming alive, disgorging an unworldly series of pipe-organ shrieks and moans. Rising and falling. Final approach, gear and full flaps confirmed, adjusting the power to eighty-eight per cent. One mile. The runway threshold emerging from the afternoon haze . . . The black scrub marks where thousands of tyres had made contact. Just before touchdown, raising the drag-chute handle on the left side of the bucket seat, setting it securely into its detent.

And down. Rumbling and shaking.

And chute.

And coming off the adrenalin rush.

Mars to mortal in the blink of an eye. One of the ways you could tell an aviator. Eyes.

Not so much the crow's-feet – the result of blinking back too many suns, or the lightning flashes of night storms that had sought to kill you – but the eyes themselves. Sometimes so distant and sad that one might consider they had glimpsed the secrets of eternity and longed to return . . . Forever. Winter, in his quiet moments, found comfort in such thoughts. And there were many quiet moments in these places. The week-ends especially, the time when the military magically ceased to exist.

It had been late that Sunday afternoon when the unsigned note was hand-delivered to his second-floor room at the Caravelle Hotel on Saigon's Lam Son Square. The meeting place was the only give-away. Winter's team had always met there. And of that original team there were only three, possibly four, left. The point being, who? And how did they know he was here? More especially, how did they know he was travelling on a passport with the name, 'William Durack'?

The intrigue finally gave way to more practical matters. He had showered and was laying boric-acid traps. Trails of white powder under the bed, along the skirting boards and, lastly, around the edges of the bathroom floor. Boric acid, deadly poison to cockroaches, and in this part of the world all hotels had them. Giant-size. Satisfied with his work, Winter ran the water in the sink until it was hot and began to wash his hands.

He looked up and saw his reflection in the mirror – the tiny webs in the tanned skin spreading down from beneath the eyes, like the crazing that takes over Perspex in old aircraft. The deeper lines – acid-etched – that ran down from the sides of his nose; the forehead creases, the blond hair – turning grey. The nagging doubts, more frequent now. Sometimes he could see it quite plainly, flying through the sound of dying autumn, through the last dark night; and then, the last controller's voice, clear, precise, accentless: 'Sibelius One descend at pilot's discretion, maintain four thousand.' He was there now: 4,000 feet. How many minutes before he was cleared for the approach? One more frequency change, two at the most.

John Templeton Smith

Mortality.

His clothes were laid out on the bed. Khaki shirt and pants, stone-coloured sleeveless bush jacket, canvas money belt worn next to the skin, brown-leather ankle boots. He dressed quickly and stared at himself in the mirror. The Leica camera hanging around his neck gave him the appearance of a war correspondent, right down to the motor-drive that was refitted with nylon gears for silence, and a remote-activation capability up to one hundred metres; the 3200-ASA Kodak black-and-white film was particularly good at night without a flash, providing there was adequate artificial lighting. When he picked up the Israeli Army-issue short commando knife in the sheath from the dressing table and slipped it into the back of his waistband, his appearance grew more ominous. Even more so, perhaps, had any observer known that the bush jacket had a customized inner lining of Aramid ballistic fibres. Body armour.

Satisfied he had everything he needed, Winter took the elevator to the lobby, smiled at a pretty Vietnamese girl through the open door of the Air France office, and stepped out into the warm night. He would be two hours early for his scheduled meeting but this was so he could observe the rendezvous point to see if other watchers might be there – looking for him. And, not unnaturally, to see who had sent the invitation before he committed himself. In a hostile environment – whether real or imagined – the ex-SAS man was still at large because he took no chances.

'What is this?' Red Stevens said, tasting the soup that had been put before him. The Australian, always a colourful dresser, was wearing a pink short-sleeved shirt, red lightweight-cotton trousers and white slip-on shoes. A gold chain hung around his neck.

Winter shrugged, and picked up the grubby white card menu. Vietnamese. No translations. 'Looks like goat's penis in a special hot Chinese sauce.'

Stevens dropped his spoon as if it had bitten him, a look of disgust spreading across his face. 'Oh, shit!' he exploded, and took a half-corona from his shirt pocket. 'What is it with these bloody people and normality?'

'Depends whose normality you want to define.'

'Mind if I smoke?'

'Go ahead. Anyway, I thought Aussies weren't squeamish,' Winter said between mouthfuls. 'You should try it, though, it's very good . . . besides which, it's supposed to be an aphrodisiac.'

Stevens patted his pockets and found a box of matches. 'Very bloody funny, especially as my wife is eight thousand miles away.'

They were in the Binh Soup Shop on Ly Chunh Thang Street in District 3; a few metres removed from the constant hustle and bustle of the sidewalk, solid traffic, car horns and choking exhaust fumes. A cheap and shabby stopover for locals. Any tourists who ventured there did so because of its history. During the war it had been the secret headquarters of the Viet Cong in Saigon. A place where the enemy, posing as waiters, had planned their attack on the US Embassy and other places in the city during the Tet offensive of 1968. A few American soldiers, convinced they had a safe billet, unknowingly closer to the enemy than the infantry grunts up around Ben Hai River more than

1100 kliks to the north. An area of names like Con Thien Firebase, Camp Carroll, The Rockpile, Hill 1015. Places that used up body bags faster than they could be supplied. Now a barren area, where only a few scrubs managed to survive in the chemically burned soil. Testament to the effectiveness of Agents White, Blue and Orange. Home to legions of unnamed graves. Some of Vietnam's 300,000 MIAs.

'So how did you know where to find me?' Winter asked.

The Australian puffed on his cigar and stared down into his cup of greasy black coffee. 'Maria contacted me . . . Told me what had happened, that you were on your way to Saigon.'

'What about the name change? How did she know that? I never mentioned it.'

'Said she'd seen a pile of your passports. Made a note of the names. I called the Caravelle first, figuring you would go there, and ran through a few names with the lady on the front desk. Third time lucky, for real.'

Winter thought of the 'Mather' passport he had used to travel to Bangkok, Vientiane and Taipei before switching to the more 'legitimate' Durack passport. Durack the orphan, the nomad, the ferry pilot. Another careful man from his past. Careful enough to stay on the outside of shooting wars, being nothing more than one of the delivery boys for different kinds of aeroplanes. One of which had killed him one fine sunny morning on a French island in the south Pacific. Winter had been scrounging a lift and was occupying the right seat. He walked out of the wreckage without a scratch. *Lucky man.*

'How is she?'

'Fine. She said you got her that job flying cargo out of Miami.'

'Favour through Si Harish, you remember him. Philippines. Nineteen seventy-something.'

'Sure. Him and Jack Crane and Charlie Riker. Back to Manila on Friday night . . . All the San Migs you could drink, all the tarts you could screw. Not you, though. Didn't you used to shack up with a Philippine Airlines stew?'

'What a memory you've got . . . Anyway, how's Maria liking the big jets?'

'I got the idea that she'd rather be here with you.'

Winter finished his soup and pushed the bowl aside. 'No place for a woman, Red.'

'What about Colombia? She saved your neck there.'

Evaluating the players. Too old. Too young. Too soft . . . Wouldn't be able to make it without food and rest . . . Now, that one . . . He might have a chance, but I'm not sure if he's crazy enough. 'Circumstances. She happened to be at a wrong place in time.' His voice dropped. 'The life span in our business is too short. I decided she needed better.'

'Did you ever think that she'd rather have a few exciting years with you than a lifetime without?'

'Did she tell you about the wife I had back in the States?'

'She told me.'

'Another reason. Loose talk costs lives. She wormed that information out of Charlie Riker. She didn't need to know.'

Stevens brushed cigar ash from the front of his shirt. 'Is it that important?'

'Of course it is. You start talking about the nonstrategic things, spreading gossip, and before you know it, it's grown to the really important matters. That's when you become a risk to the entire operation.'

'And that was the reason you didn't bring her here? Because she talks too much?'

'Partly. What happened to your first wife?'

'We divorced.'

'And your second, in Caracas. How long have you been married to her?'

'Nine . . . ten years.'

'Would you have allowed either one of them to get involved in this business?'

'Not the point. Neither of them are pilots. Maria is.'

'And that makes her immune? To what? She's safer flying straight and level in a 707, or whatever else they use for cargo-hauling these days, than flying fighter aircraft for the wrong side . . . for any side, come to that.'

'Did you ever think of letting her make up her own mind?'

Winter reached into his bush jacket pocket and took out a pack of unfiltered Particulares. He liked the Argentine cigarettes. The black, strong tobacco. Or perhaps it was the ties to his past. The good-old, bad-old days. He lit one and thought: *Of all of us Stevens has changed the least.* Beneath the layer of fat, behind the slackened muscle of incipient middle age, there was still the ghost of the skinny Australian with a mop of red hair, looking for reason where none existed. He who had joined the mercenary game more than a quarter of a century earlier. An ex-Force pilot who had seen action in Vietnam, following which he had gone back to Civvy Street and a job selling washing machines. Three years of that was enough to convince him to seek a more exciting life. He had found Winter. Not that he had been the best fighter jock. Yet he was popular. Fighter pilots were superstitious, and somehow the word got around that Red Stevens brought good luck. So they looked after him, covered his mistakes. Later on he had been used as a Forward Air Controller. Guiding the strikes. Something he had been good at. After that, intelligence gathering. Even better.

Then, when the quart-size adrenalin rushes were seen as a liability to his remaining years, he had slipped away to Venezuela, found a new wife, and turned to the selling game he had thrown aside all those years earlier. With the difference that instead of washing machines he now traded in general-aviation aeroplanes. That he had helped Winter out nine months earlier in Colombia was seen as nothing more than a favour for old time's sake. Now, unexpectedly, he was here.

'You think I should have?' Winter asked.

Stevens ran a hand through his thinning hair. Mostly grey now. 'Ah, shit! I don't know . . . Maybe you're right. All I know is, that woman loves you. But then, perhaps what you're doing is kinder in the long run.' A flicker of a smile. 'You know, Wint, there are days when I hate growing old. It's all too bloody serious.'

'And if you could go back to the beginning, what would you do?'

Infectious laughter. Almost youthful. The ghost still clinging. 'Exactly the same . . . Jeez, I don't bloody know. Still, I suppose we're the lucky ones. How many of us left?'

Winter ignored the question. Preferred exorcism to self-flagellation. 'You never told me why you came?'

'Sounded like you needed help.'

'Maria told you about the money?'

'She said that your offshore accounts had been found and frozen. That you had a deal working out here to get yourself back into funds, that's all. How much did you lose?'

'A lifetime's savings.'

'How much is that?'

Winter thought of the millions he had salted away using all the careful planning of a miser. A grand pension scheme involving couriers carrying cash handouts every six months to the widows and orphans of the men he had employed over the years. A little put aside for himself – if he survived. 'A lot.'

'Any idea who was responsible?'

'CIA.'

'You're sure?'

A nod of the head.

'Backhanded favour for helping them out in Colombia . . . Bastards. How did they track it?'

'I'm not sure. I thought I'd have one more try at going legit. I instructed my accountant in Martinique to find a way to wash the funds. Move them over to Europe. Seems he spoke to the wrong banker.'

'Sure he didn't screw you?'

'Seems a banker he'd done business with before might have turned him in . . . Besides that, he was the one who put me on to this deal.'

'So, Feds then.'

'Remember me telling you about a CIA guy in Colombia by the name of Williams?'

'Vaguely.'

'I could be wrong but I have a feeling he's at the bottom of all this. He struck me as a very thorough man.'

Stevens dropped his cigar into the ashtray and spread his hands on the tabletop. The backs were thick with freckles and tufts of reddish-gold hair. 'Any chance of getting the money back, or is that a dumb question?'

'What do you think? No . . . no chance.'

'So what's the game plan?'

'A shipment to the Middle East for two old friends of mine.'

'Anyone I know?'

'Colonel Vin.'

'Old Hoppy, you mean? He still around?'

'Pushing a pen for the Ministry of Defence.'

'Need to watch your back with that kiddy. Talks out of both sides of his mouth at the same time.'

'I know.'

'Who's the other friend?'

'You wouldn't know him. Let's just say he's a long-time buddy of Colonel Vin's.'

'And the shipment?'

'I need to move an F-4 Phantom from Bien Hoa to Iraq.'

No surprise at the destination. Or if there was, nothing showed. 'What are you carrying?'

'Carrying?'

'Sure . . . No one with money is going to buy antique hardware for their first line of defence, and I'm betting any amount of arms dealers would be quite willing to take letters of credit from Saddam for something a bit more up to date.'

Winter glanced around the shop. An old man with a wispy beard at the corner table, drinking soup with a shaking hand. Two boys with ageless faces, talking animatedly behind the counter. Smells of spicy food mingling with cigar and cigarette smoke. 'Are you in?'

'Course I'm in. Why d'you think I'm sitting in this shitty hole on the slanty-eyed side of the planet? Not for the bloody cuisine, that's for sure.'

Need-to-know information. Nothing more. Winter said, 'Uranium-235.'

One beat. Two. 'Are you fucking serious?' Face momentarily drawn. The look of a frightened man.

'Of course I'm serious.'

'There's a moral issue here . . .'

'There's a what?'

'You heard.'

'So whose morals do you want? The western powers, or Saddam Hussein's? What if I told you they were both the same?'

'How'd you figure that?'

'Do you remember why President Carter didn't win a second term?'

'Not offhand.'

'The Iranians were holding American hostages. Carter's administration managed to bungle both diplomacy and a military rescue attempt. Reagan comes into office and succeeds in getting the hostages released. Not only that, he backs Saddam in his newly started war against Iran . . . no doubt made some loose promises along the way concerning Iraq's borders. Iraq, with some US backing, wins the war. Saddam misreads Reagan's promises and years later invades Kuwait . . . And bear in mind the reason for that! In

1990 the Kuwaitis began exceeding their OPEC oil-production quota, which held the barrel price down artificially, hurting Iraq's economy; not only that but the Kuwaitis were found to be stealing oil from the Iraqi portion of the oilfield that straddled the border. Saddam tries the peaceful way to resolve the differences – through legal negotiations; the Kuwaitis, backed by the West, make no effort to resolve a problem that they themselves have created. So, Saddam takes the only option left to him. He invades. And suddenly his ally, America, does a one-eighty. It's not about weaponry, Red. It's about money. They want Saddam to remain a Third World nonentity. They don't want him in the club, or perhaps the Saudis are insisting he be kept out. His oil? That's something else, *that*'s what the West and the Kuwaitis and the Saudis want. Once they've found a way to get rid of Saddam there'll be a puppet dictator in Baghdad, one who will serve the interests of the cartel; like Visa and MasterCard, both serviced through the same banks. No competition. Just a pin-striped Mafia that controls billions of credit cards and billions of working people's lives.'

'And that justifies it, you mean.'

'The CIA stole my money. I gave them the opportunity to give it back. They refused. Besides, you're missing the historic dimension of the occasion.'

'Like becoming the world's most wanted terrorist, photo plastered in every newspaper and on every television screen on the planet.'

Winter offered a close approximation of the truth. 'Like the Chechen *Mafiya* knocking off a nuclear reactor site in Tbilisi and stealing the uranium from under the noses of the Yanks and the Brits. And then transporting it to Vietnam, who have put together a deal to supply it to Iraq. And only a few years ago the US signing normalization treaties with Hanoi, enabling them to borrow money from the International Monetary Fund to work a series of joint-venture business partnerships. Some of that money is being used to pay the Chechen boys.'

'Yeah, well, we know how really trustworthy *they* are, don't we? Both ends against the middle . . . You never told me how much of that Armageddon material you plan to move.'

Winter said, 'Three hundred kilos.'

Stevens shook his head. His eyes wide. Disbelief. 'How many people know?'

'Too many, in all probability . . . Part of the risk.'

Another shake of the head. As though it was a nervous tic developing. 'You know how much a shipment like that is worth? How many millions? You realize that every thief and his dog will have us at the top of their hit list once the word gets out?'

'They'll have to find us first.'

'Question. Why send it all the way out here? Why not straight to the end-user?'

'Why do you think? Invisible middlemen and invisible profits.'

'How did they transport it here?'

'Russian military plane direct to Bien Hoa.'

'What type?'

'Ilyushin Il-38 . . . Turboprop . . . What NATO code-named "May". It's been converted to a tanker.'

'And they want to avoid getting their hands dirty. So they contract to an outside company, right?'

'Loopholes. New game, old rules.'

'Paying well?'

'Enough. I've got a small logistics problem, though, mainly concerned with overflights.'

'Hang on a minute,' Stevens said, scratching his head. 'How did you get the Ilyushin out of Russia?'

'I bought it, along with the Phantom that's here.'

'With what?'

'A bit of "earnest money" put up by the Iraqis. The colonel helped out there. Shuffled the paper-work through the right channels . . . unofficially, of course.'

'And you're planning to use the Ilyushin to refuel the Phantom?'

'Affirmative.'

'Russian crew?'

'No. They've gone home. I've got a ferry crew coming in tomorrow from the States. They'll refuel us en route and then go on to Europe.'

'And the Phantom?'

Winter waited as the old man with the wispy beard and shaking hands shuffled past their table. A few seconds of traffic noise and street-side music as he opened the door and slipped out in to the night. 'Dump it in Iraq, unless you can find a buyer.'

'Nah, probably best left . . . How'd you find the ferry crew?'

'Maria. Frenette, the pilot, is an old friend of hers. Comes from New England.'

Stevens rescued the half-smoked cigar from the ashtray. 'When did you say they get in?'

'Tomorrow, from Singapore.'

'What about compatibility on the tanker and the

Phantom? You know that the Navy and the Air Force had different systems?'

'This is the Air Force system. No problem, I'm told. They're doing a few ground checks now, should be finished tomorrow night. I'll do a test flight Tuesday morning.'

'When you planning to leave?'

'Saturday.'

'This coming Saturday? Six days from now?'

'Yes.'

Stevens struck a match and relit the soggy cigar. 'So, you file as a ferry flight on the Phantom to somewhere like Bahrain. Pick up the tanker west of Karachi, refuel, and then go ahead and land at Bahrain. After Bahrain . . .' The Australian stopped, visualizing the Arabian Gulf, the haul up to Kuwait, and on into southern Iraq. All blanketed with NATO fighters and AWACS radar cover and satellite surveillance. 'Won't work,' he said finally.

Winter disagreed. 'It will, using my routing. But, for now, let's not worry about the final leg. The first part is more or less what I had in mind: airways flight plan to Bahrain. As far as Frenette and his crew are concerned, the situation is as follows: both aeroplanes have been sold to a British company called Warbirds (UK) Limited. We are delivering the aircraft to their base at Coventry for inclusion in their air museum. That the Ilyushin will probably get there okay, and the Phantom will not, is just one of those things. As they haven't paid for either plane yet no one is going to get too excited. Going back to the facts, as you pointed out, every thief and his dog will be looking for us by now, which includes the CIA, the FSK, and no doubt a few other agencies. Meaning I'm assuming the worst. Namely, that every air force from here to Iraq will be on the lookout for an unmarked Phantom westbound from this part of the world.'

'Ahhh! . . . Now that is a toughie. Take Thailand, for instance: they've got a pretty effective defence force . . . the word is, F-16s equipped with AMRAAMs. Then again, if you're planning to overfly India and Pakistan, you'll probably get bounced, especially after their recent fun and games with A-bomb testing. Both countries are as close to red alert as they've ever been.'

'Can you get me charts on their defence structures?'

'Sure, but that's not going to help. Of course, you could try and route around the north.'

Winter had already looked at that route: north towards Hanoi, across the top of Burma, running up the Chinese border, into Russia near Samarkand . . . the Caspian Sea . . . A quick burn across north-west Iran. 'Difficult one, isn't it?' he said, picking some shreds of loose tobacco from his tongue and stubbing out the cigarette butt in the ashtray.

'Not as easy as it used to be, that's for sure. Leave it with me, I'll sleep on it, might come up with an angle. What ferry range on the Phantom?'

'Normally seventeen hundred nauticals with a thirty-minute reserve. I've had a lot of gear removed, though, not least the 20mm cannon and the 600-odd rounds that go with it. With the extra fuel I can now carry that gives me a range of around 2,500 nauticals . . . A bit more if I'm really conservative.'

'What does the Ilyushin cruise at?'

'Around 300 knots.'

Stevens rubbed his chin. 'So you're only going to get

the chance to refuel once . . . You could be running on fumes by the end of it, you know.'

A movement of the eyes. Information copied.

'Is that all you need?'

'More or less.'

'You're aware of the odds.'

'Slim you mean.'

'Impossible.'

'Not according to the Gorsky factor.'

'The what . . . What's that?'

'I'll tell you one of these days.'

'And after this is all over, what then?'

'Oh, I don't know. Something that Charlie Riker suggested to me once . . . La Paz, Bolivia. I'll get a little house up there and drink iced coffee and read my morning newspaper at the Cafe Le Paz, and in the evening watch the sun go down over the Altoplano flatlands. Charlie always said the Cafe Le Paz made the best cheese pastries on the planet.'

Stevens chuckled. 'And when it gets to the bottom line, that's it isn't it? A quiet existence and the best cheese pastries. We'd have laughed at that idea once, right? Still, you could do worse.'

'I know.'

'I mean, how long have we been playing these bloody games?'

'Mercenaries, you mean? Depends how far you want to go back. The Persian Cambyses conquering Egypt in 525 BC, Alexander the Great in the same place in 332 BC . . . The Romans! Then again, take this little corner of the world: we were doubtless employed by the Chinese when they conquered the Red River Delta in the second century BC, or hired by the other side during the Hai Ba Trung rebellion in AD 40.'

'I'm impressed.'

'At what?'

'Your knowledge of history.'

Winter shook his head. A sad smile. 'Don't be. The result of being on the run for most of my life. No televisions or radios, or pubs to anaesthetize the recurring eight-hour memory of the workplace, just some death-smelling old battlefield and a sleeping bag. I used to carry history books instead of surplus rations, escaping into the past . . . A prophylactic against what might be coming tomorrow.'

'Pity about your teaching job back in the States . . . And your wife getting killed like that!'

Julia. Dear, sweet Julia. More than a year since her death. The memory distorting more with each passing day. The dreams becoming less frequent. The last one, two months earlier. It had been the first dream in which he had retained a sense of smell. He could see the pictures now: the white house on the dark night. Rain falling. Walking up the short driveway at the side of the house. Through the back door. A small utility room of sorts. On through the kitchen, into the front hallway. The staircase against the far wall.

And then, like in the movies, *dissolving* to another scene.

They were in bed together, a street light making animal shadows on a wall. And as he turned to take her in his arms, the smell of her perfume. So powerful it took his breath away. So powerful that when he awoke in the morning, he could swear he could still smell it. So powerful, he could have cried. 'No, Red, I had a few years of civilization. A good woman. I'm grateful for that.'

Stevens was thoughtful for a long moment. 'Look, it might not be much but why not kick this into touch. Come back to Venezuela with me. You can have a stake in my sales business, not going to make you a millionaire but it's comfortable enough, plus the fact it's safe. No one shooting at you.'

'Might take you up on that.'

'I'm serious.'

'I know.'

'And you're bloody stubborn . . . You never told me who's flying back-seater on the F-4?'

'No one. Thought I'd go solo.'

'Bad idea, with your navigation. Now take me, undoubtedly the finest navigator since Chris Columbus. The compass-and-stopwatch king of Kyabra Creek, been known to find a pub from thirty thousand feet on a night as black as a foot up an Abo's bum. Bloody legendary.'

'Too dangerous.'

'Too dangerous! If you think you're going to have all the bloody fun and leave me on the ground . . . No way.'

Winter smiled and shook his head. Took a sip of his coffee. 'Where are you staying, by the way?'

'Emperor Hotel on Nguyen Dinh Chieu. Just up the road from here. Cheap and cheerful, but I figured safer than moving into the same place as you.'

'Be careful when you're placing phone calls, the lines could be tapped.'

'Yeah, figured that as all the hotels are half-owned by the generals they'd still be paranoid about people talking to each other. Speaking of which, there's a Russian advisor staying at the Emperor. Oldish guy. Long white hair. I think he tried to follow me when I left the hotel. I'd never have known but I heard the desk clerk muttering *Lien Xo* to his buddy when the guy came in to the lobby . . . I think they hate the bastards more than we ever did.'

'But you gave him the slip?'

'No problem . . . Even so, I thought they'd got rid of them all, along with the hammer and sickle on the flags.'

'So did I.'

'So, what happens tomorrow?'

'I'm going out to Bien Hoa to meet with Colonel Vin. I'd ask you along, but I've got a job for you here in the city.'

Outside, the sound of stereo speakers filled the night with a flat thumping beat. Cars, scooters, cyclos, bicycles, motorbikes: all playing a kind of suicide ballet in time to the music. All of it light years away from the traditional beauty of an ancient culture of pagodas where monks prayed and incense burned. 'Forgotten how shitty the traffic fumes were,' Stevens shouted above the blast of an unsilenced motorbike as it took a short cut across the pavement.

'Know what you mean.'

'What was the job you wanted me to do?'

'Two, actually. Pick up Frenette and his crew at the airport. They're scheduled to arrive at noon, ex-Singapore, not sure of the carrier. Could be Silk Air if they operate here. You might want to fix them up with rooms at your hotel.'

'And the second thing?'

'Check up on prisons here in Saigon.'

'Prisons?'

'Any place the army might take political dissidents.'

'Any one in particular, or are you thinking about future accommodation?' Stevens laughed at his little joke.

'Tran Van Can . . . *Viet Kieu*. Arrested at Tan Son Nhat on Friday. Colonel Vin said he was being held for questioning.'

Another laugh. 'And if you believe that, you'd believe the bastards were telling the truth when they said they'd returned all the American MIAs. When you and I know they had the poor sods working in those zinc mines at Cao Bang on the Chinese border for years . . . Anyway, have you thought he might have been sent to Hanoi? Whatever else Ho Chi Minh may have done, he sure as hell created a very effective police state in the north. I was talking to a kiddy today who was hauling me around in a cyclo, he said they have a network of secret informers up there . . . They detain monks, priests, landowners and anyone else seen as a potential threat to the government. No trials: just throw-away-the-bloody-key incarceration . . . Any reason for wanting this guy?'

'He's an American citizen.'

'*Viet Kieu*, you said.'

'The colonel's words, not mine.'

'Friend of yours, is he?'

'Sort of.'

'And do I get to know the reason why I'll be wasting my time looking for him?'

'He might be able to help with the routing to Iraq.'

'Pilot, is he?'

'No, but he may know a way to make me invisible long enough to overfly the countries we were talking about.'

'And if the kiddy's in jail, like you're saying . . .'

'Find a way to get him out . . . Top priority.'

'You want a bit of advice?'

'No, but I feel I'm going to get it anyway.'

'Don't get involved in local politics: this is still a communist stronghold, every bit as fucked-up as the old Soviet Union . . . Start probing into the daily workings of the Politburo and you'll suffer the same fate as the American kiddy you're talking about.'

'As I said, I'm not looking for advice. Just information.'

'That's what I like about working for you,' Stevens said. 'Autocratic leadership. Not paid to think, just do . . . Besides that, you never thanked me for coming to save your worthless neck.'

Winter shrugged. 'Keep an eye out for your friendly *Lien Xo*, or I might be coming to save yours.'

Stevens turned and walked away, his contagious laughter lingering for a moment above the ever-changing street sounds.

The light rain that had carried on the wind earlier had gone. The clouds also. Faint stars glimmered in the night sky. A distant white flash on the southern horizon: tropical lightning. The raw smells of night-time Saigon. Winter walked down Hai Ba Trung Boulevard, keeping generally to the main streets, the better-lit places. A tourist would have taken a taxi. A mercenary on the wrong side of fifty needed all the exercise he could get. This was the time when the joints started to creak, when the ears and eyes began to lose their youthful acuity. The wrong side of the 'summer hill', as he had thought of it in recent years, descending with gravity; the higher speed creating some kind of localized miniature time warp – the result being that time seemed to fly by, leaving too few hours in the day. Imagination, or scientific fact? Something that analytical – or lonely – minds did.

He turned right on Han Thuyen. Not so well lit. A quiet street. Quiet enough to hear the breeze rustling through the casuarinas and eucalyptus trees as he passed a walled garden. A hundred metres further and he arrived at Notre Dame, the cathedral built by the French more than a century earlier. He walked across to the small square, past the statue of the Virgin Mary, and on into Dong Khoi Street, lined with silk shops and bookshops and camera shops and cafés and karaoke lounges. Followed every step of the way by insidious noise. Draining. The Vietnamese, apparently, immune. The music: a lunatic mix of east and west. And any café that didn't have an eardrum-splitting bank of speakers had difficulty attracting customers. Locals, at least. Fortunately most of the noise was beginning to ease up now. It was after ten p.m., the time the city dwellers made for their beds.

It all came back. Some things you simply danced into. No effort required. It was as though he had never been away to witness the days and years in between. A gravitational collapse that had formed a black hole over his past.

The Air France girl had left when he arrived at the

hotel, so no more friendly smiles. He took the stairs to the second floor, two and three at a time. More exercise.

The first thing he noticed when he entered his room was that it was too tidy. The cushioned rattan chairs with the gleam of old ivory neatly aligned around the low glass-topped coffee table, the magazines and books and personal papers in a different order than he had purposely left them. An extension of his old field training: a leaf in the door jamb, stones arranged in a certain order on a footpath, empty bottles or tin cans strategically placed on a doorstep. Nothing stolen, but it was obvious the room had been searched. And, probably, bugged. Colonel Vin keeping tabs. Or one of the colonel's enemies looking for evidence.

He took the dog-eared red folder from the top of the pile and sat in one of the rattan chairs. The folder was marked OCU/MLA, his last course in the Masters Liberal Arts programme at the small American university where he had taught medieval European history for six years. He opened the folder and flicked through the spiral-bound pages, stopping at a chapter headed: 'Cistercians – 12th Century – The Golden Age'. The Roman Catholic monastic order founded in 1098 at Cîteaux, France. Monks who demanded severe asceticism and reintroduced manual labour, making it a principal feature of their lives. They performed devotions seven times in every twenty-four hours. Nocturn, Matins, Terce, Sext, Nones, Vespers and, at seven in the evening, Compline. After Compline all conversation was prohibited, and the monks silently retired to rest in the dormitory, a long barrack-style room, where each brother had his own bed furnished with a mat, blanket, coverlet, and a pillow not exceeding one and a half feet in length. Six hours' sleep – and at two in the morning the cycle would begin again.

A soldier's discipline. Without the violence.

8

Old habits die hard.

That was why Edeyrn Owens had instructed the taxi driver to take him to the fountain on Thanon Pangkham that Sunday night. Pangkham Street. A shabby thoroughfare in Vientiane, capital of Laos. The fountain, one of the few places left where ruthless men and deadbeats still congregated, people who, for a free beer, would talk your ears off with stories governments conceal and newspapers never print. Something they call the other truth. Something that men like Edeyrn Owens understood and preserved: the secret fears of Prime Ministers and Presidents.

The rusted old Honda with a noisy exhaust jerked to a stop and dropped its solitary passenger. The city was suffering a blackout, a common occurrence during the rainy season. Owens stood, lightweight suit jacket draped over his arm, suitcase at his feet, watching the taxi drive away. The look of a well-fed tourist from civilization. A well-filled-out five-nine frame, where even the thinning grey hair – trimmed neatly at the sides – had the appearance of good health. He loosened his tie and undid the top button of his shirt. Inhaled the tropical darkness, the raw smells of traffic fumes mixed with rotting vegetation, the faint cooking aromas of fried rice and fish; a hint of the Asian monsoon in the air, perhaps. A few oil lamps gleaming from nearby restaurant windows gave the only light.

This was Owens's meeting place. The place to which he had come in his younger days. He didn't move for a number of minutes, other than to shoo away a few locals who wanted to carry his suitcase somewhere – anywhere – for a few *kip*, or an American dollar bill. Enough time for one of the curious onlookers gathered around the fountain to finally move out of the deep shadows.

'Looking for a hotel?' The accent was American, the man's face as black as the night. He was dressed in jeans and a white T-shirt. Scuffed trainers on his feet. No wristwatch. Nondescript.

Owens shook his head from side to side. 'Now why am I not surprised to find you waiting here?' He held out a hand.

'What were you expecting?'

'Oh, I don't know,' Owens said in his lilting Welsh accent. 'Old Mr Davies at Tonypandy Grammar School. Whisky on his breath and a leer in his frosty eye as he coveted the exposed white thighs of Miss Llewellyn, the games mistress, as she played netball with her girls. Or, better yet, the Marquis de Casalduero: the skeletons of the last two oxen still yoked to the wheel; the Pool of Sighs in the shade of the calabash trees . . . Anything but an antique dealer from Washington DC.'

Saigon Express

Tanner Williams picked up Owens's suitcase and the two men started walking. One, the son of a coal miner from the Rhondda Valley, the other – the many-times-great-grandson of a Nigerian Hausa man sold into slavery. Both in the game of secrets. Both getting on in years. They often played a kind of intellectual trivia, testing each other's brilliance. Like now.

Williams said, 'Gabriel Garcia Marquez.'

'What?'

'Marquis de Casalduero; the skeletons of the last two oxen . . .'

'Very good, Tanner. But which novel?'

'*Love in the Time of Cholera*? . . . *The Autumn of the Patriarch*? . . . *One Hundred Years of Solitude*?'

'Isn't this the way to the river?' Owens asked.

'Yes. We've got rooms at the Inter Hotel . . . Only decent place I could find.'

'I think I've stayed there in the past.'

'Not much better than Colombia, is it? You remember that hotel in Santa Marta?'

'I remember it was very noisy and it cost me a bottle of cognac . . . Your first time here, in Laos?'

'Yeah, not much different than what I remember of 'Nam, though.'

'Oh, I don't know, I always felt this was one of the most enigmatic countries in Asia, known from antiquity as Lan Xang, or Land of a Million Elephants . . . Or, as the Indochina War-era journalists used to say, a Million Irrelevants. How did you know about the fountain, by the way?'

'Somebody from your side mentioned it was your rendezvous point in the old days.'

'*Dates and itinerary arranged*,' mumbled Owens.

'What was that?'

'Did it come from Jaggers?'

'I don't know.'

'Not important.'

They reached the end of Pangkham Street and turned right by the Laos Foreign Trade Bank. Walked on in silence for a while. Lights flickered from boats on the Mekong River. The raw night smells growing stronger. The strobing white lights of a jet airliner in a climbing turn from Wattay airport disappearing into unseen clouds. Traffic sounds. Snatches of voices and music from a café on the opposite side of the road.

'What do you know about an individual called William Mather?' Owens asked.

'Not only Mather, Winter as well.' No preamble. As sharp as a knife thrust.

'John Winter?' Disbelief.

'It seems he tricked everybody on that flight out of Colombia.'

'He's still alive, you mean?'

'Not only that, we think he's involved with Mather on this Tbilisi matter?'

Williams outlined the scant information received from his old boss, Eberhart, and the suppositions being kicked around Langley by the Deputy Director for Intelligence (DDI), the head of the CIA's analytic directorate, which evaluates, weighs, and summarizes raw intelligence reports.

'So you think it was Mather who came here to link up with Winter?'

'We ran a check with all the airlines at Bangkok. Mather's name came up on a Thai Air manifest last Thursday morning: Bangkok – Vientiane.'

'What about the uranium shipment? Hardly bring it along as personal baggage, could he?'

Williams said, 'I raised the same question. No one seems to have an answer to that. All we know is, Winter originally mailed his letters from here . . . Probably from the post office on Khu Vieng Street. That's the only one I've located.' Adding as an afterthought, 'A kind of republic of thieves and murderers, this place, isn't it?'

'Indeed . . . So the consensus is that Mather stole the shipment, and that Winter is setting up the sale?'

'Lot of money involved.'

Owens recalled his meeting with Timothy Jaggers. *Hardly worth risking everything for a few kilos of uranium, is it?* How far did you have to move the decimal point to make the risk worthwhile?

'Did you ever think that giving Winter his money back might have saved a few red faces?'

Williams transferred the suitcase to his left hand. 'Langley did, but by the time they had come to that conclusion it was too late. The deadline had been passed.'

'Oh, dear,' Owens murmured. 'First you break your promise on the amnesty you offered him in Colombia in exchange for information on the Cali Cartel, even though he completed his side of the bargain. And then you follow up by stealing the piggy bank with his life's savings.'

'Blood money.'

'By whose definition?'

'So, what are you suggesting?'

'I'm not quite that far yet. I'm still trying to visualize Winter out here somewhere with a consignment . . .

How much uranium did you say?'

'Three hundred kilos.'

'With three hundred kilos of Uranium-235. Planning to do what?'

'Sell it to the highest bidder, perhaps.'

Owens was silent. Concentrating on finding his footing on the uneven pavement. Thinking of Winter. The man was no ordinary soldier of fortune. He was a long way beyond that. An intellectual killer. 'Any other leads?' he asked.

'We're working on it.'

'You never went up against the Russians in the old days, did you?'

'Only their friends.'

'This is not the same. You're not working with South American middlemen this time. This is a European manoeuvre, classic as Clausewitz in its way. The Russians know how to exploit an enemy's patience.'

'And we are the enemy?'

'Why not?'

'You think they engineered the entire fiasco.'

'They've been selling off every bit of junk ever since the Berlin Wall was pulled down. Everything not anchored to the planet. Makes sense, boyo. *Homo Sovieticus*, extinct race. Couple that to the fact that they are the world's most cunning liars – it's a cultural trait, you see. They can lie themselves into belief. That, after all, is the necessary precondition of their ideology.'

'And you really believe Winter is working for them? And who are they, exactly? Mafia? Georgians? Chechens? Politicians?'

'Does it matter? He obviously still has a good contact source.'

'And his being here in South-East Asia is nothing more than a diversionary tactic!'

'I didn't say that. The problem with Winter is that he's very complex.'

'Remember what I said in Colombia. I said you overrated the man. I think you're still doing it. So he pulled a stunt and faked a plane crash.'

Owens said, 'Fooled everybody, though, didn't he?'

Williams was silent.

'Why didn't you retire, by the way?'

Williams laughed for the first time that evening. 'I did. This operation is a favour for the Director.'

'Didn't realize you were that fond of him.'

'I'm not. But the pay is very good.'

'Ah.'

'Of course, it's not all about money . . . I was taken with his eloquent summation concerning covert activity in South-East Asia: "The entire fucking region is still the supreme tar baby".'

Owens chuckled. 'An articulate man, your Director.'

'Then again, he did mention the Brits were putting their most valuable South-East Asia asset out here.'

Most valuable asset. Timothy Jaggers's phrasing. 'Did he, indeed.'

Williams said, 'Of course, have you considered that if your hypothesis on the Russians is correct the consignment is probably in the hands of the new owner already?'

'Not Winter's way of doing business. This time he'll make sure that those who need to know will know.'

'Subtlety and violence combined, you mean?'

Owens said, 'A mirror reflecting a mirror. It ends in a vanishing point. We need to find the point and set our traps before he gets there and disappears.'

'Have you eaten today?'

'Picked at airline food, that's all.'

'I'll buy you dinner, then. I found a very good Indian restaurant up by the fountain . . . if you feel up to spicy food.'

'What about the blackout?'

'They have gas cookers . . . Same thing happened a few nights ago.'

'Anyway, I must say you seem very relaxed about all of this. Being retired – or is it semi-retired – must have its benefits.'

'It does.'

'And your wife is happy with you being out here?'

'I bought her a new BMW.'

'And that did the trick?'

'And sent her and her sister on a shopping spree to New York.'

'Sounds expensive.'

'Exactly what I told Eberhart.'

Owens chuckled. 'Going back to Winter, I know your feelings on this. That it cannot be exactly like the last time. That we cannot be seduced by déjà vu. The reality, however, is that Winter makes the rules, meaning he will give us more information as time goes by, little clues. You did say he sent the letter to the Director at Langley. Why would he do that if it wasn't you he wanted out here in the field? Eberhart didn't recruit you, Tanner. Winter did.'

They stopped outside the Inter Hotel. The doors were open. Candlelight flickered in the gloomy interior. The scent of joss sticks on the humid night air. Like a darkened church welcoming the faithful.

'Existential free fall, you mean?'

'The psychological school of trait theorists believes that traits are embedded in the nervous system, that they steer or guide us to behave consistently.'

'So what are you suggesting? That he's tough-minded, practical . . . controlled?'

'Tough-minded? Yes. Controlled and practical? He proved that to us in Colombia.'

'What about his expectancies, Edeyrn? "If-then" statements, or personal predictions about the outcome. Expectations about what will happen if he behaves in certain ways based upon his observation of us . . . Except competencies influence expectancies. How competent can one man be?'

'Competent enough to kill you, perhaps!'

Williams laughed. 'He's still an ex-army sergeant, Edeyrn.'

'Armies are run by sergeants.'

'Not our kind.'

Owens dropped his head. 'The book by Marquez was *Of Love and Other Demons*, by the way.'

'At least I was half right.'

It was a trick as old as orthodoxy: to snare the suspect in small heresies, paradoxes of dogma that even the prophet could not reconcile. 'Like saying Winter is an ex-army sergeant, when he in fact belonged to the elite Special Air Service,' Owens replied.

Williams was silent.

'Do you think he's still here . . . In Vientiane?' Owens asked.

'He could be, we don't know. But it seems that

Mather only had a three-hour layover here before catching a flight to Taipei.'

'Really? You think Winter went with him?'

'Possibly.'

'Anything more from Taipei?'

'On Mather? No. He disappeared. Vanished into thin air. Something arranged by Winter, I'm sure. He's very good at that, isn't he?' Williams smiled – showing even white teeth – then turned on his heel and marched into the hotel.

Owens followed. No smiles from him. He was afraid of Winter, afraid of even the idea of jungle warfare with such a man. You might make a fool of him once, but twice! It was as though Tanner had tripped a wire and he, following, had spotted the grenade . . . live now. Knowing it was too late . . . His mind saying, *Run, duck, evaporate.* Body unable to react fast enough. It was like sliding on ice. No way to stop, and nowhere to go but in the direction gravity carried you.

9

At 7.30 on that Monday morning, downtown Saigon had the look of a French provincial city. Pleasant, colourless and characterless. It also had the roar of traffic competing with jackhammers clearing sites for new high-rise buildings. Joint-venture projects. Your money, our blessing. High-stakes poker with a Soviet-trained communist government.

Winter, wearing the same type of tropical kit as on the previous evening, including the camera slung around his neck, had bought a two-day-old *Herald Tribune International* newspaper from the bookshop on Dong Khoi Street and was making his way back to the Caravelle when he saw the white-haired Russian. He was sitting at a sidewalk table outside the Continental Hotel on the opposite side of Lam Son Square. Two cups of coffee were on the table before him. The white Toyota staff car with the red number plates was parked at the head of the taxi rank, its driver, a young soldier, sitting on the kerb, smoking a cigarette.

Winter went over to the Russian and pulled out a chair. Sat down without a word.

Yuri the Yid looked up and grinned. 'No need for cigarettes, eh Wint? Traffic fumes kill you just as fucking quick.' He was a big flabby man, short of breath even when talking. Round wire-rimmed spectacles on a hooked, fleshy nose. Pale grey inquisitive eyes. Shoulder-length grey hair. Beige bush jacket – short sleeves, matching pants. Suede desert boots. Yuri Alexsandr Becker. A man who had once known by heart every stop on the two-thousand-mile trans-Siberian rail journey to Novosibirsk, courtesy of a freezing cattle car crammed with other prisoners. He, who had a small blue Orthodox cross tattooed on his left breast, a crescent moon beneath the cross bar – a thief's tattoo. He, one of the *Vory v Zakone* – the thieves-in-law, royalty in the old *Soyuz* camps and jails and prisons. Other than that, he was a Jew. Which was why he had been known as Yuri the Yid. In the days of his youth.

Winter said, 'Why the kids on the motor bikes wear face masks with filters. Sensible. Anyway, I thought you were picking me up at nine.'

'I was. But I thought I'd like to come into the city early. Take coffee outside the famous Continental. Watch the people.'

'Where you staying?'

'At the colonel's house. He insisted it is better for security. Nice place, out by the airport. I think I will buy myself one just like it.'

'Here?'

'Hell, no. Spain or Portugal. Is better.'

'And the two cups of coffee?'

Yuri the Yid shrugged. 'Oh, some old saying, "When the day's been good to you, order two drinks – one for yourself and one for humanity. Sooner or later humanity will come and join you for the other". I thought I'd get an early start on the day. Make some luck.'

Winter took a pack of Particulares from his pocket and offered one to the Russian. Took one himself. Lit them.

Yuri said, 'What of the airplane, the Phantom? The colonel said you flew it.'

'On Friday.'

'Any problems?'

'Old aeroplanes, Yuri, no guarantees, but we'll keep our fingers crossed. Speaking of which, you never told me how you spirited that shipment out of Tbilisi.'

The Russian scratched the side of his big nose. 'How do you think? Money. Dollars, pounds, francs, marks. Not roubles. Real money. We are the new capitalists, all of Russia, all the Independent States. The director of the shut-down nuclear reactor at Tbilisi no different than the rest of us who were the technicians. One day the paychecks stopped coming, like the army when the money ran out and the soldiers started to leave, taking their weapons with them. So why should he be any different, especially when we know that Mikhail Sergeyvich Gorbachev was the great traitor who conspired to destroy the Soyuz at the orders of his American and Zionist paymasters. And where is Mikhail Sergeyvich now? I tell you where he is, he is in New York, drinking champagne, making speeches. And back in Moscow, Boris Yeltsin is permanently pissed because he can't bear to focus on the greatest fucked-up country in the world. The director and the scientists and the workers at Tbilisi were once princes of the Soyuz, heroes of the people. Now they are starving. And that, my friend, is always the best time to buy people.' No short answers with Yuri the Yid. The typical soulful Russian. Far worse after a skinful of vodka.

Winter said, 'Not much different to sixteenth-century England when Henry the Eighth implemented the final dissolution of the abbeys and monasteries. They took the gold and silver. Even sold the libraries to Belgium or France. The best one was the church bells: they were gambled for. The winners sold them to Russia.'

'That is true?'

'Every word. Henry and his new religious order waging war on the monks, or what he termed soldiers of the Vatican; leaving the English peasants to face similar problems as today's citizens of the old Soviet Union. Pauperism increasing, because the whole body of the poor had been supported by the monks. One day there was bread on the table, education for the children. The next, full-scale disaster.'

'Could have been a soulmate of Lenin, your King Henry.'

'Or, as he was reputed to have spawned more than fifty illegitimate children, perhaps Lenin was genetically linked.'

'Frightening.'

'For the poor, at least,' Winter agreed. 'Anyway, what happened to the director at Tbilisi?'

'What do you think? He took the down payment and the letter of credit on the Swiss bank for the final payment next week, and ran as fast as his short fat legs would carry him. I switched the lead-lined containers. Too simple. Took the original to the airport as you instructed and handed it over to Sasha and his guys from Dneprepetrovsk. They loaded it on their jet. Last I saw of it. Then, as instructed, I came here.' Yuri finished his coffee. Wiped his mouth with the back of his hand. 'So! How did you like the Ukraine?'

'Dneprepetrovsk, you mean? I think it might have been a nice place once, especially the old part of the town, where the trees make an avenue down the centre of the main boulevard. The old houses must have been quite something in the Czarist times: homes of the rich merchants, I suppose. Bit run-down now.'

The Russian laughed. 'I think you are being polite. It's like all the other cities, fucked up and falling apart. You saw the river, of course?'

'Stayed in a hotel right next to it. Imported beer five dollars a bottle at the little café on the river footpath.'

'Sounds right, tourist prices. Did you know that river runs downstream from Chernobyl, and that the water is as toxic as hell? And the people are so poor they catch fish from it, and cook them and eat them? Shit, would you go out of your way to eat radioactive fish?'

'Probably did.'

'Not enough to kill you, though.'

'Didn't you work at Chernobyl once?'

'Sure. What do you want to know? You want a history of uranium and all that goes with it?'

Winter shook his head. 'Too early in the day for me.'

'You're right, better over a few vodkas, then you can see the funny side of caesium and strontium getting

89

into the human food chain. Fast food, faster cancer. Five hundred million victims over the next fifty years. A scientific estimate, you understand, it could be double or treble that.' A pause to catch his breath. A shrug of the broad shoulders. Coupled with a look of resignation. Russian acceptance. Nearly. 'You know why Russians don't really care about radioactive fallout and cancer? I tell you. It's because they are all alcoholics. They know that nine times out of ten they'll suffer liver failure first. So, what is it you now want me to do?'

'Help me with some of the shipping paperwork. The easy bit, Yuri.'

The Russian was thoughtful as he helped himself to another Particulares from the pack that was lying on the table. He lit it with the butt of the other one. 'You obviously had no problems with Customs when the jet got to Dneprepetrovsk.'

Winter sipped the lukewarm coffee. Thought of his cousin Sasha, who owned the Dnepre Pipe Company – the operators who had transported the newly labelled 'pipe parts' from Georgia in their Yak-40. Paid off Customs officials. Moving the crate to a hangar opposite the terminal where they had left him alone to fork-lift the crate on to a steel roller-bed, and from there into the open nose section of a modified underwing fuel drop-tank. Once inside and secured, he had used a tig-welder to run a seam around the mated parts. When it had cooled sufficiently, he had spray-painted over the seam. Matching drab green – like the rest of the tank. That night the drop-tank had been driven to Zhukovsky, an airfield near Moscow. And airlifted away on the Ilyushin-38 to Vietnam. 'Not me. Colonel Vin. He took care of everything.'

'And the colonel is dealing with the Iraqis?'

'Yes.'

'Military or civilian?'

'Possibly both. Why?'

'They're like the Chechens, that's why. Stalin was right about those bastards; send them east with the rest of the yellow pagan hordes. Dangerous people to deal with. Anyway, you think the Iraqis enjoy handing money to an unbeliever like you? An infidel.'

A small smile. 'Anybody out there you trust, Yuri?'

The Russian prodded his chest with a stubby forefinger. 'I trust Yuri Alexsandr, why I am still here. Apprenticed in my youth at Cold Mountain and the finest Siberian gulags. Why I outlived the old KGB. The OBKhSS. The apparatchik.'

'What was the OBKhSS?'

'Police Department for the Fight Against the Theft of Socialist Property. Okay for the party leaders to rob the fucking country blind. Not the citizens, eh!'

Winter half-turned in his seat and watched the early morning traffic turning into Le Loi Boulevard. A million or more people on the streets at the same time. Each driving to their own interpretation of the rules of the road. Girls in white *ao dais*, long hair flowing, high heels working the brake pedals of their Honda motorbikes as they weaved in and out of the moving lines of cars. Amazing there were so few accidents. 'How would you feel about going back to Russia?'

Yuri's eyes blinked. Like a startled owl. 'I can't go back . . . Not yet, at least.'

'Why not?'

'Why do you think! After Tbilisi the word will have

got around that Yuri disappeared at the same time as the uranium consignment . . . Even Russians can put two and two together. And when I go back the Organizatsiya – the *Mafiya* – will want a piece of the action, following which I get the heart attack . . . You know, the one caused by a knife between the fifth and six ribs.' More truth in that than he wanted to think about. Skulov, the policeman he had double-crossed in Tbilisi. Skulov, the simple cop coming up for retirement, to whom the promise of a fat pay day was too much to resist. Except Yuri'd skipped town without paying him. Skulov, more than one knife thrust. *The man who goes down gets skinned seven times, and then they stamp on him until he resembles nothing more than a week-old road kill.*

Winter said, 'Moscow, not Tbilisi. A quick in-and-out job. I'll get you new papers.'

Yuri the Yid scratched his nose again. Nervous. 'How long would I need to be there?'

'One night. One day. Max.'

'Same job as the one we're doing now?'

Winter nodded. 'More or less.'

'There's nobody else?'

'No.'

'What's it about, exactly?'

'Paperwork, that's all. Like the British passport you picked up for me in Tbilisi and sent to the Ukraine on the Yak.'

'I'd forgotten about that. Obviously you got it okay?'

'What about the owner? No trouble.'

The Russian's breathing rattled in his chest, came out as a faint whistle between his teeth. *Winter had insisted on no rough stuff.* He waved a hand impatiently.

'Nothing to do with the owner. I bribed one of the girls who take the passports and give you the hotel card. The hotel unfortunately "lost" the passport. As the guest was registered for another four or five days I figured that would give you the time you needed to get out of there.'

'How did you get my photograph laminated in so quickly?'

'I planned it that way. Besides, I didn't want to hang around.'

Winter took a pen from his shirt pocket and began writing coded instructions and numbers on the cigarette packet. 'Something else that's simple,' he said eventually, sliding the pack of Particulares across the table. 'Same code we used for Tbilisi.'

The Russian studied the packet for a moment. Squinting from time to time at the small print, trying to decipher the text. Finally he said, 'Why Moscow, if all I have to do is send two faxes? Why not from here?'

'Protection for the colonel, among other things. If the authorities intercepted a fax to Iraq . . . A remote possibility, but you see what I'm getting at?'

'But it would be in code, no?'

'And you think the local authorities wouldn't see that?'

'Okay. Then, if not from here, why not send the faxes from Paris or London?'

'That's the way the colonel set up the deal with the Iraqis. Even gave them a hotel fax number in Moscow where the fax would originate from and a precise time. I agree with what you're saying, but to try and change things now could cause serious problems, like the Iraqis thinking security had been breached. That could kill the deal.'

'Shit.'

'A matter of hours in Moscow, no more. A lot of money at stake.'

'What about the contents of the faxes?'

'I'll give you that before you leave.'

Yuri frowned and compressed his lips into a thin hard line. Shook his head from side to side. 'And my new papers?'

'There's an old Frenchman who lives not far from here. He was a double agent. Spied for the French *and* the Viet Minh back in the fifties. He's quite an exceptional forger. If he's still alive.'

'And if not?'

'We'll find someone.'

'Only the best,' Yuri the Yid said anxiously. 'I'm not going back to Moscow, not even for a day, unless I have genuine papers.'

'Get your hair cut short, dyed blond. New business suit. Half a dozen passport photos. I'll make contact with Frenchie today. If he's still in business I'll leave an envelope with the concierge at the Rex first thing in the morning. Instructions how to get to his house.'

'When am I leaving?'

'Wednesday.'

Two cups of coffee. One for himself, one for humanity. Some fucking joke. Yuri squinted at the cigarette packet again. 'What is this GSM phone?'

'I'll let you have it tomorrow. Memorize those two numbers: the first one is yours, the second, mine.'

'Not a problem.'

'Red Stevens saw you at the Emperor last night, by the way. Thought you might be following him.'

'Campbell. He's travelling as "Neil Campbell". How

94

did he find out who I was?'

'One of the desk clerks mentioned you were a *Lien Xo*. So he thinks you're a Russian adviser working for the Hanoi boys, that's all. I thought you would have paid off all the desk clerks.'

'Only the manager.'

'How'd you find him?'

'Names and aliases you gave me. Checked them against a daily list I get from a Customs officer at the airport. I was going to phone you at the Caravelle, but I figured he would already have been in touch.'

'Anything?'

'He arrived on Saturday morning. 11.30. Came in the same way as you, from Taipei on an EVA flight. Two phone calls: one Saturday, one yesterday. Both to his wife in Caracas.'

'You listened in?'

'Better. All his calls are recorded. Apart from his pet dog being sick and his wife telling him she missed him and asking a dozen times when will he be home, nothing. Looks clean to me.'

'Good.'

'Frenette and his crew will be arriving at noon today.'

'I know. I'll keep an eye on them.'

The Russian laughed. 'And you ask me who is out there I trust!'

'Business, Yuri.'

Yuri the Yid rocked gently back and forwards in his chair. *Business. Moscow. Skulov.* 'Shit,' he whispered to himself.

10

Timothy Jaggers was staring through the plate-glass window of the airport terminal, as if willing the early-morning light to break through the low cloud and drizzle that persisted over the Warsaw Plain.

He turned to the man at his side, Sam Yeo. The man with the scarred eyebrows and the flattened nose – the ugly American. A Louisiana accent as thick as molasses. Even so, he was appropriately dressed, thank God (the previous evening he had been dressed in jeans, sweater, sneakers and a baseball cap – which had precluded them from dining in a decent restaurant). Conservative suit, dark overcoat. Briefcase. Another Monday-morning businessman, off to somewhere. 'I assume you're flying back to Tbilisi this morning?'

'Hell no, sir.' Except he pronounced it 'suh'. 'Back Stateside. Whatever was in Georgia is long gone, mark my words.'

Jaggers checked his tie was straight in his reflection in the window. Turned back to Yeo. One gloved hand covering the other on the umbrella handle being used as a support to lean on. *Whatever was in Georgia is long gone, mark my words.* He didn't altogether agree. But then, he found it hard to agree with Americans at the best of times. He didn't like them. Too loud. Too brash. 'You're quite sure it was Mather?'

'Not me, Stonecipher. Worked for your people in the old days.'

'Did he really?' Jaggers said innocently.

Yeo looked around. Gauging the distance to the nearest passengers. Businessmen, mostly. Heads buried in newspapers. One or two pecking away at laptop computers. He lowered his voice. 'Probably before your time. Anyway your guy Mather checked out of his hotel. Told the desk clerk he would be back after the weekend, and that he'd like a more comfortable room. Only reason he was remembered, it seems: complained a lot about the service. Beyond that, all we know for certain is that Mather travelled to Bangkok, Vientiane, and on to Taipei. After Taipei, no movements.'

'And from what you told me last night you have reason to believe that Mather may have joined up with John Winter in Vientiane.'

'Supposition, predicated on the fact that the letters Winter sent to Langley and your people in London tie in quite nicely with the present scenario. Seems he plays a pretty sophisticated kind of ball game, wouldn't you say?'

Jaggers sneered. 'He's just another thug.'

'Ex-British SAS. Very successful mercenary. Retired some years ago and took up a teaching job in Oklahoma City at a small Methodist university, married a television journalist. She was killed eighteen months later by a drug gang. The university professor drops his disguise and promptly takes out the entire gang, one by one. Following that, he heads south to Colombia and virtually single-handedly wipes out the Cali Cartel; a bit more than a thug, in my book!'

Jaggers lapsed into one of his long silences. He checked the briefcase at his feet. The toes of his black Oxford brogues. The building was becoming too warm. Uncomfortable. He considered removing his raincoat and his gloves, glanced at his Longines watch and decided it was hardly worth the effort: the flight would be called soon. Finally: 'And the package! Why weren't we made aware of the exact amount being transferred?'

'You're asking me?' Yeo managed a cynical little laugh. 'Some secret deal cooked up between President Clinton and your Prime Minister. I doubt if Langley was kept up to speed on half of what was going on. Until the shit hit the fan, at least. Then everyone was shredding documents and pointing fingers. All I can tell you is that no one really knows how much fissionable material is now under loose guard in the former Soviet Union. KGB guards at nuclear plants have been replaced by pensioners carrying rusting World War Two rifles. Other than that, Minatom is so goddamned broke it can't even conduct inventories in its laboratories, let alone pay its scientists, technicians and security people . . . That's the reason they agreed to move various smaller packages to Tbilisi, for collection as one consignment. As the plant was being closed down it was considered a good low-key move.'

Jaggers's mind focused on Minatom, Russia's Atomic Energy Ministry. The weak link, as far as he was concerned. 'So who was providing security at Tbilisi?'

'Good question. The Georgians. Except they're blaming our people and your people, saying we agreed to collect it. What they're forgetting to say is that the package was switched no more than forty-eight hours before the official handover.'

Jaggers suppressed a yawn. He needed sleep. 'You didn't say that last night.'

'I didn't say what?'

'That the package was switched forty-eight hours before the handover.'

'It couldn't have happened any other way, because that was the time the smaller shipments were consolidated into the one packing crate.'

'What about the British consignment?'

'That was in a detachable end-frame of the container. Separation was supposed to occur at the airport on the day that the two flights were due to airlift the cargo out.'

'And the contents were as described?'

'Uranium-235, yeah.'

'Anything else you can add?'

Glass doors sighed open nearby. Stewardesses pulling their collapsible wheeled baggage-haulers. Happy pretty faces. Non-stop chatter. A faint hint of perfume caught in the whirlpooling damp air that followed them into the terminal.

Yeo watched them for a moment, then went back to considering the jumbled facts running around in his mind. Not least of which was his briefing on Uranium-

238, or 'yellow cake' as it was known, which fuelled nuclear reactors. And his knowledge that the 235 was contained within the 238, but achieving isotope separation was not only very slow but very difficult – and seriously expensive. He shook his head. 'Not really. Except that if Saddam gets his hands on it we've got big troubles.'

'They've been working on bomb-engineering for some time now, you mean?'

'Exactly. With this package they could have their first bomb in place within months. After that, no one is going to dare suggest they leave Kuwait a second time. In fact, we'll probably give it to them by way of a peace offering.'

Jaggers turned back to the window and peered out at the cerebral morning. His breath misted the glass. 'So that's more or less everything?'

'Except for the Tbilisi director and one of the technicians being reported as missing. I gave you the details last night.'

'Quite, quite.'

'It was suggested to me that Mather's buddy might have been involved, at least as a fall guy.'

'His buddy!' Jaggers winced. 'May one enquire who that might be?'

'Jack Giles.'

'Giles was a Member of Parliament. That he happened to be on the board of Prometheus Limited, Mather's company, does not necessarily implicate him in any subversive plot. Her Majesty's Government would be at the very least displeased should unfounded rumours of that nature make their way into the press. I do hope I'm making myself quite clear?'

'You figure that Giles's death was suicide, then?'

'I'm not a policeman, Sam.'

'Then again, there's the money.'

'Money?'

'Somebody's going to pay Winter and Mather a great deal of that.'

'And you think we can trace such a payment?'

Yeo was thinking of his drinking buddy Mehdizadeh in Nassau, a man who knew a thing or two about capital flight. 'Anything's possible, Tim.'

Twenty minutes later Jaggers was sitting in an aisle seat in the Club Class section of a British Airways Boeing 757, recapping on the weekend events. The meeting in Brussels with an old chum who had been up at Oxford with him. That he was now a Euro-minister was all the better. Someone to advise him on the new strategies about intelligence agencies being mooted by the member countries. Cutbacks being considered a very real threat for the twenty-first century. From that meeting, the sudden opportunity to meet with Yeo on Sunday night in Warsaw. Arranging to leave his car at the embassy until the following weekend; an excuse that would, he hoped, lead to picking up where he'd left off with his old Magdalen ally.

Reading up the American's file on the Sunday-evening flight to the Polish capital. Yeo, a man who had worked for the CIA Moscow station years earlier under Paul Stombaugh, the case officer for aviation expert Adolf Tolkachev, the Soviet mole who had provided critical intelligence for years on Soviet research into stealth/radar-defeating technology. It was after Stombaugh was arrested, along with four other CIA undercover agents, and expelled for spying that Yeo slipped in and obtained the final pieces of the stealth technology puzzle. Not a moment too soon. Tolkachev was arrested the following day and executed. Yeo returned to the west with the last pieces of the puzzle. Enough to start the American techno-crats down the road code-named 'Have Blue' and 'Senior Trend' that led to the development and acquisition of the first very-low-observable combat aircraft – the F-117A.

A good man in his day.

But what about now?

And what contributions had he made in this latest fiasco? Nothing they didn't already know. Which left what? He had seen field reports from the new self-proclaimed Chechnya Republic. Home to the largest open-air weapons market in the former Soviet Union. Buyers came from every corner of the world to bid on the weapons looted from the Red Army by its own men. Rifles, hand grenades, howitzers, rocket-launchers, all the way up to helicopters and fighter planes. And now the serious side of the inventory. The nuclear side. Jaggers wondered how Mather and possibly Giles (God forbid) had become involved in such things.

Then again, there was always Stonecipher.

Perhaps he knew more than he was telling!

11

The War Crimes Museum was once known as the 'Museum of American War Crimes'. It is housed in the former US Information Service building at 28 Vo Van Tan Street, at the intersection with Le Qui Don. In the yard of the museum, US armoured vehicles, artillery pieces, bombs and infantry weapons vie for space. There is also a guillotine, which the French used to deal with Viet Minh troublemakers. And models of the notorious tiger cages used by the South Vietnamese military to house VC prisoners on Con Son Island.

Winter arrived outside the museum a little after seven o'clock that evening, at the same time the storm hit the downtown area. Tropical rain, pounding the streets. A ghostly image of wind-driven surf-spray caught in the street-lights. High-frequency sheet lightning flickering white and orange and yellow, picking out the threatening lines of towering cumulonimbus clouds. It was the season when all the illnesses of the spirit seemed to hang heavy in the air.

An emaciated Chinese shuffled to the museum gate

and began to fiddle with the lock. He looked as thin as
the soaking wet clothes he wore. The gate opened and
the old man looked up, 'Mis-ta Win-ta, this way,
please . . . Mis-ta Red, this way, please.' He bowed as
Winter slipped quickly through the gate and waited
while it was secured. He watched the man, noticing
the sunken cheeks, the tiny wrists, arms like those of a
young girl, and wondered how many opium pipes – or
whatever else they used these days – it had taken to
whittle him down to almost a shadow.

The man moved past him, through the puddles,
weaving through the killing machinery. Winter
followed. The artillery pieces strobing in and out of
the lightning-lit darkness. Images that threw up other
images from the distorted shadows; not unlike a Nick
Ashe course on the Brecon Beacons in his army days.
The reflex-action exercise: standing face-to-face one
metre apart. Ashe holding his massive arms forward,
calloused palms together, fingers pointing at Winter's
chest. The assignment: to strike your instructor's
hands before he jerked them out of range. The penalty
for failure – a free hit for the instructor. A hit that
would make your eyes water. Winter flinched at the
memory. Real. Too real.

Through the smells of rain and vegetation and
untreated sewage, he picked out the scent of the cigar
long before he reached its owner. 'I hear you sell
planes,' he called out.

Laughter. 'Sure I do,' the Aussie accent called back
from the doorway shelter of a watchman's tin-roofed
hootch.

'What colour?'

'Blue and white. God's colours.'

'My favourite.'

Stevens laughed again, and held the canvas sheet aside, 'No beer, but we've got the kettle on.'

Inside the hootch was a small table with three chairs. A young man – little more than a boy – was sitting in one of them. His face half-turned away from the yellow light of the lantern. Rain dripped through the roof, splashing off the edge of the table.

Stevens motioned him to a chair.

Winter sat. 'What's the big panic, then?'

Stevens pointed to the young man. 'Your mate, TC.'

Winter looked again; the boyish face turned towards him. He hadn't recognized him. Something was missing, or perhaps it was the badly swollen face, the cut lips caked in dried blood. The black hair cropped to the skull. The rags he was dressed in. He held out a hand. 'Hello, TC. Good to see you again.' A soft comforting voice.

'Thank you, Mister Winter, I really appreciate your help.' He spoke with a Californian accent – nervous, uncertain, anxious to please.

'Call me Wint, we don't stand on ceremony. No thanks necessary, believe me; we don't like bully boys, that's all. No broken bones, I take it?'

The young American nodded to confirm Winter's supposition and mumbled, 'No, fine.' And continued to look scared to death.

Stevens said, 'Bloody lucky you asked me to try and find him today. Seems they were planning to ship him out to Hanoi tomorrow morning, to Hoa Lo Prison. You know, the old Hanoi Hilton.'

Winter took a damp pack of Particulares from his shirt pocket and lit one. The snare-drum sound of rain on the tin roof increased its tempo. 'How did you manage . . .' he started.

'Long story, we can talk about that later. Right now I need that grand. You got it?'

Winter unfastened the lower buttons of his shirt and opened one of the pouches of his money belt. He counted off ten one-hundred-dollar bills and passed them to the Australian who promptly disappeared back out into the rain. He returned a few seconds later, sat down and tried to re-light his soggy cigar. It caught at the third attempt and he took a few puffs. 'The Chinese guy,' he said, by way of explanation. 'He wanted two grand for helping to spring TC here, that's why I phoned you at the base a couple of hours ago. I only had a thou, and the old bugger wouldn't take a cheque or an IOU.'

'So what happens when they find TC missing from wherever you lifted him?'

'They already have. I think you could say we've got problems.'

Winter looked from Stevens to TC and back again. Something he hadn't quite bargained for. Usually bribes were enough to make people forget they'd ever known a prisoner. The bigger the bribe, the longer the sudden attack of amnesia lasted. After that, and with the bureaucratic red tape in this part of the world, it would have been a year or more before anyone discovered anything was amiss. Even then no one would care too much, or if they did they would never show it. Saving face. 'Were you seen by the army or police?'

'Both.'

'You need to check out of your hotel. First priority.'

Stevens jerked a thumb towards the corner of the

hootch. Two suitcases. 'Already did that. You want tea?'

'Thanks.'

Stevens clucked out something in Vietnamese and an old woman emerged from a dark corner, set three places, and poured the steamy liquid over the crystal-line sugar in the bottom of the cups.

'What's your idea?' Winter asked.

Stevens turned to the old woman. '*Di di mau,*' he said sharply, and she disappeared through the canvas flap into the rain. He turned back to Winter. 'She's offered us the use of her simple home. We return the courtesy in dollars.'

'She can be trusted?'

'Only if she hears nothing. I doubt she understands English but it's not worth the risk.'

'Who is she? Relation of the Chinaman?'

'No, but he knew of her. That's why he suggested this place for the exchange.'

Winter wondered how long the good faith would last now that the money had been handed over. 'Not wise to stay too long.'

'Roger that.'

Winter took a sip of the tea. The sweetness coated his mouth like a sickness. He put the cup back on the table and lit another cigarette from the old one. Dropped the butt on the floor. It fizzled out on the wet earth. 'I'll get hold of the colonel. Perhaps he can fix you and TC up with quarters at the base.'

'You think that's safe?' Concern in every word. 'I mean, I know the colour of the tiger and I know which end the teeth are on, but I don't necessarily want to chance my bloody arm sleeping in the cage, do I?'

'Last place they'd think of looking, Red.'

Stevens puffed at his cigar. 'Nothing else we can do, then?'

'Not at short notice.' Winter turned to TC. 'I imagine they've still got your passport and all your personal belongings?' That soft voice again.

The American put his hand to his face. 'And my glasses.' *The missing something.* 'Except,' he added, reaching down by the side of the table. 'My mother's ashes, I got those. I'd like to take them to the temple before I leave. That's why I came, after all.' He put the willow-patterned urn on the table.

'How did you get that back?'

'He hit a guard across the head with a bloody chair,' Stevens snapped.

'He what?'

'The guard was trying to stop him getting it.'

'It was an accident,' TC mumbled.

Winter said, 'Anything else I should know?'

Stevens took a deep breath, held it, then exhaled very slowly. 'I think he killed him.'

'You think . . .'

'I didn't have long, but I checked his pulse. Nothing.'

'Shit.'

'More or less what I said.'

It was two hours later when they arrived at the Bien Hoa airbase. *Doc Lap, Tu Do, Hanh Phuc,* painted in black letters on the outer entrance concrete arch – Independence, Freedom, Happiness. The national slogan.

Fortress Bien Hoa. Searchlights. Twelve-feet-high

cinder-block walls topped with razor wire. Heavy-gauge solid steel gates. Armed soldiers with guard dogs. And, once airside, the headlights of the car picking out lines of clapped-out corrosion-riddled Skyraider aircraft parked in concrete revetments and a ramp full of C-130 Hercules transports, most sitting at drunken angles due to flat tyres. Soldiers squatting under the wings out of the weather. Guarding what? A near-thirty-year-old tinker's yard, where the scrap-metal price would hardly pay the cutting and moving expenses. Winter thought about mentioning it, but the colonel wasn't having a particularly good evening. He had even driven his own staff car that night, afraid to let his regular driver in on anything that appeared non-procedural. Out of the ordinary.

He dropped the three of them outside a barrack hut set in a stand of trees, a few hundred metres east of the maintenance hangar that housed the Ilyushin-38 and the F-4 Phantom.

'I will wait for you,' he said to Winter. 'Five minutes, then we must go.' A nervous man.

Winter would ease his mind on the drive back to Saigon. The banking transactions they were putting in place the following morning at the Vietcombank – something to make him sleep a little easier.

Stevens was the first inside. He found the switches by the door. Low-watt light bounced off cracked brown linoleum and cream-washed walls. The smell of rotting vegetation and raw sewage through a broken window-pane. No lampshades.

Winter said, 'On the hoteliers' star-rating system this place is listed as a dusty, off-course meteor in the galaxy of African Rest Houses and Sherpa way stations.' He paused and, when TC continued to look blank, he explained: 'A joke.'

'Sorry.'

'Forget it.'

Red Stevens was already at the far end of the barrack room. 'I'll check the windows and doors out back,' he shouted, before disappearing through a doorway.

Winter sat down on the end of one of the beds. The rooms were barren, with cold linoleum floors, rickety wardrobes, low iron beds and stained, lumpy mattresses with the musty damp smell of the tropics. There were no televisions or telephones. No kitchen to cook meals. The bathrooms, he had noticed as he came down the corridor, were communal, with rows of metal shower stalls, seatless toilets and long pig-trough sinks. The only good thing about the former American-built barracks was that it was dry and free and, hopefully, safe. 'Did you ever serve in the army, TC?'

TC was looking around the Spartan barrack room, as if trying to come to terms with some terrible nightmare he had found himself trapped in. The reality of third worlds: you either loved them or hated them, there was no halfway. Black and white. Period. 'No.'

No. He should have known. Too soft. Too gentle. *Me, I grew up in places like this. All my worldly possessions in a tallboy and a bedside locker. Terrible food, the worst pay in the world. Discipline.* 'Do you want a cigarette?' TC reached out and took one. Winter lit it. 'Not quite LA, is it?'

'I've been thinking that ever since I arrived. My parents were both Vietnamese, but I haven't a clue what's going on in this country. I mean, I just couldn't imagine the filth and squalor that these people live in.

It's as if they don't care.' TC put his hand to his jaw. Gently rubbing at some invisible pain.

'Oh, I think they do, except their priorities are not neat little homes with perfectly cut Bermuda-grass lawns and a two-car garage complete with the latest-model autos. This is one of those seriously troubled third-world countries, ruled by so-called benevolent dictators or governments of the same ilk. The priority here is how to get enough rice to fill your belly day after day.'

'Yes, I suppose . . .'

'Did you ask your army captors if you could see someone from the American Consulate?'

'About a hundred times a day.'

'What did they say?'

'They laughed. Called me a *Viet Kieu.*'

'You know what that is?'

'Sure. My father wasn't one, either. Just someone who didn't believe in communism. Seems he was right all along, wouldn't you say?'

'Quite possibly.'

'They . . . they told me that my father had worked for the American CIA, that he'd helped them in the mass assassination of fifty thousand Vietnamese. Something they called the Phoenix Programme.'

'I've heard of it, but I think they probably try the same interrogation procedure on anyone they pick up. Salve for a festering wound. Or perhaps saving face at any price.'

TC dabbed at his cracked and bleeding lips with the sleeve of his dirty shirt.

'If it hurts to much to talk, we can leave it until tomorrow.'

'No . . . It's nothing . . . I thought perhaps now I'm free I could go to the American embassy. Surely they'd get me on a flight back home?'

Winter stared into the young man's eyes. 'Except you've killed a Vietnamese national. They'd be forced to hand you over to the local authorities.'

'It was an accident . . .'

'Maybe, maybe.' Winter shook his head sadly. 'But it's your word only. What did Red say?'

'Nothing. He was too angry.'

'Understandable. You probably frightened him to death. The point is, we're here on semi-official government business. That we are now harbouring a wanted man puts us in a very difficult position.'

A gentle nod of the head: like a man suffering a hangover. Confusion in the young eyes.

'Looking on the bright side, we're leaving here in the not too distant future. Ferrying two aircraft to Europe. If we can keep you hidden away until then we'll drop you somewhere up the route, a place where there's an American embassy. They'll take care of you, get you a temporary passport sorted out, airline ticket home. In fact, we can probably have a whip-round of all my aircrew guys, make sure you've got some money in your pocket.'

'What about my mother's ashes?'

'I'll take them to the temple myself, don't worry.'

'What would have happened if I'd gone to Hanoi in the morning as planned?'

'The truth?'

'Sure.'

'Bullet in the back of the head.'

'You serious?'

'Always.'

TC rubbed the side of his face. 'My father used to tell me stories like this, about people being picked up for questioning and never coming home again . . . I always thought he was exaggerating.'

'Your father's dead as well as your mother?'

'Yes.'

'Any brothers or sisters?'

'One brother. I had an elder sister but she was killed as my parents were leaving Saigon . . . One of those crazy days at the embassy when they were airlifting people from the roof of the building. She was nearly one year old. My mother was carrying her. She was hit by a stray bullet.'

'I'm sorry. Must be tough for you now.'

'Not too bad, I have my brother.'

'We'll have you back before you know it.'

A look of relief. 'I don't know how to thank you . . .'

'Not necessary. Although there might be something you could advise us on.'

'Yes.'

'On the flight in from Taipei you mentioned you were a computer programmer. That right?'

'Yes.'

'As I mentioned, we have to move a couple of aeroplanes out of here; the problem is we may be routing over unfriendly countries – unfriendly to us, that is. My thinking was, if we could hack into the country's defence net and plant a virus, it might shut down some of their radar systems and allow us to get the aeroplanes across the country in question before anyone realizes.'

'That sounds very difficult.'

'But possible?'

'Perhaps.'

'Something that you could work on?'

TC hesitated. 'It's . . . it's not exactly legal, is it? I mean . . .'

'Killing a Vietnamese national isn't "exactly legal", either. We're not trying to start a war, TC. We simply need to slip away from here unseen.'

The young man looked stricken. 'I don't know . . . You see, I'm involved in writing video games, something altogether different. What I do is work in C-language. Quick and dirty assembly kind of thing, that's like three-letter mnemonics and stuff like that. It's pretty basic.'

'So there's no way . . .'

'Oh sure, there are ways. The problem is that it's very difficult. For instance, to break into the server of an agency such as the Department of Defence you would have to know their phone numbers, how to access their systems – and exactly what security measures they have, like passwords, voice, photo ID. Then again, you have to know exactly what items you're looking for, as well as where those items will be located in the system. Most big companies and agencies have employees whose only job is to monitor the computer system – who's doing what, where and how . . . When do you need this for?'

'Saturday.'

'Saturday! You mean Saturday this week?'

'Five days from now, yes.'

'Impossible.'

'But you understand viruses?'

'Yes . . . But . . .'

Winter went over to the nearest window, opened it,

and flicked his cigarette butt out into the night. 'Why not sleep on it? Give it a little thought. I'll pick you up a laptop computer tomorrow.'

A flicker of interest in the eyes.

'I'd need a modem.'

'Not a problem. I've got a GSM cell phone, though: problem with that is that I can call most places in the world but not the US.'

'Perhaps I can hook up a phone patch through a friend in Tokyo . . . He was at UCLA with me.'

'I'll leave that one with you, then. And I'll pick you up some clothes as well; can't have you walking around like a tramp, can we?'

A weak smile.

'Not too secure, this building,' Stevens said, returning through the end door.

Winter turned round. 'American-built, temporary structure for the period of hostilities only. It's lasted quite well. You saw the security, though, no one in their right mind is going to try and get on to the base. I think you're pretty safe.'

'As long as the buggers let us go when the time comes.'

'The colonel will take care of that. Did you eat earlier, by the way?'

'No. Not since breakfast.'

'I'll get Colonel Vin to send out one of his boys from the guardroom to find you some food.'

'A few Tiger beers wouldn't go amiss . . . And maybe a first-aid kit. Something to put on TC's cuts.'

'See what I can do.' Winter turned to TC. 'If you get a desire to go outside for a walk, keep out of the grass. Snakes.'

115

The young American pulled a face. 'What sort?'

'Aggressive ones: that right, Red?'

Stevens, who was checking the beds to find the most comfortable mattress, looked up. 'Sure. Only one I remember is a brown bastard about four feet long. The Yanks used to call it the seven-pace snake . . . If it bit you, you managed another seven steps before you keeled over.'

'Do they come inside buildings?' TC asked nervously.

Stevens smiled across at Winter and gave a conspiratorial wink. 'Too bloody right. They like dark places to sleep. When you've got your bed made up it's always a good thing to check it every night before you turn in.'

TC looked quite pale.

It was as Winter was leaving that the Australian said, 'Oh, shit.'

He stopped and turned. 'What?'

Stevens sat down on the end of one of the bed frames and took a fresh cigar from his shirt pocket. 'Forgot to tell you in all the bloody excitement. Went out to the airport and picked up Frenette and Priest – he's the boom operator. And you'll never guess who the co-pilot is.'

'Try me.'

Stevens bit off the end of the cigar and spat it out. 'Don't get mad at me, will you? I mean, I didn't know anything about this.'

'About what?'

'Maria.'

'Maria what?'

'She's the co-pilot'

Winter shook his head in disbelief. 'Now how the hell did she . . . No, never mind. Where are they staying?'

'I put them in the Emperor initially. Then, after this afternoon's little fracas, I told them to move to your hotel.'

'They didn't expect anything?'

'Nah, I said the Caravelle had suddenly got three spare rooms, and that they'd find it a bit more comfortable.'

'Good. See you tomorrow, then.'

'Don't forget the beers.'

Winter raised a hand and went to join the little colonel for the drive back to the city.

The rain had stopped by the time Winter was dropped off at the Caravelle. It was a few minutes after one o'clock. The air was pleasantly cool. Twigs, leaves, paper, plastic cups and flattened tin cans, so much flotsam from the earlier storm, washed up on the pavement outside the hotel. No people. No traffic. Psychological arrows of time – a street from any third-world past you cared to choose.

He took the elevator to the fourth floor, going over the different ways to tell Maria that she was on the first eastbound airliner home. That what was happening here was more than 'ferrying' a couple of aeroplanes across a part of the world. Dangerous. More so than it had been in Colombia. There the enemy had been a known and limited quantity. Here the mission was a panacea for all the wrong formulas that could nonetheless easily turn through a hundred and eighty degrees.

Winter opened the door quietly and slipped inside. A bedside light threw a soft glow across the room. Gleams of old ivory from the rattan furniture, the faint shushing sound from the air-conditioning system, magazines and books scattered untidily across the table. A black leather handbag rested against the leg of one of the chairs. Past the bathroom door, the room opened out. It was then that he saw her. Fast asleep, black hair spread across the pillows. Exhaustion had obviously overtaken her. Jet lag. It would keep until the morning.

He laid out fresh clothes, then pulled a chair up to the window and drew the curtains back. Lastly, he switched off the bedside light and kissed her gently on the forehead.

He returned to the chair and sat, watching the empty street below for a few minutes, running over the day in his mind, what had to be done tomorrow. And as tiredness crept over him, the promise that he had made to himself all those years ago that he would not get involved with any woman while he was playing this particular game. He had witnessed the heartache that marriage could bring, to the ones who were left, at least.

Except he hadn't counted on meeting someone like Maria Espinosa. Nine months earlier she had literally flown into his life at a deserted airport in the Florida Keys . . . and from there a dangerous low-level night flight to an uncharted airstrip in north-east Colombia. The few words she had exchanged with him tempered with a drug runner's reticence in talking to strangers. Observing her features in the dim red glow of instrument-panel lights, how the pretty face carried some of the hardness of the voice. The faintest hint of danger.

And, as the days unfolded, discovering a forty-year-old woman with an obsession for airplanes. A woman born in Cali and raised in California, the daughter of a Vietnam vet – a fighter jock – a man who had returned from the war and lost himself in a bottle. A man who had walked out one day leaving an invalid wife and six children to fend for themselves. Maria had been the eldest child. She had taken charge; left school, found a job – two jobs. Her dreams of flight relegated to the back burner. But no further.

She eventually learned to fly and gained a commercial ticket and an instrument rating. The problem that followed was that no operators wanted low-time pilots. Especially low-time women pilots of South American extraction with Hispanic accents. The reason she ended up working for a shady character out of the Florida Everglades. Running drugs. Doing *anything* that would guarantee her a precious few hours in the sky.

And later, when he found he was falling in love with her, how he had found her a job flying jets out of Miami. He had thought that would be enough. That her obsession with flight would allow him to slip quietly away to his singles-only world. The world with no room for love and commitment.

It seemed he had been wrong.

12

'How long did you spend in this part of the world?'

Owens blinked at the bedside light, which had suddenly been switched on. 'How . . . What time is it?'

Williams pulled up a chair and sat down. He tugged his green silk dressing gown about him, shivering slightly. The night had turned chilly. Finally he glanced at his watch. 'One o'clock.'

'And you couldn't sleep, I suppose.'

'I went down to see the night porter guy, to get him to make me some coffee. The curry we had earlier didn't seem to agree with me.'

'Which one did you have?'

'Prawns.'

'Ah well, there you are, you see, a bad one. All it takes. Best to stick with the vegetarian dishes in these places: they don't seem to understand that dead meat of any description has a finite life. Have you taken something?'

'Pepto Bismol, all I've got.'

'Don't worry, boyo, I'll keep an eye on you.

Anything goes dramatically wrong, I'll take care of the funeral arrangements. You won't mind if I choose the hymns, will you? Welsh, you see, known for our fine singing voices.'

'Very funny.'

'At one in the morning, I rather thought so. The answer to your question, by the way, was all my working life, give or take the odd year in Scandinavia at the end of things. What some people would call too long. Me, I suppose I enjoyed it in my own way. More than Wales – or England, come to that. Had the time to read a lot of the great books, learn some of the obscure oriental languages. Back in the UK I would have doubtless fallen into the old trap of walking the dog, dropping in at the pub, and consuming too much television. Instead, I became the career tourist, an international troubleshooter for the high and the mighty. Not bad for a raggedy-arsed kid from the Rhondda Valley, even if I do say so myself. So, what's your next question? Would I like a game of chess? Or perhaps you're going to read me the Tarot cards.'

Williams took the gold Dunhill cigarette lighter from his dressing-gown pocket and turned it over in his fingers. His eyes were temporarily glazed. Lost in thought. It wasn't about Winter or Mather, though: it was a story that his Grandmother Baba had told him when he was a boy. Something about his ancestor, the Hausa man, and the night journey in chains to a holding camp of sorts on the coast, and the slave ship at anchor on a silver sea. Being branded on the breast, the red-hot iron carrying the name of the British company trading in the transport of human misery. The ship that had carried him, on what was known as the Middle Voyage, to Barbados. There they had decided he was too small, physically too weak, and he was sent on to South Carolina where he was purchased by a man called Washington, a young man who had done rather well by marrying a plain-looking widow of great wealth – Martha. Young George Washington who had invested his new-found fortune in a tobacco crop – the promise of a great profit from England. A business decision that had nearly bankrupted him. Personal history never discussed outside the immediate family. Blurred phrases and images. A common link with Owens's working-class upbringing. Against all the odds. He shook his head and dismissed the old ghosts that had shaped his life. 'I've got a pot of coffee next door. Would you like a cup?'

'Not particularly. So, what's the problem?'

'I just received a fax message. If I deciphered it right, it would appear Winter's in Vietnam.'

Owens sat bolt upright. 'Really? How very interesting. What about Mather? He's with him, I assume?'

'Nothing on Mather, only that Winter is in Ho Chi Minh City. It appears he's working for – or with – the Vietnamese government.'

'Good God.'

'Better yet, it appears the customer for the uranium *is* Iraq.'

'How did you find him, exactly?'

'An old enquiry I instigated back in the States.'

Owens said, 'So the Hanoi government, who are on good terms with their former Russian partners, get embroiled in some dirty little scheme to sell off weapons-grade uranium, is that what you're saying?'

'Raw intel. Even so, not a particularly clever move

by the wise men in Hanoi.'

'How about, Vietnam is one of the poorest countries on the planet. Average per capita income about three hundred dollars.'

'But why jeopardize normalization treaties signed with the West in recent years?'

'An observation.' Owens's hand fluttered in the air. 'No moral scruples here, Tanner. Business is business. You make money any way you can. Lie, cheat, steal, kill. It makes no difference.'

'The reason Winter chose Vietnam as a likely venue, you mean?'

'Perhaps,' Owens replied thoughtfully. A moment's pause before going on. 'When we were in Santa Marta earlier this year, the manager of that dreadful hotel we stayed at told me an interesting little story. He said that around the Caribbean there was a tale of a pirate ship, its sails torn by winds, masts chewed by sea worms, still looking for the course to Guadeloupe after two hundred years.'

'Local folklore.'

'Of course, but a lot of islanders – fishermen and so on – would swear blind that they have seen the ship, and that it exists. We, of course, know it is so much fantasy because master mariners – pirates or not – never get lost, and even if they do become temporarily uncertain of their position they most certainly would have resolved the situation after two centuries, right?'

'Seems logical,' Williams answered.

'Which brings me to your fax message. Winter is in Ho Chi Minh City, working for the Vietnamese government. What is wrong with this picture?'

Williams, arms folded across his chest, considered

the question. The ghosts of Grandmother Baba gone, replaced by those of the present. Eminently more sinister. 'A master mariner would not get lost for two hundred years; ergo the pirate ship is a figment of the imagination, whereas Winter is not . . . Which presupposes his course is very tightly plotted. But why would he show the transverse-Mercator chart and the carefully drawn rhumb-line tracks thereon to his enemy? Is that what you're saying?'

'He's two parts charlatan, one part black magician, and the rest unknown. The last part is what you should be worrying about, boyo.'

'Why we're going to Hanoi tomorrow,' Williams announced.

Owens smiled. 'Reason?'

The American, keeping his voice barely above a whisper, said, 'I have a small team of former KR guys there. We might be able to use them.'

Owens felt his smile freeze on his face. KR. Khmer Rouge. Primary opposition to the erstwhile Communist regime in Cambodia – a puppet of Vietnam. Also Communist, the KR had been a notoriously savage group, killing as many as three million Cambodians during the time it ruled the country in the late 1970s. 'Sounds tricky, if you intend to use them in-country, that is. Diplomatic backlash, that sort of thing.' He managed to keep his tone light, offhand.

'Not necessarily, Edeyrn. The reason we set up Black Ops. Quite simply, this is not CIA.'

'Plausible deniability restored,' Owens murmured. 'The Great Satan disguised in a brown habit with the cord of Saint Francis around his waist, swinging a penitent's rattle among the Sunday crowds at the public market.'

'At the very least.'

'There's still a risk.'

'Not really. I've learned from the last time, I do assure you.'

'You've got somebody on the inside, you mean?'

Williams stood up and moved towards the door. Smiling. 'The flight for Hanoi leaves at 1300 hours.'

Owens lay awake for a long time after Williams had left. Worrying. An intelligence officer's intense focus is known to skew the perspective. Sacrifice the background. The better to see the target.

But was it the right target?

PART THREE
Capital Flight

13

Mehdizadeh had had a bad day. He had lost twenty million dollars of the bank's money. A Black Monday, of sorts. A day when near-panic had swept through the world's $1.5 trillion-a-day foreign-exchange market and driven the dollar to a 21-month low against the mark, and a 12-month nadir against the yen. Mehdizadeh's bank had been one of the short-yen long-dollar losers. The rationale: a worldwide decline fuelled in part by hedge funds scrambling to unwind so-called carry trades after Tokyo made moves to ease the country's credit crunch, sparking rallies in the yen and Tokyo stocks.

One of the reasons Mehdizadeh went to the British Colonial Hotel on the corner of Bay Street and Cumberland Street that evening to meet Sam Yeo for a drink. He needed it.

It was a business arrangement that had developed into a friendship.

Yeo, the CIA spook, who had long haunted the corridors of domestic and international finance institutions.

Mehdizadeh, the banker, who funnelled millions of dollars through his bank for CIA covert operations in foreign lands.

In exchange for the banker's assistance, the Langley people turned a blind eye to the occasional side deal Mehdizadeh carried out, with the proviso that such side deals should not be with *known* felons or, if they were, that they would be subject to careful vetting.

He found the American at a quiet table by a window overlooking the harbour. The faint smell of new paint, new carpets, in the century-old structure.

Facelifts for forgotten corners of Empire.

'So,' Mehdizadeh said, between sips of his Cuba Libre, 'how was the European trip?'

'Like I told you before I left. A waste of time. Whatever happened there, and whoever instigated it, long gone.'

'Ah.' The banker looked understandably worried. Laundering money had its drawbacks, not least to do with the people who were involved. Informing on such people could be life threatening. 'So the man Sibelius – Winter, the one you told me about before you left – is still out there. And he knows that my bank turned over the information on his account to . . .' He glanced quickly around, his voice dropping to a whisper. 'To the CIA?'

'Seems more than likely.'

'I will get protection . . . You have always assured me that would be the case if there were any threats . . .'

Yeo raised a hand. 'Sure, sure. Reason I'm here . . . and something else.'

'Something else!' The banker didn't like the sound of that.

'Off the record, you understand,' Yeo said.

'Of course.'

Sam Yeo was generally a man who thought before he spoke. Especially when the subject matter was serious. He was thinking now. Looking for the words to simplify a complex matter.

'Let us say that this guy Winter wanted his money back, much as I outlined to you last week, and that as a way to twist our arm he bought a large cache of weapons from Russia and set up a deal to sell it to the Iraqis. He offers us an ultimatum: Return my money and I won't deal with Saddam.'

'A delicate matter.'

'I agree. Unfortunately, it's gone beyond that. You see, we had a deadline to open negotiations. Regrettably, by the time we'd checked the facts the deadline had passed.'

'Which means this man Winter is now selling his arms to Iraq. So how can I help in this?'

'I think the key to what I'm chasing could be financial: you understand what I'm saying?'

Mehdizadeh did. Only too well. 'How much?'

'Certainly not nickels and dimes. We feel the Swiss might be involved. They always seem to be in such matters.'

'And you think large amounts are more traceable than small amounts?'

'You tell me.'

'All I can tell you is that *any* amount would need to be specifically identified.'

'What does that mean, exactly?'

'It means that, despite some patchwork tightening of disclosure provisions in the 1980s to head off the bank secrecy referendum, it's still lawful – in Switzerland, for example – for deposits to be held in the name of attorneys and trustees acting on behalf of anonymous depositors. All they need to do is declare that, to the best of their knowledge, their clients are not engaged in unlawful behaviour. Further to that the money could be deposited in the name of an offshore ghost company. Impossible to access. Bearing that in mind, it would remain to be proved that what your individual did was a crime under Swiss law.'

'So, there is no way to monitor such amounts being transferred?'

'Not if the transfers are, er, clandestine, shall we say.'

'You've done it before.'

'Certainly, but in those instances I've had a lot more information. Exact sums being telegraphically transferred, originating bank, that kind of thing.'

'If we had all that we wouldn't need you.'

'Maybe, maybe not. But what you need to bear in mind is that you – your Company – have screwed up time after time on foreign funding deals.'

'How would you see such a deal being played out?'

Mehdizadeh rattled the ice cubes in his empty glass. 'A few years after the end of Desert Storm, Iraq was granted permission by the UN to sell off a certain amount of oil to enable them to buy foodstuffs and medical supplies. So perhaps they are not transferring money after all. Perhaps they are transferring oil.'

'Can you get information on the previous transfers, the ones sanctioned by the UN?'

'Yes. But you must remember this is only an idea. It is more than likely that Iraq has large, secret offshore accounts like most of the drug czars have. A rainy-day fund. Something to facilitate the Russian deal we are talking about.'

'In which case we may never know where the money went.'

'No.'

'You must have examples of similar transactions.'

'A thousand of them. Which ones would you like to check out? To cover every possible angle could take months, years.'

'The Federal Reserve monitors all large transactions: this is correct?'

'Legal ones. I think if your man Winter, or "Sibelius" as we call him, is in any way involved you can kiss goodbye to the money.'

'So, no simple scenarios on oil deals.'

'Not my field. Barrel prices are low, though, due to a worldwide glut. I read somewhere that Venezuela, among others, is dumping oil as cheap as seventy-five cents a barrel on the US market. I think it would be difficult to sell in such a climate.'

'But it must be easier to track large shipments of oil, rather than large amounts of money. That right?'

'I don't know. It could simply be moved through a chain of offshore companies. Impossible to trace.'

'Meaning we're in the same situation we were at the beginning of this conversation. What about European connections? You must have some of them.'

Mehdizadeh stroked his beard and considered his early days in the banking business.

Carrying illegal currency.

Rushing around different banks on rainy afternoons in Milano, changing dollars into lira, and when the day was darkening and all the money changed, finding a cheap little hotel on a street called the Santo Spirito and climbing some dusty back stairs. Knocking on a door. Waiting. Two leather-jacketed young thugs, doing a poor impersonation of members of the human race. Mean faces. Skull-cropped hair. Scarred knuckles. Frightening. Another man sitting in the shadows. The suitcase being laid on the bed, the man in the shadows clicking his fingers at one of the minders. Watching while every bundle was counted. No words passed between them. In fact, he had never known with whom he was dealing at the Italian end. There were rumours, of course. Mafia. Even that a number of Catholic priests were local Mafia *capos*, washing money through the Vatican bank.

At the British end, something altogether different: a respectable merchant bank in the City of London, a bank with a branch in the tiny Channel Island of Guernsey – one of those quiet, conservative, offshore tax havens. Someone with connections in both camps. It was the chairman of that bank who owed Mehdizadeh a favour. 'One man, with good connections. Mafia, I think.'

'Who is he?'

Mehdizadeh shook his head slowly. His analytical thinking again. 'First things first. The ten per cent reward I was promised three months back for locating the Sibelius account.'

'I can't do anything until tomorrow. Even then it may take time.'

'One step at a time, Sam. When I'm paid for the last job, I'll see what I can do to help with this other matter.' The banker stood up. He had had enough for one day. 'You know where to find me.'

14

Maria Espinosa heard the faint traffic sounds first. She was lost for a moment in that long-haul pilot's nightmare of day-time-location. A few panic-filled seconds of associating the sound with that of aircraft engines – believing she had fallen victim to micro-sleep; body jolting awake with an intensity that can be frightening. Grabbing for imaginary controls, only to find as the eyes flicker open it is an illusion. There follows relief, and sometimes when the exhaustion of the previous duty period's flying has not quite worn off, turning over and burying one's head in the pillow. But not this morning. Her eyes had half-focused on the pale morning light at the window. And on the outline of a man.

'Good morning,' he said, turning his head towards her.

'How did you know I was awake?'

'Your breathing pattern changed.'

'How long have you been listening?'

'I showered and dressed about thirty minutes ago. Since then, I suppose.'

'Why didn't you wake me when you got back?'

'Too late,' he said. He got up from the chair, moved over to the bed and kissed her lightly on the forehead.

'You are angry.' Her Spanish accent more notice-able.

'Why should I be?'

'My being here.'

'Not if you get on a flight and go home today.'

'Cam Frenette needed a co-pilot: I am working for him.'

'And he's working for me.'

'He told me it was a ferry flight, nothing more.'

Winter went back to the window and looked down on the square. Beyond the Municipal Theatre towards the Continental Hotel. The traffic already flying down Dong Khoi Street, turning right, streaming into Le Loi Boulevard. 6.45 a.m. He wondered where everyone was going at such an early hour. Western thinking. In these places work started with the first light of day, much as it had in Europe before the invention of electricity. They would catch up eventually. 'But you know differently, is that it?'

'I didn't. Red told me yesterday when I arrived.'

'He didn't say anything to the other crew, did he?'

'No.'

'You're sure?'

'He only told me because he is worried about you.'

'In that case you know this isn't exactly a game.'

'I also know that you need a full crew for the tanker and that our ETD is late Friday night. Difficult to find a replacement at such short notice, I think.'

Winter ran his hand through his hair. He thought: *You believed you were so clever, finding her a flying job in Miami. Why didn't you leave it at that? Why confide in her about the money? The job in Vietnam? Perhaps because you love her,* a little voice told him. He tried not to listen. Love was a luxury he could not afford. 'This is very dangerous, you have no idea . . .'

'Colombia was dangerous,' Maria replied quickly. 'But if you do not want me here I will go.' He saw the dark eyes flash. The impatient gesture with her head as she flicked hair from her eyes.

He stood motionless at the window for perhaps half a minute: he with his hand to his hair, she propped up on one elbow watching him. The sheet had slipped from her bare shoulder. The honey-coloured skin, the small breasts with the dark nipples, brought a catch to his throat. He turned away, glancing back out of the window.

Across the square, a white army staff car pulled up. He saw Colonel Vin get out and hurry into the Continental.

'We have no time for this.' He spoke quickly. 'I have a meeting across the street. Can you get the crew together? Make sure they have a good breakfast, I'll arrange a car to pick you up at 9.30. It will take you to Bien Hoa . . . with luck we'll get the first flight tests out of the way by this afternoon.'

'Do I get a kiss before you leave?'

An impossible woman, he decided. *Totally impossible.*

The Vietcombank is on Ben Choung Street. The street borders the Ben Nghe Channel, which runs out of the nearby Saigon River. The bank itself is one of those magnificent marble palaces with Doric columns and high vaulted ceilings. The interior is vast; the tellers working from a central island – which realtors might be tempted to quote in acres – hemmed in by bars and bulletproof glass. Customers mill around a wide rotunda of sorts, trading in dollars and francs and kip and yen and dong. Electronic counting machines sit on the customer side of the counters, essential for those changing their hard currency into a blizzard of local money, where one dollar American gets you more than ten thousand Vietnamese dong. Even the air smells clean and healthy and prosperous. It is so much at odds with the outside world of squalor and disease that it seems to possess the make-believe ambience of a Hollywood movie set.

'Beautiful building,' Winter remarked as they came up the marble steps into the bank.

'Something we inherited from the French,' the little colonel replied with a smile. 'Sometimes I think it pays to be occupied for a hundred years.'

They found a small table and two chairs up against a wall, away from the early business rush. Winter put the metallic blue Puma sports bag he had been carrying on the table, unzipped it, and removed a pink-coloured file. They sat down, facing each other.

'So,' the colonel began, 'the airplanes now have their papers complete, no? You now need to transfer the dollars to the MoD account. Once that is done Customs will clear both airplanes to leave from Bien Hoa.'

Winter opened his file and removed the printed statement he had collected from the bank late the previous Friday afternoon.

Saigon Express

Vietcombank
29 Ben Chuong Street, District One,
Ho Chi Minh City
Telephone: 848 291490 Fax: 848 297228

Statement

Account name:	John Paul Winter
Account No:	362.414.37.7.4641
Type of Account:	US Dollars
Balance:	$425,000.00

He pushed the paper across the table. 'The amount left from the original $500,000 deposit paid by our customers. I gave Yuri twelve thousand five hundred for his expenses. I took a similar amount. The fifty thousand went to Sergei Grishin, the Director at Tbilisi, as a down payment for his services. Satisfied?'

'Of course. And you have the MoD account for the two aircraft?'

Winter removed the two white Ministry of Defence bills of sale (completed in triplicate), one for the F-4 Phantom, the other for the Ilyushin-38. The total price for the two ageing military aircraft – $350,000. 'I don't know how you got the gentlemen in Russia to release the aircraft without being paid up front, but whatever you did, I'm impressed.'

The colonel waved a hand dismissively. 'They were not that trusting, believe me. I arranged for a letter of credit against the MoD account. Like giving them a young girl for the night. A matter of comfort.'

'Even so, a lot of people won't accept LCs these days . . . Anyway, carrying on with this matter. I'll transfer the money to the MoD account right now. When will

Customs clear the aircraft?'

'Today. Tomorrow. I will take care of it. If you need the papers post-dated or backdated this is not a problem.'

Winter produced a green sheet of A4 paper from the file. 'The next part is the difficult one. That is, the balance of the money for the "cargo".'

'You think the Iraqis will not move the money as agreed?'

'Oh no, that's not the problem. The problem is that after today it is out of our hands. It lies squarely with a number of banks: we have to hope that they do what they are supposed to do on the agreed dates.' He turned the green paper around so the colonel could see the pencilled figures and simple flow-chart diagrams. 'I can show you this once only, colonel, then it will be destroyed. Safer in my skull, you understand?'

A discreet movement of the colonel's head. 'One thing I do not understand is how such a large sum of money will be moved in total secrecy.'

'With the help of the Roman Catholic Church.'

The colonel looked surprised. 'This is possible?'

'Putting the money lenders back in the Temple, certainly.' Winter went on to explain how the world's most sanctimonious offshore banking centre and tax haven sat in the heart of Rome, and had emerged from a meeting in 1929 between the Italian dictator Benito Mussolini and Pope Pius XI. A meeting that had laid the foundations for the creation of an institution through which Italian state finances could be subverted, capital flight encouraged, and Mafia money washed. The key to all this being the Lateran Treaty – recognition of the Vatican as a sovereign state. Aware that future economic and therefore political power would derive from financial assets rather than from landholdings, the Vatican's financial advisers put its Lateran Treaty wealth into gold, Italian financial and industrial assets, and Swiss-based international financial holdings. Somewhere in the middle of all this investment was the growing arms industry.

'I understand that. But I still do not see how the funds can leave Iraq, with so many embargoes on trade.'

'Your friend, the cousin of the Iraq Finance Minister.' Winter said softly. Using a pen as a marker he pointed to the top of the green sheet. 'He has a company in Paris called Occidental Petroleum (Paris) S.A., which I have noted here as OPP. This company will be trading a block of oil at an agreed futures price with the Vatican Bank. The value of the oil is 100 million dollars. However, OPP have agreed to sell this block to the Vatican Bank at half that price, 50 million.

'Bear in mind that the value of our "cargo" to Iraq was put at $100 million, and that we decided that if we had to take payment in oil it would cause a problem due to the current glut of crude worldwide. But if we offered it at fifty per cent of the price we would perhaps find a buyer. We did. The Vatican Bank. With me so far?'

The colonel motioned with his hand. A slight movement that said, 'You have my undivided attention. Please continue.'

Winter moved the pen down the paper. 'Now here we have a company called Occidental Petroleum (Luxembourg) Limited, or OPL as I have shown it. This is *our* company, a Panamanian-registered corporate tax entity. You will note the similarity in names with the Paris company. Except that is all it is – a similarity.

'So, today we issue Bills of Lading to our customer.' The pen indicated a line that stated: CUSTOMER: IRAQ GOVT. BAGHDAD. 'Once they have these documents, duly stamped by the Vietnam Ministry of Defence, showing that the "cargo" is loaded at Bien Hoa, they will notify OPP, the Paris company, who will commence the oil transaction with the Vatican Bank.

'The Vatican Bank has established a back-to-back irrevocable letter of credit with Credit Suisse in Zurich for $50 million.

'That is, Credit Suisse have an instruction to immediately pay that $50 million to OPL, the Luxembourg company.'

'And the Vatican, of course, gets the oil,' the colonel noted. 'At half the price. A very good deal for them, no?'

'A very good deal. Absolutely.' The pen moved across the flow chart to indicate the movement of oil and money and the uranium consignment. 'Of course, the $50 million paid out by Credit Suisse has to be in our Luxembourg bank by close of business Friday. We cannot leave here if that has failed to happen. This is something you will need to confirm before the bank closes on Friday afternoon.'

'I understand. And, assuming it has been paid, what then?'

'Next Monday, the twelfth of October, our Luxembourg bank, shown here, will transfer the $50 million to Bank Julius Baer in Zurich to the account of John Winter, shown to be the owner of OPL, the

Luxembourg company. Once this transfer has taken place, OPL – Occidental Petroleum (Luxembourg) Limited – will cease to exist.' Winter paused to check his surroundings. That no one was getting close enough to overhear any part of the conversation. That no one was in such a position that they could lip-read.

A counting machine at a nearby counter clicked its way through a wad of money. The low murmur of voices. The soft whir of ceiling fans.

'The last part is the best, or at least I think so.'

The pen swept down the green sheet to a block entitled *Final Transaction.* 'The final transaction takes place on Tuesday morning, the thirteenth of October. Bank Julius Baer on my already issued written instruction – that is, the written instruction of John Winter – will transfer three amounts of money from that account. The three amounts are for $15 million each. One will go to Yuri's private bank in Liechtenstein, another to your private bank in Geneva, and mine, in the name of William Durack, to a similar institution. The three sums will be routed through a Liechtenstein attorney, which means our names do not appear on any bank records as beneficiaries. The balance of $5 million will remain on deposit in Winter's account at Bank Julius Baer in Zurich. Already lodged in a safety deposit box at that same bank, and in the name of Winter, are a number of documents showing the $5 million to be the net figure for the sale of the uranium to our customer. The point of this is that, should the trail of this transaction be picked up, now or in the future, it will *end* at Bank Julius Baer.'

'Except the account is in the name of "John Winter".'

You! What happens if you are arrested? Next week! Next year!'

Winter took a maroon-coloured British passport from the pocket of his bush jacket. He slid it across the table. The colonel picked it up, flicked through the pages. Stopping at the last one. Plastic-covered. The page was headed: United Kingdom of Great Britain and Northern Ireland. Beneath that the passport type was designated as 'P', the code of the issuing State as GBR, and then came the passport number – 702102178. It was in the name of Durack, William – British Citizen, and had been issued some five and a half years earlier by the British Embassy in Washington DC (a renewal of Durack's last ten-year passport). To the left of the typed information the image of John Winter stared up at the colonel. 'So you have a new identity,' he observed, 'Except I think a false passport is little protection.'

A deception that had its origins in eleventh-century England. How King Harold II had been apparently slain at the Battle of Hastings. But how two of his elder canons, Osegode and Ailric, had been unable to find his body on the battlefield. With the Conqueror's permission they returned with Harold's mistress, Editha Swanneshals (Edith with the swan's neck). She, it was said, recognized the body of her lover by secret marks known only to herself. The corpse was removed to Waltham and buried with honour in the choir of the Abbey Church. *Except there was another truth:* the badly injured Harold was discovered among a heap of corpses by a group of Saxon women. He was still breathing. Recognized by two of his countrymen, he was taken to Winchester (the place – curiously enough

– that Editha Swanneshals retired to after the 'death' of her lover) where he remained in concealment for two years. At the end of that time, having recovered from his wounds, he went to Germany in the hope of raising an army from the old Saxons and Norwegians. A plan that failed. Even so, he survived. Lived on into old age with the beautiful Editha.

Footnotes to history.

'Very true,' Winter agreed. 'Except it is not a false passport. It is very genuine. Durack and I were involved in an aeroplane crash many years ago on the island of New Caledonia in the South Pacific. As we were very similar in features and as at that time I was on a lot of blacklists around the world, I traded places. To the point that the French authorities in Noumea, New Caledonia, have on file a copy of the death certificate of John Winter. There's also a grave in his name in the local cemetery.'

'What if they exhumed the body? Would there be a way to find out? Through your army records, perhaps. You understand what I am saying, no?'

'The control column went through Durack's chest in the crash. He was quite dead. I got the passenger door open and climbed out on the wing, reaching back behind the seat for my flight bag. It was after I'd gone a hundred metres or so from the plane – going to find help – that it started to burn. To cut a long story short, Durack was cremated. As for the flight bag I'd picked up, I found out I had taken his by mistake. Easy enough to do: most flight bags are plain black leather. That was when the idea to change identities came to me.'

'You have used this identity before?'

'No. After I left New Caledonia I decided to find a new line of work as a teacher. But as Durack was a career ferry pilot that made it difficult. So I borrowed the identity of a man called Carroll who was killed in a car accident in England. Carroll was a history professor. Medieval European history specifically, and as the subject has always been my hobby I took his identity, went to the United States and found a teaching position at a small Midwest university.'

'And then your wife died!'

Brutally raped and murdered by a drug gang. And for what? Investigating drug pushers targeting metro city schools in the American Midwest – material for a series of television programmes. An idea that he had given her. 'A long story, colonel. I'll tell you about it over a drink one evening.'

'As you wish.'

Winter pointed to the flow chart. 'Going back to the funding operation, the $5 million remains here . . . at Bank Julius Baer, Zurich.'

The colonel looked concerned. 'I think that $5 million dollars is a lot of money to leave behind.'

'A lot of money, I agree. And that is precisely the reason why any interested third party tracing it that far will not bother to go any further. Which leaves you and me and Yuri with healthy retirement pensions.'

'I have three questions. What of the $500,000 deposit we have been paid by our customer? What of the payment to the ferry pilots? And how is the final payment made to the Director from Tbilisi?'

'The pilots' pay has been arranged from my personal bank account: payment will be made once my share has been received at my overseas bank next week.

146

Similarly, our friend Sergei Grishin, the Tbilisi director, will receive the balance of his one million dollar fee from my account. Written instructions are in place for both of these matters. I'll send you and Yuri a copy of the accounts at some point, and you can each send me a cheque, if that's fair.'

'Very fair. And the $500,000 deposit? Why did you not make our customer pay us the final sum less this half a million?'

'The best part, I was getting to that. The finance minister's cousin, who is the president of Occidental Petroleum in Paris, will receive that amount from Winter's account at Bank Julius Baer, Zurich. A letter of credit is already in place to effect the transaction. Finally, a personal letter, from Winter, will be mailed to the gentleman in question at the time of the money transfer. The text states that this is the refund of the half-million loan against the *total* purchase price of $5 million. There will, of course, be a copy of the letter in Winter's safety deposit box at the Zurich bank.'

'What will he make of the letter when he receives it? He will know the figure, the total purchase price, was much larger than five million.'

'Not important. He may see $5 million as a typing error. What is important, to us at least, is that it verifies that the money in Winter's account *is* the total payment for the cargo. And even if the president of the Paris company stepped forward to dispute that, which is extremely unlikely, who is going to take the word of an Iraqi, especially one who is related to Saddam's Finance Minister?'

The little colonel grinned. 'And your share of the money! What do you intend to do with all that?'

Winter thought of the fifteen million dollars. How seven million of that would be wired to an account in Panama for the attention of his accountant Patrick Van Fleteren – a man about whom he still had serious doubts. The balance of eight million, being the exact amount seized by the US government – that he would have to make certain payments from that amount to the Tbilisi director, to his cousin Sasha and to the pilots was a small price to pay. At least his pension fund would be back in place. At least the widows and orphans of the men who had fought alongside him over the years would not suffer. 'Do?' He smiled. 'I hadn't really thought about it.'

PART FOUR
Flight Test

15

There should be such days in every life.

Breathtaking mountains to climb, twisting, eye-aching, meringue-sided valleys to explore, pillars of vertical sunlight propping up chaotic skies from the shifting dragon-filled waters of the South China Sea; birdless sanctuaries full of dawn-of-creation silence, unrehearsed wind-song and, on those other days when the Gods of the East were at their most cantankerous, the borrowed symphonic scores of Wagner, when with a little imagination one might believe one had exchanged fates with the Flying Dutchman: traded the ghostly schooner for an aeroplane that never stopped travelling, waved goodbye to the land for ever, and yet still remembered, as one passed over the Rat Islands in the Aleutians, to mail the postcard to the tousle-haired boy who sat shivering under a 1940s street lamp in a Euclidean time-locked England, keeping himself warm with his dreams of flight.

Winter's thoughts on that October afternoon.

He had forgotten about Red Stevens. At least until

the Aussie accented voice drifted over the ICS. 'When did you last do this?'

Winter was looking down through a hole at the rags and tatters of stratus cloud that loitered along the south-central coastline as it tracked north towards Da Nang. Six miles below lay the South China Sea. Twenty miles back in his six o'clock – Phan Thiet: Stevens had spotted that as they had gone 'feet wet', mentioned being there at the end of the war and how the entire region was one of the most arid in Nam, plagued with swarms of flies. 'Home from home for Aussies,' he had joked. *When did you last do this?* Good question. 'Refuelling, you mean?'

'Yes.'

'First time.'

'Are you serious?'

'Yes.'

'Shit.'

'I've read the book, though.'

'What book?'

'There was one on the Russian plane.'

'In English?'

'No.'

'Do you read Russian?'

'No . . . But I understood the pictures.'

'What pictures?'

'Well . . . There was this naked woman-wrestler type doing strange things with a vodka bottle . . .'

'Shit . . . You trying to frighten me to death?'

'I offered you the trained-killer's seat.'

'Jesus! And I thought I'd be rusty. Do you think this is a good idea?'

'How difficult is it, Red? I mean, you used to do it

once . . . You told me it was a piece of cake . . .'

The Ilyushin came up on frequency, breaking into the lighthearted deprecating humour known to military pilots the world over.

'Sibelius One, Tango Four Two.' Maria from the right seat of the tanker. Hispanic accent. Hard. Impersonal.

'Tango Four Two, Sibelius One, go.'

'Roger, Four Two is in a right-hand race track, five zero miles east of Phan Thiet, level two five zero, true airspeed two zero zero, advise contact and state fuel . . . Go ahead.'

'Sibelius copies, ten thousand on the fuel . . . And we're commencing climb out of two zero zero at this time.' Eyes outside, scanning the area of clear sky above – the backside of what was left of the frontal system – from his ten o'clock to his two o'clock. Getting the feeling he was a little way behind the aeroplane today. Too many other matters to deal with, not enough time to do a thorough pre-flight check, to get attuned to the machinery's wavelength. *Get yourself together, old son.* He began easing the throttles back. Reducing speed.

Stevens picked up the tiny dark shape of the four-engined turboprop first. 'Come left twenty degrees, six miles . . . High.'

'Thanks.' He picked it up immediately. Thumbed the transmit button. 'Tango Four Two, Sibelius is tally.'

'Roger that, Sibelius One . . . Tango Four Two is commencing turn . . . Maintaining flight level two five zero, speed two hundred knots . . . Advise in trail.'

'Roger.' He watched the tanker rolling into his turn,

gauging his own closure. Through the first ninety degrees of turn the relative closure went from ten miles per minute down to three, paring the distance to slightly more than a mile. He continued his turn, closure becoming more and more a matter of speed differential – initially 150 knots, but decreasing as he decelerated – to where it was eighty knots with ninety degrees of turn remaining. At a quarter of a mile out, and with forty-five degrees of turn remaining, Winter popped the speed brakes. Deceleration from putting out the brakes was crisp at higher speeds, but as the speed bled off, their effect diminished.

The airframe entered into a gentle pre-stall buffet at 240 knots true airspeed that grew more insistent as he slowed to match tanker speed. The flaps-up stall speed of the Phantom with drop tanks was about 175 knots, rising to close to 180 knots because of the extra weight at the completion of refuelling. At a refuelling speed of 200 knots, this was not dangerously close to the stall – but there were other problems.

First, the plane was on the wrong side of the lift/drag curve – needing more power to fly slower because of increased drag. And whereas the Phantom was burning 8,000 pounds of fuel per hour in cruise, on the tanker he would be averaging 12,000 to 14,000 per hour, or more than 200 pounds of fuel a minute. From the refuel amount of 10,000 pounds supplied by the tanker he would burn a thousand in the process of joining, tanking and departing. Part of the price paid. Not that it was a critical factor today: more of a systems check. Machinery and operators.

Of more immediate concern to Winter was the deterioration of the F-4's handling qualities, a function of reduced airspeed. At 200 knots with the flaps up, even a 'clean' Phantom could be something of a handful for close-quarter manoeuvring. A bunch of esoteric factors like angle of attack, centre of pressure, induced drag, Dutch roll, and a dozen more, plotting against you. The trick was to do as little as possible with the stick, which provided primary inputs for pitch-and-roll commands. Once displacements in pitch and roll occurred, the sensation was something like being in a three-dimensional rocking chair. Entertaining – bordering on dangerous – to the uninitiated. A time when the pilot could suddenly suffer spatial disorientation – vertigo – and when at worst he could 'lose it' and ram the tanker. Not many people survived mid-air collisions. It was about plateaus on the learning curve, those that occurred when you accepted the perspective that allowed you no growth. Flying a fighter required brute force *and* finesse. Balancing the two was the trick. You didn't get there in a hurry, but if you stayed with the programme you would eventually and that was the time when, through experience, you began to realize that physical limits were truly there and that the only way around them was through use of the imagination. The fact that you could not see the ragged edge of the envelope did not mean it wasn't there, but if you tried to find it rationally, nine times of ten you failed. It was when you looked inside yourself that you found it, because intuition, attuned to the threshold whispers of all the receptors, was the supreme evaluator.

The closing rate had slowed to a walk now until, as the tanker rolled level on a westbound heading, Winter stabilized in the 'box' – an imaginary cube of air with roughly twenty-metre dimensions. Once there, you held station on the aircraft in front by doing everything he did. The image in the windshield must not change. A secondary aid to that was the two lines of fore-and-aft lights on the tanker's belly. Green, you were good. Red, too far forward or too far aft. Slip outside the box and you automatically disengaged and switched off fuel transfer. A major headache if you were fuel critical.

Winter picked out the flat glass window (no distortion) in the tanker's belly, saw the wild-eyed Hod Priest looking down on him. The overweight Boston man – who was already complaining about the absence of fast food, especially his favourite hot dogs – lying prone in his little bay under the tanker's floor, waiting to release the boom with its swept wings and by the use of a small joystick 'fly' it down into the Phantom's receptacle, which was aft of the cockpit in the spine of the upper fuselage. Male into female. His voice was up now, a nasal, almost English accent. He had taken over communications from Maria. 'Sibelius One, Tango Four Two, how do you read?'

'Sibelius is reading you strength five . . . How me?'

'Fives also.'

Winter picked up the boom in his scan, flying back to meet him. His breathing was very shallow. All his faculties concentrating on keeping the aircraft in the perfect trail position. Even though the air was relatively smooth it was no 'gimme', especially for a pilot badly out of practice.

'Looking good . . . Looking good,' Red chanted over the ICS. Reading his mind.

In tandem at 200 knots.

Winter portraying the unblinking, canyon-deep calm of a sitting idol – at least on the outside – almost afraid to breathe now, unless expansion of the chest should accidentally transmit itself through the shoulder, the arm, the hand . . . the stick. This was as close to transcendental meditation as one purposely got in a fighter.

Priest's voice: 'Tango Four Two, contact.'

Winter simultaneously picked up the green light that had lit up on his instrument panel. 'Sibelius, contact.'

Next would be Maria, who was monitoring transmissions. She would activate the necessary switch to commence transfer. Winter waited. One eye picking up the fuel counter in his rapid scan, waiting for it to start increasing. Waiting for Priest to call: 'Sibelius One completing ten thousand pounds, on my count disconnect . . . Three . . . Two . . . One . . . Disconnect.'

He was running through the normal procedures in his mind, maintaining station slightly below the sooty trails from the four Ivchenko engines of the Ilyushin. Close enough to count the rivet lines on the mammoth empennage that danced gently beyond the highly tempered bulletproof windshield of the Phantom, when Priest's voice leapt across the ether. 'Sibelius One . . . EMERGENCY DISCONNECT . . . GO.' Winter suffered that microsecond of doubt. Of not believing what he had heard. Then he initiated disconnect, coming back on the throttles, dropping aft, stick forward into a gentle dive. The Ilyushin simultaneously increased power to all four of its engines and started to pull away and climb.

Winter let out a shaky breath, brought in the dive

brakes and, increasing power to the two General Electric J-79 engines, climbed out to the left of the tanker. 'Tango Four Two . . . You got problems?'

Momentary pause, then Maria said, 'Looks as though a transfer valve has failed . . . RTB.'

RTB. Return to base. 'Roger that, see you on the ground.'

A double-click on the transmit button.

The Ilyushin shrank to a tiny black dot as the Phantom went supersonic in a gentle westbound climb.

They had levelled at flight level 360 – approximately 36,000 feet – when Stevens said, 'I bloody knew it.'

'Knew what?'

'Russian technology, what do you think? Reminds me of an old Abo rainmaker whirling his bull roarer to rouse the sleeping spirits of water and life . . . That never worked, either.'

'Where's your sense of adventure?'

'Had it removed, now I'm a gibbering wreck like the rest of the nine-to-five ground-pounders . . . Just let's say I have an aversion to emergencies, real or otherwise, especially up here.'

'It is better to return home bearing terror of the battle than not to have returned at all. Lunacy can be treated, death is incurable.'

'A pearl of Oriental wisdom, no doubt. Who said that? Chairman Mao?'

'Winston Churchill.'

16

Timothy Jaggers watched the professor hurrying along the pathway in the direction of Magdalen's Founder's Tower. A tall man dressed in a brown tweed suit, leather patches on the elbows, sturdy brown shoes. The white shirt collar showed signs of fraying, as did the mustard-coloured wool tie. The black leather briefcase was tucked under his arm, carried in this awkward fashion because of a handle broken two years earlier, something that he had never found the time to get repaired.

Oxford Rules in October: beginning of the Michaelmas term. The crowds of tourists and language-school students had left. The undergraduates had just arrived, full of enthusiasm and good intentions. Professors' workloads at the beginning of a new academic year were bearable – best time to talk to them.

Jaggers stepped out in front of the man. 'Professor Mather?'

The professor stopped, his startling green eyes observing the slightly taller man in a dark overcoat, holding a furled umbrella, the swept-back dark hair – overlong, the mouth turned down in a permanent sneer. 'Yes?'

'My name is Jaggers, Professor. I'm with the Foreign and Commonwealth Office. I telephoned you yesterday, regarding your brother.'

'I understood the meeting was at eleven o'clock this morning!' Mather's voice was clipped and dry.

'My apologies, but I have to be in London by then: something rather urgent came up at the last moment. I won't keep you long.'

The professor gazed at him. 'I can give you five minutes, Mr Jaggers. I'm already late for a tutorial.' An exception to Oxford Rules, perhaps.

'Yes, well, we only recently found out that William Mather had a brother and as he is unmarried there were no other relations that we were aware of. To put it bluntly, Professor, your brother seems to have disappeared. We were wondering if perhaps you had heard from him recently.'

The professor looked out across the Cloisters – Matthew Arnold's 'last enchantment of the Middle Age' – towards the Bell Tower. 'When did he "disappear", as you put it?'

'Sometime last week.'

'Yes. Always in a hurry, young William. I quite remember my father chastising him for what he called his unrepentant haste. Where was he when you lost him? I assume he was doing something for the government – he always seemed to be, at least.'

'In Eastern Europe, which is as much as I can tell you at the moment, I'm afraid.'

'Not in any trouble or anything like that, I take it?'

'No, no. Very decent chap. We, er, think very highly of him.'

'Yes, of course. It's just that I haven't seen him for years. Always sends me a Christmas card, though. But curiously enough, just lately he seems to have acquired one of those signature-stamp gadgets. Too busy to use a pen, you see.'

'And you haven't heard from him recently?'

'Last Christmas. Not since.'

'Would he call you if anything was wrong?'

'Never has in the past . . . And I don't think he will now.'

'Any good reason to think that?'

'Oh, didn't you know? We're identical twins.'

'Ah.' Jaggers looked vague. 'Is that significant?'

'I think he's dead, Mr Jaggers.'

Jaggers stared at the professor for a long time. Then he opened his mouth as if to say something but all that emerged was a sigh.

'I know what you're thinking,' the professor went on quickly. 'But unless you're an identical twin you could never understand. We are two halves of the same whole, you see. It was a week last Saturday – early in the morning, I suffered a very severe chest pain. It lasted only for a minute or so, but when it had gone I knew instantly what had happened. When you telephoned yesterday I thought you were coming along to confirm my suspicions.'

'We haven't found a body,' Jaggers explained. 'He merely disappeared from the hotel he was staying at.'

'I quite understand. I'm sorry I couldn't be of more help. Perhaps you will let me know when you find him.'

'Of course.'

'Jaggers,' the professor said absently, 'Used to know a Jaggers at Winchester . . . Relation, perhaps?'

A family tradition. All Jaggers attended Winchester. And Professor Mather, what age was he? Early forties – looked ten years older. 'My elder brother, in all probability.'

'Played the French horn, as I recall.'

'Still does, from time to time.'

A contortion of the briefcase-clutching arm to check his wristwatch. 'Late. Must dash. My best wishes to your brother.'

'I'll pass them on. Thank you for your time, Professor.' Jaggers watched him go. Head down. Briefcase tucked under his arm. Rapid footsteps. *Unrepentant haste.*

He turned to leave. Somewhere close by the choir was practising. Voices carrying on the damp October morning – a hint of woodsmoke in the air.

> *Te Deum Patrem colimus,*
> *Te Laudibus prosequimus,*
> *Qui corpus cibo reficis,*
> *Coelesti mentem gratia . . .*

To someone who had taken a good degree in the sciences at Magdalen fifteen years earlier, coming back and hearing the *Hymnus Eucharisticus* might have stirred old feelings.

Jaggers, however, had other things on his mind. Not least of which, the supposition that William Mather was dead! Which, in a roundabout way, brought his thinking back to the phone call from Century House that morning.

Something about a Special Branch report on the late Jack Giles MP. A very damning report.

17

Colonel Vin's office was a shrine to Ho Chi Minh, one of the better-known of the fifty aliases of Nguyen Tat Thanh, founder of the Vietnamese Communist Party and President of the Democratic Republic of Vietnam from 1946 until his death in 1969. Framed pictures of Bac Ho (Uncle Ho) hung from every wall. Uncle Ho who had travelled the world in his time; working as a teacher, cook, gardener, snow-sweeper, waiter, photo-retoucher and stoker, before his political conscious-ness began to develop. Uncle Ho the legend – a good man to bear allegiance to, especially if it was a cover for adventures in capitalism at the expense of one's own government.

The little colonel had left shortly after Winter's return from the abortive refuelling mission. He was sending his wife and daughter to Paris that afternoon. The beginnings of a new life. The colonel, with a new set of papers, would follow them that Saturday morning, a few hours after the Ilyushin and the Phantom had taken off. From Paris the family would move to a secret address in Northern Spain.

The office in the meantime had been turned into a pilots' crew room of sorts. Cups of coffee, cigarette smoke, airways charts spread out on tables, bone-domes, flying gloves, survival vests.

Cam Frenette, the white-bearded New Englander, had found a seat in the corner of the room and was poring over schematic diagrams of the Ilyushin's refuelling system. He was an old man. Seventy if he was a day, according to Stevens. A pilot and a licensed A & P mechanic. His right hand was gnarled and deformed, the result of an accident working a lathe many years earlier. A serious, unsmiling man, one who from the brief conversations Winter had had with him indicated that he had been around the block so many times he had worn a groove in the pavement.

Maria was discussing join-up procedures with Red. Flying hands prescribing delicate ballet movements between two military aircraft with a combined weight approaching 200,000 pounds.

Winter looked at the wall-clock – symmetrically placed between two framed pictures of Uncle Ho. 1600 hours alpha. The day had practically gone. He had meant to talk to TC about the computer virus idea, but that would have to wait until the morning. There were more pressing matters, such as aircraft unserviceability and his later meeting with Yuri.

The seriously overweight – five foot five and 240 pounds – Hod Priest. Late forties. Wild, frightened eyes – the result, it was said, of being shot down many years earlier by a MiG fighter when he had strayed into Angolan airspace on a single-engined ferry flight from the United States to South Africa. A number of months being tortured (as an American spy) in an Angolan prison before the US government, pressured by Priest's family, had secured his release. Even so, you had the feeling they had been too late. Something had happened to turn Priest's mind. Not completely, but enough to let you know that you were not dealing with a totally rational human being.

It was Priest now who picked up a dusty army boot from the corner of the colonel's desk and turned to Winter. 'Unusual pen holder,' he said, twisting the pen-filled plastic cup that was fitted into the boot. Nasal voice. Thin. Almost a whine.

'Indeed. You've noticed the colonel's limp.'

'Sure.'

'He lost his left foot to a landmine at the end of the war. What you're holding is the foot that got blown off.'

Priest grinned and inspected the boot even closer. 'Radical.'

'If you shake it you can hear bits of bone rattling around. In the old days it used to smell to high heaven, but once the flesh had decomposed and someone had thrown in a few mothballs, it became more bearable.'

Priest shook it. Like a kid with a new toy. 'Quite a character, huh?'

'A colonel in the army of the People's Republic of Vietnam. I doubt any of them are "characters", Hod. Not in the way you think, at least. The reason for keeping it probably has deep religious significance.'

'Ah, yeah, hadn't considered that.'

Frenette closed the Ilyushin's technical manual and came over to join them. 'From what I can gather,' he said, 'It seems that they robbed most of the refuelling system out of a KC135. Probably from one we left behind at the end of the war.'

'And the problem?' Winter asked.

'Looks like a hydraulic shuttle valve. You think they've got any spares in the hangars? We must have left thousands of tons of equipment behind on this base alone.'

'I'll check with Colonel Vin. How soon to rectify the squawk once you have the right part?'

Frenette scratched his beard. 'Hard to say. Old military equipment was built with a pretty high maintenance man-hour-per-flight-hour spec.' Except he said, 'MH-slash-FH.' The jargon used by aviation technical journalists. Or ex-military flyers.

'A day!' Winter proposed.

'Oh, yes. That would be a worst-case scenario.'

'Which likely rules out tomorrow for flying. Meaning we need to slate the final airtests for Thursday.'

'What about Friday?'

'No, I'd rather leave that as a rest day. You need to be airborne at midnight, and I'll be departing at 0200 with the Phantom. Anything else?'

'Number two engine is running at a higher ITT than normal. Two main wheel tyres badly worn. Half the instrument panel lights don't seem to work, more than likely a rheostat. Plus we don't seem to have the engine logs. Any idea of times since the last hot sections?'

'Afraid not. Still, looking on the bright side, we only have to get it to the UK and its flying days are over.'

'Let's hope that engine doesn't fail before then.'

'But if it did we could still do a three-engine ferry, couldn't we?'

'We could,' Frenette said unhappily, 'But you'd have to say goodbye to your refuelling operations. Need to keep the weight down, which means minimum trip fuel.'

'How many hours have you got? Ferrying, that is.'

'Twenty-five thousand and some change. Enough to know better than to fly antique Russian hardware, right!'

'I'll trade you the F-4.'

Frenette shook his head. Mock laughter. 'I have plans to die in my own bed at a ripe old age surrounded by my grandchildren and great-grandchildren. Forty-year-old transports are one thing, forty-year-old fighters something else altogether. Put another way, I'm not that brave.'

'Or foolish!'

'At least it's got a good paint job,' Frenette said lightly.

'Ah yes, shiny paint distracting the eye from more meaningful things.'

'You got it. In the meantime Hod and I had better get the flight planning out of the way tonight. One tech stop in Bahrain for both aircraft, that the idea?'

'Yes. As we have a tanker we might as well keep the costs down – besides which, the museum at Coventry is not too cash-rich. I've agreed a fixed price on delivery based on air-to-air refuelling: anything over that comes out of my pocket, and I'm about as broke as the rest of you!'

At least Frenette understood that. He had been ferrying aircraft long enough to know that cost-cutting was the main object of the exercise. At retirement this should leave any ferry driver with two basic rewards.

The first: enough money to stave off terminal starvation.

The second: enough wisdom not to have killed oneself by the aforesaid cost-cutting.

Thin red lines.

The New Englander said, 'I saw a bunch of old Hercs as I came in to land, ten or more. Southside of the base. We converted some of those to tankers during the bad old days. If any had that mod done I might be able find a compatible part. Long shot, but worth a try.'

'The colonel should be back soon. I'm sure he'll arrange for you to go and have a look. When do you want to start?'

'Now. ASAP. Another thing: Red mentioned he was staying on the base. Any chance Hod and I could move over here? The one-hour drive each way to the city is a waste of time as far as I'm concerned. If I was here I could work on the plane through part of the night.'

'Bit rough and ready. I'm not sure if there's hot water, even.'

'As long as there's a bed.'

'And enough food,' suggested Hod.

'I'll see what I can do,' Winter promised. 'If we can arrange it, you can move out here tomorrow.'

18

Yuri the Yid had been to the Rex early that morning. The hotel barber had cropped the shoulder-length hair and dyed it ash-blond. A manicurist had worked on his ragged finger-nails at the same time. Then he had collected his two hand-made medium-weight wool suits – measured up the previous day – from the hotel tailor (a fifty per cent bonus payment had ensured the slightly quicker than normal service). Finally he had stopped at a local photographer – a one-hour service for passport photographs. As the photographer also doubled as an optician he took an eye test and ordered a pair of blue-tinted sunglasses.

Now, early evening, he was waiting in the muddy alleys between the tightly packed houses guarded by crumbling walls, some overgrown with tumbling vines: the backstreets of Saigon. Here and there yellow light silhouetted a figure watching from an upper-floor window. The police did not venture into these places often. Westerners were never seen here, except perhaps during the war when deserters had sought refuge, knowing that the military police did not have the balls to follow them. These were the places where lawlessness was more powerful than war, where people died unnoticed and no one even bothered to count the bodies.

In these places the raw night smells of the city were at their most powerful. Most vile. The localized silence was the real frightener. Yuri tried to shrink his bulk further into the shadows of the wall, all the time watching. Thinking. Remembering. This area was much like those he had known in his younger days. The poor, desolate, empty places that had filled his poor, desolate, empty years. He had been born in a small basement room in Moscow. His mother had had a job sweeping the streets so she could take care of her invalid husband and her young son. Yuri's father told him, years later, how he would awake early and find the bed already empty, and how he would lie there, and through the top part of the dirty window-pane that looked out on to the street would come the sound of the big, stiff brush, moving back and forth on the roadway. She was outside every day of her life. All weathers. She died twelve years after the victory fireworks, worn out by physical labour. That was the time Yuri had to stop his schooling and find work to support his sick and, by now, alcoholic father. Stealing had been the easiest way.

As it had become again.

Him and Skulov in Tbilisi. The plan to steal a passport made more complex because he knew that William Mather was a high-level businessman doing a deal on behalf of the British government: gossip, everybody at the Tbilisi plant knew. And to steal a passport meant you had to recruit the assistance of one of the clerks at Mather's hotel. Reason: all foreign visitors' passports were held by the hotels. The problem was he didn't know any hotel employees well enough that he would put a hundred per cent trust in them.

And as any good Russian would tell you: The *chekisti* still live – those who snoop into other people's lives, grass to the cops.

Skulov was different.

Yuri had known Fyodor Ipatovich Skulov since he was a kid. The reason that he confided *everything* to the bent policeman, the agreement being a fifty-fifty split of all monies received. (A million US dollars at least, Yuri had assured him.) But even Skulov had agreed there were informers everywhere. Which was why they had evolved the elaborate plan of a phone call from Minatom in Ordzhonikidze early that Saturday morning, a way to get the Englishman to check out of the hotel.

So that he could disappear.

As for killing him: not as drastic as it sounded, according to Skulov. Wouldn't his disappearance point accusatory fingers concerning the missing uranium in his direction? An even better plan to Skulov's way of thinking than Winter's, which had merely hinged on an Englishman with similar features and build – hair and eye colour being easy enough to change – and a borrowed passport with which to safely leave Russia and disappear. Too many loose ends.

Finally, how he had tricked the idiot Skulov out of his share of the money – a lie about a planned meeting in a bar in the old town the following Monday evening to hand over the money. A small lie inside a bigger one, as Yuri had not yet been paid. And as he would never be going back to the city on the Kura river! And as Skulov could not 'finger' him without implicating himself!

Kulak psychology: founded on pathological greed. He hoped to God that Skulov remained a long way from Moscow.

A sound.

He froze. Pricked up his ears. Strained to hear something. Anything! The distant hum of city traffic. The pulse beating in his head. He moved away from the wall, turning his head, screwing his eyes to focus through the thick lenses of his glasses into the darkness. Nothing: his imagination, perhaps.

The commando blade touched his cheek. A quiet voice: 'Yuri?' Too late to stop his heart ricocheting painfully off his ribcage. Nearly too late to stop his bladder from giving up the ghost.

'Who do you fucking think . . . You nearly frightened me to death,' he said, gasping for breath.

'Just making sure,' Winter replied, slipping the dagger back into its sheath.

'How do you do that?'

'Do what?'

'The caretaker from hell thing, appearing from nowhere . . . I was looking . . . How could I not see you?'

Winter's old SAS instructor – Nick Ashe – at the Lines in Hereford. Someone who had spent years in the East and had married the skills of British soldiering with yoga and transcendental meditation.

John Templeton Smith

Who had taught the lucky few about energy centres called 'chakras' and 'prana'. How to observe and interpret the colour of auras that everyone carries with them like the clothes on their back. Enough mental energy to redirect another person's focus in a totally different direction. Long enough to come up behind them unnoticed and slit their throats. Closely guarded secrets, lest the knowledge be turned on oneself. 'Old army training. Been waiting long?'

'Long enough. Not a good idea in these places.'

'I'm impressed with the haircut. A new man.'

'Makes me feel light-headed,' Yuri complained.

They started walking. Yuri had taken off his glasses and was cleaning them with a grubby handkerchief as he stumbled along the dark alleyway. He said, 'I had a friend who was beaten to death in a place like this.'

'Here in Saigon?'

'No, back in Russia, at a settlement I once lived in. His name was Yegor; he liked animals. He kept some swans at a place called Black Lake, clipped their wings so they couldn't leave . . . said they decorated life. He went out to visit them every day to make sure they were okay. Then, one night, some guys from the village went out and killed them. Cut off their heads and plucked them – to sell, you understand. Yegor caught up with them in a back alley in the village, told them he wanted their papers, that he was going to take them to the police. So they beat him senseless . . . My uncle found him bleeding to death, called the police. And you know what? He knew who the guys were, but he never said. Just, with his dying breath, that he forgave them. Makes you wonder, doesn't it?'

'Yuri the philosopher: I never knew.'

Yuri had been thinking of Skulov as he spoke. A simple policeman who was also known for his violent temper. A man who might well skin you alive – and chop off your head – for a lot less than the small fortune Yuri had cheated him out of. 'Stolichnaya writes the script . . . That's the other trick to surviving Russia. And this place, come to that: you drink enough to relax, but not enough to lose your focus.'

The house was much like the rest of them; built on a minimum plot, surrounded by an eight-foot-high wall. Decay was all around. Except in this yard there was the smell of blossoming frangipani, partially disguising the stench of open drains. Unbearable became bearable.

Winter followed the Russian into the small yard and waited while he secured the steel gate.

'You've seen Frenchie?'

'Sure, I brought the photographs this afternoon. He showed me how to work the lock.'

They went up a short flight of steps and through the back door of the house. Three rooms noticeable instantly, linked by doorway openings with the doors removed, or perhaps there had never been the money or the desire to fit doors. The first room had a small cot, draped with a bright multi-coloured blanket, pushed up against the wall. Three hard-backed chairs, the seats and the backs covered in light blue plastic, faded, discoloured with a faint sheen of tobacco brown – American kitsch circa the 1950s. One of the chairs was by the desk – an old roll-top antique with a green-shaded desk lamp. Rows of ink bottles, a long wooden box overflowing with calligraphy pens, a stack of

175

different-coloured passports (held together by an elastic band), magnifying glasses, Customs stamps with ink pads – all the colours of the spectrum. A forger's place of business.

The old man, Valerie Boulanger, who had left his native Paris a number of lifetimes ago, shuffled into the room. Somewhere in his eighties now. Dressed in a grubby white shirt and wrinkled grey flannel trousers. The light tan carpet slippers long since worn out, his toes peeping through. He was a tall man with a pronounced stoop. Unbelievably thin. The shadows in the badly lit room accentuating his facial bone structure. Grey hair, dry as straw. Thin bloodless lips, moist eyes. The smell of camphor. Old age.

'*Bonsoir, Monsieur Winter, il y a longtemps, n'est-ce pas?*

Winter shook the old man's hand. Felt the paper-thin skin slipping over the bones. '*Plusieurs ans, Monsieur Boulanger, mais vous avez gardé votre santé.*'

'*C'est le vin.*' A twinkle in the old eyes.

'*Mais oui,*' Winter said, adding in English, 'You know Yuri, of course.'

'But of course.' The Frenchman smiled at the Russian, went over to his desk, opened one of the drawers and took out a bottle of vodka. 'Especially for you, Monsieur Becker,' he said. 'Please take a seat. I will get some glasses.' He shuffled slowly out of the room.

Winter and Yuri sat down. 'He has the passport ready?' Yuri asked.

'He didn't say.'

The Frenchman came back and poured the vodka.

'*A votre santé*,' he pronounced, raising his glass.

'To you, Valerie, good health for more years yet.'

They drank. And the glasses were refilled.

After three toasts the old man went to his chair at the desk, sat down and shuffled through the pile of passports. He selected a dark blue one embossed with the legend *New Zealand*, and handed it to the Russian.

'Very good. Really, very good,' Yuri exclaimed. 'How did you get the Vietnamese stamp?'

The Frenchman smiled. 'From a Vietnamese Customs officer. We split my fees fifty-fifty. A good arrangement, yes?'

The payment was made. The business concluded. And then the Frenchman pulled a small chest out from under the bed and removed an old and worn photo album. It was a part of the ritual. You bought a forged passport; you listened to some of the war stories. Of the French and the Viet Minh.

Tonight it was the tunnels at Cu Chi, north-west of Saigon. The tunnels that stretched all the way to the Cambodian border. Those started in the 1940s, burrowed deep in the red earth, built over two and a half decades, the improvised response of a poorly equipped peasant army to its enemy's high-tech ordnance: artillery, bombers, chemical weapons. The same tunnels used against the French came back to haunt the Americans, not least with the stunning attacks in the South Vietnamese capital itself during the 1968 Tet Offensive which were planned and launched by the Viet Cong from Cu Chi. Lastly came the sepia photos of Boulanger with Uncle Ho and various generals from both sides. There was even one with the English author Graham Greene, at the

John Templeton Smith

Continental Hotel in the 1950s, signed: '*A Valerie, avec les souhaits meilleuts, Graham Greene – l'homme anglais discret.*'

It was after they had left and were making their way out of the labyrinth of back alleys towards the main streets of District One that Yuri said breathlessly, 'You want to get drunk?'

'That bad, uh?'

Skin you alive . . . Chop off your head. 'I was thinking about Frenchie,' he lied.

'Being here, you mean?'

'Hell of a place to stack your bones.'

That cold wind again. Incipient. Full of voices from the past.

'One drink only,' Winter said. 'I might have to fly tomorrow.'

'Stolichnaya?'

'Sure.'

'Two.'

They went to the Rex. And drank a bottle.

19

They met as Winter was crossing Lam Son Square. It was midnight.

'Not safe to be out on the streets alone after dark,' he said, catching up with her.

'That is what Cam and Hod told me. I told them I could look after myself.' Maria turned her head as she spoke. Looking up at him. Her large dark eyes glittering in the street lights. The faintest hint of perfume. French, expensive. 'Your meeting went well?'

'Fine . . . Cam and Hod over at the Continental?'

'Yes, we only got back from the base an hour ago. Hod had found out the food was very good at their restaurant.'

'And was it?'

'I was too tired to notice. I stopped after the soup course, left them to their talking.' Her voice was sharp. Impersonal.

Winter knew only a little about body language – but enough to grasp the sense of a message. The problem was, what message? Wearily, he followed her into the

Caravelle and up in the elevator to their room.

He was sitting in one of the rattan chairs, taking off his shoes, when he said, 'Are you all right?'

'What do you mean?'

'You don't seem very happy.'

She had taken off her sage-green nylon flight jacket, hung it over the back of a chair. Which left her *uniform*: blue jeans, white T-shirt, no bra – she never wore one. She had been folding the bed sheets back and fluffing the pillows when he spoke. Now she turned to face him, a cool look. 'Have you considered Red's offer?'

Female psychology, he thought. You wish to share my bed – you had better give the right answers. And this was her skill, after all. Steering the conversation around to no-go areas.

When tired and facing another long day tomorrow – agree.

'What offer would that be?'

'Going into the sales business with him in Venezuela.'

'How did you know about that?'

'He told me this afternoon, while you were discussing the tanker problems with Cam. So what do you think?'

He got up and took her arm and steered her towards the bathroom. 'I think you should come into my office.'

In the bathroom Winter turned on the cold-water taps in the sink and in the shower. He sat on the edge of the bath, close to the taps – the most noise – and motioned her to sit by him. 'Anything you say is being listened to, do you understand?' Mouth to ear conversation. Her perfume, intoxicating.

'How do you know?'

'This room was searched the other evening. They probably used the visit as an excuse to plant bugging – listening – devices.'

'What kind of people go round bugging respectable hotel rooms?'

'The government, perhaps . . . They're still emerging from their own kind of cold war, after all.'

She thought about that. Returned to the earlier theme. 'And Venezuela, what of that?'

'I'll certainly go and have a look at the operation. Might even like Caracas.'

'When?'

'When what?'

'When will you go?'

'Whenever Red says.'

'What if he said tomorrow?'

The bottom line. The big dark eyes, challenging. The long fingers – unmanicured, unadorned – beating a tattoo on her jean-covered thighs.

'You know that is impossible.'

'I know nothing of the sort.' She reached down and tugged off her ankle boots. Tossed them aside. A sign of anger.

The wrong answer.

'A certain group of people, shall we say, stole every penny I had ever worked for in my life. This came after I had helped them to resolve a particularly messy problem they had in South America; you were there, so you know that to be true. I made them an offer: my money for the cargo that is now in my possession.

They didn't even bother to reply.'

'And you think selling uranium to Iraq is the answer? You realize they will never stop hunting you after this.'

'They've been doing that for the best part of my life. They haven't caught me yet.'

'What about us? You told me you loved me.'

Pillow talk. When they had been making love. When, in the darkness, he had seen and touched and smelled his wife. He still dreamt of her. Imagined he always would. Love! He didn't know if he could go through that much pain again. 'What's love got to do with a simple business transaction?'

'Everything. Besides, it is hardly simple. You said yourself that you had given them the opportunity to buy the cargo. What does that mean? Does it mean you have told them where you are? The same way you played your little games in South America?'

Winter said nothing.

'Charlie once told me that this was an occupation for young men, that staying in it too long could prove fatal . . . I would rather have you alive and poor than rich and dead.'

'It's not about money, Maria. Don't you understand? It's about principles. Honour.'

'*Es el colmo*. Where is the honour in trading in stolen uranium? '

Winter smiled. He thought of the millions the American government had stolen from him. *Thou shalt not steal.* Which version of honour?

She noticed the grin. 'What is funny?'

'Nothing.'

Another mistake. A non-answer.

182

'I think perhaps I will leave, after all,' she said irritably.

'If that's what you want.'

'You are not going to try and stop me?'

'No.'

Her face was angry now. The lethal covenant between a highly reactive brain and a body that is preparing to attack. Deep, thin wrinkles appearing in the face, engraved emotional war paint. Most noticeable, a disgust dimple caused by the emotional right side of the brain pulling up the small muscles on the left side of the lower cheek.

At the very least he expected a slap across the face. She was good at that. Instead she picked up one of her ankle boots and, as she stood, flung it at him. It missed, but knocked a glass from the side of the wash basin. It shattered on the floor. She stormed out of the bathroom, slamming the door so hard that flakes of whitewash drifted down from the ceiling.

He closed his eyes and pictured a study in a quiet house, hidden away in snow-covered northern woodland. And heard the opening of Sibelius's Seventh Symphony . . . The shuddering note of mystery developing into an utterance of passionate intensity.

Secret places.

Places to hide.

PART FIVE
Quick and Dirty

20

'As I see it, we've got four problem areas,' Stevens said, laying a number of computer printouts on the bed. They were maps of various countries. With a difference. They showed deployment of their air forces, right down to the squadrons and equipment being operated. Military intelligence.

Winter, a mug of coffee in one hand and a cigarette in the other, glanced at the detailed pages. 'I'm impressed. How did you get all that together at such short notice?'

'Not me, your mate TC.' He motioned his head towards the end of the barrack room. The young American had set up a makeshift workstation. Two bedside lockers pushed together under a window serving as a desk. He was there now, fingers flying over the keyboard of the new Compaq Presario laptop Winter had bought him the previous day. 'I don't think he's left that chair since you gave it to him. Not even to go to bed. You and him should get on like a house on fire.'

187

'Why so?'

'Why'd you think? You both seem to suffer from bloody insomnia. I mean, what time is it now? . . . Seven in the morning. I bet the colonel didn't come out with you.'

'No, he loaned me his car and driver.'

'Exactly. He understands that the human body needs rest. Needs to recharge the batteries. You know what time I went to bed last night? I was out in the Herky graveyard until ten. Then, after we found a valve that Cam reckoned would work, he and the team headed back to the hotel and left yours truly to remove the u/s part off the tanker. Two o'clock before I turned in.'

'Look on the bright side. You're getting paid well enough.'

'I am? You never told me how much.'

'We'll talk about it tonight. If you and Cam can get the tanker serviceable and we're able to get a flight test in this afternoon, we'll be ahead for the first time. Also, I'll buy everyone dinner at Maxim's. Colonel Vin included. We need to be seen to be taking care of him, especially as we're just concluding a two-aircraft sales deal with the Ministry of Defence.'

'Keep the masters up north happy, right.'

'Object of the exercise.'

The Australian lifted his left boot on to the end of the bed and began tying the lace. 'Left to right on the paperwork,' he said – nodding down at the pages he had laid out. 'I've based it on the assumption that we're moving in the general direction of Bahrain. As you'll see on page one, a direct GPS track to Karachi takes us close to Bangkok as we overfly Thailand. Two

F-16 squadrons. One at Nakhon Ratchasima and the other at Takhli.'

Winter put his coffee down and picked up the paper. It was headed:

THAILAND'S AIR FORCE
DATA BASED ON INFORMATION AVAILABLE

'Helicopter bases, flight training schools, the Royal Rain Making Flight, 103 Squadron based at Nakhon Ratchasima, 403 Squadron at Takhli . . . Very comprehensive.'

'Only plus I can see,' Stevens said, tying off the other bootlace, 'is that due to Thailand's rocky economy, the air force has probably suffered cutbacks. Having to count the pennies, or the *baht* if you want to be picky. The point being that a regular airways flight shouldn't cause any problems, assuming, as you said earlier, that the CIA and other foreign agencies and air forces have not been alerted.'

'With luck TC will come up with something in time to create enough confusion at least until we're past Karachi.'

'Planting viruses in the respective air defence systems, you mean?'

'Yes.'

'He figures it's impossible in the time-frame allowed.'

Winter put the Thai Air Force paper back on the bed and retrieved his coffee. 'He's thinking like a civilian, Red. I'll get him up to a speed he never knew he had by lunchtime.'

'I have no doubts. Going on with our little journey to

the land of the bed-sheet blokes. Pages two and three deal with India and Pakistan respectively. We have the same intel there as we have on Thailand, so there's not much point going through it. The fourth problem area is the one that's got me really worried. The Middle East. Used to know another Englishman years ago, he would have called it a bugger's muddle. About right for that part of the world. So, we rendezvous with the tanker west of Karachi, and proceed on the airway towards Bahrain. Which throws up the question: what US aircraft carriers are currently cruising around the Arabian Gulf area?' He picked up a photocopied double page from an atlas, held together with paper clips. It carried the legend: *The Near and Middle East.* 'Once you get to Bahrain, there's no option but to land. I mean, we can't actually overfly and keep heading north-west, can we? Thirty years ago we could have – daylight or dark – because whatever primary radar they had was only for the terminal areas of a handful of airports. Now we have NATO forces patrolling the north and south of Iraq. No way in. And even if we legitimately negotiate the airways to Bahrain and then try to make a run for it, we've got a little matter of about 600 nauticals to Baghdad. Which is where you start to believe that every F-14 or F-15 in the area has got a good lock-on, and you're about to kiss Mother Earth goodbye.'

'We're not going that way,' Winter said quietly.

Stevens put the map pages back on the bed. Finished his coffee. Wiped his lips with the back of his hand. 'What do you mean, we're not going that way? What other way is there? Unless you're talking about routing north-west into Russia and dropping south-west over the Caspian Sea – down the Turkish border. They've still got a no-fly zone up there, you know.'

Winter put his coffee mug on the bedside locker, stubbed out his cigarette in a red plastic ashtray advertising the Emperor Hotel (obviously borrowed by Stevens on his recent visit), and took the pages from the bed. 'After refuelling west of Karachi we continue west along the airway towards the Gulf of Oman. Abeam Chah Bahar at sixty-one degrees east . . . About here,' he pointed, 'we alter heading right and track towards Sa'idabad. At the same time we switch off our transponder and begin a rapid descent. It'll be night, of course. At Sa'idabad we'll be flying visual – there's a full moon that night, I've checked the *Air Almanac* – once over that checkpoint, which looks to be about 1500 metres above sea level, we come left approximately ten degrees and track low-level through the mountains – the Kudha-ye Zagros – towards Shahr-a Kord, a small town eighty kilometres south-west of Esfahan. At Sharh-a Kord we come hard left to 275 degrees . . . After about five kliks we climb over the Zagros mountains – spot height in that area indicates 4548 metres . . . Once clear we drop down low-level and cross checkpoint Chogha Zambile. Notable feature here is the ziggurat; original height fifty metres, now it's reported as about thirty to thirty-five . . . I mention this as we'll be flying at no more than 30 metres a.g.l. . . . We might want to keep a good lookout for it. Once past the pyramid, 200 kilometres to the next checkpoint. This is across the border in Iraq and at the bend in the Tigris, east of Al Kut. Final leg to Baghdad – 225 kliks.'

Stevens had taken a half-corona from a box on his

bedside locker. He had been chewing it as he listened. His eyes wide. His face quite pale. He spat the cigar out. 'IRAN! You're planning to over-fucking-fly Iran . . . Tell me you're not serious.'

'I'm always serious . . . What's the problem?'

The Australian snorted in disbelief. 'The problem. Singular! How about problems plural, as in too fucking many? Firstly, flying through unfamiliar mountain valleys is tricky enough in broad daylight. At night, hoping the full moon hasn't set by the time we get there, or that the weather hasn't clamped the entire area, is crazy. Secondly, American AWACS could and probably will still pick us up: whether or not they will do, or can do, anything about it is another matter. Thirdly, and most importantly, Iran has an air force, amazing as it may seem. It's more than likely western Iran is also well equipped with missile sites, for no other reason than that a few miles away to their west is Iraq. No love lost after the last war they had, right? So, some slick radar operators pick up a fast-mover near the Iran/Iraq border, and guess what? Both sides end up thinking it is the other side about to do something they shouldn't. Which means that we could be targeted by the people we're doing business with as well as the Iranians.'

Aeronautical letters of disenchantment.

Winter understood. Red Stevens was a careful man. The reason he was not a good fighter pilot. He had perspective – a civilian thing. In a military environment perspective would eventually kill you. 'Baghdad has been given an e.t.a. for the border. They've assigned us the call sign "Babylon Six".' The sixth pillar of Islam – *jihad* – striving in the way of God. What else!

'And that's it. *That* is the grand plan?'

'Why not? We arrive in Iranian airspace during the early hours of Saturday, local time. Which follows a hard day of praying by the locals.'

'Every day's a hard day of praying.'

'Granted, except the majority of the faithful attend their local mosque on Friday noon and then spend a long day with their family.'

'So they'll all be safely tucked up in bed with the *Qu'ran*. Yeah, I get the point.'

'Element of surprise, Red.'

'Quite possibly. What about Iraq? They'll probably only give us a plus or minus three-minute time slot for the border. Can we be that accurate?'

'You're the navigator, you tell me.'

Stevens stretched, rubbed his eyes with his fists. Yawned. 'Then again, there's the fuel. If we're operating low-level in the mountains we might not have enough to even make the Iraq border. Then what? We bang out over Iran. I don't think the Iranians will smile too kindly on an American warplane flown by two guys wearing civilian clothes under their flight-suits. They do nasty things to "spies". And what about the uranium? The contamination! I mean, I may not be a bloody saint, but I'd hate to think that I'd screwed up thousands of lives with wholesale cancer . . . Especially the lives of kids. Lastly, there's Bahrain. What happens when we disappear? Everyone will assume we've crashed. What about Cam and his team?'

'Once on the ground in Baghdad we phone Bahrain air traffic control and advise them we're in Karachi: that we had a radio failure and diverted to the nearest international airport. Then we'll send a similar confusing message to Karachi. Either way, it will take a day or two before anyone realizes that we have truly disappeared, by which time the Ilyushin will be in Coventry, the crew paid off, and you'll be home in Caracas with your wife.'

Stevens pulled on his bush jacket. His face unusually serious. 'You know,' he said, striding towards the door that led to the exit corridor, 'I'd give real money for just one ounce of your optimism.'

'Where are you going?'

'Over to the hangar to check the fuel capacity and burn figures on the Phantom.'

'Good thinking.'

'You're sure there are no military bases on our planned route over Iran?'

'Don't you trust me?'

'I'll let you know,' the Aussie voice shouted back. No laughter this morning.

Winter refilled his coffee mug and lit his second cigarette of the morning. A bad diet for a man of his age. As for the military bases, his reassurance to Stevens had not been quite true. The ziggurat at Chogha Zambile, near the ancient ruins of Susa, was in a restricted military area. And what was in that area was anybody's guess. Even so, the Iranian soldiers would be watching for 'incoming' from the west, the direction of Iraq. A jet suddenly and dramatically appearing over their base heading *towards* Iraq would initially indicate it was one of theirs. By the time the duty officer had rushed to awake his commander – who would then put a phone call through to the nearest air force base to check what exercises they were carrying out and why he, the army commander at

Susa had not been informed – it would, hopefully, be too late. The Phantom would have made its pre-arranged radio call on the assigned Iraqi frequency and be safely across the border. *Least said, soonest mended. At least for now.*

Winter walked down the long room towards the sound of fingers attacking a computer keyboard. Reminiscent of clicking knitting needles. 'Well done on the defence-net information, TC.'

The young American, dressed in his new blue jeans, red sweatshirt and Nike trainers – another part of Winter's shopping list the previous day – turned from the computer and smiled. His eyes screwed up. Trying to focus without his glasses. The bruising, cuts and swelling around his face seemed to be improving. Healing scabs covered his lower lip and chin. The injuries not quite as noticeable as they had been two days earlier. 'Not a problem . . . There's plenty of that available. Just knowing where to look.'

'Any more thoughts on the virus idea we discussed on Monday night?'

'A lot. Something I found out from a guy in Tokyo . . . we went to college together. I told him I was writing a new high-tech game with a military flavour. Sort of, you get to fly an airplane of your choice, and you have to fly it through a real-world scenario, over-flying enemy countries, trying to evade their radar and so on. He said there were a lot of games out there, that might follow that protocol.'

Winter could see the enthusiasm in the young American's eyes. TC: the loner, the odd one out. Spending all his life in front of a computer screen, no social awkwardness there. Just complete control. Time? It didn't exist. Here, in front of a small fold-up screen, you could exercise the power of the Wizard of Oz over any imaginary kingdom you wished to invent. *A matter of finding common ground. Trust.* 'What computer programming language do gamers use? I think you told me the other day, but you'd better count me as computer-illiterate.'

TC turned back towards the screen, eyes squinting slightly, as though its pale grey light offered some mysterious, soul-bending, vaporous elixir. Known by most of the world as self-confidence. 'Well, uh, generally it's done in C and, I guess, it would really depend on what context it's in. Like on the console systems they normally start out with a very quick-and-dirty assembler. And that's like, the lowest level you can go . . . We actually get to the binary level. That's three-letter mnemonics and stuff like that. It's, like, move-call, move-call.'

'Press this key, then this will happen, you mean?'

'Yeah, stuff like that. Well, it's actually more of a mathematical thing and it has to do with the registers and addresses in the system . . . And you're actually manipulating the CPU's instructions. Like with Basic. Basic is a high-level language, OK? It's like: "Print this Message", "Go to this message", stuff like that. And assembly is mainly just like move to this register, pull from this address, poke to this . . . things like that. On the consoles, where I have my main experience, we usually have just quick-and-dirty. And that just means that there aren't any windows or processes you have to go through. You just kink off, run a program and stick in a code, and then you assemble it from there.'

Winter put his coffee mug down on the end of the
desk and took the pack of Particulares from his shirt
pocket. 'Want one of these?'

The American looked up and smiled shyly.
'Thanks.' Winter lit it for him. 'How about a cup of
coffee?' he asked the youngster.

TC shook his head. 'Red got me some bottled water.
I prefer that.'

Winter put the cigarettes back in his pocket.
Wondered where this new generation got their fun.
'What sort of games have you assembled, or written, or
whatever you call it? Have you got something new, not
yet off the drawing board, something we could use . . .
download to someone's computer via e-mail?'

Maybe the kid was boring and shy. But his mind was
lightning fast. 'You think that would appeal to the
analysts in the foreign countries you were talking
about? I mean, it would be no good in English, we'd
have to translate.'

'How long would that take?'

'Too long. Even if we can gain access we have to get
them to open the file and with the VPI systems these
days . . .'

'What's a VPI?'

'A virus protection program.'

'Who makes those up?'

TC turned from the computer screen and looked at
Winter. 'What did you say?'

'Who produces the virus protection programs? Local
government employees? Top experts in their field?'

'In the US, yes.'

'And in foreign, third-world countries? Those
friendly with the US.'

TC's face froze in a picture of pure delight. 'Oh shit,' he murmured. 'How clever . . . how very clever.'

21

Paris of the Orient.

Hanoi: the capital of the Socialist Republic of Vietnam. A city of lakes, shaded boulevards and verdant parks. And, in the tradition of Lenin and Stalin, where Ho Chi Minh, encased in a glass sarcophagus, is set deep in the bowels of a concrete monument that has become a site of pilgrimage. A place where honour guards in snowy white uniforms are stationed at five-metre intervals, giving a macabre Doctor Strangelove air to the tableau of the embalmed little body with its wispy white hair.

Edeyrn Owens, dressed in tropical white cotton shirt and trousers, was enjoying breakfast at the restaurant in the Dong Loi Hotel. A place with thick linen napkins and heavy silver cutlery, where waiters dressed in crisp white uniforms moved quickly and efficiently about their business, seating customers, producing menus, whipping away covers from hot food like stagehands shuffling props in a fast-moving breakfast theatre. Even so, as Tanner Williams had observed the previous day, after they had checked in and were enjoying a late lunch, 'All this courtesy and efficiency costs'. And it did: the Dong Loi was one of the more expensive hotels in Hanoi.

Owens buttered his last piece of toast, glancing casually around the restaurant as he did so. And, as happens in those far-off places, there was a European couple sitting at one of the tables. Early middle age. Smart. Respectable. But it was more than that which had caught his eye. It was the woman's face and eyes. Her cropped red hair. Her slim figure, the elegant way she dressed. She was so like his late wife Eleanor that he couldn't believe what he was seeing. The disbelief gave way to a moment of feeling quite ill. A cold prickly sweat breaking out on his forehead. He put his hand to his chest and looked away.

Remembering.

The day she had died from an overdose of barbiturates, he had been away in a place like this. He had flown home immediately, mentally planning all the things that one associated with dying: undertaker, florist, church, hymns, obituary for the newspaper, family solicitor, stonemason . . .

Except, when he reached their home in Surrey, he found that Eleanor's sister Rebecca had already arrived and taken charge. A formidable woman, who had lost her husband Dicky some years earlier.

She moved about his house like a whirlwind. He had stayed in the background, marvelling at the energy the woman possessed. At the end of it all, Eleanor's coffin was taken by hearse to Kent and interred next to her mother and father in the village cemetery of Wingham near Canterbury. 'Eleanor wanted it this way,' Rebecca had said to him in that strident voice of hers when he had questioned the choice of cemeteries. 'She must have mentioned it to you.'

'Perhaps. I forget.'

'Did she tell you she arranged a plot here for you also?'

'Not that I recall.'

Rebecca cluck-clucked as though inferring that her sister had been throwing good money after bad. 'Anyway, it's there, although with the places that you seem to live in it might be rather expensive to bring you home. Have you thought about that?'

He hadn't. He was thinking about Eleanor, young Eleanor, middle-aged Eleanor, and the last Eleanor, the one he had never really known. But he had loved her, in his own peculiar way he had loved her very much. 'I'll let my company know: I'm sure they'll make the arrangements if necessary.'

'Don't you mean the Service?'

'Arbuthnots, the medical-supply people. They're quite big overseas.'

The strident voice lifted. 'Eleanor said you went into the Soviet Union.' She was prying again.

'No, no. China once in a while. I've never been to Russia. Come to that, I don't think I'd want to, all those terrible camps they have. Wicked, isn't it?'

It was after the funeral that Rebecca had taken him to Canterbury and put him on the London train. 'One last thing, Edeyrn. Flowers. I take care of mother's and father's graves. I'm quite willing to look after Eleanor as well, but you will need to send me some money. The florists charge a great deal these days, and I'm not that well off any more. Dicky's fault, of course: he never planned for the future.'

Poor old Dicky, as maligned in death as he had been in life. 'I'll send a little from time to time,' he promised.

She gave him a frosty stare. 'Make sure you do. As you didn't do too good a job as a husband for her in life, it would be rather nice if you made the extra effort now that she's gone . . .'

'Are you all right, Edeyrn?'

'What . . .' Owens looked up quickly. Startled eyes. It was Williams.

'You look like you've seen a ghost.'

'No, no, I'm fine . . . I was just thinking about something . . . Nothing important.' A stolen glance across the restaurant. But the couple had left. *Nothing important.* Perhaps Rebecca had been closer to the mark than he had realized. Than he had cared to admit. *As you didn't do too good a job as a husband for her in life . . .*

'You're sure?' Williams asked, sitting down opposite.

'Absolutely.' He picked up his cup and sipped his tea. His hand was shaking.

Williams ordered coffee and toast and sat back in his chair. He was dressed in a lightweight grey wool suit, white shirt, and a moss-green tie. A totally different image from Vientiane. All business.

Owens said, 'You should try the kippers. Out of a tin, of course, but really quite good.'

'Too English for me. Like that awful oatmeal.'

'It's called porridge. Blame the Scots for that.'

'Rather pleasant here, isn't it?'

'French, Tanner. They occupied the place for close

to a hundred years. And as they're the most stylish and elegant people in the world, is it any wonder that their mark still lingers?'

'No argument from me on that.' Williams had taken the gold Dunhill lighter from his jacket pocket, was absently turning it over between his fingers as he spoke.

'So. Did you get through to your locals?'

'Not since the phone call yesterday. I've tried the number six times this morning. No reply. How does four o'clock yesterday afternoon translate to eight o'clock this morning . . . and still holding.'

'Nice thing about the East. Speed. Or should I say lack of it. Kipling wrote some pretty terrible doggerel in that direction.'

'Not up to Dylan Thomas, you mean?'

'No, I never really liked Thomas. Preferred Sylvia Plath, in my younger days. Depth, you see. A shame she committed suicide.'

'Not suicide, Edeyrn. Ms Plath would have called it murder in the one hundred and eightieth degree, destruction of the alter ego responsible for whatever pain and hopelessness it had visited upon the finer and more noble half. A matter of artistic inter-pretation.'

'Weakness, all the same,' Owens pronounced.

'Morbid subject over breakfast!'

'I agree. We're still leaving for Ho Chi Minh City this morning, I take it? I mean, not much time, is there? If the information you've been passed is correct, that Winter and his team are leaving on Friday night.'

Not much time indeed. Something that had kept Williams up half the night. Thinking. The goal of the intelligence officer is to put the other side to sleep, make them feel confident, secure, inattentive. Followed by a line from the CIA guerilla-warfare manual: 'If possible, professional criminals will be hired to carry out selective jobs.' *Analytic judgement based on intercept material.*

The white-uniformed waiter served the coffee and toast, bowed, and disappeared.

Owens said, 'A brave man, your Director.'

'Why'd you say that?'

'Sending you out here after the Colombian business – I'm betting he was questioned by your House Intelligence Committee over that. He wouldn't want to find himself in the hot seat again within months, would he?'

Williams remembered the top-secret closed-door session before all fifteen members of that committee. There had been a lot of rancour. He had been there as well as Eberhart. And from there they had gone to the Senate Intelligence Committee's secure hearing room and sat at the long witness table. The members of the committee had sat around a white horseshoe-shaped table. The chairman pointing out that they did not swear witnesses as it was felt this promoted an atmosphere of free exchange. *Grilling was closer to the mark.* 'He's a hard man. He likes taking risks.'

'And you think picking up Winter, if your intel is on the mark, will result in finding out where lies Pandora's box?'

The American dropped the gold lighter back into his jacket pocket and took a sip of the coffee. 'Not bad,' he said to himself. 'I'm sorry, Edeyrn, what were you saying?'

'Picking up Winter . . .'

'Ah yes. Why not? We know where he is. We know he's purchased two ex-military planes from the Ministry of Defence. And all indications are he's planning to depart Bien Hoa on Friday night for Iraq. The only detail outstanding is the exact location of the cargo.'

'Which will doubtless be on one of the aircraft on Friday night.' Owens poured himself more tea. Added a little milk. Stirred it. Civilized, after blacked-out Vientiane. 'You never told me your information source,' he ventured. 'Someone in Hanoi, perhaps?'

'Perhaps.'

'If the government is as involved as it appears to be, it would seem more than likely that the cargo is on the Bien Hoa military base, right?'

'Possibly.'

'And if Winter confirmed it, what then? We can hardly drive on to one of their bases and take it out in the back of a truck, can we?'

'Something for our diplomatic staffers to sort out. Shouldn't be too difficult, should it? I mean, once the cat's out of the bag, the members of the Politburo are hardly going to cause any scenes, are they? Naturally, they'll lay the blame elsewhere, and we'll nod sympathetic heads in agreement.'

'And all will be well with the world.'

Williams waved a hand. As though he was brushing away an imaginary fly. 'Justice and injustice. The Scylla and Charybdis of human existence.'

'And Winter's interpretation of justice!'

'Egoistic. The antithesis of justice that is human, universal, innate to the absolute majority.'

'He doesn't stand a chance, you mean?'

'He's a scholar of history. He should know that better than most.'

'What if your KR man . . . what's his name?'

'Pham Chi Tin.'

'Right. What if he fails to put in an appearance this morning?'

'What would you suggest? This is your part of the world, after all.'

'What did you offer him when you called him yesterday?'

'US citizenship.'

'You can do that?'

'Act of 1949. The CIA may admit up to 100 aliens per year into permanent residence in the United States if deemed essential to the national security or intelligence missions, bypassing normal immigration procedures.'

'How long to have it sanctioned?'

'Immediate.'

'I'm impressed. So what did he say?'

'Not interested. He wants money to fight for his cause.'

'How much?'

'I don't know yet. Although I have the feeling it will be a lot.'

'So who did you say you were?'

'A rich American businessman with connections in Congress and the Senate. You think I look the part?'

'Most certainly.'

'So, what would you suggest if he doesn't show?'

Owens looked down at his plate and the remnants of his breakfast. Silent for a while. Covert-action operations and activities. No rules. Creative Thinking 101. Better than the *Telegraph* crossword. 'I think we'd better leave for Ho Chi Minh City as planned on the one o'clock flight. I'll make an appointment to see Andrew Pitter at the British Consulate down there.'

'You know him?'

'I knew his father.'

'What can he do?'

'Introduce us to somebody who can in turn introduce us to somebody else. As long as it's at arm's length no one will mind too much . . . You really should try the kippers, you know: we'll probably miss lunch, and if the flight is delayed you might regret it.'

Williams bit into his toast and chewed for a while. Took another mouthful of coffee.

Owens went on, 'Of course, we're still at a distinct disadvantage – you do understand that? Mather. William Mather. Now he concerns me. Or at least his continued absence does.'

'Nothing new from London, then?'

'No.'

Williams toyed with his cutlery. 'Although your guy Jaggers is still of the opinion that Mather has nothing to do with this. Isn't that what he said?'

More or less. And in his own deferential way had listened for ideas. The bad ones he would discard, the good ones he'd claim for his own. The way of all successful men. Theft in the first degree. Owens knew, had met enough of them in his time. 'Indeed, Jaggers believes Mather might even be dead. Puts the blame squarely with Winter and the two officials who disappeared from the plant in Georgia.'

'Except Mather was one of the few people who knew

what was going on in Georgia. Is Jaggers a friend of his or something? Misguided loyalty, perhaps.'

'Oh no,' Owens murmured. 'Much more than that. They went to the same school.'

The cutlery stopped moving. 'They what?'

'Winchester. One of England's better public schools. Closer than the Masons, those boyos.'

22

Century House lies south of the River Thames, between London's Elephant and Castle and the Old Kent Road, and is the unfashionable address of the British Secret Intelligence Service. It was there in the early hours of Wednesday morning (a few minutes before two o'clock) that Timothy Jaggers finished reading the report.

It had been Special Branch who had uncovered the whole sorry affair. From whence it had found its way, via various departments to the Permanent Under Secretary of the Foreign Office in Whitehall, and from there to Sir Peter Wishart, Chief of the SIS. From Sir Peter's office on the top floor, a few hours earlier, it had made its way to Jaggers. It had all taken time. And now there was a feeling that time was running out. Especially with the news from their colleagues at the American Embassy in Grosvenor Square, that Winter was in Vietnam, and that unconfirmed reports stated that he and his team might be transporting the missing consignment of uranium to Iraq on Friday or Saturday of that week. The possible involvement of the Vietnamese government in the transaction added to the tension surrounding the whole three-ringed circus – as one of the CIA people had so quaintly put it.

And as if that wasn't enough, Saddam Hussein had once again – and within the last seventy-two hours – banned UNSCOM (UN weapons inspectors) from checking sites for suspected weapons of mass destruction. This inspection had been subject to a written agreement relating to lifting the trade embargo on his country (something Saddam knew from caveats engraved in stone was not about to happen unless a clean bill of health was granted by UNSCOM). Which all seemed too much of a coincidence. A coincidence predicated on the pending (secret) arrival of 300 kilograms of Uranium-235, perhaps!

Consequently the world press had reported that the United States and Britain had issued immediate warnings of possible military strikes to force Iraq into cooperating.

As for the Special Branch report: that had brought terrors of its own. How private possessions at Giles's north London flat had included letters, and a very comprehensive diary, written in a beautiful copperplate hand: Jack Giles, the back bench Labour MP, had been the gay lover of William Mather. They had had a violent argument earlier in the year over a holiday they had planned. It had to be cancelled at the last moment, due to Mather's business commitments. *One of which was recorded as a visit to Tbilisi, Georgia, to arrange the shipment of Uranium-235 to Dounreay, Scotland, later in the year.* How Giles had gone out that night to a popular gay bar in Soho and picked up a Frenchman by the name of Patrick Van Fleteren. An accountant from Martinique, who was visiting the UK and the Channel Islands on business matters for his clients. (In the margin of the report was a small hand-written note: 'Money laundering, perhaps.') The same Van Fleteren, it would appear (according to words Jaggers had initially had with Clarke Miracle, deputy head, European division, CIA), who was the account-ant of John Winter aka 'Sibelius'. The more than likely link to Winter discovering the top-secret plans to move the uranium.

As for Giles's suicide, there had been no note. Police reports, however, indicated that the MP, who had initially been questioned by Special Branch a few days after Mather's reported disappearance in Georgia, was in a highly distressed state. Quite possibly Giles had reasoned (from the nature of the Special Branch ques-tions) that it was about more than the disappearance of just one man. He might well have decided, in his own mind at least, that the top-secret information he had divulged to the Frenchman Van Fleteren lay at the heart of the matter. The passing hours would have thrown up all kinds of horrors. There would have been anguish. Tears, even. The end of careers!

Giles, in a highly charged emotional state, had, quite simply, taken it a step further and thrown himself under a train at the Euston Underground station. The end of lives.

And, if leaked to the press, the possible downfall of the Labour government!

Jaggers picked up the phone and placed a call to Sam

John Templeton Smith

Yeo in Nassau. Something the ugly American had mentioned in Warsaw. Something about a great deal of money.

23

Seven time zones east of GMT, Tan Son Nhat airport was relatively quiet. At least inside the terminal building. Winter and Yuri the Yid were seated at the bar of the small fast-food concession service next to the Duty Free shop, drinking Pepsis – the Russian's drink diluted 70/30 with Stolichnaya from a personal supply he had in his carry-on luggage.

The terminal building itself was clean, colourful and carried the stamp of 1960s architecture – concrete, glass, simplicity. It had seen numerous facelifts since the time of the Americans. Across the hallway and through the massive plate-glass windows could still be seen the temporary open-ended hangars the United States Air Force had erected years earlier, when Beach Boys music had blasted from the speakers as mechanics worked on their warplanes. Shabby now. Mostly unused. A few Russian-built airliners in the blue-and-white livery of Vietnam Airlines were parked around the apron. A military helicopter passed overhead. Low. The familiar flat two-blade *wap-wap-wap* sound of a Huey.

'You're clear on the procedures?' Winter asked.

The Russian, elegantly turned out in one of his new dark blue medium weight suits, white shirt, striped tie, and a new pair of prescription sunglasses with a soft blue tint, said nothing. He was thinking of Skulov again. Worrying.

Winter repeated the question.

Yuri looked up. Scratched his big hooked nose. 'Couldn't be simpler. Nothing left to chance, eh?'

'There's no higher glory than dying for one's country, so my old army told me . . . Except it is advisable to leave a will.'

'And what of yours? Who will inherit your fortune? You have a family?'

Winter thought of all the widows and orphans scattered across the world. 'Of sorts.'

'Make sure they don't get it too soon, then. I think, as you told me before, that those airplanes are a little old, a little dangerous.'

'I'll be careful.'

'And after this, I think you kiss them goodbye, yes?'

I tried once, but they kept calling me back. Worse than any woman. 'Getting too old, Yuri. As a friend of mine used to say: It's a young man's game.'

'Like screwing, you mean.'

They both laughed.

Yuri went on, 'Of course, nuclear waste is the biggest risk to health, you know that. You know what I find funny?'

'What?'

The Russian scratched his nose again, and adjusted his glasses. 'How some governments have convinced the people that nuclear power is the cheapest form of

energy available. Bullshit. I read a study from the
United States last year detailing high-level and low-
level waste. You know how much money the Nuclear
Waste Policy Act called for from the Department of
Energy in the United States alone? Thirty billion
dollars. Thirty billion dollars! . . . A nuclear-waste
fund to cover the cost of developing and operating the
deep repositories to store the fucking stuff.'

'You're sure of the figures?'

'Sure I'm sure.'

Winter took a packet of Particulares from his pocket
and offered one to the Russian. He lit them. 'Don't
forget to make contact with the colonel's wife in Paris.
And try and pick up an overcoat and some gloves, it'll
be chilly in Moscow.'

'You should have been a general, Wint. Your
soldiers would have loved you. All this care and
attention.'

'Make sure you remember that when you're sitting
on the balcony of your Spanish villa, drinking your
vodka.'

'Vintage champagne,' Yuri pronounced. 'No more
dreams of proletarian *dachas*, with their tiny veget-
able gardens and outhouses, stuck on the edge of a
forest of birch and spruce trees. Oh, they were real
dreams . . . I used to know those places years ago . . .
The route from the room I had in Moscow when I was
studying. Street by miserable street, until I was going
north on Yaroslavskoye Highway . . . Life's great
ambition. To own a *dacha*. Simple tastes we Russians
had . . .'

The Bangkok flight was called.

They finished their Pepsis, stubbed out their

cigarettes, and went across to the top of the stairs where a line was forming, ready to be led down to the exit door and the bus that would whisk them across the ramp to the waiting airliner.

'Give me the procedure again,' Winter said.

Yuri, out of breath from the short walk, hoisted the strap of the wardrobe bag across his shoulder: another purchase – Italian soft leather, very expensive. 'You call me on my GSM cell phone on Friday night. Eight p.m. local time Moscow,' he said breathlessly.

'The number of your cell phone?'

'Netherlands number . . . Country code 31 . . . Number 655 386108.'

'And my number?'

'Same, except transpose the last two digits.'

'And after I've called?'

'I send two faxes.'

'Good.'

'I've known harder ways to make money.'

'And if I don't phone you for any reason?'

And if you do and I don't answer because I've run into Skulov!

The line started moving. Passengers struggling down the stairs with armfuls of carry-on baggage. Oriental voices twittering with excitement. Like exotic birds.

A shake of the head. 'I know . . . I know. Do not worry, Yuri Alexsandr will take care of everything.'

24

'Seems that things are generally more hopeful than I thought,' Sam Yeo said, rubbing his hands together to generate warmth. The Caribbean night had turned chilly.

'The reason we left the ladies at the hotel!' Mehdizadeh replied unhappily, waiting for the guard to open the door to the bank. The uniformed Bahamian saluted as the two men walked into the marble-floored lobby.

'So why couldn't we have had this conversation in your room at the hotel?' the banker continued as they entered his office. He switched on the lights and waved Yeo to a chair on the other side of his desk.

'Call it paranoia,' Yeo said. 'Imagining everywhere is bugged.' He went on quickly to outline the phone call he had received from London when he had gone back to his room to pick up his wallet. They had been planning to take the ladies to a casino. His cell phone had been on the dressing table. It started ringing the moment he walked into the room.

Mehdizadeh straightened the lapels of his white suit jacket. 'And you think the Frenchman knows more than he has told you?'

The phone call. Timothy Jaggers in London had thought so. 'More than likely. Van Fleteren picked up the information on the Tbilisi transaction during his visit to London earlier this year and his meeting with a gay Member of Parliament guy. He thinks no more about it. Until? Until he accidentally causes one of his best clients to become a pauper overnight. Naturally, he is a man who prides himself on his professionalism, except this time he has got it very wrong. So what does he do? He makes amends. He tells Winter about the Tbilisi plans. A way to balance the books. Winter sees an opportunity. Orchestrates the theft of the uranium. Except it goes a step further than that. The Frenchman has been Winter's accountant for a number of years, perhaps the only one. Even following the disaster of Winter's fortune being seized, is the Englishman, at this late stage in his life, going to change horses in midstream? I think not. I think he will stay with the man he knows. The man he trusts. He knows that he's not going to make the same mistake again. Perhaps it is more than that. Perhaps Winter gave him a number of weeks or months to come up with something or he would be fed to the fish somewhere off Martinique. Whichever way, I truly believe that the little French guy knows every last detail of the financial transactions about to take place over the sale of that uranium.'

'A substantial amount of money,' the banker observed.

'Has to be.'

'And your intentions?'

'Phone one of our people in Martinique, ask them to put Van Fleteren on the first flight to Nassau in the morning. Failing any scheduled traffic, they can charter a plane to bring him.'

'Why not go there?'

'I need him here at your bank, with every piece of paper and computer disk he has on Winter. We need your infrastructure to put things in place in a hurry.'

'What if he doesn't cooperate after he gets here?'

'We rent a Cessna from the flight school. Take him for a ride down the Exuma chain, on the pretext of buying him lunch at one of the islands down there. Halfway point, we hang him out the door . . . He'll get the message.'

That caught the banker's attention. His eyes flew wide open. He waited for signs of humour. A smile. A laugh. And, when nothing came, he said, 'You expect me to be involved in *that*?'

'You *are* involved, Mez. Have been for years. Besides, if we go I need a pilot. You've got your private ticket. How long you had that?'

'Ten years. Doesn't mean a thing, though. I've only got about three hundred hours, and I haven't flown for six months or more.'

'Like swimming, they tell me . . . You never forget. Anyway, all you'll be doing is flying straight and level. I'll sit in the right seat on take-off, then go back to join the French guy once we're on the way . . . You don't even have to turn round.'

'I've never flown with a door open before . . . It could be dangerous.'

'You're worrying too much, Mez. This is all

hypothetical. Once Frenchie is here he'll talk. I guarantee it.'

'Then again, why do I get the feeling that I'll be the last person he wants to see?'

'Don't worry about that. He knows nothing of your involvement in Winter's accounts being seized. As far as he's concerned, we were already following him. The fact that he came to see you has now caused you an unnecessary amount of grief. I'm the government agent. I can even indicate that you're both facing a hefty jail sentence if I don't get the answers I'm looking for.'

'And if there are no answers? If he really knows nothing?'

'We'll fall back on whatever you had in mind.'

Mehdizadeh thought about that. The favour from a colleague in London, a man whom he had since found out was enjoying semi-retirement on the island of Guernsey. 'What about the reward money from the Winter deal in June?'

'Being processed.'

'So you keep telling me.'

'What if I can get it wired here first thing in the morning?'

'Then you have my help . . . Not the airplane, though. I'm not getting involved with that.'

Yeo grinned. 'Still want to take the ladies to the casino?'

'What about your phone call to Martinique?'

Yeo pulled a cell phone from his inside pocket. 'Nice thing about the modern age . . . very mobile. Come on, I'll call my guys as we're walking back to the hotel.'

25

Saigon Express.

The newly painted legend on the nose of the Phantom. Winter stood back and admired the handiwork of Corporal Thien Tri who had made up the stencil and sprayed it with white paint. Something his old friend Charlie Riker would have done had he still been around.

The repaired Ilyushin-38 had departed five minutes earlier for the same waypoint as the previous day, east of Phan Thiet over the South China Sea. A block of airspace promulgated by the Ministry of Aviation as a military training area, sea level to 40,000 feet, sunrise to sunset daily. Except, since the People's Republic did not have much of an air force, it was rarely used in its intended fighter-pilot role of practice intercepts (PIs) and air-to-air gunnery.

Maria had failed to show, so Stevens had taken her seat, leaving Winter to fly the Phantom solo. Which was just as well, as it now gave him the time he needed to switch one of the drop tanks with the help of

Corporal Tri. Part of the plan, nothing more. Changing the left outboard tank for the tank that had been airlifted in from Russia. No one of importance present to witness the switch. No one present to ask questions. Need-to-know information. Even Yuri had been unaware how the uranium had been transported. Colonel Vin was the only other man who knew. Simple reason: the colonel had dozens of surplus drop tanks at the Bien Hoa base. 500-gallon tanks compatible with the F-4. Other than that, you had to trust somebody.

It took them twenty minutes. The old tank showed a small weeping drip. Something Winter had doctored with the help of a tool he had found on a workbench in the hangar, and which resembled a miniature ice-pick. It had taken him a couple of minutes early that morning before he had left to drive to Tan Son Nhat to see Yuri off. The plane had been in the hangar, Red Stevens in the mechanics' crewroom going over fuel and range numbers in the F-4 Pilot's Notes. With the help of a hammer he had tapped a pinhole aperture in the aluminium next to the drain plug. Simple sabotage.

Now Winter began his walk-round inspection. Patting the newly fitted drab green drop tank as he passed it. It matched the rest. An ugly combination, all the same. A battleship-grey aeroplane and green underwing tanks. He climbed the steps to the cockpit and settled himself in, while the mechanic removed the top pin from the Martin Baker ejector seat and showed it to him. Winter passed him the lower pin that he had removed. The pins were stowed. Seat live.

Three minutes later he was airborne. On course for

Saigon Express

Phan Thiet. And the South China Sea. The afternoon had turned cloudy, an October mix of stratus, altostratus, stratocumulus, embedded nimbus. Rain showers washed the sky. Vivid green and swathes of red earth below. Monsoon grey above. And, through 18,000 feet, patches of Wedgwood blue and warm sunshine. Streets of ice-crystal cirrus arched across the heavens.

It took half an hour to make the join-up. Smooth air again at 25,000 feet. Steven's voice, terse, businesslike. Being handed off to Priest – seeing his wild eyes peering down as he flew the boom.

The colonel's words from an earlier meeting: 'I do not think much of the crew you have picked, John Win-ta.' His reply: 'I can see why you might say that. Frenette, too old, too frail, a little forgetful, perhaps, prone to nod off without warning; Priest, wild-eyed, too out of shape, too slow, looks like he's heading for a coronary. The sharp-tongued Maria, a former drug runner who's always picking holes in the operation. Stevens, who is so cautious you get the idea he could never make a command decision until it's too late and all the participants of the flight he was conducting have been consigned to a smoking hole in the ground. Apart from that, no slick airline uniforms. Yes, you're right, colonel: they're a bunch of gypsies, not bright enough to get the good jobs flying the big jets, never quite able to fit in to society's norm of what a professional pilot should be. Other than that, they do a job no sane person would even entertain: flying seriously dangerous old aeroplanes anywhere you ask them to go. But they're survivors . . . blessed with an inordinate amount of luck. In this business, that's all that counts.'

10,000 pounds uplifted. By the book. Everything going perfectly. Dropping away astern, then going to afterburners and climbing to 36,000 feet. No more ghosts. Just the freedom of solo flight in an empty sky. Magical. And, at seven miles above the earth, rolling to the inverted and sliding down the back side of the parabolic arc towards Bien Hoa.

The weather had worsened. A heavy rain shower, some miles in extent, passing over the field. Cloud base 200 feet. Visibility: half a mile. The controller asked if he'd like a GCA (Ground-Controlled Approach). Winter accepted, knowing that he needed the instrument-flying practice.

'Sibelius One, continue descent to two thousand five hundred, turn left on one eight zero. Lost communications procedures follow. In the event of no transmissions for one minute in the pattern or five seconds on final, proceed in accordance with ILS/DME procedures, landing runway two seven. Copy?' The slightly American-accented English unable to disguise the fact that the controller was Vietnamese. Enunciation too perfect to be an American. Or an Englishman, come to that.

'Sibelius One, roger lost com.' Winter checked the chinagraphed frequencies and headings on the plastic window on the right thigh of his flightsuit. The ILS and DME was already set up. Which meant that if he lost the controller on the approach, he would continue by use of the instrument landing system. Essentially two needles. The vertical one kept you on the extended centreline of the runway, the horizontal one on an approximate three-degree glideslope. Keep the two needles in the perfect cross and you would arrive at your decision height – in this case – of 200 feet with the runway dead ahead and the threshold less than half a mile away.

At ten miles east of the field Winter was fast arriving at the extended runway centreline, descending through 4,000 feet on his way to 2,500 feet. Speed 300 knots.

'Sibelius One, turn right to two seven zero, perform landing cockpit checks, and reduce to approach speed. You are now seven miles from touchdown, approaching the glidepath.'

Winter checked the speed. 220 knots. He selected gear down. Waited for the three-greens indication. At 170 knots he selected full flaps and increased the power . . . First to eighty-eight per cent and then, as the speed bled off to 145 knots, to ninety-two per cent. 'Sibelius One, cockpit checks complete. All green.'

'Roger, Sibelius One, no need to acknowledge further transmissions . . . you are five miles from touchdown . . . Slightly right of course . . . approaching glideslope. Come left to heading two six zero.'

Slight to moderate turbulence in the solid overcast. Total concentration.

'Still right of course heading two six zero, closing . . . Coming on to glideslope . . . Adjust your rate of descent.'

Winter keeping up a rapid instrument scan, reduced power to eighty-nine per cent, giving him a 700-feet-per-minute rate of descent. A light sweat had broken out on his forehead. High workload. Especially for someone who was out of current instrument flying-practice.

225

'You're approaching the centreline, Sibelius One, come right ten degrees . . . Two seven zero your new heading . . . Three and one half miles from touchdown . . . On the centreline, on the glideslope.'

The steady stream of instructions kept coming.

'Two miles . . . On centreline . . . On glideslope.'

Winter's scan picked up the 170 knots and the 700-feet-per-minute rate of descent . . . Peripheral vision confirmed three greens – gear down and locked.

'You're at one mile, Sibelius One . . . On course, on glideslope. Tower has you in sight. Cleared to land this frequency . . . Be advised standing water . . . Braking action poor.'

Winter went head up. At first he saw nothing. Then the lead-in lights emerging from the gloom . . . Then the runway glistening like a river of liquid pitch. Approaching the fence . . . Quick check of the speed . . . A bit hot . . . Raising the drag chute handle on the left side of the bucket seat, setting it in its detent.

All over but the landing.

A perfect flight, where everything had worked according to plan. Except it couldn't last.

Touchdown . . . The normal rumbling and shaking.

And the tower controller's voice: 'Sibelius One, you have a streamer.'

SHIT.

The brake parachute had failed to deploy cleanly.

And why not today! When the speed had been a little hot on the approach, which had translated to a higher-than-normal touchdown speed on a very slippery runway. And now this. Barrelling down the runway. 110 knots at the midfield point . . . Too fast to touch the brakes yet. At the 3,000-feet-to-go marker the speed was ninety. Enough for a gentle application of the toe brakes . . . Now . . . Gingerly . . . Easy . . . Easy . . . Watch for aquaplaning . . . 2,000 feet to go . . . Sixty knots . . . Brakes feeling better . . . 1,000-foot marker . . . Speed approaching thirty . . .

Turn-off speed came up with less than fifty feet to spare.

'Sibelius One clear of the active, taxi maintenance.'

'Cleared, Sibelius One.'

Releasing the chute with an adrenalin-shaky hand when clear of the runway for the ground crew to pick up. Taxiing slowly in to the ramp area. Shutdown checks. The steps being hooked on the side by a ground crewman. The refitting of the ejector-seat pins. The tug being positioned by the nose, ready to tow the aircraft back in to the hangar.

Winter climbed down. Felt the momentary strangeness of solid ground beneath his feet. Still with the adrenalin rush. Doing a quick walk round the aircraft, checking for leaks or bits that might have fallen off – unsecured access panels, forgotten by a mechanic and overlooked by a pilot on his pre-flight inspection were the usual. But there were no signs of ailments, other than the failed brake chute. No sickness. Rosy-cheeked rude health in children. 'Satis' – satisfactory – in aeroplanes.

He went to the side of the hangar and lit a cigarette, his mind dwelling on those unexpected little things in aeroplanes that seemed hell-bent on killing the occupant.

And when his pulse had returned to near normal he went over to the barracks to find a cup of coffee. And some spare beds.

Unexpected little things.

In adversity the resourceful mercenary always seeks security.

26

The Air Vietnam Tupolev from Hanoi to Ho Chi Minh
City was effectively doing a two-for-one. That was, as
the fourth of the five services per day, it had only been
showing a fifty per cent payload factor on the
passenger manifest. It had therefore been decided to
delay its departure by two hours. This resulted in the
service picking up passengers from the last scheduled
southbound flight, and the cancellation of the fourth
service. Even then the aircraft had empty seats, which
was the reason for the unscheduled landing at Danang.
It was now airborne again en route to Ho Chi Minh
City. This time it was packed to capacity.

'One of the poorest nations in the world. Makes you
wonder where they find the money to fly, doesn't it?'
Owens said, half-turning his head to indicate the
locals who made up more than ninety-five per cent of
the passengers.

'It had crossed my mind,' Williams said, staring out
of the window. A saltpetre sunset between layers of
cloud. 'Looks like rain in the south.'

'I always liked rain in this part of the world. Soft and warm, nothing like England. Lucky that Pham Chi Tin appeared when he did, wasn't it? Talk about eleventh hour.'

'He'd have been a fool not to. A big pay day for him and his team.'

'No doubts on his ability, then? You are obviously aware of his background.'

Williams turned and looked at the Welshman whose talk and manner suggested a retired diplomat or a connoisseur who had run through a fortune. Anything but the son of a Welsh coal miner. The American's voice was low. 'I have no doubts on his need for money. You heard what he said about his father. He had a big restaurant in Saigon until the Hanoi mob moved in and catalogued every table, chair, chopstick, glass, plate and dish. And, if he broke a glass, he had to pay for it, even though everything had originally been purchased with his money. And in the end the Hanoi guys took his business and his bank accounts. As for his background: a soldier of the Khmer Rouge who spent years pulling night-time raids on Vietnamese villages and massacring the inhabitants, until the Vietnamese army invaded Cambodia in 1979 and ousted them from power. So he's a tough little guy. What we need.'

'More than tough, Tanner, he's psychotic. He and his friends are difficult people to control. They're killers who hate the Vietnamese with a passion that's hard to comprehend. If they find out what Winter's up to, and the nature of the *cargo* he's planning to move, we'll have another thief to contend with. And the price for its return – should he get his hands on it –

would be funding from America for the KR's renewed war against Vietnam. The Mekong Delta was once part of the Khmer kingdom, after all. And where is this new-found sympathy going to lie? With the Marxist-Leninist old farts in the north, who sent an entire generation to re-education camps in Russia to learn to toe the party line while being taught the not-so-subtle nuances of the Russian language and an Orwellian dependence on two hundred and thirty-one different brands of vodka? Or with a group of desperate men who possess a very dangerous cargo? It could get a lot worse, of course: they could eclipse everything that has gone before and try and do a deal with the Chinese. Something you've considered, naturally?'

Williams said, 'You remember Frank Murchek who helped us out in South America?'

'The ex-Marine? Of course.'

'He's meeting up with us in Ho Chi Minh City.'

'Your contact source?'

'He's been in the loop all the way along. A good man to work closely with Pham Chi Tin.'

'To keep an eye on the shop. Why not?' Owens said scratching his head. 'And your plan?'

'Once they've picked up Winter and we've found the answers to what we're looking for, turn them in to the authorities.'

'While confronting the same authorities with their own misdemeanours, you mean. A way out for the Hanoi mandarins.'

Williams said, 'Of the thirty or more countries I've been to, Vietnam is quite possibly the most beautiful. I've seen more shades of green here than I ever knew existed. Rice fields tended from dawn to dusk, forest-covered mountains, pristine deserted beaches. What price all that?'

'To them, a great deal.'

'Exactly. In much the same way as their age-old custom of saving face. Therefore, once we have Winter, and once we know the location of the cargo, we bring in the diplomats. They open a dialogue with Hanoi . . . Something along the lines: "We have caught a group of KRs who have in their possession a large cargo of rather interesting – and extremely dangerous – material. With the assistance of foreign mercenaries, they have sought to implicate your honourable government in this matter, by using the purchase of aircraft as a front to access one of your military bases . . ." Et cetera. You get the drift, of course.'

'Naturally.'

Williams pondered his strategy a little longer. A move which the diplomats could, hopefully, keep away from the Department of Defence who would pass it on to the Joint Chiefs of Staff as an OPREP (Operational Report). Military moves. Usually starting out as a narrative report transmitted via AUTODIN or the Worldwide Military Command and Control System (WWMCCS) Intercomputer Network. Of the five levels of report, only OPREP-3 was implemented worldwide continually. The very last course of action Eberhart would want. He would see that as failure. He wouldn't survive the House and Senate Intelligence Committees a second time around.

'And what time does Pham Chi Tin get in tonight?' Owens asked.

'He and his guys had seats on Pacific Air. ETA

around twenty hundred.'

'Seems too easy, doesn't it?'

'Winter, you mean? Why shouldn't it be? We found him in Colombia, didn't we?'

'Except he knew we were coming.'

'He got lucky.'

Luck! Something the Oxford Dictionary might refer to as: *Chance as bestower of good or ill fortune.* Nothing about stealthy SAS-trained assassins. 'And this time?'

'This time it's our turn.'

Owens said, 'Even so, I'm still trying to imagine how the enigmatic Sergeant Winter could benefit from all of this. From your boys finding him.'

Williams chose not to answer. He turned back to the window. Staring out into the no man's land between the cloud layers, the pewter-coloured light all but gone now. *I'm still trying to imagine how the enigmatic Sergeant Winter could benefit from all of this.* An odd choice of words! He had been thinking *neutralize.*

Or

Realigning the threads of the woof and warp of the tapestry of illusions.

Or

In the words of the Company: pre-emptive self-defence.

27

The speciality was snake wine – *ruou ran*. A rice wine with a snake floating in it. Or, as the little colonel explained, snake meat was supposed to possess tonic properties, and drinking snake wine was said to cure everything from night blindness to impotence. The more poisonous the snake, the better for your health. The colonel, however, took it a stage further. He had a live cobra brought to the table, where its head was chopped off and the blood drained into a cup. Small amounts of the blood were mixed with everyone's rice wine. At which point the little colonel made a toast to the pilots who were guests in his country: a wish for a safe journey to their Motherland. The glasses were raised.

Wine with aphrodisiac properties.

Except for Red Stevens who, even though he had had a few bottles of *Saigon Export* beer with *Hanoi Vodka* chasers, had sobered up very quickly at the sight of the hissing cobra. His features, turning quite pale, became covered in a thin sheen of sweat. He was careful enough not to lose face or insult the colonel, however, mentioning that he couldn't mix his drinks any more without making himself ill. But that the next time they went out for dinner he would welcome the opportunity to try the wine.

The dead snake, meanwhile, had been removed to the kitchen to be stir-fried with vegetables and noodles. A Viet Cong guide to thrifty housekeeping: make one thing serve two purposes.

They were at Maxim's Dinner Theatre on Dong Khoi Street. A dimly lit restaurant supplemented with candles on the tables, an even darker nightclub upstairs where a live band was playing sixties music. Colonel Vin, dressed in his dark suit, white shirt and favourite red tie, was at the head of the table. He was in conversation with an elderly waiter who was struggling to translate the menu – which was in French and Chinese only – moving it ever closer to the candle at that end of the table, while ranging his eyes further and further away. All the ingredients of a comedy. Or, as Stevens had suggested moments earlier, perhaps the waiter was part of the floor show.

Frenette and Priest sitting opposite each other. Talking aviation – airways routings, climatology for the time of year all the way to UK; what deferred defects they could carry on the Ilyushin should the need arise, crew duty times to Bahrain, handling agents at Bahrain and the need to get a fax off tomorrow morning. The ancient Frenette wearing khaki slacks and a dark blue shirt. His partner, sporting grey trousers and a grey open-necked shirt. A change for both of them after the sweaty flightsuits of the past two days.

Next came Maria who, for one of the few times since Winter had known her, was wearing a dress. White. A simple sleeveless design. Scooped neck. Flared knee-length skirt. She was reading the French menu out to Red Stevens. The Australian's emerald-green trousers and canary-yellow shirt had been voted fashion statement of the evening by Hod Priest. Everyone was in good spirits.

Winter, in a freshly laundered change of khaki bush-kit, sat quietly at the opposite end of the table to the colonel. Watching and listening. Feeling very much like a Soviet political officer must have felt when escorting a group of his fellow countrymen on over-seas visits. All dressed up for a night on the town. Loose talk, getting drunk, possible defections. Staying sober while everyone else had a good time. Waiting for somebody to step out of line. Except, of course, TC was absent. No way could they have brought him into the city: even Red Stevens was a risk following his involvement in the jailbreak. Especially with his attention-getting laughter. He stood out in any crowd.

As for Maria! No real surprise there. She often had a change of heart. This time she had decided that as she had come all this way she might as well stay for another forty-eight hours. Fly the tanker with Frenette to the UK. Get paid for doing it.

And what about himself in these latter days? A fore-boding of what was to come, as if everything he had worked for could quite easily evaporate back to nothing. Soldiers of fortune were loners by design. Living by the code of survivors, trusting nothing, even at times speaking in code to warn each other never to give out precise information, that the smallest slip-up could be the last. Men who had been conditioned over a lifetime to walk side by side with death. Something that could result in a black aura about them. The eye didn't need to be trained to see it. Ordinary people would still sense a chilling something. Enough to warn them off. Enough to tell them that the man standing in front of them was dangerous. Not the civilian understanding of danger, though. This was the military trained-killer version, which made hell appear as an extended vacation in Hawaii.

'You are quiet,' Maria said, leaning towards him. Red Stevens had finally placed his order with the stoop-shouldered long-sighted old waiter, and was involved in a conversation at the other end of the table.

'Making plans.' An adequate enough answer.

'And what sort of plans would they be?'

'We all move out to the base tonight.'

Raised eyebrows. 'You are not serious. Red told me there is no hot water out there – the reason he came to the hotel tonight for a shower. And he wanted to buy a sleeping bag at the Chinese market in Cholon. Why do you want us out at the base?'

Keeping everyone – including those on your own team – slightly off balance. SAS training again. 'Security.'

'And that is an order?'

'A suggestion.'

The dark eyes flickered. The old anger resurfacing? Or perhaps a trick of the candlelight? She smiled instead. Something close to a smile, at least. 'Yes, perhaps you are right. You have an unfortunate way of attracting the wrong people, I think.'

'The reason I asked you to go back to the States.'
Careful. This was supposed to be a civilized evening.

The eyes registered their dislike of his choice of words. 'You know what I meant. How can you expect your own people to observe strict security when you send invitation cards to the very people we are told we should be avoiding?'

'You're talking about Colombia, of course.'

'Of course. The *Federales.* More dangerous than the cartel *cabrons.*'

Cabrons. Assholes. Appropriate as a reference to the trained gorillas who worked for the drug czars. But it was more than that; it was when she started to slip back into her native *Castellano* that he got worried. 'The reason we're moving out to the base tonight. The best security in the country.'

'I hope you are right.'

'I didn't tell you earlier, but you look very beautiful. Lovely dress.'

Her voice lifted half an octave. 'Changing the subject so soon.'

'Not at all.'

'You don't remember?'

'Remember what?'

'The dress. It is one you bought me in Caracas. Or, at least, the one that Red's wife bought for me with your money.'

'I never saw you wear it.'

'It is hardly suitable for flying an airplane.'

Another mistake. Perhaps he should stop talking altogether.

Maria continued: 'What are you having?

'Having? Food, you mean?'

'Yes.'

'Sea slug and duck web.'

She pulled a face.

He laughed. And the tension eased. 'I'd have rather gone with Red's suggestion of the Aussie-style restaurant up near the New World Hotel. Apparently they do imported meat pies, with mashed potatoes, peas, and gravy; but then, this is the colonel's evening.'

'Very diplomatic.'

'I thought so.'

She picked up her glass of rice wine and took a sip. Keeping the glass in front of her face. Her eyes watching him over the rim. 'Tell me, who is the Vietnamese-American at the base, the one I saw working on a computer in the barracks yesterday?'

From the nightclub upstairs, the muted sounds of the band, starting a new set. An old Beatles number filtering down through the building.

> 'One day, you'll look, to see I've gone . . .
> But tomorrow may rain so
> I'll follow the sun.
> Someday, you'll know, I was the one . . .
> But tomorrow may rain so
> I'll follow the sun . . .'

What was the question? Who is the Vietnamese-American? She sounded like a newspaper reporter looking for a story. 'A friend of mine.'

'One of the crew?'

'No, we're just giving him a lift out of here.'

'And the computer work? Red said he thought it was

something to do with flight planning.'

'It's more than that.' He explained how TC had come to Vietnam to bring back the ashes of his mother. His arrest at the airport.

'So how did he get released?'

'We did a deal.'

'What sort of deal?'

'What do you think? We paid money to someone to help get him out.'

She rolled her eyes. 'Oh, come on, Wint, it is more than that.'

'The police are looking for him; that's why we're giving him a ride westbound. Get him out of here.'

'You do not think you have enough troubles without this? What if they discover he is on the base? What will happen to you? To us?'

'They're not going to find out.'

'You think it is that simple!'

'Nothing is simple in a communist country, Maria. In the old Soviet Union they would send you to one of the gulags for *thinking* of committing a crime. This country is not a long way behind that mindset, believe me. The maxim for survival: deaf, dumb, and mute. The point is, no one knows, except me and Red. And now you.'

'And the colonel?'

'Naturally. He arranged to hide TC on the base.'

'Because of his involvement with the uranium you are taking.'

More than that. How the colonel – as a young man – had fought for the South Vietnamese Army (ARVN) at the end of the war. How he had lost his foot to an anti-personnel mine as the NVA poured into Saigon. How he had later found out that the NVA had executed his entire family – selected them from thousands of refugees fleeing along National Highway 1. And from that day a simple plan: changing allegiance to the Communist Party and, although crippled, rising to the rank of colonel in the army of the People's Republic of Vietnam. The good soldier. He had planned his revenge very carefully. Waited nearly a lifetime for the right opportunity to present itself. Had put a price on all the pain and suffering. And something more.

'Have you ever heard of Vietnamese ancestor-worship?'

'No.'

'It's something to do with the cult of the ancestors being based on the belief that the soul lives on after death and becomes the protector of its descendants. These spirits exert a great influence on the living.'

'So what has that got to do with anything?'

'The Vietnamese venerate and honour the spirits of their ancestors on a regular basis. That honour could mean righting a wrong that was visited on the spirit in question, or exacting revenge against the wrongdoers or the wrongdoers' spirits.'

'You believe that?'

'Doesn't matter what I believe. It's what they believe.'

'And how does being involved in something like this right any wrong?'

Winter shook his head slowly from side to side. 'Saving face with the dead! Money to help the Overseas League of Vietnamese Boat People? I don't know, but whatever it is you have to believe he has his reasons. Anyway, let's just call what he's doing simply

241

his involvement with the aircraft we are ferrying: I'd hate anyone to overhear something to the contrary.'

'And you trust him?'

'Why shouldn't I?'

She was about to answer his question when the first course was served. And more rice wine. And the Vietnamese Beatles upstairs, still going strong:

> And now the time has come
> And so my love I must go . . .
> And though I lose a friend
> In the end you will know . . .
> . . . oh . . . oh . . . oh . . .

'You never told me about that Grobchek, or whatever his name was,' Stevens said, his voice slurring.

Dinner was over, finished off by a delicious vanilla soufflé. The colonel had taken Maria, Frenette and Priest upstairs to see the nightclub. Winter and Stevens had declined. Preferring a cigarette and a cup of coffee and talking about any subject that came to mind. 'Who's Grobchek?'

'You know . . . You said nothing's impossible or something . . . Called it the Grobchek factor.'

'Gorsky,' Winter corrected him.

'Close enough. So who was he?'

'Do you remember when Neil Armstrong first walked on the moon, and gave his "One small step for man, one giant leap for mankind" speech?'

Stevens belched. 'Sure I do.'

'Just before he re-entered the lander, for lift-off, he made the remark: "Good luck, Mr Gorsky." NASA thought he was passing his best wishes to a Soviet cosmonaut. He wasn't. Seems that when he was a kid he was playing baseball with a friend in the backyard. His friend hit a flyball, which landed in the flower bed in front of his neighbours' bedroom window. His neighbours were Mr and Mrs Gorsky. As he leaned down to pick up the ball, young Armstrong heard Mrs Gorsky shouting at Mr Gorsky: "Oral sex! You want oral sex? You'll get oral sex when the kid next door walks on the moon."'

Stevens laughed. And took a half-corona from his shirt pocket and lit it. 'True story?'

'Who knows?'

'Speaking of the feminine persuasion, how you getting on with Maria?'

'As well as can be expected.' Noticeable uncertainty.

Stevens leaned back in his chair and puffed on his cigar. He grinned. 'Hot blood, those Latinos . . . You should marry her.'

'Is that the best suggestion you have?'

'Oh, it's not too bad. You can have the wedding in Caracas. Take her to Brazil or Argentina for a honeymoon.'

'And then set up house in La Paz, you mean.'

'Sure. Buy her a little airplane. A Cessna Turbo Centurion should handle the altitude okay. Some of the early marques had a 310-horsepower engine . . . That's the one you need.'

'And you just happen to have one in stock, I suppose.'

'As a matter of fact, I do. 1978 model. Low-time motor. Collins avionics. Hundred and fifty grand. Good buy.'

'I'll think about it.'

Stevens chuckled. 'Sure you will. Same way you're thinking about coming into the sales business with me.'

'You still think this deal is a bad one.'

Stevens jammed the cigar in the corner of his mouth and counted off on his fingers. 'Angola. Southern Philippines. Bolivia. Yemen. Afghanistan. Five operations out of a lot more that ran like oiled silk. Reason? We were not threatening the western powers like NATO. The first-world governments. The banking cartels who keep the first-world countries on top. This,' he took the cigar from between his teeth, 'this has all the misplaced optimism of that hundred-and-fifty-year-old journey over Razor Back Mountain in Australia when the immigrants expected to find a land of perpetual sunshine. Instead all they got was wild rains and winds and blowing mountain snows. To most of them it was the coldest place they'd ever known. The early settlers said New South Wales was no land for loving. They were right. It still isn't.'

'So, like Maria, you still think I should walk away from this?'

'I'm not pressuring you.'

'I know,' Winter said. 'And I appreciate it.' He pushed the plate of candy over to the Australian. 'You should try one, they're really very good.'

'What are they?'

'Petits fours.'

'Posh way of saying sweets, you mean, and you get charged twice as much.'

'Quite likely. The old waiter brought them. Perhaps they're free. Or perhaps he's an undercover agent for the Hanoi government.'

Stevens took a chocolate-covered candy and put it in his mouth. 'He's what . . .?'

'Undercover agent with the local KGB. Already found out what we're up to. Been sent to take care of us . . . You know, inject the petits fours with poison.'

'Oh shit!' Stevens spat the remains of the chocolate into his napkin. 'Jesus Christ, Wint. There are times I question your fucking sanity.'

Winter and Maria left half an hour later and walked to the Caravelle. The colonel had arranged for a car to take Frenette, Priest and Red Stevens out to the base. The car would return and collect them from the hotel.

'How long before the car gets back?' she asked.

'Two hours, perhaps. Depends on the traffic. If there's been an accident and the road's blocked . . . Well, you've seen it. One narrow, potholed, unlit road once you're outside the city. Then again, the driver might stop on the way back to visit his wife or girlfriend. Why do you ask?'

'No reason.'

They walked on in silence. Her arm linked through his. Her sage-green flight jacket draped over her shoulders. A tiny figure clattering along on too-high high heels. He'd noticed those, too. And the black stockings. Something else he had bought her in Caracas without knowing, perhaps! They moved slowly down Dong Khoi street, the place the French had known as Rue Catinat, towards Lam Son Square and the Municipal Theatre, their eyes taking in everything from the thinning traffic to the shopkeepers pulling down the shutters, examining the shadows of the doorways.

His thoughts drifted to Colombia. The taste of her skin as they had lain together in the quivering heat of that dark shelter at the Hill Station base. Bodies softened by sweat. Hands exploring each other. Events spinning out of control.

And then they were at the hotel. Going up in the hotel elevator in silence. He followed her down the corridor, watched as she turned the key in the lock. Then they were inside. Maria, slipping the safety chain on the door. Turning to him. The only light was that from the street, falling softly across the room. He felt his chest swell, his throat, his mind become paralysed. Her mouth was soft and wet, then harder as it pressed against his. She groaned when their tongues met.

They moved back towards the bed. A stumbling waltz. Each trying to undress the other as though time – every unforgiving second – was vital. He pulled back the sheet and lowered her gently on to the bed. Felt himself growing hard as he searched deeply in her soft mouth. The feel of her breasts against his skin. A way to dispel the pains of the day. The pains of a lifetime.

She was on top of him, showering him with kisses. Her hand reaching down, gripping him. Squeezing him. He sat up suddenly, holding her shoulders as he kissed her neck, her breasts. The concave curve beneath her rib cage as she leaned back and moaned. And then he was rolling over her, and they were one. Rocking and gasping and crushing their mouths together until their fingernails dug into each other's flesh in the last, violent moment of frenzy.

Long moments passed while their breathing returned

slowly to normal. She beneath him, hugging him. Contented. He, pleased that she was there. Forgotten for the moment the thoughts that she had never fired a weapon, knew nothing of sabotage, could not fly a fighter aircraft in its intended role, or fight with a commando knife. She had never run through a flaming obstacle course on the Brecon Beacons while masochistic instructors fired live rounds at her feet. She probably couldn't tell Semtex from kid's Silly Putty, or a Tomcat from a Foxbat. And she certainly hadn't attended one of Nick Ashe's famous seminars. Even so, he was glad she was here. He kissed her forehead.

'Shouldn't we be packing our things . . . The driver!' she murmured sleepily.

'He'll wait.'

She hugged him even tighter.

PART SIX
Pre-emptive Self-Defence

28

Soldiers suffer mental wounds in their work. Given time, a period to convalesce, the wounds 'scar' over. Except that the recipients have nightmares for months, possibly years. Blood guilt has to be allowed to work itself out. Giving the individual time in the corrupting environment to make his accommodation with it is essential, or else he will carry the corruption with him forever.

Winter had had such a nightmare the previous night at the base, after he and Maria had finally arrived back there from the Caravelle Hotel. He had spent most of the day reliving it. Watching Charlie Riker raising a gloved hand in salute, moments before his aircraft spiralled out of control towards the Colombian plains. He was a man who should never have been in an aeroplane. Had been totally unfit. An alcoholic who hadn't really known what he had been doing half the time. A man Winter had pressured, cajoled, belittled, just to recruit him for a mission that had been nothing more than a personal vendetta.

And the thought that he was doing the same thing all over again with Red and Maria. Colonel Vin and Yuri, that was different, they were joint-venture partners. Thirty-three per cent money and risk takers.

Which was why he was performing two humanitarian acts late that afternoon. The first had been to drop an envelope at the reception desk at the Rex Hotel, addressed to Senator Whitethorne. The second was the errand he was presently running: he was now going to the Phung Son Pagoda to deliver TC's mother's ashes to a monk and sit through a service of blessing. Making an atonement of sorts. Assuaging a feeling of guilt.

TC had, of course, wanted to come but his face was too well known by the military and civil police. Winter had left Red in charge, saying he had a few supplies he needed to collect for the following night's flight. Maria had insisted on going with him.

The colonel's driver pulled to the side of 3 Thang 2 Boulevard, near its intersection with Hung Vuong. 'That is the place you need, sir.' He pointed to the pagoda.

'Can you wait?' he asked the driver.

'How long, sir?'

'Thirty minutes . . . Perhaps one hour.'

'I will wait.'

Maria said, 'Do you want me to come in with you?'

'No. You stay here with the driver. I'll be as quick as I can.'

He got out. Took his wristwatch from his pocket – the best place to keep it in third-world countries, especially if it was an expensive watch, where you ran the risk of having a drive-by thief try and rip it from your wrist. It was five o'clock. The tail end of a muggy afternoon. The main entrance to the pagoda was locked (the usual preventative measure against theft) but he found a side entrance. A short way inside the building two young women were at a desk. One of them took the details of the deceased and entered it in a ledger. Winter made a donation of two hundred dollars on behalf of Tran Van Can. It was recorded. He was then escorted by a young monk – dressed in a simple saffron-coloured robe and open-toed sandals – from the main sanctuary to a place with an open-air courtyard in the middle and an altar with four statues on it, including a standing bronze Thich Ca Buddha. To its right was an altar on which there was a glass case containing a statue made of sandalwood – Long Vuong, who was said to bring rain.

The ceremony with incense burning and murmured prayers lasted no more than ten minutes. In Buddhism there is no mourning for the dead in the Western sense of the word. Sorrow for the parting is relieved by the prospect of rebirth. Death has no terrors for the Buddhist. More like quiet acceptance, perhaps: the book is closed, life goes on. After the prayers, the urn – named and numbered – was taken to a wall of shelves and a place found for it.

Winter left the monk at the door of the pagoda. The young holy man with the shaved head, now selling talismans to a group of Australian tourists, offering to tell their fortunes or perform acupuncture. To Winter he sounded a very convincing salesman.

The white staff car had gone. Half expected. The driver and Maria had had an hour to kill. He'd probably taken

253

her to Cholon to do some shopping at the market: she'd mentioned picking up some food for flight rations on the drive in. Winter lit a cigarette and took his watch from his pocket. Five-thirty. She would be back by six. After that they could stop at the Continental for a beer before heading back to Bien Hoa.

The cigarette was finished. The butt tossed in the gutter. Five minutes elapsed time . . . close to. And the young woman across the street in the white blouse and the black silk pants was still watching him from the shadow of a doorway. A prostitute? Winter thought not. A prostitute would not have stood and watched a tourist from the West for five minutes: she would have been offering him her services within thirty seconds. He moved his eyes but not his head. Checking the street through the streaming traffic and exhaust smoke, which hung as a blue haze in the fading afternoon light.

A tickling sensation at the back of his neck.

Something was not right. He checked his watch again, then sauntered back to the side door of the pagoda. Aware of eyes following him. The monk who had been inside the doorway, selling talismans, had gone. The two young girls at the table had also disappeared. There was no electricity, it seemed, just the flickering light from a few candles. In the main sanctuary to the left of the dais, an altar with a statue of Boddhi Dharma, the founder of Zen Buddhism.

He was planning to go to the open-air courtyard to find another way out when he heard the soft sound of a sandal on the tiled floor. He turned. It was the woman from across the street. Short black hair framing a pale round face and large dark eyes. 'Mis-ta Win-ta? You are waiting for your driver?'

His mind was asking the question – 'Who are you?' – as she moved towards him and, even though the light was poor, he saw that the white blouse was see-through. His eyes focused on her small firm breasts and the dark nipples.

One of the last things he remembered.

That, and something very hard hitting him across the back of the head. And seeing bright flashes. Something like Cerenkov radiation. A form of light called an electron shower. Gamma-ray bursts that looked like flashes of lightning in a night sky.

29

The white house at 261 Dien Bien Phu Street lay back from the road and was partially obscured from view by a high wall, trees and shrubs. The brass plaque on one of the white gate pillars simply stated: MARATHON OIL COMPANY LIMITED. The building was, in fact, the temporary quarters of the British Consulate in Ho Chi Minh City. A fact made more obvious for anyone trying to gain access through the small side gate and past a stone gatehouse manned by two armed guards who required ID. After that, walking up the driveway and witnessing the vast array of aerials and state-of-the-art satellite dishes on the flat roof of the building made it obvious it was anything but an oil company's headquarters.

It was at that building one hour later, shortly before seven o'clock, that Edeyrn Owens met with Andrew Pitter, the son of Edward Pitter who had been with the Foreign and Commonwealth Office in Owens's time.

'So nice of you to call in,' Pitter said in an accentless

voice. A pink-faced young man with horn-rimmed glasses. A tweed jacket over his shirt and tie. A gold chain dropping from the buttonhole in his left lapel to his top pocket. An air of practised control. He looked more like a schoolteacher than an SIS man and he was still young enough to consider that as a possible change of careers, should this one begin to pall at any point in the near future. They were sitting in his cluttered little office on the ground floor, white walls, a high shuttered window, neon strip-lighting on the high ceiling, grey box files piled high on every flat surface it seemed. No pictures on the walls. No framed photographs on the desk. No vases of flowers, or pot-plants, to lend the place the look and feel of home. It had the air-conditioned chilliness and antiseptic air of a morgue anteroom. The Englishman noticed the cursory inspection and added, 'Temporary quarters, we're planning to move back to our old HQ in a few months.'

An understanding smile. 'Your father's well?' Owens asked.

'Enjoying retirement. Spends a lot of time fishing in Scotland.'

'Yes, always was keen on that, wasn't he. Where does he go exactly.'

'Somewhere close to Inverness. I went a couple of times when I was a boy. Never much liked it. Especially the fly-fishing. My wife agrees, thinks it's as exciting as watching paint dry.'

'I feel the same way about golf, can never quite understand the fascination with hitting a little white ball and walking for miles . . . Or even driving after it in a golf cart.'

'Indeed. Are you here long?'

'Oh no. Few days holiday, you know the sort of thing. How about you?'

'My third month and I'm still looking for a house to rent. Mind you, you were lucky to catch me. Just got back from a few days in the Delta.'

'Anything interesting?'

'Oil exploration . . . Looks promising.'

'The reason the hotel prices are so high,' Owens said. 'Every geologist in the world is out here.'

'A lot of Americans, that's for sure,' Pitter replied. He got up from his desk. 'Anyway, let me show you around.'

They went to the communications room, Pitter securing the steel door behind them. 'Only place we can talk,' he said casually.

Owens understood. The foreign government paranoia concerning eavesdropping. The building was wired. More 'bugs' inside than outside in the gardens. The reason why overseas embassies carried their own building maintenance people wherever possible. The communications room would be the only place that was 'swept' on a daily basis. Safe.

Andrew Pitter was a product of Manchester Grammar School and London University – where he had read Oriental Languages. He was one of those intelligence officers with an overseas posting to an embassy. Apart from 'Illegals', those who worked completely outside this cover, there were two other categories: 'Declared' or 'Undeclared'. A declared officer – or brass-plate operator – is one whose real function is known. This was particularly fruitful during the Cold War period in attracting dissidents from the communist side. In the new world order, brass-plate officers have become unacceptably high-profile. Andrew Pitter was therefore 'Undeclared'. In fact, he was also an executive director of Marathon Oil Limited which was working alongside British Gas who had offices along the same street at number 124.

They sat down at the end of a long console of radio equipment. The sort of thing Owens had been familiar with once. COMSEC – communications security: protective measures taken to deny unauthorized persons information derived from telecommunications of the government related to national security and to ensure authenticity. A secure worldwide communications system operated by GCHQ in Gloucestershire, which works very closely with America's National Security Agency (NSA). A time-division multiplex channel-packing system used for transmission of signals intelligence information. Codes, ciphers, authenticators, call signs. Satellites with operational support worldwide, from Cheltenham, RAF Oakhanger and Menwith Hill in the UK to Bad Aibling in Germany, Akrotiri in Cyprus and Thule AB in Greenland to Alice Springs (Pine Gap) in Australia. A world within a world. 'You've spoken with Jaggers, then?'

'Not since last night.' He had a way of enunciating his words. Mobile lips.

'We've picked up Winter.'

'Really. When?'

'About an hour ago.'

'Where is he now?'

'With Williams's team. A safe house in Cholon.'

'Nothing new on Mather, I take it?'

'No.'

'The cargo?'

'Williams assures me it's just a matter of time before Winter lets us in on that.'

'And who he's dealing with in Hanoi? We are assuming that to be the case . . . .'

'Yes. You might include in your message to London that I'm planning to leave on the first available flight home. Nothing more I can do here, is there.'

'No, quite right. You've done more than enough.'

'Not me, Williams. It seems our American cousins had some good intelligence on this.'

'I hope they're right.'

Owens said mockingly, 'There's always a first time you mean.'

A hint of a smile. Quickly gone. 'Precisely. Your feelings?'

'I think we could be in serious trouble.'

Pitter frowned. 'Why do you say that?'

'I was listening to the BBC World Service earlier today. Picked up the latest situation on Iraq. It seems we are suddenly back to an impasse, with Tariq Aziz jumping up and down shouting that any attack on them would be considered the sheer aggression of criminals. Any new reasons why Saddam kicked the UN boyos out again?'

Pitter fiddled with his glasses. Repositioning them on the bridge of his nose. 'No. Usual thing. Saddam moving stuff around, playing the old shell game. Needs a few weeks to hide it in a new place. He then invites us back and we start the search all over again. And while he and his soldiers are doing that, he sends out the over-excitable Mr Aziz who swears on

Muhammad's reputation as the true prophet of Allah that Iraq has no weapons of mass destruction. Which leaves the illiterate ninety per cent of Iraq believing it must be true, and the educated remainder shaking their heads in dismay. There does seem to be some consolation this time, however; neighbouring states are saying that the government of Saddam Hussein will be responsible for the consequences of any forthcoming air strikes by NATO forces.'

'I think it's more than that this time.'

'Such as?'

'Winter, on behalf of the Vietnamese government, is apparently planning to move 300 kilos of uranium to Baghdad – more likely to be dropping it off there than delivering it to an out-of-the-way military base. Lose it in the crowd, you see. Even so, with UN inspectors crawling over everything it could prove problematical, so what does Saddam do? He kicks out the UN a few days before the shipment is due to take place. A window of opportunity to receive it and hide it away.'

'Except you've forgotten the increased security on the southern and northern no-fly zones. How does Winter get the cargo in?'

'Good question. I don't know. The military might have an idea on that, though. What I do know is that Winter is very sophisticated. The fact that we haven't found Mather worries me even more. Winter is making all the moves and we're following him. The question is, what is Mather doing?'

'Jaggers is of the opinion that he could be dead.'

'He's wrong. My gut feeling tells me differently.'

Pitter managed a weak smile. *Gut feelings. Bloody hell, how unoriginal.* 'Interesting. I'll make a note of it in my report. Where are you staying, by the way?'

'The Rex.'

'Very exclusive.'

'Timothy's idea, said I should have a few days in the sun.'

Pitter scratched his chin. His eyes thoughtful. 'What do you think Mather is doing? Assuming you're on the right track, of course.'

'Second line of reasoning. Assume you are right in thinking that no aircraft could penetrate Iraqi airspace without being picked up by American radar and shot down. I must then conclude that Mather is sitting on the uranium somewhere in Russia. Waiting to deliver it to Iraq by road.'

'He's the hard target, you mean? Not Winter?'

'Perhaps.'

'Except the Americans are convinced that it came out of Russia on an Ilyushin aircraft. One that is now at Bien Hoa.'

'Except we haven't seen the cargo. Neither have they.'

Pitter edged his glasses up his nose again. A compulsive mover. Nervous energy. 'I think sending it by road would be even more difficult than trying to fly it in. Too many checkpoints, plus the Americans have their J-STAR aircraft on patrol. They're fitted with downward- and sideways-looking radar: they can pick up almost any piece of metal that begins to move.'

'The BBC went on to say that the UN pullback began in earnest yesterday. Apart from the inspectors, that includes one-third of the 450 humanitarian workers. The departure of aid workers is likely to reduce the effectiveness of programmes to help Iraq's 22 million people.'

Pitter chewed on his lower lip. He wasn't following Owens's line of reasoning. 'Meaning?'

'UN, Red Cross, world church organizations . . . There'll be a lot of metal moving back and forward across the border. Food, medical supplies. How effective is the policing?'

'Damned effective,' Pitter blustered. 'No one is going to haul 300 kilos of anything over the border in a lorry without our knowing about it, believe me.'

'How about ten-kilo units on camels? The SAS moved men freely into Iraq on intelligence work during the Gulf War disguised as Bedouins . . . Winter is ex-SAS. You see where I'm going with this, Andrew?'

Pitter didn't really care. And he didn't like old men with gut feelings rambling on about hypothetical situations that better suited children's tales from the *Arabian Nights*. 'I do, and I appreciate your time, Edeyrn. I will make sure London is made aware of your feelings on the subject. I would add, however, that we have a tricky situation of our own right here. We have an American Senator in town. Some of his staffers are staying at the Rex, as a matter of fact. He's the chairman of the MIA Senate Committee. He's presently meeting with Vietnamese officials, and he's promising all kinds of hell if he doesn't get answers on the 2,000 or more American boys still unaccounted for. With the apparent implications of Hanoi being a party to this Iraq deal, you can see the diplomats are treading a very delicate line.'

'I'm not overly concerned with the diplomats, Andrew. I'm concerned with Saddam. Can you imagine the problems we will face if he gets his 300 kilos of uranium?'

Pitter removed his glasses, took a handkerchief from his jacket pocket, and began to polish the lenses. 'Your observations are extremely valuable, Edeyrn. The reason London sent you out here. Perhaps once we have something more tangible to go on. You understand?'

The door opened. It was a staffer with a tray and two mugs.

'Oh, good,' Pitter said, smiling. 'Tea.'

30

Mehdizadeh met Sam Yeo just before nine for breakfast at the Colonial. He ordered eggs – over easy – bacon, whole-wheat toast, coffee and orange juice.

'You should do this more often,' Yeo said.

'I prefer to cook my own breakfast; besides, do I want to pay double the price for the same meal I can make at home? More importantly, how hygienic is their kitchen?'

'What about the pretty girls serving you?'

'Don't talk to me about pretty girls.'

'You worry too much. So they'd left by the time we got back to the hotel last night. Don't worry, they'll be back at the bar tonight. We'll celebrate, take them out to dinner.'

'I think that sounds premature; the Frenchman hasn't even arrived yet.'

'No, but he's on his way. He'll be here around noon.'

'And he's going to have all the answers! You forget he already lost Sibelius's fortune once. To do it again . . .'

'Would show serious disregard for his own life, is that what you were going to say?'

'This man Sibelius, or Winter if you prefer, is a wanted terrorist. Your words. Why wouldn't he kill Van Fleteren if he gave away his money a second time?' *And come after me, perhaps, he almost added.*

Yeo poured himself more tea and squeezed in a little lemon juice. He glanced around the dining room, but at nine o'clock in the morning it was relatively empty. A large number of visiting business people stayed at the Colonial, and by nine they had left for meetings. The remainder were middle-aged-to-elderly well-heeled tourists who wanted class rather than the usual beach-side hotels that catered more for young families and singles and anyone who liked noise and an endless supply of free Bahama-Mamas during the Happy Hour. 'The reason we will be celebrating tonight, Mez. I spoke with Langley this morning, less than hour ago, in fact. It seems that Winter a.k.a. Sibelius was picked up in Ho Chi Minh City about two hours ago by one of our people.'

A pretty young Bahamian waitress poured coffee for Mehdizadeh, gave him a winning smile and moved away. He added half a packet of sweetener and stirred it. Felt a wave of relief pass over him. 'Thank God.'

'Puts the Frenchman in an easier position to deal.'

'Except I was under the impression that the transaction was not going to take place until this weekend. As you now have this man Sibelius that seems unlikely. So, what of the money?'

'I've already considered that. Winter is a pretty smart guy; you would need to be to amass the millions that he did over the years. Therefore I can only assume that he would conduct the business in question with the country in question in the same manner that my people would.'

'Which is?'

'Money up front.'

'Why not in escrow, so that when the cargo is delivered the money is transferred?'

'Fine under normal circumstances. Dealing with normal people in normal countries. His customer is a long way from normal, at least by our interpretation of the word. No, the way I would have put that deal together would be the same way we've done deals, through your bank I might add, with South American customers. *We* produce all the paperwork, including the bills of lading and the Customs declarations . . . *You* send the money. Normally as safe as a bank because: (a) you have Customs declarations showing the goods have been checked and sealed and are now safely stowed in a Customs warehouse, pending imminent loading on to the cargo carrier in question, and (b) you have full insurance to site. Of course, in this instance I hardly think that Lloyds of London or anyone else is going to step up to the plate and underwrite a cargo like this one. So if the ship sinks or the aircraft crashes, it's going to smart for a few days. But then, with the oil reserves of the country concerned, it shouldn't hurt for too long.'

'You're forgetting the embargo. They're not doing so well on oil exports right now.'

'The rich stay rich, Mez, you should know that at the very least. Those guys out there are not really hurting . . . Sure, the people might be. Food, medical supplies, all running short. The poor people dying a bit quicker

267

than normal, that's all. The Iraqi government is using the embargo as a propaganda tool to try and win support from their Arab neighbours. So far they haven't got it.'

'There is another problem,' the banker observed.

'Which is?'

'Assuming the money has already been paid as you think it has . . .'

Yeo raised a hand. 'Or the oil. As I've mentioned on other occasions, it could well be that they have a way of sanction busting, in which case it would be easier for them to trade than to deal in hard currency. Even if they've got secret Swiss accounts they'll hardly want to deplete them.'

'I understand that. My point was, if we assume the money has been paid to a Sibelius account anywhere in the world, my bank ceases to be a factor in the transaction. You can activate the wheels of the justice system to seize it, much in the same way you did with the Sibelius account out of Martinique.'

'True . . .' Yeo started, and fell silent as the pretty waitress returned and served Mehdizadeh his breakfast.

The banker started on the piping hot food immediately.

'Big appetite this morning,' Yeo said.

'All that drinking, walking and talking we did until the early hours of this morning. Anyway, you were saying.'

The Louisiana man sipped his lemon tea. 'It occurs to me that we might be in an enviable position concerning Winter's money. I made some mental notes this morning on the way I would have handled

Saigon Express

the deal he was putting together. The intel we have is that the delivery flight was due out on Friday night from Vietnam. That would be about eleven o'clock on Friday morning here in Nassau. I would not let a flight leave without payment. But by the same token, and as we have done in the past, the customer is entitled to all the necessary paperwork. Now, maybe it is not possible to get American Customs officials to postdate bills of lading and suchlike, but South-East Asia, that's something else all together. A few hundred dollars in the pocket of the right man is all it takes. Assuming all the foregoing to be correct, and I have to, bearing in mind Winter's track record, it brings us to his account. The funds are there, wherever *there* might be, and he's been grabbed off the street in a far-off foreign city. Hell, he could even be dead. Naturally enough, our guys will, or should, be able to stop the shipment at the last moment. As for the money, if we fail to get our hands on it pretty quickly, it could be floating around in some numbered account for the rest of eternity.'

The banker finished off his eggs and bacon and started on the toast and marmalade. 'It had occurred to me. How much money, do you think?'

'No way of knowing. It has to be millions, though.'

'If we could locate it, it would initially come through my bank?'

'Of course.'

Mehdizadeh thought about that. A welcome deposit, after recent events. The flight capital appearing on the bank's balance sheets would, in accounting terms, be no different from any other deposits. But, as the banker had long known, flight capital did not always behave like other deposits. It was, in fact, *de*

269

jure a deposit, but *de facto* part of the capital of the banking system. Or debt that insists on behaving like equity. It was easy enough to modify accounting procedures to conform to this economic reality. Especially when you were the president of the bank. Especially if he could hold on to it a little longer than normal.

A few more dollars on the credit side of the ledger.

The meeting early that afternoon was run on strict guidelines. Sam Yeo sitting in the banker's chair, the one that had the view of the blossoming poinciana tree through the side window. Mehdizadeh and Van Fleteren in chairs drawn up on the other side of the desk. A ceiling fan whirred softly.

The Frenchman, dressed in a lightweight wool beige suit and open-necked cerise shirt with matching Italian leather slip-on shoes, had been escorted to Nassau by a CIA agent and looked suitably frightened. Mehdizadeh could quite understand. Yeo had transformed himself. The black suit, white shirt and black tie, the flattened nose, the scarred eyebrows, the scowling face, all contrived to strike fear into the heart. A long way beyond a mere CIA man. An executioner, perhaps.

The Louisiana man glared at Van Fleteren. 'I'm going to keep this very simple,' he snapped. The voice razor sharp. Violent. 'I am going to begin with an opening statement. Following that I will ask you questions. As I know the answers to most of them, this is a way to check if you're lying. How do I know most of the answers? A matter of hours ago your client John Paul Winter was arrested by American colleagues of mine in Ho Chi Minh City, Vietnam. As it appears he was involved with the Vietnamese government in a large-scale nuclear arms deal with Iraq, it may well follow that the local authorities will want him tried in their own country. The seriousness of this issue is naturally causing grave concern; therefore the US government may well accept some kind of plea bargain from the Vietnamese government. This would no doubt result in Winter being made an example of. Quite simply, the death penalty. As for the Vietnamese government themselves, this is a matter for the United Nations, perhaps. Not my problem. So, as I've already stated, I know the answers to most of the questions. For every lie there will be a penalty. The penalties are very serious, I can assure you . . . In fact, I'll go a stage further: they are life-threatening. Do you understand?'

'I have not been told what this has to do with me,' Van Fleteren said nervously.

'Yes or no, Mr Van Fleteren. Do you understand?'

'Yes.'

'In the event that you are wondering why Mr Mehdizadeh is attending this meeting, the reason is quite simple. We consider he may have concealed certain facts about the Winter/Sibelius accounts . . . in the past. Your answers during this interview will have a significant bearing upon *his* future as well as your own. You understand?'

'Yes.'

'Good. Bear in mind that this interview will be taped. A matter of record. I have prerecorded the date and the subject, so we can begin.' Yeo started reading from a sheaf of papers spread out on the desk in front of him. 'Your name is Patrick Alain Van Fleteren. Your age is thirty-eight. Religious affiliations: Catholic, non-practising. Your mother is dead. Your father lives at 3, Boulevard Blanqui, Paris, France. He is a retired surgeon. You live at a house known as "Broken Glass" in the town of Fort-de-France, Martinique. Your profession is Chartered Accountant. You live with your gay lover Douglas Noli.' The last sentence was uttered with disgust, as though Yeo had just realized he had trodden in dog shit and now had to clean it from his shoe. Scare tactics. 'Noli is aged fifty-three, and is an artist and a poet. The name of the house is, in fact, taken from the title of one his poems. In your business activities you are known to favour working for tax exiles. You are expert in setting up corporate tax companies. You are suspected of money laundering on a large scale. Do you have anything to correct in what I've just presented to you? Think about what I said earlier: I have no time for untruths.'

'No.'

'Excellent. We will be finished all the more quickly . . . providing you continue to cooperate.' The CIA man shuffled the papers for a moment until he found what he was looking for. 'Do you know a man named John Paul Winter, also known as Sibelius?'

'Yes.'

'Isn't it true that you were involved in the matter of a large account for Winter's company, Sibelius Holdings Limited, which was seized by the United States authorities earlier this year?'

'I . . . I was unaware . . .'

Violence crackled around the Louisiana man like lightning in a summer storm. He slammed his fist down on the desk. So hard that a pen-holder toppled off the desk, scattering pencils and ballpoints on the floor. 'Leave them,' he hissed. 'Yes or no?'

'Yes.'

'Do you currently have dealings with Winter, financial or otherwise, over the Vietnam business, which I will state here and for the record concerns a stolen shipment of Uranium-235 from Tbilisi, Georgia?'

'Financial . . . I . . . I am handling his account,' the Frenchman stammered.

'And what is the name of that account?'

'The company is called Seventh Symphony Limited . . . the bank account is in Panama.'

'You have brought all the details of this company and the company's bank with you?'

'Yes.'

'Who are the directors of that company?'

'Mr Winter and myself.'

'Is it a joint bank account? Does it need the consent of both signatories, that is?'

'Yes. But I have power of attorney to act for Mr Winter, should anything go wrong.'

Yeo shuffled the thin sheaf of papers before him. Impatience in every gesture. 'Such as?'

'If he were involved in an accident.'

'Have any funds been transferred to this account from the Iraq deal that was scheduled to be completed by this Friday or Saturday, October the ninth or October the tenth, that is?'

'The money has been paid . . . I do not have all the details of how. I have been told payment will be received on Tuesday the thirteenth at the company's Panamanian bank.'

'The thirteenth of this month?'

'Yes . . . next Tuesday.'

'Are you aware of the amount being transferred?'

'Could I please have a glass of water? My mouth is very dry.'

Yeo turned to Mehdizadeh and snapped his fingers. 'Could you . . .' The banker was already out of his chair. He hurried through to his private bathroom and came back with a glass of water. Handed it to the Frenchman. He then sat down.

'My question was . . .' Yeo exploded.

'Seven million US dollars,' Van Fleteren blurted out, then drank quickly from the glass. All the time his eyes never left the man behind the desk. Almost as if he was mesmerized with fear.

Yeo never blinked. Seven million dollars could have been seven million pebbles on a beach. 'You are sure of that amount?'

'At the Panama bank . . . yes.'

'And the origin of this money?'

'A bank in Liechtenstein, I think.'

'You think? Or you know?'

'I received a phone call from Mr Winter. He told me that seven million US dollars would arrive in the Panama bank on Tuesday the thirteenth. I asked him if it would be coming from Switzerland. He said Liechtenstein. That is the truth, I swear it.'

Yeo waved a hand dismissively. 'The seven million . . . Is that all the money that is involved in this transaction?'

The Frenchman thought about that for a moment, took another sip of his water.

'Think carefully, Mr Van Fleteren. As I have already

274

indicated, we have Winter in custody. Withholding evidence will cost you dearly. On the other hand, a frank and forthright exchange of information will be seen in an altogether different light . . . one that could, and in all probability will, result in a substantial reward being paid for the recovery of the funds being discussed.'

'There is another account in Zurich which . . . as from Monday the twelfth of October . . . next Monday, will hold five . . . no, four and a half million dollars . . . The account is in the name of John Winter.'

'Why isn't that amount being transferred to Panama with the rest of the money?'

'My client did not want to have his accounts seized again. He planned to leave this amount in Zurich with paperwork showing it to be the total payment for the transaction . . . That way, should any government agency trace it that far they would think there was nothing else.'

'Are you a signatory on that account?'

'No.'

'Is there any way you know of whereby that amount could be transferred along with the seven million dollars to Panama?'

'No.'

'How about you, Mr Mehdizadeh? You're an international banker. How could we legally transfer that sum to the company account in Panama?'

The banker had blinked more than once. Seven million. He had long stopped listening. He was already working on ways to get the funds transferred to his bank. Rates of interest.

Yeo's tone became even more unfriendly. 'What do

you think, Mr Mehdizadeh? Can we legitimately move those funds to Panama?'

The banker managed an annoyed shrug. Playing along at being an innocent victim. 'I don't see the purpose. You are a part of the Federal government: why should it cause you undue concern? Zurich is easier than Panama in this instance.'

Yeo folded his arms and leaned back in his chair. 'I'm the one asking the questions, Mr Mehdizadeh.' He glowered at the banker and then turned the look on Van Fleteren. The Frenchman seemed to shrivel up in his chair. 'However, I can tell you this much. Should Iraq, the country in question in this interview, find out exactly where the money has gone, and to whom, they will put the names of the offenders on their blacklist. They will also ensure that those names are passed to friends of theirs around the world. The *raison d'être* is simple enough. The Arabs have got long memories. They will keep the names of the offenders fresh in their minds, and at an appropriate moment they will strike. Cars or airliners or city skyscrapers, it makes little difference to them where they place their bombs. More simply, if we can spirit the money away . . . make it untraceable, with all the indicators pointing to Winter as the sole architect, then the Iraqis can do little but focus on him. That he will be incarcerated or dead is one of those indicators.'

'No terrorist threats against the United States government or agents thereof, is that what you're saying?' Mehdizadeh asked.

'Precisely . . . and if we have to bring action against a Swiss bank to seize the four and one half million dollars, it will obviously indicate to Iraq that we have, in all probability, the rest of the money. So, once again, Mr Van Fleteren, what would you normally need to move those funds from Zurich?'

'Mr Winter's authorization.'

'You have documents with you, documents carrying his signature?'

'Yes.'

'So if we had Winter's signature on the appropriate document it could be faxed to Zurich to instigate the transfer?'

'N-no.'

'What do you mean, no?'

'It needs to be a hard-copy document with an original signature.'

Yeo rubbed his chin thoughtfully. 'Could you take Mr Van Fleteren out to the lobby, Mr Mehdizadeh, perhaps find him a cup of coffee. I need to make a private phone call . . . It will be made on my credit card, of course.'

'Yes, of course.'

Yeo looked at his watch, then said to the recorder, 'The time is 1307 hours. Interview terminated at this time.' He looked up as the two men stood to leave. 'Perhaps you could bring me a cup of coffee at the same time. Thank you.'

'There was s-something I wish to make clear,' the Frenchman said nervously. He was halfway across the office, and had stopped and turned back to face Yeo. 'At the beginning of the interview you stated that Mr Winter was involved with the Vietnamese government over this Iraq matter. My understanding is quite different . . .'

Yeo said, 'Go on.'

'He's working with a man called Colonel Vin. He works in the Ministry of Defence in Ho Chi Minh City . . . I don't think it has anything to do with the government.'

'Why not? The colonel works for the Ministry. The Ministry is part of the government.'

'Not exactly. Colonel Vin's name appears on some of the paperwork . . . I think he's a partner with Winter.'

'Do you . . . Are there any other names?'

'One more . . . a Russian. His name, I think, is Becker. I would need to check my papers . . .'

'Have your coffee, Mr Van Fleteren, we will go through the documentation after that. And while you're drinking your coffee you may want to ponder the answers you have given me thus far. If you think you have been anything less than truthful you may want to consider if you've been saved by Jesus because, I do assure you, *He* will be all you have left.' The hands joined together in a prayer-like posture before his face. 'You do understand what I am saying?' he added. Most certainly the executioner.

Van Fleteren said, 'Yes, s-sir.' He looked quite ill.

Yeo was sitting at the banker's desk, making notes in his pocket diary, when Mehdizadeh came back into the room with the coffee. Their eyes met and they both started laughing. 'Eleven and a half million dollars,' he said with a broad grin, 'The good Lord has blessed us this day, Mez . . . He surely has.'

'What about the Frenchman? He knows a great deal. Can he be trusted?'

Yeo got up from the desk. 'Need to use your bath-room . . . Drain the dragon. Takes me that way sometimes – excitement, that is. As for Frenchie, not a problem: I'll invite him to one of my little prayer meetings.'

'And the Vietnamese government and the man Colonel Vin. Something you need to report?'

'We'll arrange the transfer of the funds first. One slow and careful step at a time, something I learned from you . . . You *did* get that reward money this morning, I take it?'

'Yes, never got around to thanking you.'

'Not a problem, I phoned the ladies and told them we'd meet them at eight. You know, I think I might just get a little bourboned out tonight.'

31

Timothy Jaggers was checking the street for unusual activity. It was cold in Munich that late Thursday afternoon. Raining. No snow, but the afternoon light had that mottled look of winter when it remained unchanged all day. The sidewalk cafes were empty of tourists whilst the *Munchners*, shrouded in wool and leather, were preparing, it seemed, for the snow-slicked streets that were just around the corner.

The message – a reply to an enquiry instigated by Jaggers – had come from Stonecipher. Real name: Max Lehmann. A former GSG9 – West German anti-terrorist team – member. He had since retired, but had been used from time to time by the SIS during the latter stages of the Cold War. He was an asset. Had an ear to the street. More than that, he was very dependable. The text of the message had been brief: 'Know whereabouts of William Mather. Are you interested?' A price had been agreed. Rather high for the SIS, but under the circumstances deemed acceptable.

The reason Timothy Jaggers found himself standing

in Unter Sendling that Thursday afternoon. It was three o'clock when he paid off the taxi driver. Waited as the diesel-engined Mercedes clattered away around a corner. Discreetly checked his surroundings. The apartment building a hundred metres up the street. The flat was on the second floor.

Jaggers was sitting in the modern little kitchen, sipping a mug of tea. The grey afternoon light leaking through the partially opened slats of the Venetian blind at the solitary window. From an adjoining room a radio played softly. Gershwin's *Rhapsody in Blue*.

The German, a heavy-set man with blue eyes and wavy white-blond hair sat down, poured a bottle of mineral water into a straight glass. He was fifty, but looked ten years younger. Very fit. Very active. His old GSG9 training. 'It's been a long time, Timothy. I hear they have given you a promotion.'

'Something like that. And you? What are you doing?'

'Buying and selling. Same as always. Except instead of the KGB it is now the *Mafiya*. Funny world.'

'Yes, Max, I have heard it said.'

'So,' Lehmann said, more brightly, 'You brought the money?'

Jaggers lifted his briefcase from the side of his chair and laid it on the Formica-topped table, began to realign the two combination locks. A recurring theme on the date of the Battle of Hastings, hence 106 610 – something that had survived from his prep school days. A date known by every English schoolboy, much as old soldiers never forgot their service numbers. He removed the sealed blue plastic packs from the briefcase and slid them over to the German. 'One hundred and fifty thousand pounds sterling, as agreed.'

Lehmann tore away a corner of each packet and peeped inside.

'Aren't you going to count it?'

'No. I trust you. If it had been the CIA, I'd have counted every last note. They have a habit of short-changing you.'

Jaggers liked that. He nearly smiled. 'The reason you didn't pass the information to Sam Yeo in Tbilisi!'

Lehmann said, 'You think I would rather work with the mighty *Spionage* service of Her Majesty?'

'Let's not get into semantics.'

An amiable grin. 'Just small talk. I was thinking of the last time I saw you. Kirkenes, Norway. The Russian Gate. Long time ago, of course.'

Jaggers nodded politely. Listened to a story he had all but forgotten. The Lap farmer, Vonka, his herd of reindeer straying across the border from northern Norway into Russia . . . The Russian guards allowing Vonka to come over and get them. *Easy crossing point for Murmansk.*

Jaggers held out a hand at the first opportunity. 'The information, Max.'

Lehmann pushed a slim manila envelope back across the table to the Englishman. Jaggers opened it. Standard situation report. He read through the five and a half pages quickly. Looked up at the German. 'You're sure about this?'

'I just got back from Tbilisi, of course I'm sure. A local policeman took me to the grave. There was a spade there, covered with fingerprints. They tallied with the prints of a technician from the Tbilisi nuclear plant. I personally checked the records.'

'And the body?'

'I identified it and covered it back over.'

'Jesus.'

'He's dead, Timothy. He's not going to mind a few more days in the soil. Besides, I can't afford to be directly involved in a diplomatic incident. That, my friend, is *your* job.'

Jaggers turned back to the report, flipped through the pages. Stopped at the third one. 'What else do you know about this man Becker?'

'Not a lot. A technician at the Tbilisi nuclear facility, he doubled as a driver at the weekends. It seems he disappeared at the same time as the uranium consignment, along with the Director of the plant – Sergei Grishin. And, of course, Mather.'

'Any known reason why Mather checked out of his hotel?'

'Ah, the great mystery. No. It does seem likely, though, that a man fitting Becker's description was seen leaving the hotel with him early on the Saturday morning in question.'

'And Mather's belongings?'

'What do you think! Gone.'

Jaggers finished his tea. Put the mug down on the table. 'Is the policeman who passed you this information a detective?'

The German laughed. 'Skulov. Nothing so grand. A simple policeman all his life. Apparently, this last year he has been given a car to drive because he suffers with bad feet – they wanted to keep him going until retirement.'

'Oh, when's that?'

'Next week, I think.'

'Would you say he's an intelligent man?'

'Are you serious! No, he's just a dumb Russian without even the brains to make sergeant. Thirty years on the force and still on the bottom rung of the ladder.'

Jaggers was quiet for a minute, lost in his own thoughts. Finally he said, 'Curious that such a man should suddenly become so informed, when all the top men in Tbilisi haven't even come close to finding the body.'

'You need a bit of luck in this life, Timothy. It seems the old man finally got his. After that CIA guy Sam Yeo had been poking around asking questions, and generally putting everyone's backs up, Skulov was up in the old town. Picked up a drunk. The guy worked at the nuclear plant. It seems he knew a man who was involved with Becker in some shady dealings. A man who had been promised a pay-off. Except he didn't get it. Becker skipped town. The drunk told Skulov the location of Mather's body, a way to *finger* Becker on behalf of his friend. Skulov drove out to the place in question, not believing a word. When he found the grave he drove back to the city. I happened to run into him before he reported the information. Asked him if there was any more news on the Englishman, Mather; told him there was a reward – on the quiet, of course. I bought him a drink at a local bar. That's when he told me what had happened. I explained the diplomatic consequences and suggested that, with his retirement being so close, it might be wiser to forget all about it for the time being.'

'And he accepted without question!'

'I paid him a few dollars. Don't worry, he'll keep his mouth closed.' *A few dollars.* Two thousand the old fox had twisted out of him.

The music ended in the next room. A German DJ with a smooth 'Desmond Carrington'-style voice carrying his listeners effortlessly to the next number – Duke Ellington's *Sophisticated Lady.*

'But nothing more on the missing uranium?'

'No.'

Jaggers slipped the sitrep into an inside pocket. Checked his watch.

Lehmann said, 'Need a lift to the airport?'

'Taxi will be fine.'

'Turn left out of the building, walk down to the corner. Plenty of taxis looking for a fare at this time of the afternoon.'

Jaggers paused in the open doorway. 'Was he Georgian? Becker.'

'No. A Muscovite.'

'You don't think he might have gone back to Moscow?'

'For what?'

'To lie low. Easier to disappear in a big city. Especially if it's one you know well.'

'You want me to make enquiries?'

'You think it's worth it?'

'No. Not a chance in hell.'

'More or less my feelings. You might let someone in Tbilisi know about Mather's body, though . . . anonymously. I think his brother might like him back. Decent burial service in England, that sort of thing.'

'Of course. Goodbye, Timothy.'

'*Auf Wiedersehen,* Max.'

32

Winter was seated on a hard-wooden chair, hands cuffed behind his back. Behind the chair, too, so that his shoulders were wrenched painfully back. His head throbbed – which was, in a way, good, as it took away some of the shoulder and chest pain he was feeling by being racked over the chair back. He sagged forward a little, and found his arms rode up slightly, taking off some of the pressure.

The two local men who had secured him to the chair had long since left. The woman he recognized from the Pagoda came in once. Sat in a chair on the other side of the room and smoked a cigarette and then left. She switched off the light as she did so. Standard procedure. Hot windowless room. Stale air. No water. Leaving you alone to allow your imagination to go to work. What happened? How? Who are they? What had Red Stevens said on the first night they had met at the Soup Shop? Every thief and his dog! Maybe.

An hour or two later they were back. The door was

opened and the light switched on. The handcuffs were removed. He was rubbing his wrists when the African-American came through the door. Dark lightweight suit jacket across his arm. Cool white shirt. Immaculate green silk tie. Colombia, nine months earlier.

'Life's full of surprises,' Winter said. 'Long way off your regular beat, Mr Williams.'

Williams walked across the room. Leaned against the wall. Heard the soft voice, imagined he saw the trace of a smile on the Englishman's lips. The genius of the barren politics of survival. Here! In front of him. A man, it was said, who had travelled the world in his time. From the Hindu bazaars of the East to the icy barrens of the Arctic. From the dusty backstreets and brothels of Tashkent to the volcanic cities of Central America – from the dangerous Isthmus to the perfumed islands of the South Seas. Any place where wars and rumours of wars brought military men to fight their battles. To kill their enemies. Anything for a handful of gold.

'Except the roles are reversed this time. No surprises with pressure switches and 500-pound bombs.'

'A pity your people didn't respond to the letter I sent,' Winter replied. 'If they'd returned my money it would have saved us all a great deal of trouble.'

'No trouble, I assure you. Now we have you, and shortly we'll have the missing uranium.'

Winter looked suitably blank. 'Missing uranium?'

'We're not playing games . . .'

'Somebody is. You see, I'm here with my crews to ferry two aircraft to an aviation museum in the UK. A place called Coventry.'

'And the letter to Langley concerning the three

287

hundred kilos of uranium was just a bluff, you mean!'

'Why not?'

'Let's say we know differently.'

'We? You and your two local gangsters here, you mean. Or are there more of you?'

'Not important.'

'No, perhaps not.'

'Easy way or hard way, Mr Winter. We know the uranium is somewhere on the military base at Bien Hoa. You give us the exact location and you walk.'

'Wrong man, I'm afraid.'

Williams hesitated. He was like a miser with a counting house full of priceless information: parting with each fact was agony, lest he said too much. Or too little. 'We know you transferred it to Bien Hoa on an Ilyushin aircraft from Russia. We therefore know it's on the base. Where are you taking it? What is the route?'

'Your intelligence is still as suspect as ever.'

'Easy way or hard way,' Williams repeated. 'It makes no difference to me. You see, sooner or later you are going to tell us everything you know.'

'I've already told you. We are here to ferry two aircraft to the UK.'

'We also know that you are working with a Colonel Vin from the Ministry of Defence.'

'That's right. He's the man who has taken care of the paperwork for the two aircraft. Check with the government in Hanoi, they'll confirm it.'

'Do you deny you were recently in Russia?'

'No, of course not. I was arranging for a tanker aircraft to be flown to Vietnam.'

'And the reason?'

'To refuel an F-4 Phantom on a ferry flight to the UK, to the museum I mentioned.'

Winter watched the American pacing the small room. Reading the footsteps, the look on the man's face, the line of questioning. Interrogations can enlighten those being questioned as much as the questioners. From what Williams was asking, Winter could measure the extent of his knowledge. It was obvious he knew about the aircraft at Bien Hoa. And no doubt the fact that they were about to be ferried to England. The uranium? Guesswork! Based on the letters he had sent, and the fact that by now they knew that 300 kilos of Uranium-235 had disappeared from Tbilisi.

'You're an intelligent man, Mr Winter. Take comfort from the fact that we credit you with that. Do you think we'd have bothered if you had been like that lush Riker who was with you in South America? I'm betting you could keep this up for hours. The problem is that we don't have hours. Other than that, you *will* eventually tell us everything you know . . . So why make it hard on yourself?'

Winter thought of the anonymous letter he had written to the American Senator. The one he had dropped off at the Rex Hotel for one of his staffers to forward to the politician. 'Senator Whitethorne, I applaud your efforts in trying to resolve the MIA situation. Perhaps you should ask the Hanoi government to take you to the zinc mines at Cao Bang, near the Chinese border. Up until ten years ago there were still as many as two hundred American POWs working there. If they are not alive today, perhaps you should have a UN team investigate this site. Those Americans who died working at Cao Bang were buried in the walls of the mine. If you require confirmation, try and contact ex-Sergeant Joe York in Vientiane. (He's one of the MIA's who managed to escape. He lives off the local economy with his Laotian wife and children. Send one man only – unarmed – to make enquiries from the people who congregate at the fountain on Thanon Pangkham. Your man should say Sibelius sent him.) Your time will not be wasted, I guarantee it. Good luck.'

There had been no good reason to write that letter. He wasn't even an American. Besides, many other mercenaries knew the fate of a large body of American MIAs in Vietnam. Except no one had ever stepped forward. Or, if they had, their word had not been taken seriously, simply because information would have had to be forwarded under the same shield of anonymity that he had used. Unsubstantiated evidence. Not worth considering to the majority of lawyers, and as most politicians were lawyers the American people got what they paid for – nervous reticence, the stuff of fair-weather sailors when confronted by darkening skies. But he had written it. As though some heart's code had sensed trouble and was offering him a form of protection.

Why make it hard on yourself? A good question. 'As you're so convinced that there is a large consignment of uranium at Bien Hoa, why not speak to the government? Ask for permission to carry out a search. It's easy enough. There are foreign businessmen out there most days, inspecting helicopter engines still sealed in cans from the war days.'

Williams continued pacing around the cell. Winter

was bluffing, of course. Part of his game. As Owens had once told Williams: *I think he might be a frightening chess player.* Or better yet: poker.

'Do you remember Murchek? He was with me in Colombia.'

'Frank Murchek, I remember.'

Williams was behind Winter's chair. Winter could feel the hot breath on the back of his neck. The smells of aftershave and body sweat. The whispered voice. 'He's here with me. In fact, he's in charge of this operation. And you know the problem with Murchek? He still thinks he's a marine – the alpha-dog in country. Other than that, you made a fool out of him in Colombia . . . Help me with this, and I can keep him out of the loop. Give you protection. You have my word.'

'Like the amnesty document you promised me in South America! What happened to that?'

'Not my fault, I assure you. My boss didn't see fit to process the paperwork.'

Satan's slippery prosecutor, uncovering and digging out everything; tangling up the thread of truth until it became indecipherable. A solicitous assassin. 'And why would he think differently now?'

'I work for someone else.' Williams straightened up and continued pacing around the cell. 'So . . . Where is the uranium? What is its destination? What is the route?'

'Which truth do you want?'

'There's only one.'

The government man. Turning lying into a universal principle: a servant of the Law belongs to the Law, and as such is beyond human judgement. 'You should have been a lawyer.'

'Where is the uranium? What is its destination? What is the route?'

The same three questions continued for minutes that seemed to stretch into hours – quantum fluctuations. And at the end of it, the door opened and the white-faced man with the blond crew-cut came in. Prominent ears. Pale eyes. Brutal. Instantly recognizable. Murchek. A very fit man. Jeans and sweatshirt. Rippling biceps. *The alpha-dog in country.* He smells fear, he's going to come after you hard. He's going to try and make you lose focus on the questions and answers. He's going to yell, he's going to posture. And if you try and go at him with your tail up, his tail's going to be higher. When you growl, he'll growl louder. When you bark, he'll jump on you and kick you to the ground.

Ex-Marine!

At least you knew there wouldn't be any meaningful conversations.

Murchek said to Williams, 'Did you get your full, signed confession?'

'No. He's not in the mood today.'

'My turn, then.'

Williams left as quietly as he had arrived.

'Another surprise,' Winter said. 'Mr Murchek.'

Murchek prowled around the cell. 'The problem with Williams,' he snarled, 'is that he's ex-Navy. Too fucking soft. Thinks that because he once studied Psychology 101 at Yale he can induce your better self to see reason and tell all. Me? I know that's a crock of shit. I know that people like you don't have a better self. Scum, Winter, that's what you are.'

'Shaking the tree, eh, Frank? It *is* Frank, isn't it? Something they taught you in the Marines? Quantico, perhaps! Except you've got the wrong tree.'

Murchek glanced across at one of the local men. 'His name is Pham Chi Tin, former Khmer Rouge. Something of an expert in getting answers out of uncooperative prisoners.'

Winter looked at the man. Small, wiry, very tough. Short unruly black hair. Prominent cheekbones. Inscrutable unsmiling eyes. An old scar on his chin. The look of a trained soldier.

'The other man is his brother. He takes over when Mr Tin gets tired.'

'And you?'

Murchek grinned. 'When they've finished with you, I get to tear your fucking heart out and eat it.'

He turned and nodded at Pham Chi Tin. The little KR man slowly extended his fingers in front of Winter's face, then brought the hand arcing down. A karate blow to the kidneys. He had been expecting it, but it did little to lessen the white pain that shot through him. He rolled off the chair to the concrete floor, knees pulled tightly in to his stomach, and began to retch.

He was dragged back to the chair. He waited for the next blow . . . No, that was a mistake . . . The trick was to focus on something else . . . *He thought about climbing a mountain in Afghanistan. He did not need ropes or caribiners or pitons. He had chosen the face well. It was only sixty or seventy degrees at the worst spots, with plenty of solid hand- or footholds. There was a danger, however . . .*

'Where is the uranium consignment?'

'Wrong tree, Frank . . . you're not listening.'

Another blow to the kidneys.

On the floor again. Feeling the bile burning its way up his throat. The taste. The smell. The terrible pain.

The gloating voice: 'You'll be pissing blood for the rest of your fucking life.'

The mountain again . . . the danger was, however . . . the sun. It was bright like the heart of an atom, yet as it sucked the fluid from your body you hardly seemed to sweat, for even as the water gushed from your pores it was instantly evaporated. The apparently cool breeze was a devil's lie. The sun could turn good muscle to jelly without warning. It could sear the alveolae of your lungs. Beneath the shade of a hat brim, it could cause a condensed rivulet to wash an eye with salt, making you see true rock where there was only sand, forcing your hand to reach for false security.

Like the hand reaching out now to help him up . . . and seeing too late the brass knuckledusters . . . and the swinging blow that crashed into his jaw.

Back on the floor. This time, tongue exploring the inside of his mouth. He spat out part of a tooth. Noticed the saliva was dyed pink with his blood.

The KR man dragged him back to the chair. For a man of his size he was surprisingly strong.

'How long do you think you can last?'

'Long enough.' Winter's mouth was swollen. He talked as though he had had a novocaine injection.

Murchek didn't bother to answer at first. Then he said, 'We have Miss Espinosa.'

The bargaining chip. Emotional blackmail. *What had they done to her? Stay calm*, he told himself, *stay calm, stay calm, stay calm.* 'She's here to fly one of the aircraft to the UK.'

'So she says.'

'It might be in your better interests to let her go.'

Murchek laughed. 'When you tell us what we want to know.'

'You do realize you're making a mistake . . .'

'In what way?'

'Kidnapping is a federal offence.'

'In America, perhaps. Where is the uranium? What is its destination? What is the route?'

Those same three questions again.

'Go to hell.'

Pham Chi Tin hit him again. Same spot. But harder. Much harder. He didn't faint, not immediately. Then the KR man stepped aside and he slid to the floor. A trail of vomit trailing across the dirty concrete. He tried to reach up, and that was when the pain kicked in. That was when he lost consciousness.

They left him shortly after, bleeding and soaked in his own urine, huddled on the floor. His hands had been cuffed behind his back. Moments later, the woman returned, snapped on a pair of surgical gloves and inspected his mouth. He could taste the latex dust. *So that was her role! A doctor!* A natural addition – skilled hands to ensure the patient is kept alive. It was the pale skin, of course. The Vietnamese consider pale skin to be beautiful. On sunny days the trendier local women could often be seen carrying an umbrella in order to keep from tanning. As in nineteenth-century Europe, peasants got tanned and those who could afford it did not. *Like lady doctors.* She took a plastic bottle –

hydrogen peroxide, he guessed – from the pocket of her jacket, along with some cotton swabs, and cleaned up his face as best she could. The stinging sensation was a pleasant relief from the pain of the beating. Finally she gave him an injection in his left arm. He felt absurdly grateful as he sensed the pain beginning to wash away. His eyelids flickered against the white light of the solitary bare bulb that burned high above him. As she left the room it was switched off. Blackness.

He was slipping away when he heard the high-pitched two-note sound – insistent in the darkness. At first he didn't understand what it was. Where it was coming from. Then he realized it was his wristwatch alarm. They hadn't searched his pockets. Or if they had, they had only been looking for weapons – like the sheathed dagger he carried in the back of his waistband. A wristwatch alarm that was set for six a.m. A safeguard against oversleeping.

Six o'clock. Six o'clock, Friday morning . . . It had to be. The aircraft were still at the base. The only reason Murchek was asking the same questions over and over again. He needed to hold out for eighteen more hours. Until midnight. Until the Ilyushin departed. Hopefully with everybody on board – a part of his brief to Red Stevens:

If anything happens to me all the crews will depart on the Ilyushin at the scheduled e.t.d. (earlier if deemed critical to safety).

Eighteen hours! How many minutes was that?

He was struggling to come up with an answer as the floor dissolved beneath him.

33

Andrew Pitter, rumpled tweed jacket looking as though he had slept in it, blinked calmly behind his horn-rimmed glasses. 'Good of you to drop in,' he said to Owens as he secured the steel door of the communications room and offered the Welshman the same seat he had occupied the previous evening. 'I understand you're on the afternoon flight to Bangkok. Four o'clock, isn't it?'

'Four oh five, yes.'

'It's just that I've had a message from London. They wondered if perhaps you could delay your departure.'

'Problems?'

'Yes and no. Some interesting news, however: it seems that our chap Mather turned up late yesterday. He was found in a shallow grave a few kilometres outside Tbilisi. Seems he'd been robbed. Body's a bit of a mess, apparently . . . decomposing. More or less in line with Jaggers's thinking. Which of course rules out your idea about Mather being the hard target . . . As a matter of interest, I never got around to mentioning

297

that. They beat me to the punch, as it were. So I suppose we can say all's well that ends well.'

'I'm pleased for Timothy. Should do his promotion chances the world of good.'

'He does have an uncanny knack of . . .'

'Acting against the synapse, not the sinew, perhaps,' Owens suggested.

'. . . Getting his finger on the right pulse,' Pitter concluded, more simply.

'Not the chess master who surrounds you, cuts you off, and leaves you stranded alone with your doubts, then!'

Pitter managed a weak smile. He fiddled with his tie. Intellectuals bothered him. He sensed the Welshman was playing games. This was hardly the time for in-house politics.

Owens continued. 'It still leaves us with the interesting question of who used Mather's passport to travel to Taiwan.'

'In all probability, the mugger. Got hold of a wallet full of credit cards and decided to fly out to Taiwan to buy a few gross of radios and video cameras to ship back to Russia and sell for a tidy profit.'

'An interesting theory.'

'More than interesting, it seems to be common practice with the Russian *Mafiya*. Twenty-eight reported cases so far this year, mainly from Moscow. French, Chinese, Colombians, Americans – mostly business-men who went out on the town one night and never returned. By the time their bodies were discovered their credit card accounts had been milked for hundreds of thousands of dollars.'

'Very interesting,' Owens said.

'Nothing more from your tame CIA chap, I take it?'

'Afraid not. It seems that Winter is sticking to his story that he and his people are here to deliver two rather old military aircraft to an aviation museum in Coventry.'

Pitter played with his glasses. 'Yes . . . I'm afraid that's all been confirmed by London . . . They're also a bit confused as to the identity of this chap Winter. The chap responsible for delivering the aircraft to Coventry is, in fact, someone known as William Durack.'

'False passport.'

'Seems not. Durack is a professional ferry pilot, been in the business for donkey's years. Actually undertaken contract work for the RAF, the Civil Aviation Authority, and the Israeli Air Force, among others. He has an address in England – somewhere down in Dorset, pays his taxes, his bills . . . and so on.'

'Even so, it's the same sort of game Winter was up to in the United States when he was teaching at a university in Oklahoma. Except this time, instead of using the identity of one who's slipped this mortal coil, he's borrowed the ID of someone who's still alive and kicking. Any chance of finding the real Durack?'

'Who knows? Even so, it seems our American might have jumped the gun.'

'Williams! I don't think so, Andrew. He's really quite a brilliant chap. I'm quite certain he's at least halfway down the right road. What about authority to get on the Bien Hoa base and check the aircraft?'

'Ah . . . Up to yesterday we had no problems in that area. Regrettably, we've had a little upset since then. Do you remember I mentioned the American Senator who is over here to follow up on the MIA issue? Senator Whitethorne.'

Owens nodded his head.

'Well, last night he issued a public statement accusing the Vietnamese government of lying to the American people for the past twenty-five years. He went on to say he has irrefutable proof that the Vietnamese government, in conjunction with the army, had vast numbers of American prisoners of war working as slave labour.'

'Good heavens, was he drunk?'

'Apparently not. He even added a postscript along the lines of knowing where a number of "our brave boys", as he put it, are buried.'

'Locals? Have we got someone we can send on to the base?'

'We do, but I don't think we're going to be overly lucky. Aviation experts with a working knowledge of radioactive material are pretty thin on the ground.'

'Williams would have been the man for the job. You're sure there's no way we can get him into Bien Hoa?'

'Not after the Senator's outburst last night. I should think the repercussions will take some months to calm down.'

'His first time out here, I take it?'

'Yes. And his last.'

'Unless he's on to something, of course.'

'Yes, well, there's always that,' Pitter murmured.

'What about Williams briefing one of your local people? Would that help?'

'Possibly. Do you want to phone him?'

'When? Now?'

'A tight time frame, I agree. We went public yesterday with news of Iraq's secret committee, the one
responsible for hiding weapons of mass destruction.
The news has been confirmed by Wafiq al-Samarai . . .
the exiled ex-head of Saddam's military intelligence.'

'And the reason?'

'Support for the Americans. They're launching a
squadron of B-52s tonight from Diego Garcia in the
southern Indian Ocean.'

'And by weapons of mass destruction I assume
we're still talking about the biological stuff?'

'The press release stated: 600 tons of three precursor
chemicals for the production of the VX nerve agent.
On the biological front, information from defectors
indicates Iraqi scientists have experimented with
campelpox, which is genetically close to smallpox,
and with the bacteria *yersinia pestis*, which cause
bubonic and pneumonic plague. Also, that they have
the technology to produce anthrax on a large scale. No
mention of their nuclear build-up, naturally.'

'Naturally . . . Saddam's still not backing down,
then?'

'Quite the contrary. Although I can't see what he
hopes to achieve by inviting air strikes, can you?'

Coincidence! The early hours of Saturday, October
the tenth. Planned air strikes against Baghdad on the
very night that Winter was due to leave with his
aircraft for the UK! A connection? 'Depends. Anything
from London on a route into Iraq that is not covered by
the allied forces? Assuming Winter was still going
ahead with the delivery flight, and assuming the
uranium consignment was on board?'

'Only option they could see would be from the east.

That means overflying Iran, which really is a non-starter. I mean, anyone overflying Iran without clearance would promptly get shot down.'

'Perhaps. I remember Winter getting into the United States, though, on such a night flight, when everyone thought his plane had crashed.'

'And you think he could do the same thing there?'

'More than likely . . . What about Williams?'

'We have a Miss Hei,' Pitter said. 'A typist. She has a brother in the army, stationed out at Bien Hoa. Perhaps Williams could stop by and brief her.'

'When?'

'Now. She's here until four.'

'Worth a try.'

'I'll go and pick Williams up from the Rex. I said I'd meet him there for lunch at one. I'll bring him straight back here: lunch can wait.'

They both got up from their chairs and started to walk towards the door. Pitter said, 'You might want to give some thought to how we can best handle this, assuming the worst comes to the worst and we find that uranium at Bien Hoa. I'm thinking of the current situation with Senator Whitethorne and the MIA fracas.'

'Best if we could take care of everything at arm's length, you mean.'

'The longer the arm, the better.'

Owens walked down the driveway deep in thought. Pondering endgame strategies. And although he was only Oriental by experience and sometimes inclination, he played the game rather well. It was forming in his mind even now. A plan that violated all the common assumptions. And that was its elegance. It would be too direct to be seen as contrived. And in the world of ambiguity, the obvious was quite often the cleverest sleight of hand.

34

Career travellers. Red Stevens was watching Frenette and Priest doing a walk-round of the Ilyushin-38. They were checking every inspection plate, every flying control, and every propeller blade. Aware the flight that night was more dependent upon the machinery remaining serviceable than on any other single factor. Like the F-4 Phantom that was still tucked away inside the hangar. Old airplanes. Bloody dangerous.

The two Americans finally completed their task and strolled across to the open hangar doors, where Stevens had pulled up a chair – borrowed from the crewroom – and was enjoying the sunny day. A cool wind from the north made it all the more pleasant. 'All right for some,' Frenette said.

'I'm just the navigator on this trip, and as I've got a pair of hand held GPSs, there's not a lot to do.'

'Except hope all the satellites don't fall out of orbit at the same time.'

'Back to VORs, NDBs, all that terrible stuff, you mean? Although it could be worse. How would you like to be plunged back into the dark days of carrying navigators who worked out air plots?'

'And wireless operators who tapped out Morse. We've come a long way, haven't we?'

'Too right,' Stevens replied. 'Anything on the route weather?'

'Mixed bag. Nothing to worry about until we're in the region of Bhopal . . . about halfway between Calcutta and Karachi. After that, scattered thunderstorms over most of the route, up as far as the Iranian coast. Could be a problem.'

Stevens took a cigar from his shirt pocket, rolled it by his ear, checking for dryness. 'Have to keep an eye on it, that's for sure.'

'Seen Wint this morning?'

Stevens jabbed his cigar in the direction of the road that led to the guardroom. Maria had been found quarters in the former officers' club. Converted to sleeping accommodation for VIP guests. Winter had moved in with her. 'It's his Viking blood,' he joked. 'Something about screwing fair maidens every other day.'

Frenette smiled with what the Australian considered Bostonian politeness. 'Have you eaten?'

'Nah, but I've got our friendly mechanic in there,' Stevens nodded his head back in the direction of the darkened hangar, 'on standby with his truck. He's going to take us up the road . . . Local food, but he reckons it's good. No snake or dog, just healthy roast chicken.'

'What about TC, is he coming?'

The overweight Priest jogged away towards the barracks. He shouted back. 'I'll go and check . . . Two minutes . . . Don't leave without me.'

'Only time he moves quickly,' Frenette explained. 'When somebody mentions food.'

'I'd noticed. How's the ship? Any squawks?'

'Only real problem is the number two engine. I might shut it down once we're in the cruise tonight. Do an air start just before you rendezvous in the F-4.'

'How much would that slow you down?'

'About forty knots, which means that we would need to depart an hour earlier at 2300, to be over Karachi at the scheduled time . . . Any problem with that?'

'No. Might need to clear it with Wint, but go ahead and file your flight plan for the new time . . . Give Corporal Tri a call, will you? He's in the hangar somewhere.'

Frenette wandered off to look for the soldier.

Stevens looked out at the massive Ilyushin. He'd glanced through the pilot's notes. Wingspan – 122 feet, 8.5 inches. Length – 129 feet, 10 inches. Height – 33 feet, 4 inches. Empty weight – 83,775 pounds. Maximum All Up – 134,480 pounds. So much worthless trivia to most. Not to the Australian. As an airplane salesman he had always made it his business to know every last detail of the aircraft he was selling. Something of an obsession that overspilled into peripheral areas – every aircraft he was involved with.

Not unlike career travellers who possessed that undying optimism that drove them to seek gold or land or different skies. Not much different in a way from his great-grandfather who, as a boy, had travelled with his father and uncles up the Warrego and across the Cuttaburra, and out on to the sandy, treeless plains of the Paroo. Country of little use for cattle as they had hoped. Stevens had been there once, in his younger days. At least, he had flown over it with a flying-doctor friend. During the drought. Hot winds stirring the dust. Whirlwinds spinning red columns against a cloudless sky. Career travellers never gave up. His great-grandfather never had: he had gone to Australia to seek his fortune and had died from sunstroke at the age of thirty-seven, clearing scrub at his Thylungra selection – leaving a wife and nine children who luckily had the same bloody-mindedness when it came to winning. They kept going.

Like Winter. Although with him it wasn't about money. It was something altogether different. A quality of life not sought by ordinary people. Living every day on the edge. Avoiding comfort zones.

35

Dreams.

It was an old recurring vision. Something between a dream and a nightmare. One that Maria Espinosa had once a year, perhaps, sometimes more. One that she had been having for longer than she could remember.

It began in a place that was very similar – in a geographical sense – to Narssarssuaq in southern Greenland. With a difference: she was in an airplane departing the deserted airstrip, the next tech stop Iceland. It was nearly dark. And then came the advice from a voice over the radio saying that if she went to the right – to the east – over a spit of icy land, and swung north up the coast, she would find an easier route. A land of the midnight sun, where it never went totally dark. The weather was better that way. The route – it seemed – was favoured by the Gulf Stream. Some way up the coast there was an airport (no name that she could remember, anyway it was fictional, as were the route and the confused topographical details). She landed for fuel. It was that arctic twilight

308

that you find in mid-summer. She cleared the runway and stopped. There was a man – a ferry pilot she had run into over the years on the northern route – standing at the intersection of two taxiways, a few hundred yards from the terminal. He was dressed in a black leather jacket, collar turned down. Dark trousers and shoes. He looked very smart.

She got out of the plane and went to meet him. The air was chill. No wind.

'What are you doing here?' she asked.

'Oh, the usual. Survey work.' He pointed back to an old Lockheed Lodestar on the ramp, the company name on the fuselage undecipherable from that distance.

'How about you?' he asked.

'On my way to Iceland.'

'I'll buy you a cup of coffee while they refuel you.'

They turned and walked slowly down the taxiway. Talking aviation. What else!

Except she was watching herself and the survey pilot walking towards that fictional terminal on that non-existent airport near the top of a make believe world.

Nothing else. It was like catching the dying seconds of an old black-and-white movie. No way of knowing the whole story. What it meant.

Reality.

It had been too easy. Even a highly trained agent, at the right place, the right time, the correct point of weakness in their life, was open to the simple gambit. She, an unsuspecting civilian, had never stood a chance. Whatever defences she might have had were down the moment the Vietnamese woman, bowing at the open car window, said in perfect English, and with a charming smile, 'Mr Winter asks if you would join him.'

She had left the car and hurried towards the side door. A backward glance – seeing the local woman talking animatedly to the driver, who then started the engine of the white staff car and drove off in the direction of District One. Nothing registered until she went through the doorway of the Phung Son Pagoda and a Vietnamese man with a scarred chin and a grip of steel held the rag soaked in chloroform against her mouth. But by then it was too late.

The room had a window, and even though it was barred it looked out on to a small garden of trees and flowering shrubs. The room itself had lime-green walls – a broken wall-lamp hanging from one of them, and a tiled floor, a cot with a sheet and a pillow, one chair and a small bedside table. The badly fitted wall-mounted air-conditioning unit emitted a loud buzz and rattled from time to time like bad plumbing, but at least it kept the temperature down to a comfortable seventy degrees. Other than that, there was a small en suite toilet and a handbasin. Clean towels and a bar of soap had been laid out on the end of the cot.

Then again, there was the American, Tanner Williams. The smiles and quiet voice had failed to hide the toughness, the hard edge to the eyes. Imperturbable. Almost cold. Something she had noticed in Winter. The CIA man had been very clear in his discussion with her that morning. He had been sitting on a hard-backed chair at the side of the bed.

'You are here for your own safety,' he confided. 'As an American citizen I have a duty to protect you.'

She was in bed. Naked. She didn't know who had undressed her. She pulled the sheet up tight about her neck. Her eyes flashed. 'Protect me from what? I was kidnapped . . . You understand that? . . . Kidnapped and drugged. I wish to see the police.' A trace of hysteria in the voice.

Williams spoke quietly. 'I apologize for the way that was handled. Our instructions were that you should be quietly advised of a very real threat from certain foreign nationals, and asked to accompany our agents to this safe house. Regrettably, our local people misunderstood their instructions . . . They have been suitably reprimanded, I assure you.'

'And I am supposed to believe that?' she spat angrily.

'I can take you now to see a very senior Vietnamese government official who will confirm it.'

'How . . . I have no clothes.'

'I'll make sure they are returned to you immediately. I'm sure they were taken to be washed and pressed.'

There was no real answer to that.

Williams continued. 'Time is running out, you do realize that?'

She had told Wint that it was dangerous. Begged him to take Red's offer and go back to Venezuela. 'I am here to ferry an aircraft to Europe.'

'To Coventry, England: we know. Except that on the way you intend to deliver a small cargo to Iraq. This cargo, as I'm sure you're aware, is 300 kilograms of Uranium-235. It's really very simple, Miss Espinosa. We have Mr Winter here in this very building . . . under our protection, of course.'

311

'Protection from what?'

'Unfriendly elements, shall we say . . . We thought you would like to help us.'

'What unfriendly elements? What do you mean?'

Williams rubbed his hands together. Uncertainty in his eyes. As though he were considering disclosing some grave secret of national importance. 'Unofficially . . . we believe them to be Russian *Mafiya*. We don't know the extent of their knowledge, except they are here looking for Winter . . . and, we assume, his associates.'

'Why not ask him?'

'You haven't been told?' A look of total surprise.

'Told what?'

'Yesterday afternoon at the pagoda, Winter was lured out of the back of the building. We got there in time, but he was quite badly beaten up . . . Nothing to worry about, except he has been heavily sedated ever since.'

'When can I see him?'

'Immediately,' Williams offered. 'Well, as soon as I get your clothes returned.' A smile, almost fatherly.

'You said you thought I could help you. How?'

'We need to know the exact location of the uranium at Bien Hoa. I can assure you that any charges against John Winter and anyone involved with him in this matter will be dropped . . . We are more concerned in ensuring that the uranium is removed to a safe storage facility in the United States.'

'And I am supposed to believe you? What of his bank accounts? What about the money you took from him?'

'Not strictly true. Yes, the accounts are frozen, but

we haven't actually confiscated them, rather we are conducting investigations to ascertain the provenance of that money. If it turns out to be legitimate, as seems very likely, it will be returned.'

'So why seize them in the first place, if you now think the money is legitimate?'

'A good question. A very reasonable question. It seems that an accountant working for Winter was involved in some money-laundering operations, perhaps even using Winter's money. The accountant spoke to the wrong banker. The banker reported the matter to our people. Naturally, we had to follow up and alert the appropriate authorities.'

She watched him. Trying to come to terms with what she was hearing.

'Which brings us to the uranium,' Williams said. 'Do you know where it is?'

She took a breath. 'No . . . he has never told me where it is hidden.'

'You're quite sure?'

'Yes.'

'You realize the information could save his life?'

She shook her head sadly. 'I know nothing . . . I swear it.'

Williams smiled again. He got up from the chair and moved towards the door. 'I'll arrange for your clothes to be sent in.'

'And then I can see Wint?'

'As I have already told you, Miss Espinosa, we are only trying to protect you.'

He left the room. The key grating in the lock seemed to contradict everything he had said.

36

Williams was going into the Rex Hotel as Owens arrived in a taxi. He waited by the door as the Welshman paid off the driver. 'How did your meeting go?' he asked as they moved into the lobby. Mellowed kitsch dating from the time it served as a hotel for US military officers. Still a popular watering hole for ex-pats, especially around sunset.

Owens loosened his tie and shrugged the light-weight suit jacket into a more comfortable position on his shoulders as he felt his body sweat being chilled by the fierce air-conditioning system. 'Not so well. Looks as though I'm here for another day at least.' Owens went on to outline briefly the discussion he had had with Pitter.

'Sure I'll talk to her,' Williams agreed, when Owens had finished. 'But I don't think it's going to help. Unless your Miss Hei can get me on the base.'

'I doubt that.'

'Worth a try, though.'

'Have you got plenty of dollars?'

'How much is plenty?'

'A few hundred at least. That might make somebody forget they've seen you for an hour or two. Risky, though, boyo.'

'When do you want to go?'

'Now. She's waiting at the Consulate. Have you got your cell phone with you?'

'Yes.'

'Give me a call when you get out there. I'll stay on at the Consulate.'

'What's the number?'

Owens took Pitter's card from his pocket. 'Two numbers on there, either one. Ask for me.'

'Pity about lunch.'

'Do you want to get a sandwich in the coffee shop.'

'No. A Pepsi, maybe.'

'How about an ice cream?'

'Even better.'

'You want to get changed before we leave?' Owens asked, indicating the American's charcoal-grey suit. Summer weight. Pure wool. But it still looked uncomfortably hot.

Williams smiled. 'My Hausa genes. Hadn't noticed.'

Owens chuckled and steered the American back out of the door. 'Kem Bach Dang, a block this way,' he said. 'Best ice cream in town.'

'You've tried it.'

'Every day.'

They sidestepped a group of beggars. Children, five to ten years old. Barefoot, filthy, in rags.

Owens said, 'What did you get from Winter? Anything more than name, rank and serial number?'

'Not really.'

'I told you he was good, didn't I? What about the Spanish lady?'

'Colombian-American.'

'Close.'

'I don't think she knows anything. Winter doesn't trust his people very much, does he?'

A middle-aged woman shuffled up to them, thrusting a cage containing a small monkey in their faces. The animal was nearly dead from dehydration. Its tiny hand reaching out through the thin wooden bars. Owens said, '*Toi khong muon.*' The woman, lacking affect – a possible side effect of drugs – moved on. Her steps slow and measured. Not unlike those of a sleepwalker.

'Remind you of San Diego yet?'

'Really.' Except Williams stretched the word into a near-sentence. The Californian way.

'Pitter thinks you've got the wrong man.'

'He what?'

'He's done some checking with London. Convinced the man you have isn't Winter at all. Thinks it's some-one called Durack. William Durack. A British citizen.'

'And the potted bushes shaped like animals on the fifth-floor verandah back at the Rex really are animals pretending to be bushes.' More than a hint of sarcasm.

'He was adamant.'

'What did you say?'

'I supported your judgement, naturally.'

'What else did he say, this Pitter guy?'

'Doesn't want any trouble on his manor; that's what the London coppers call their turf.'

'Political, then?'

'Just let's say American isn't exactly the flavour of

the month,' Owens replied, leading him in to the ice-cream parlour.

Williams had caught the news on the hotel radio in his room that morning.

> *The Voice of Vietnam: 'A new political firestorm erupted last night concerning the American MIA issue in Vietnam. US Senator Joseph Whitethorne, the new chairman of the Senate committee exploring the MIA issue, and who is presently in Ho Chi Minh City on a fact-finding tour, last night accused the Hanoi government of a shameful cover-up over the fate of more than 2,000 American servicemen. Senator Whitethorne stated that he had irrefutable proof, if not of surviving prisoners of war, then of their grave sites . . .'*

The story went out in Vietnamese, English, French and Russian. It was also carried by Radio Australia, the BBC World Service and the Voice of America. As well as Reuters putting it out on their wire service worldwide. 'Senator Whitethorne?'

'Senator Whitethorne.'

Williams handed Pitter's card back to Owens. 'Better idea. Why don't I brief you on what to look for and you go to the base with Miss Hei?'

'You think that's a good idea?'

'Light skin is not as noticeable as black. Besides, you speak the language.'

'And if we find what we're looking for! What about Winter?'

The gold cigarette lighter was out, tumbling through Williams's fingers, glinting in the harsh sunlight that streamed through the plate-glass window. 'Remember Kafka's *The Trial*? What would you have in the final chapter if you removed the psychological and philosophic implications; if, say, it was a straightforward thriller as distinct from being symbolic literature?'

Owens thought for a moment. 'Two pale men, if I remember rightly, who collected Joseph K from his lodgings and killed him.'

'But not outside his lodgings . . .'

Or in the town itself, Owens thought. Suddenly understanding. Similar to something he had had in mind. 'Tell me more, Tanner.'

37

It was nearly twenty-four hours after her abduction that Maria Espinosa was handed her freshly laundered clothes by the Vietnamese lady doctor and ordered to dress. It took her about two minutes, after which her hands were handcuffed behind her back. She was then blindfolded and led from the building, where she was lowered gently to the floor of a car in what she later thought was the space between the back and front seats.

Two men, as far as she could guess: the driver, and the other one sitting in the back, resting his foot on her. After about two blocks they seemed to get stuck in a traffic jam. The man in the back screaming something at the driver. The driver yelling back. She didn't understand a word, but the tone in their voices told her they were frightened men. Frightened of being stopped by the police, perhaps?

They started to move again. Driving for a very long while before they left the noise of the city. The road became bumpier. More potholes. The choking exhaust fumes being replaced by fresher air. She took a deep breath and exhaled very slowly through her mouth. Trying to regain her composure.

On a number of occasions she felt like asking where she was being taken, that she had been promised she could see Winter, but she was too afraid. She had read newspaper accounts of such abductions in her native Colombia, when the cartels had taken away their blindfolded victims to some remote spots miles from anywhere and shot them, execution style, in the back of the head.

The car finally stopped and the handcuffs were removed. 'We are putting you out of the car now,' the voice said. 'You will keep your blindfold on and count to two hundred. After two hundred you can remove it. To do so before that time will mean you will be killed. Do you understand?'

Maria nodded her head. 'Yes.'

She was led a number of paces from the car into what felt like a grassy area under her feet. A smell of woodsmoke. She was ordered to begin counting. She did as she was told. Listening as the car was driven away at high speed.

When she removed the blindfold she found it was nearly dark. A few yellow lights flickering through a grey-blue haze about half a mile up the tree-lined road. She began to run towards them. It was only when she reached the scattering of buildings that she realized she was outside the main entrance to the Bien Hoa airbase.

38

The plan was a simple one.

The reason that Yuri the Yid's footsteps echoed on the brown marble floor of Moscow's Sheremetyevo II airport that Friday morning, twelve hours later than Winter had suggested, was simple: because this way he did not need to spend the night in a hotel – which would have meant handing in his passport. And although the photograph inside that passport portrayed a new sophisticated Yuri Becker, it might not have been enough to fool someone who was *seriously* looking for him.

Skulov! Who else? He had been thinking about him all the way from South-East Asia. Imagining the gaunt face with the unsmiling eyes lurking around every corner. Of course it was ridiculous: Skulov was too simple. Besides, he was the one who had killed the Englishman – shot him in the chest at near-point-blank range. He wouldn't talk. He'd be a fool to. His retirement, his pension, why throw all that away?

Yuri handed his passport to the Customs officer.

Still thinking. *Aktivniye meropriyatiya. I arrive Friday morning. Then I take a taxi along the Leningrad Highway that connects Sheremetyevo II with Moscow. The taxi driver drops me at the Slavyanskaya Radisson – Moscow's most luxurious Western-style hotel (and the one from which the faxes need to be transmitted later in the day). A word with the manager to check availability of fax machines. Any problems – because you are not a guest – you slip him a hundred dollars. After that you remain in the residents' lounge all day, reading a newspaper. You take lunch. More reading. Phone call from Winter early evening. Send faxes. Taxi back to the airport. Return flight to Paris.*

Aktivniye meropriyatiya – active measures.

Simple.

'Your visit is business or pleasure, Mr Melvin?'

Melvin! Yuri looked blankly at the uniformed woman before him, the dark blue passport in her hands. What was she saying? Melvin. *Ronald Melvin. New Zealand national.* Shit! That was him. Tight steel bands were squeezing his chest. Panic. 'Business,' he wheezed. 'Business. I have a meeting in Moscow . . . My ears . . . The fast descent in the aeroplane, you understand . . . It makes me deaf.'

The young woman Customs officer, on her third day in her new job and who had never flown in her life, gave him a suspicious look and waved him on to the inspection station.

No problems there: his only luggage was a briefcase.

Walking away now, feeling the official eyes boring into him. The prickly sensation in his scalp. The sweat breaking out on his forehead. This was not good. Not good. Had the Customs officer suspected something?

Why had she looked at him in that way? Why had she taken so long looking at his passport?

And now the voices:

'The photograph, you mean?'

'Of course, the fucking photograph, what else?'

'So why didn't they arrest me?'

'Perhaps they are waiting outside the terminal. A quick trial in the street, you understand . . . The shortage of money is responsible: in short, you, Yuri Alexsandr, are accused of premeditated murder with aggravating circumstances, in accordance with Article One Hundred and Three of the Criminal Code of the RSFSR. Do you understand?'

'Piss off, there's no RSFSR any more.'

'You're dead lucky then, comrade. Congratulations!'

'What does that mean . . . Congratulations?'

'It means you're still living.' Laughter. Like broken glass. Fading away.

He got on the escalator and went down to the airport lobby. Recessed lighting, most of the bulbs burned out. The unmistakable stink of disinfectant. He could sense the lethargy that seemed to hang in the air. Feel it soaking into his clothes, his skin. The glorious old Soyuz, where else!

He looked around, checking for anything out of the ordinary. A group of foreigners were laughing with a tour guide. Two soldiers, smoking cigarettes, were chatting up a plump girl at a duty-free kiosk; one of them noticed him watching, returned his stare. He hurried out through the lobby doors. The chill air hit him. Now he knew he was home. In a few weeks the Moskva would be frozen, and if he were still here he would need to buy boots, hat, a warm coat. A few weeks! He laughed. A few hours, more like.

He pulled the black raincoat tighter around his body. Inadequate, but the only off-the-peg size close to his own that he had found at the airport shop in Paris. Even so, it was tight under the armpits. He went to the taxi at the head of the line. Told the driver his destination. Sank back in the rear seat. Closed his eyes. So far, so good. Besides, how difficult could it be? A few hours sitting in a comfortable hotel, reading a newspaper. It wasn't as if he was facing interrogations and beatings and solitary, was it?

The humming of tyres on the Leningrad Highway changed to the metallic click of railway wheels.

The train that had shipped him across the Ukraine to the Kharkov Central Distribution Prison, the place the thieves called 'Cold Mountain'. Three days later he was sentenced to two years' hard labour and immediately began the seven-day, two-thousand-mile Trans-Siberian rail journey to Novosibirsk. He had been eighteen years old. A skinny, pimply-faced kid, who had been transferred at Novosibirsk to a train that had taken him to the fairy-tale city of Tomsk, and from there farther north to the detention camp in the isolated logging town of Kolpashevo. He remembered some old lag welcoming him and handing him a large glass of oily *samogon*, home-brewed vodka, asking him what he was there for. He told him. The old lag laughed. 'Selling a few misplaced pieces of clothing to make a few extra roubles gets you here, eh? Always the rich getting richer and the poor getting more fucked up, so that the day shit is worth money, poor people will be born without an asshole . . . Have another drink.' And how that night the same old man had tried to climb in his bunk and fuck him. Not much laughter there. Besides, there were a lot of old men. He didn't last long.

'Your first time in Moscow?' the taxi driver asked, in passable English.

Yuri started. 'What?'

'You have been to Moscow before?'

'No,' Yuri lied. 'The very first time.'

'It's a beautiful city.'

What are you talking about? It's a gutted paradise. I could tell you stories, boy. I could tell you stories.

'You would like to do some sightseeing?' the taxi driver continued.

'Haven't the time. I'm only here for the day . . . on business.'

'No one comes to Moscow just for the day.' Surprise in the voice. 'Perhaps you will change your mind.'

Yuri closed his eyes.

Change my mind! Some fucking joke.

39

Winter was breathing with difficulty in the near-airless heat. Trying to count the hours until midnight without reference to a watch or the sun. Something the Cistercian monks had been able to do with amazing accuracy. A train of thought to keep the mind focused.

It was night, by his calculations, when the key grated in the lock and the door was opened. The smallest pool of cool damp air eddied across the floor. He opened his parched lips and sucked it in. The light was switched on and the handcuffs were removed. He was helped to the chair. The lady doctor pushed a mug of strong sweet tea into his hand. He drank a little, recognized the sickly-sweet taste of condensed milk. She slipped quietly away.

'I apologize for Murchek,' Williams said, coming into the cell. 'But I did warn you.'

'Your concern is noted, Mr Williams.'

'But you haven't reconsidered.'

'I've told you everything I know.'

'I understand.' Williams took a fresh pack of

cigarettes from his shirt pocket, opened it, and gave one to Winter, lighting it with his gold Dunhill. Winter inhaled deeply, noticing that the American had not taken one, understanding they were merely a part of the 'soft' man's props. 'Even so, Miss Espinosa told me earlier today that you had the uranium. That it was on the base.'

'She's mistaken.'

'Why would she say that?'

'She probably misunderstood what I told her about a little joke I played in an attempt to get my money returned . . . the letters I sent.'

'Of course. But what of William Mather? He was very real. Of course you remember him. *Your* man in Tbilisi! The person responsible for transferring 300 kilos of Uranium-235 from the plant in Tbilisi to the UK and the US . . . The man you got to! Did a deal with? So what happened? Somebody got too greedy. Decided that once he'd helped out, he was surplus to requirements.'

'Never heard of him.'

'He was found twenty-four hours ago in a shallow grave somewhere outside Tbilisi. According to the post-mortem he was buried alive. There was dirt in his lungs.'

A pause. What had Yuri told him? Not a problem! We paid the girl at the hotel to have five minutes alone and the key to the drawer that held the guests' passports. 'I've never heard of him.'

'What about Yuri Becker? The technician who worked at the Tbilisi Nuclear Plant. You must know him . . . What he did?'

A longer pause. 'Enlighten me.'

'It seems more than likely that he was the man who killed Mather. Buried him twenty kilometres outside Tbilisi, by the side of the Georgian Military Highway.'

Satan's slippery prosecutor, uncovering and digging out everything, tangling up the thread of truth until it became indecipherable. That Yuri was a thief was one thing. That professional thieves – according to some unwritten law of the underworld – were not killers, something else. 'I'm here with my crews to ferry two aircraft to the United Kingdom . . . That's all there is to it.'

'And that's your last word?'

'There's nothing else.'

Williams carefully removed the cigarette from Winter's swollen lips. Dropped it on the bloodstained floor. Ground it out with the toe of a highly polished shoe. 'And you think I should be satisfied with your fables about flying carpets and whales that fed on entire ships and their crews . . . except I know you're lying. And now I'm afraid there's nothing I can do to help you. You belong to Frank Murchek. Goodbye, Mr Winter.'

Two minutes later the grinning Murchek was circling Winter's chair. The two KR men hovering in his peripheral vision. 'You know, what sticks in my craw, Winter, is you thinking you can get away with it. What was it, now? A sergeant in the British SAS, killed one of his own officers . . . shot an unarmed man when the going got tough.' The buzzing silence was shattered by the shouting voice.

'Wrong man.'

'And hasn't even got the fucking courage to admit it.

Then again, there was your wife, back in the States . . . raped and murdered by a gang of druggies? What happened? Did you run away and leave her to face them alone?'

Winter threw the mug of tea at Murchek's head. 'Leave my wife out of this.'

The ex-Marine grinned as he wiped the hot liquid from his face and moved slowly forward. 'You're a fucking dead man,' he hissed.

Strong arms grabbed him from behind. Wrenched him from the chair. And Murchek punched him in the kidneys. Again and again and again. And when he tired of that he went to work on the face.

The trick, as Nick Ashe had always told him, was to think of something else.

The Cistercian habit was a white robe with a black scapular and hood . . . Their garment was girt with a black girdle of wool; in the choir, they had over it a white cowl, and over that a hood, with a rochet hanging down . . . Bound before to the waist, in a point behind to the calf of the leg . . . When they travelled, they wore a cowl and a great hood, all black, which was also the choir habit . . .

Murchek's voice lifted. 'I'm talking to you.'

He hadn't heard.

'I'm tired of listening,' Winter mumbled.

A crashing blow to the side of the head; the hands released him and he fell to the floor. Gasping for breath now, under a hail of kicks.

How many hours left? More to the point, how much longer could he take this? *Stop thinking. Focus on rhythms caused by the brain's activity . . . Beta level . . . Analytical behaviour and concentrated problem solving . . . A place you can feel joy. Something the Cistercians had discovered in their rigorous physical order . . . They who performed their devotions together seven times in every twenty-four hours and had through discipline and routine discovered the body clock . . . Tapped into what the Chinese had known for centuries – spiritual energy, Qui . . . Wave and particle energy considered as one whole. More simply, no one was going to design and construct something as complex as a human being without building in all the necessary senses. Time being but one. The Cistercians called it divine inspiration . . . Or blessing.*

The kicks stopped and he was hauled back to the chair. This time the doctor came to him. Began the ritual of cleaning up his face. Checking the inside of his mouth. Four more broken teeth . . . He'd found those earlier, ran his tongue over the ragged edges. Checking his body . . . Feeling for broken or cracked ribs. Wincing at every touch. She went away and returned with a glass of water.

They were the only two in the room now. 'Do you speak English?' The mumbled sound was like no language he had ever heard.

Even so, she understood. 'Yes.'

'Thank you for the water.'

No reaction. Total control. She took the empty glass from his bloody hand and left the room. Switching off the light as she went. He heard muffled voices in the corridor. Fading slowly away.

He tried to get off the chair, but his legs wouldn't support him. He fell to the floor, felt his cheek against the cool stone. Closed his eyes and tried not to think about the searing hurt. Tried not to think of anything.

Focusing on the third eye. Repeating his mantra under his breath. Emptying his mind. Until he eventually found what he was looking for, or perhaps it found him. A number. Pale against the darkness. *Eleven.* Eleven o'clock.

One hour.

Thirty minutes later the light was switched back on. He blinked at the brightness. Lifted an arm to shield his eyes, as though trying to ward off blows. Tried to focus on the figure in the doorway.

'Who is it?' he mumbled through puffy lips.

'Owens.' The Welshman came slowly across the room and knelt down on one knee beside him. Looked at the unrecognizable face, which had been beaten to a red fleshy pulp. The lacerations on his forearms – and, from the dark stains that had seeped through his shirt, his shoulders and back also. The stench of blood, and stale body sweat, and urine. 'Good heavens, what have they done to you?'

'Fell off the chair,' Winter mumbled. 'Hit my face on the floor . . . Nothing too serious.'

'Why ever didn't you tell them what they wanted to know? Save yourself from all this?'

Winter sucked in a lungful of the cool night air that coursed through the open door. 'I've told them everything.'

'You're saying you never had the uranium?'

'And if I did?'

'You'd be doing your country a great disservice.'

'Which country . . . England?'

'Indeed.'

'And America, perhaps . . . your CIA friends . . . And

anyone dealing in arms and selling them to Iraq would be considered a traitor, is that what you're saying?'

'There are dangerous men in the world. Saddam Hussein is one of them.'

Winter thought about that. Henry VIII had said the same thing about the Vatican, the Vatican had said it about Henry. More than fifty per cent of the American Congress had said the same thing about President Clinton over his indiscretions with a young intern in the White House . . . *A dangerous man.* The problem was, who decided who was dangerous? Who got to choose the meaning of truth! Who played God this week? 'What do you expect me to say?'

'Nothing . . . An observation, that's all.'

Winter lowered his face back to the cool stone and closed his eyes. He was curled up on his right side, foetus-like. His body raw. His joints seized solid. His stomach convulsed, but there was nothing much left to bring up. A rank-smelling fluid dribbled from his lips.

'You've gone too far this time, boyo.'

He gasped for more cool air. 'What does that mean?'

'What do you think it means?'

It was something the British SIS had never understood. There was no point in threatening professional soldiers with death; they drank with him every day of their lives, were his blood brothers. Winter started to laugh at the idea, but it hurt too much. He started coughing instead. That hurt even more. When the spasm had passed, he said, 'Do you know who I am?'

'John Winter.'

'You've seen my record?'

'Only bits and pieces.'

'When you get back to England you might want to

look a bit more closely. Belfast would be a good place to start.'

'And what would I find there?'

The truth. How a young soldier failed to prevent one of his officers from executing two children whose only crime was having the wrong accents. A long story. One he hardly believed himself any more. 'What part of South Wales are you from?'

'Tonypandy.'

'Any of your family work down the mines?'

'All of them.'

'Except you. The second son, right? The one who was educated.'

Not common knowledge outside working-class Welsh families. 'Yes.'

'Any of your brothers killed down the pits?'

A moment's recollection. A moment's sadness in the eyes. Quickly gone. 'My father . . . A pit explosion.'

'And he knew the dangers of going underground?'

'Of course. Every miner knows that.'

'So why did he do it? . . . Why not farm the land, or work in a bank as a clerk?'

'In his blood,' Owens said. 'It's what he did, what his father had done.'

'Making the pit owners rich, you mean . . . More of your dangerous men, perhaps.'

'You're mistaken.'

'The anti-chivalry of the twentieth century, money above all else. You don't think the pit owners were in any way responsible for your father's death? Inadequate safety measures, for instance. What price that kind of morality?'

'What are you suggesting? That it's the dialectics of

the soul, it's the soul's quest, a higher demand that it makes on itself. Honesty. Dishonesty. Justice. Injustice . . . All very interesting but we haven't the time. Can you walk?'

'I hadn't been planning any more exercise today . . .'

'But you could try!'

'Any good reason?'

'They're coming for you at midnight . . . in about twenty minutes . . . Planning to fly you up to Hanoi. Hand you over to the Vietnamese secret police.'

'Who are they . . . Americans?'

'Yes.'

'And you . . .'

'The British Consulate has a problem with this. There's an American Senator in the city, on a fact-finding tour concerning American MIAs. Yesterday evening he held a press conference, accused the Vietnamese of all sorts of evil deeds. Seems he has proof of mass burial sites of American POWs.'

Winter listened in disbelief. The letter he'd delivered. Someone on the planet actually sitting up and listening at last. 'Good for him.'

'Why do you say that?'

I always thought politicians were weak-willed when it came to the important issues. Especially lacking loyalty to their fighting men and women. 'No reason . . . I like people who stand up for their beliefs, that's all.'

'Except he's very wrong in this instance. A case of an over-excitable American politician on his first official visit to South-East Asia trying to make a name for himself . . . the reason we have a car waiting outside with a driver. I suggest you make for the Cambodian border.'

'An Englishman being turned over to the Hanoi authorities . . . Is that it? Okay for the Americans to embarrass themselves but not the British . . . Better if I was picked up and shot in another country!'

'I didn't say that. It's more that we have a diplomatic corps who have worked diligently for years to foster good working relations with this country . . . They are the ones who would be very grateful if you could take your mess elsewhere.' Owens reached down for Winter's arm. 'Now, can you make it?'

'What about Maria? . . . She's here somewhere.'

'They didn't tell you?'

'Tell me what?'

'She was released about eight hours ago.'

'Where is she?'

'I don't know . . . They assured me she is safe.'

'And you believe them?'

'She's an American citizen . . . They have enough problems already. Besides, she has no criminal record.'

'Only me, you mean?'

'Can you stand?'

The night was pleasantly cool, and clear. Between the branches of the trees that lined the street stars hung like early Christmas decorations.

'Down there,' Owens pointed. 'Can you see it?'

Winter made out the sidelights of the car about twenty-five metres down the narrow road.

'You think you can make it?' the Welshman asked, removing his support from the other man's shoulder.

Winter rocked uncertainly on his feet. His voice when he spoke was little more than a whisper. 'Like your father, Mr Owens, it's in the blood. It's what I do.'

The old Welshman said, 'Ah yes, the miraculous depths of the working classes . . . I won't wish you a safe journey, but you'd understand that, wouldn't you, boyo?'

Winter turned and hobbled away into the darkness.

Headlights flashed, car horns sounded, motorbikes dived through impossible-looking spaces. The raw night smells of Saigon mixed with exhaust fumes, streamed through the open windows. Red Stevens concentrated on his driving, working his way from Cholon in District 3 along Tran Hung Dao Boulevard. Past the Cho Quan Church, paralleling Ben Chuong Duong Street and the Ben Nghe Channel; mixing with the unusually heavy late-night traffic at the round-about with the statue of Tran Nguyen Hai, emerging on to Le Loi Boulevard. About three hundred metres further on he swung left on to Nam Ky Khoi Nghia Street. A girl dressed in a white *ao dai*, long black hair flowing in the slipstream, dived in front of them on her Honda motorbike, trapped for a second in the head-lights, accelerating away, weaving from lane to lane with the finesse of a professional.

Stevens said, for the sixth time since Winter had collapsed in the front seat, 'What did those bastards do to you?' He was trying to concentrate on his driving, but every few seconds his head would turn to the right, to the passenger seat. A horrified look on his face.

Winter was in a daze. Pain, and an imminent feeling of being sick. 'Where are we going, Red?' Nothing more than a croak.

'Tan Son Nhat.'

'What's there?'

'A way out of this bloody place.'

'Maria . . . What about Maria?'

'She came back to the base late this afternoon. She had a note for me from a guy called Owens, British Consulate. Told me to be in that side road back there, at 2330 hours prompt. That you'd be waiting. After fifteen minutes I was getting worried, thought it was some kind of trap. Then I switched on the headlights and saw this nearly-doubled-over figure weaving down the middle of the road; thought it was an old drunk at first. Then I thought it was some hit man pretending to be a drunk and working his way close enough to get a shot off. Shit, man, you gave me a scare.'

'Is she still there? At Bien Hoa?'

'Nah, after I read the letter I figured it was best to stick to the game plan. Told Cam to start up and leave an hour earlier. Didn't want him hanging about too long once I'd left the base, just in case the soldier boys turned funny. Standard routing . . . Said we'd see him at the rendezvous, and that he'd probably have to sit in the holding pattern for a while.'

'What do you mean, the soldier boys turning funny?'

'Guess you didn't hear the news: that American Senator guy has apparently found the location of a mass burial site . . . American MIAs.'

'Ah, yes. Owens mentioned it.'

'Other than that, Frenette wasn't too happy about the number two engine on the tanker, thought it would be safer to shut it down in the cruise. Anyway, the real news is that the army has sealed off all the military bases. The little buggers are getting twitchy.'

'What about Maria? Was she hurt?'

'No. A bit shaken up, that's all. Then she got real upset when I told her she was leaving with Frenette and the guys . . . Tears and everything . . . She didn't want to go. I told her you were fine, that there was nothing to worry about.'

Winter felt faint again. He held his head half out of the window, drinking in the cool night air. 'Don't think we're going to make that . . . but thanks for getting her out.'

'No problem . . . So, which bastard did that to you? People the Owens guy works for?'

'A few friends of Williams.'

'The CIA guy? The one you ran up against in Colombia?'

'The same.'

'And Owens?'

'British SIS. They work together, or at least they did in South America.'

'So how'd they find you?'

'They picked me up at the Temple . . . just after I'd delivered the ashes of TC's mother to one of the monks. Think about it: TC probably told them about the urn when he was first picked up on his arrival. After his escape they simply staked out the temple . . . especially as he'd retrieved the urn.'

'Still doesn't explain how the CIA got in the loop.'

Maria. The ever-chatty Maria. Recruiting a ferry crew in the States to travel to Vietnam. Someone else being watched – phones tapped – possibly from the time he had mailed the letter to Langley informing them that he would like his money returned. 'Like you told me, every thief and his dog. Perhaps somebody saw – or heard – too much in Russia. Sold the information.'

Stevens banged the steering wheel with the flat of his hand. 'Shit . . . So, what did you tell them . . . about the cargo?'

'The truth. That we're here to ferry two planes to the UK . . . that the uranium is a figment of their imagination.'

'And they believed you and let you go, you mean.'

'I know, doesn't quite add up does it? . . . Have you checked your rear-view mirror lately?'

Stevens looked up nervously. Watched for a few seconds. 'Nothing there.'

'Might be a good idea to take the next right and switch off your lights, pull into a gateway if possible . . . you know the drill.'

Stevens did exactly that. They sat in silence, parked under a banyan tree, wedged in between a truck and a rusted panel van. The only sounds the squeaking of fruit bats in the upper branches, the flap of wings. No lights followed them down that street. After two minutes had elapsed Stevens started the engine and drove slowly around the block, still with his lights switched off. When he came back to the main airport road – Nguyen Van Troi – he switched on the lights and floored the accelerator.

A hundred metres on, the car swept over a bridge. Sewage smells from the river lasting a few seconds as the Toyota picked up speed along the deserted road.

'So, what happens at Tan Son Nhat?'

Stevens had taken a cigar from his shirt pocket and lit it. He puffed for a few seconds. 'There's no way to get back to Bien Hoa by road . . . They sealed the place up tighter than a duck's arse at twenty hundred hours this evening, along with every other military base in the country.' He swerved to miss a particularly bad pothole. 'That Yank Senator gets my vote . . . Something every fucking fighting man will applaud. About time someone did something about it, instead of fobbing off the rest of the world with political claptrap. Course, it helps that this Senator guy just happens to be an ex-Air Force jock who did a couple of tours out here in the war. Lost a good few buddies, I'm guessing . . . I heard part of an interview he gave on the radio. Sounds like a man who takes no crap.'

'What happens at Tan Son Nhat?' Winter asked for the second time.

'As I was saying, the gooks have shut up all the bases. As of 2000 hours tonight. By the time I left Bien Hoa they had all the barricades up. I got the feeling a white face was seriously unfashionable, especially when I appeared the other way . . . coming off the base, in the colonel's car. Had the distinct impression they wanted to search me, and the vehicle, and then pull me out by the side of the road and put a bullet through my head.'

'So we're not going back there?'

'Not by road.'

Winter looked across at the face tinted by the soft green light from the gauges and instruments. 'What does that mean?'

'We're borrowing a helo from the military hangar at Tan Son Nhat.'

'How did you arrange that?'

'I didn't. The colonel did. I take back all I said about

him: he's really come through, the old bugger.'

'Where is he now?'

'Waiting at the airport. He's going to have us flown over to Bien Hoa.'

'For what?'

'What do you think? We're getting out of this fucked-up place.'

'In the F-4.'

'Sure.'

'Is it refuelled?'

'Corporal Tri and his lads are waiting.'

'Except I'm not in a fit state to fly, Red.'

'We'll patch you up . . . If not, I'll fly.'

'Ever operate the machinery before?'

'Nah . . . F-86 Sabres years ago . . . You can talk me through it.'

'What about the refuelling?'

'Same deal . . . You tell me what to do, I'll do it.'

'That easy, huh?'

'What else do you suggest?'

'Owens thought we should try for the border . . . Cambodia.'

'You don't sound too convinced.'

I won't wish you a safe journey, but you'd under-stand that, wouldn't you, boyo? Owens's parting shot. Warning him off? One working-class man to another. The mention of his father, triggering an emotional tripwire! 'I think it's a trap.'

'Guaran-fucking-teed,' the Australian muttered in between puffs on his cigar. 'Machine-gunned at the border by some invisible – and recently invented – rebel faction. How very bloody convenient.'

'What about TC?'

'He's taken the cell phone you allocated him. Reckons he can shut down every military computer from here to Mars.'

'He came up with something, then?'

'Some idea you gave him, apparently. He got hold of a security-program cover-sheet document from the Pentagon; mate of his is an intern there. He told his mate he was working for the Vietnamese government, advising them on computer security, used the colonel's address and numbers at the Ministry. He's sending out a doctored copy of that official Pentagon document as e-mail to the countries you told him . . . The e-mail states it has an attachment concerning updates on military virus-protection programs. Top-secret classification. Except when the foreign analyst opens the bloody thing he gets pictures of naked ladies . . . That's when the virus is downloaded.'

'And he really believes they'll open it?'

'It's an official document, for Christ's sake. I've seen it . . . TC reckons it has a good chance, especially at this time of night when the computer minders are catching forty winks.'

'Not a word to the rest of the crew, though.'

'Nah . . . they're all on the flight deck. He's got a row of three passenger seats rigged up in the main cabin. Only time anyone would be seen back there would be any crew members going for a piss, or Hod Priest making his way back to his little hole under the floor to start the refuelling operation. Out of sight, out of mind.'

'You've still got my other cell phone, though?'

'Yeah. You need it?'

'I'd like to check the state of play with TC before we launch.'

'Any insurance is better than no insurance – right! It's in the glove compartment in front of you.'

'What's the time?'

'Midnight, give or take a minute.'

Winter pressed the cell phone's power button and extended the aerial. He punched in a series of thirteen numbers. Put the phone to his ear. Leaned his head out of the open window into the cool night. Waited.

'Any luck?' Stevens asked as Winter pulled his head back inside the car and dropped the phone into his shirt pocket. He shook his head. 'No. Must be a bad area. I'll try later.'

The Toyota staff car flew on through the night. Zig-zagging past potholes, rattling over railway crossings, sweeping past the new Omni Hotel and the dark outline of a pagoda on the opposite side of the road, passing the intersection with Hoang Van Thu, with the neon-lit Tan Son Nhat Hotel off to the right. Braking to a screeching stop at the airport tollgate. Stevens lowering his window and handing the operator a fistful of high-denomination Dong notes, snatching the receipt, accelerating up the airport road.

'You're sure about this?' Winter asked minutes later, as Stevens pulled up to the military gate.

The Australian looked at the waist-high sandbags in the headlights. The miniature soldiers in their jungle-green fatigues and tin hats, nursing old Russian-issue AK-47s. One of them shone a flashlight inside the vehicle, then pulled the driver's door open. A smell of body sweat and gun oil. He motioned with his weapon for both men to get out.

'I think we may have made a bloody mistake,'

John Templeton Smith

Stevens called back as he stepped out of the car and raised his hands.

PART SEVEN
Squawk Code A7500

[TRANSPONDER OPERATIONS – UNLAWFUL
INTERFERENCE WITH AIRCRAFT IN FLIGHT.
Should an aircraft in flight be subjected to
unlawful interference, the pilot-in-command shall
endeavour to set the transponder to Mode A Code 7500
to give indication of the situation.
(ICAO Doc 8168, Vol 1, Part VIII. 1.5.2)
*Note: The absence of a reply from the pilot will be
taken by ATC as an indication that the use of
Code 7500 is not due to an inadvertent false
code selection.*]

40

In Moscow Yuri the Yid was making a farewell tour of a few of his old haunts. He had been to Arbat Street, had bought a beer at the Rioni Café and paid tourist prices, he had strolled over Kalinisky Bridge and had found, after some searching, the street that his mother had swept for all those years. A lot of memories on that street. Eventually, having made his silent farewells, he had found his way back to the hotel. Smiling and happy. A rich man after all these years. Handing out handfuls of million-rouble notes to the beggars and the children. 'Yuri Alexsandr,' some of the older folks said admiringly, 'what a man!'

In his mind, at least.

In reality he had hidden behind an English newspaper for most of the day. An armchair in the residents' lounge. Checking his watch every five minutes. Too distraught to eat lunch. It had been the longest day of his life. By the time the eight o'clock deadline approached he was practically a nervous wreck.

No phone call. Nothing. What should he do? *Try and phone Winter!* He fought against the panic that was rising within him. Went through to the bar and ordered a vodka. And another. The third gave him that slight buzz he had been looking for.

He went to find the hotel manager. Winter's words ringing in his ears: 'In the event that I fail to contact you by 2000 hours local time Moscow, you are NOT to send the original two faxes. Instead you will send the single message with the code B1 to the fax number printed on that sheet – the recipient of this fax will know precisely what to do. There must be NO mistakes in timing. Finally, when you have left the hotel in Moscow, you will destroy all the fax sheets. I suggest you tear them up and flush them down a toilet at the airport. Lastly, you are to return to your hotel in Paris and await my phone call.'

Five minutes later, having paid the young hotel manager an extra bonus, Yuri was alone in the hotel's fax room, feeding the sheet marked B1 into the fax machine. He pressed the speaker button, pressed 9 for an outside line, and punched in the series of numbers he had pencilled in on the back of the paper. All the time wondering what had gone wrong! Wondering if this meant they would not get paid off as planned. Swearing under his breath.

A distant ringing tone came over the speaker of the fax machine. After three rings it changed to a shrill steady tone. His finger was poised over the 'Start' button when the cell phone in his suit pocket began to warble.

Shit.

He snatched the phone from his pocket, pressed the

'Talk' button, and held it to his ear. He said in a panicky voice: 'Woesheil.'

A distant voice replied calmly: 'Drincheil.'

The phone went dead.

Shit. How fucking lucky could you get? Seconds away from sending the wrong message. He pressed the 'Stop' button on the fax machine and took the original two fax sheets from his brief case.

Less than ten minutes later Yuri the Yid was hurrying out of the hotel. Walking on air. It was done. It was over. Two simple little words Winter had borrowed from the Cistercian Order of monks. Some forgotten drinking pledge from eight centuries earlier. Appropriate, perhaps. Yuri was on his way to Paris. He thought he might get drunk for a week. Maybe two.

Woesheil.

It was as he charged out of the hotel's main door that he bumped into the two militiamen. 'So sorry,' he said. 'Excuse me.'

One of the policemen muttered something. But Yuri didn't hear it, he was hurrying to the waiting taxi. It was as he was climbing into the taxi and the driver was asking him where he wanted to go that he realized what he had done. He had spoken to the policemen in Russian. Skulov again. Skulov's face. Skulov's voice. He looked back towards the hotel's main door. The two men in uniform were nowhere to be seen.

'Airport,' he told the driver, in English. 'Airport . . . as fast as you can.'

41

The little colonel had been nervous all the way from Tan Son Nhat to Bien Hoa. The soldiers at the gate had been carrying out orders direct from Hanoi to hold and question any foreigners trying to gain access to military installations. Another sixty seconds and it would have been too late. He had decided that Winter and the Australian were not coming; that they had been arrested. He had been preparing to leave in the helicopter.

As it happened, the shouting that had broken out at the main gate had brought him back. He had saved a situation in which Stevens was about to punch out a miniature soldier who had insisted in ramming the sharp end of his AK-47 in the Australian's gut. It had given them minutes. How many, it was impossible to know. Until perhaps someone checked the colonel's authorization and found it did not exist.

The low-level helicopter ride had taken seventeen minutes, following which Stevens had taken Winter to the barracks to get him cleaned up for the flight.

Saigon Express

*

'Missed your vocation,' Winter mumbled as the Australian finished dabbing his face, shoulders and upper back with cotton wool swabs soaked in hydrogen peroxide taken from the aircraft's first-aid kit before hauling him naked to the showers.

Stevens said, 'Nothing personal, you understand. But if you're flying in the same aeroplane as me I'd rather we both started out smelling nice.' No humour tonight. Just tension.

The icy jets of water and the soapy sponge were a shock to the system. Searing jolts of pain. Like electric shocks. Stevens winced at the sight of the weals across the Englishman's back, but said nothing. He had seen it all before. A part of a business he had once been in full-time. And it made him wish – not for the first time – that he was a long way away from this bloody place. Anywhere but an airbase surrounded by paddy fields, where the smell of woodsmoke drifting from the numerous evening fires – where locals were preparing food – seemed to persist late into the night. Where small men with dangerous eyes had long practised the art of the poker face, with the same degree of success as they had at slipping a stiletto into your back without scraping a rib.

Winter moved out of the shower, unable to take any more. He was practically doubled over. Stevens passed him two towels and helped him back down the corridor to the barrack room.

There were a number of thermos flasks on the bedside locker. Stevens opened one, poured chicken soup into a plastic cup and passed it to Winter. It was only then that the Englishman realized he was hungry, that he hadn't eaten for something like thirty-six hours. He had three cups in all. That was when Stevens took a small red pill from a box and snapped it in half. 'Swallow that.'

'What is it?'

'Amphetamine, what does it matter . . . it'll keep you awake tonight. I'll put the box in your flightsuit: you might want the other half at some point.'

Winter knew enough about the drug. Sometimes necessary to stay awake in a critical situation. He also knew, like most informed – and therefore alive – mercenaries, about the increased stimulating effect on the cerebral cortex and reticular activating system. In plain English: increased alertness and response to incoming stimuli. Euphoria, even.

The pain floated away.

'The matador and his dresser,' Winter said. A laugh in his voice.

Stevens went on laying out the flight paraphernalia on the bed. A man in a hurry. 'We've been bloody lucky so far. I'd hate for everything to do a one-eighty on us at the last minute . . . What's the matador and his dresser got to do with anything?'

'I was watching you laying out the battle armour and thinking that the closest I ever got to a bullfight was walking across the border between Gibraltar and La Linea in my youth and standing outside an arena, looking at the posters. A hot summer's day. I bought a poster of a past bullfight from a Spaniard who also had an interesting line in cheap watches.'

The matador and the dresser – the way he felt as Stevens passed him each item of flight kit. String vest,

352

long johns, lightweight sweatshirt, tracksuit trousers, over which went a flightsuit. Two pairs of socks and ankle boots. Next came the g-suit, an inflatable girdle covering the abdomen, thighs and calves. Laced tightly to begin with so that, when the suit inflated, blood was prevented from moving from the torso into the abdomen and legs. In jet aircraft, engine compressor bleed-air was directed to the suit by a g-suit controller when the unit sensed acceleration on the airframe in excess of a predetermined value. In the F-4 it was 2.5g (two and a half times the force of gravity). The greater the acceleration, the greater the volume of air that was directed to the suit, so that at 8g's, the effect (to the uninitiated) could be frightening – like having the life squeezed out of you by a boa constrictor. By keeping the blood from being forced to the bottom of the body, the g-effects, noticeably blackout, where the brain doesn't receive enough blood to process optic inputs, could be delayed considerably. Though the onset of blackout varied from person to person, five to six g's were generally enough to render most unaided bodies of little use to their owners. By tensing the abdomen and with the aid of a g-suit, pilots were able to withstand in excess of eight g's for considerably long periods of time. If the pilot was prepared for high-g manoeuvring, the onset of blackout was a gradual affair, where peripheral sight and colour degraded in an ever-constricting brown tunnel. Until all went black.

The torso harness was next. Fitting over the g-suit, it was designed to spread the loads from the four seat-attachment fittings over a large area of the body through a maze of criss-crossed straps connecting the various parts of the corset. During flight it kept you securely anchored to your seat – its real purpose to spread the load of parachute-opening shock following ejection. Attached to the outside of this: flashlights, D-rings, pistol restraint and flotation ring.

Apart from gloves and bone-dome, usually put on prior to climbing the steps to the cockpit or, by some, once they were settled in the cockpit, the survival vest was the last item. It was put on like a waistcoat. The vest contained more than twenty pounds of equipment, from Mae West life jacket to rappeling line, fishing line, hooks, weights, knife, mini-flares, beta light (a light-emitting crystal for map-reading at night and for use as a fishing lure), snare wire, medical supplies including potassium permanganate (water-sterilizing), condoms (which make good water bags and hold one litre apiece), candy, cigarettes, water-proof matches and pocket compass.

'What's the time?'

Stevens passed Winter his watch, which he'd rescued from his blood- and urine-soaked trousers before consigning them to the garbage bin outside the barracks. 'One-forty.'

'We going to make the 0200 departure?'

'Everything's done . . . Corporal Tri's standing by for us to climb aboard. How do you feel?'

Spacey. How do you think I feel! Except that would alarm the Australian. Understandably. He was riding in the back seat with no controls of his own. His faith pinned on the man up front. 'I'm fine.'

'Good. Did you try TC again?'

'No, I'll wait 'til we're airborne . . . Where's Colonel Vin?'

Saigon Express

'Out by the plane, last I saw of him.' Stevens handed Winter a cup of water. 'You want a cigarette?'

'No . . . I'm fine.'

A moist breeze that had started its life over the South China Sea had drifted inland as far as Bien Hoa, muting the crescendoing whine of the ground power unit. Indistinct figures carrying light-wands darted back and forth like fireflies among the dark shapes of aircraft. There had always been something about the smell of jet exhaust, jet fuel and the insides of military aeroplanes that had quickened Winter's pulse. No more so than tonight when he was drawn to the magic of the flight line and all that went with it.

Stevens was already aboard, strapping in as Winter turned to the little colonel. 'Thanks for the help in getting us here tonight, colonel.'

'My pleasure, John Win-ta. Or perhaps we should thank the American Senator who has caused a temporary diversion.'

'There's no truth in what he's saying, then?'

A sad smile. 'We are professional soldiers, you and I . . . The politicians make the mistakes and we take orders and try and cover them up. No?'

As close to an answer as he would get. Right and wrong on both sides. Good men and bad. Who draws the lines of demarcation?

'What about you?' Winter asked. 'What was the story you told the soldiers at Tan Son Nhat . . . that you were bringing me over here to escort me by military jet to Hanoi? What happens to you when they find I've left with Red?'

'I will not be here. The man flying the helicopter is

my brother's only son. My brother died some years ago and I have been taking care of the boy ever since. He is coming with me.'

'Where?'

'To a place over the Cambodian border. From there we have a car to take us north into Laos, and across to Thailand. We will be fine.'

The firing of automatic weapons in the distance. Like firecrackers.

Winter started. 'Where's that coming from?'

The colonel turned and peered across the arc-lit ramp, beyond the graveyard of derelict fighters and transports guarded by the high cinderblock walls and razor wire. 'It sounds like the main gate . . . The sentries shooting a stray dog, perhaps.'

Winter wasn't so sure. 'You did check the Luxembourg bank today . . . the money?'

'It arrived this morning.'

'That's something, at least.'

'More than something, I think.'

'Yes . . . why not?'

Another burst of gunfire rattled in the distance.

'Time to go, colonel.'

'I will see you in Spain, John Win-ta.'

'I'll be there.' The two men shook hands.

Winter watched as the little colonel limped away towards the waiting helicopter. Then he climbed aboard the F-4.

Corporal Tri removed the top ejector-seat pin. Winter handed him the lower. They were both stowed – seats live.

Strap in. A matter of attaching four quick-release fittings to the hip and shoulder rings on the torso harness, and then threading a line through the eyelets of the leg-restraint straps buckled to each leg below the knee. The purpose of the leg restraints: to draw the legs tightly against the seat during ejection (so that they would clear the instrument panel and canopy bow) and hold them there until it was time for seat separation and parachute deployment. Once firmly buckled in, with bone-dome on, oxygen mask hooked up and g-suit connected, Winter tried the intercom. 'You ready in the back?'

'Ready as I'll ever be.'

'I'll leave the radio and the nav with you . . . got your GPS hooked up?'

'Affirm.'

Winter signalled to the groundcrew man. Start air directed to the right engine . . . RPM indication ten per cent . . . Ignition button on the inboard edge of the right throttle pressed and held . . . Throttle moved forward, then inboard around the idle detent . . . Jump in EGT (exhaust gas temperature) . . . Rapid increase in RPM . . . Light off . . . Ignition button released . . . Engine spooling up to idle . . . Temps and pressures fluctuating back and forward . . . Ducts and ramps and auxiliary air doors opening and closing . . . Selecting internal electrical power . . . Waving away the ground power unit . . . Repeating the start process on the left engine . . . Rolling away from the ramp . . . A quick tap on the brakes . . . The checks continued.

'Cleared to runway 27.' Red's voice over the intercom.

'What's our call sign?'

'X-Ray Victor Hotel Lima Uniform . . . On the top of your panel.'

Winter picked out the dynotape strip in the red glow of the instrument lights: XV-HLU. 'That official?'

'What else? The colonel even had his boys stencil it on the rear fuselage . . . Standby.' Stevens went back to talking to the controller on the radio.

Winter continued running through his cockpit checks. He was near the end of the taxiway when he saw the shape of the blacked-out Huey cross over above him, caught in the reflection of the blue taxiway lights. Then it was gone into the night. *Safe flight, colonel.*

'Cleared for take-off, runway heading to three thousand, then climb on course . . . Initially cleared to one eight zero.' Red's voice.

Winter swung the Phantom on to the runway and pushed the throttles forward. The aircraft, heavy with fuel, began to gather momentum. After six seconds in dry power and an indicated speed of fifty knots he selected the throttles outboard and to the stops. The afterburners kicked in . . . Thrust jumping from 20,000 pounds to 34,000 pounds . . . Stick held aft . . . Nose wheel extending at 125 knots . . . 140 knots airborne . . . The speed was passing 180 as Winter selected gear up and began to climb . . . Leading and trailing edge flaps retracted . . . And, as speed reached 300 knots, afterburners cancelled.

Winter checked the instruments and trimmed for the climb. Running through the climb checks, planning ahead to the cruise checks, outside air temperatures at ISA plus ten conditions, fuel burn. His mind alarmingly clear. 'What's the border estimate?' he asked Stevens.

'Christ! Give me a minute . . . Still waiting for the

GPS to pick up enough satellites.'

Winter checked the nose was five degrees above the horizon, and power set at ninety-five per cent. Rate of climb indicated 2,000 feet per minute. It would be twenty minutes and one hundred and forty miles before they would get to their planned flight cruising level of 42,000 feet.

To observers on the ground, nothing more than flashing strobe lights and the thunder of jet engines. Both fading with time like a red-shifted star.

42

Yuri the Yid was frightened. The reason he asked the taxi driver to drop him off a hundred metres before the terminal building. He had a headache, he explained. The short walk in the cold night air would help. The taxi driver could have told him it was dangerous to walk anywhere alone. Especially at night. A lot of thieves were constantly on the lookout for rich-looking foreigners. But then, he wasn't his brother's keeper; this was the New World of capitalism where you took care of yourself. He took his money and a reasonable tip, and sped away.

Yuri crossed the street and entered a poorly lit car park. The police at the hotel? Nothing! Something? Skulov up to some old trick. Sure, he'd never made it to sergeant. Sure, a lot of people reckoned he was dumb. But you didn't spend all those years in the militia without learning something. *Like what?* It was Skulov who had shot the Englishman, after all. As cool as you like. Straight in the chest. And it was Skulov who had buried him . . . No! It was Yuri who had shovelled the earth into the shallow grave. Skulov had told him to grab the spade. *No gloves! No fucking gloves!* That was what he had learned. You get something on your partner just in case he tries to double-cross you. His fingerprints. Skulov had *Yuri's* fingerprints all over the handle of that spade.

Yuri checked his watch. It was late. He needed to get into the terminal, check in for the Paris flight. He moved slowly between a line of cars. Listening to the whining thunder of a jet climbing away. He looked up but couldn't see it. Wished he was in a window seat on that very flight, waving goodbye to the old Soyuz forever. *Not long*, he told himself. *Not long.* He found a place in the lines of cars where he had a good view of the front of the terminal. He squinted through the thick lenses of his glasses, working his way from one end of the terminal to the other. No militia in sight. Not a one. A few passengers. A number of cars and taxis.

A coach pulled up suddenly. The doors hissed open. People began pouring out, milling around on the sidewalk. Chattering as they waited for the driver to get their baggage. A perfect time to cross the road, to lose himself in the crowd – they could even be on the same flight.

Skulov again. *Be careful. Think what you're doing. Think.* So what if Skulov had his fingerprints; what was he going to do with them? He'd never mentioned that he would be in Moscow. Shit, he hadn't known himself until Winter had sprung it on him. So how could the dumb-fuck policeman know?

He stepped across a low barrier, eyes intent on the group around the coach. Voices arguing over baggage.

It was as he was moving forward that a voice cried loudly, 'Yuri.'

He froze, unsure at first where the voice had come from. Behind him? In the car park? The police? He felt the suffocating cold sweat breaking out on his face. *Shit.* His heart thumping in his chest. *Shit, shit, shit.* The shortness of breath, so that he was gasping for air.

What should he do? To turn and face the voice would be admitting he was him: Yuri Alexsandr Becker. To keep on walking without looking back was a chance to merge into the crowd. To slip into the terminal and disappear. His only chance. And as there was no life beyond the grave he needed to live his last remaining years to the full: there was nothing else.

The voice called his name again. Louder this time. A note of anger, even. *Shit! That bastard Skulov.* How had he known? What story had he spun to the Moscow Oblast? Or perhaps there was no story to be spun. Perhaps he had that gun again. Was looking for revenge.

Yuri lowered his chin into his chest and began to run across the road.

He didn't see the beat-up Zhiguli with one headlight out speeding towards him. In the same way the youth who was driving the car one-handed while holding a bottle of vodka to his lips with the other didn't see the pedestrian in the dark raincoat running out in to the road.

Yuri felt, or thought he felt, a sharp tap, but he couldn't be sure. Something else he couldn't be sure about was the rain that had just started. It seemed to be falling directly on to his face, into his eyes. He didn't mind too much: he felt very hot and the rain cooled him down. And then there were people gathering around. Looking down on him. Someone, in what looked like a uniform, asking questions, checking his pockets. Yuri wondered what had happened to his glasses. Perhaps he would ask his mother. She would be along shortly. Sweeping the streets with that big stiff broom.

He called her name once.

It was the last thing he said.

Yuri Alexsandr Becker would never know that the voice he had heard was that of a young man who had just parked his car and, having unloaded a number of suitcases from the trunk, had discovered that his young son had wandered off, playing games. He had been calling him.

Yuri – a common enough name.

As for the man in the uniform asking the questions, looking for identification: a scam artist, one who had learned his trade in New York. By the time the real police arrived on the scene, Yuri Becker's pockets had been picked clean.

It would be much later at the morgue that a coroner would discover that the latest John Doe had a thief's tattoo above his heart. That same coroner would decide that justice had possibly been served, and that the world was probably a better place now that it didn't have to support another deadbeat.

Had he known the net worth of the body with the thief's cross it would have taken his breath away.

43

The effects of the amphetamine were wearing off. Not enough for Winter to feel the pain in his body just yet, but enough to sense its aura. A thin armour. Getting thinner. Like the fuel. Or lack of it. They were down to their last 800 pounds. At 24,000 feet that gave them six minutes before flameout.

Six minutes.

Surrounded by thunderstorms the tanker had stabilized for the second time on an outbound track, attempting to fly a racetrack pattern in a small patch of clear air twenty miles off the Pakistan coast. Winter closed up . . . Walking pace . . . The tanker's red lights turning to green . . . Steady . . . Steady . . . Oblivious now to the threatening outlines of the thunderheads caught in the moonlight . . . To the moderate chop he felt through the seat of his pants . . . The winged boom flew down in the darkness . . .

Four minutes.

No voices now . . . Just tension, so thick you could taste its suffocating presence . . . The boom inched back over his head towards the receptacle in the F-4's spine . . . *C'mon, Hod, what's the problem, move it, move it, move it* . . . Not a valid argument . . . They hadn't practised night-time join-ups . . . Something he'd overlooked or hadn't considered important enough . . . Something that was getting away from him . . . Had got away from him . . . The confidence of youth . . . Disjointed thoughts running through his mind . . . Overflying Cambodia, Thailand, the Gulf of Martaban between Moulmein and Rangoon, out over the Bay of Bengal; feet-dry over India south-west of Calcutta, abeam Bhopal, towards the Rann of Kutch, and away to the north, near the Afghanistan border the once-British garrison of Quetta – a place his grandfather had served more than eighty years earlier; a sergeant in the REME, a man who had known the Khyber Pass, Peshawar, Simla, names that conjured up images from Kipling's novel *Kim*. The days of the White Raj . . . A once-upon-a-time world, gone forever . . . The F-4 hit a bumpy patch of air . . . The aircraft bucked and tried to roll . . . Winter anticipated, feeding in minute corrections . . . At 200 knots not an easy task . . . twenty knots above the stall . . . Slight burbling through the controls . . . Like walking a tightrope over Niagara falls in a strong wind – against the clock . . .

Three minutes.

The winged boom reappeared above his head . . . Ominous in his peripheral vision, like something out of a *Star Wars* movie . . . And was gone again . . . Seeking something he could not see . . . His face felt clammy, his hands inside his gloves were sweaty . . . More thoughts: TC's computer viruses playing havoc with air traffic control, not just military, civil as well, reducing the controllers to primary radar coverage only, delaying airline arrivals and departures. Establishing contact with the tanker on their discreet frequency, a few words with Maria. Joy at knowing the other was safe. Love unspoken, as the poet might have said. All the days ahead to prove it. Creeping around the edges of boiling thunderstorms looking for the anti-collision lights of the Ilyushin. The seconds ebbing away, until ejection had seemed the only alternative to survival . . . Now he was reaching up with his free hand, wiping sweat from his brow . . . Waiting . . . Waiting . . . A dull clunk . . . Green light flickering on . . . Fuel flow confirmed . . . Quick glance at the fuel counter . . . Working . . . More concern, worrying that the fuel was now going where it was not supposed to . . . A valve sticking could permit fuel to transfer to the external tanks from the number one feed cell – meaning you could flameout even while you were plugged in . . . The engines kept running . . . Now a matter of hanging in . . . More minutes . . . Anticipating the choppy air . . . Fingers twitching the stick . . . And, finally, the green light flickering off . . . 25,000 pounds uplifted . . . Easing back on the power . . . Dropping aft of the tanker by another 100 feet . . . Radio call: 'Tango Four Two, Lima Uniform disengaged, departing your starboard side' . . . And surfing away along the edges of the cumulonimbus . . . Back to the thinner air at 42,000 feet . . . And the lower fuel burn.

Long minutes of silence.

'Bloody close,' Stevens eventually sighed over the ICS.

Winter, beginning to feel pain in his shoulders

where the seat harness cut into the skin, was quiet, concentrating on avoiding the storm cells that circled them, looking for moonlit valleys that would offer a means of escape. Sheet lightning flickered in three cells simultaneously. Artillery fire from a foggy battle-field. Not recommended.

The tanker came up on the discreet frequency some seconds later. It was Maria. 'Lima Uniform, Tango Four Two.'

Winter was monitoring box two while Stevens was working box one with Karachi (advising them of their return to Flight Level 420). He said, 'Go ahead, Tango Four Two.'

'Roger, we have had to shut down number two engine . . . excessively high ITT . . . Do you want us to carry on to Bahrain?'

'Does Cam think it's fixable?'

'He does not know.'

'Better divert to Karachi, get a local engineer to look at it.'

'Cam thought we might be able to get a spare engine flown in from Russia?'

'I'm sure we can . . . Just takes time. I'd better have a word with him.'

'Take care of yourself.'

'And you.'

'I mean it.'

'I know.'

'What are you going to do when this flight is over?'

'Anything you want.'

'Is that a promise?'

'A proposal.'

'I do.'

'That quick.'

'I have had nine months to practise.'

Laughter. 'You'd better hand me over to Cam.'

'I love you.'

'Non-standard RT procedure.'

'Are you complaining?'

'Never . . . I'll talk to you later.'

Frenette came up moments later. 'Understand you want us to divert to Karachi.'

'Affirmative. Cheaper to go tech there than Bahrain, do you agree?'

'And there was me thinking it was only ferry pilots who counted the pennies. Yeah, you're right, much cheaper.'

'Can you also make sure TC gets to the American Embassy after you land? Red's given him money to get an airline ticket, plus his flight pay . . . Perhaps you could explain he's lost his passport to the powers that be.'

'Not a problem. Going back to the engine trouble, what do you want me to do about that at Karachi?'

'Find someone who's capable of doing an engine change, first off. I'll liaise with you from up the route. You might have to leave it there for a month or two before we can get the work done.'

'Standard operating procedure, then . . . I'll take care of it.'

'Copied.'

'I hear congratulations are in order.'

'News travels fast. Thanks, we'll invite you to the wedding . . . Safe trip, what's left of it.'

A double-click on the transmit button and he was gone. Winter switched his VHF selector to box one.

Stevens was still talking to Karachi. He'd tell him later.

The altimeter slipped silently through 35,000 where the mountains of platinum-edged clouds began to peter out. Wind-torn anvils. Knights' pennants. Camelots thrown up by adiabatic lapse rates. A full moon clearing the battlements.

Nice night.

44

In Baghdad the Deputy Prime Minister had received
the message (via his secretary) from the Slavyanskaya
Radisson Hotel fax number in Moscow, stating –
'*Nineveh confirmed. Sibelius.*' From there it had been
a matter of passing the information to the Prime
Minister. From the Prime Minister it went to Lt Gen
Abed Hamid (private secretary to Saddam). From Lt
Gen Hamid to Amir Saadi (Saddam's adviser). From
Amir Saadi to the President for his approval. And from
the President, after careful deliberation, back to the
Prime Minister who had immediately contacted the
Secretary-General of the United Nations, Kofi Annan,
and agreed to the terms outlined for allowing UN
inspectors back into Iraq to recommence their inspec-
tions of weapons sites. Confirmation was asked for.
This meant a typist was required. A clerk was sum-
moned from his bed. Time dragged on. Finally, the
typed and signed confirmation was sent by fax.

The whole procedure took more than five hours.
Iraqi military intelligence had gauged it very close.

Saigon Express

One more hour and it would have been too late.

Which was why three B-52 Stratofortresses (Buffs) on their way from Diego Garcia, a small island in the Chagos archipelago in the southern Indian Ocean, were recalled minutes after they had crossed the coast of Oman at Al Juwara. The cell of three bombers had been modified to carry Cruise missiles programmed for eleven primary targets, of which the first two were Jabul Makhul (near the central Iraqi town of Samarra, and one of eight presidential palace sites, covering ten square miles and containing ninety structures) and Al Taji (an armoured vehicle plant), nineteen miles north-west of Baghdad. And secondary targets at Takrit, Kifri, and Kirkuk.

For the crews of the Buffs, a few of whom had seen action in the Gulf War with the 4300th Bomb Wing, it was an anticlimax. And a long depressing haul back to nine degrees, fifty minutes south and seventy-five degrees east. The lat and long of Diego Garcia.

45

Pain skirted Winter's body. Probed like the lances of paladins prancing in and out of range on their iron-hoofed warhorses. Dizziness came in waves. Sickness welled in his stomach, sour bile pushed up in his throat. He forced himself to swallow. Took a few deep breaths of the 100 per cent oxygen. Felt the sweat trickling down the bridge of his nose, around the edge of his oxygen mask, across the top of his cheeks. The broken piece of the amphetamine pill, retrieved from a pocket of his flight suit, had slipped from his fingers moments earlier. Was on the cockpit floor now. A matter of inches away. Inches that might as well have been miles.

He looked outside. The cloud had gone. Moonlight bathed the Iranian coast away to the right. In between, the waters of the Arabian Sea glistened silver. Perhaps it was time to start on down. 'What's the range to Chah Bahar?'

'One hundred.'

'Let me know when it's fifty . . . We'll start descent.'

A questioning silence. As though he was speaking a foreign language. 'No need.'

'What do you mean, no need?'

'We're going on to Bahrain.'

'Are you . . .' He was going to say crazy, but he never quite got that far. It was as though pain had finally deciphered all the illusions. Discovered the sleight of hand – all the more difficult because it was never expected. The note Owens had sent with Maria back to Bien Hoa! How did Owens know Stevens was on the base? 'There never was a note, was there, Red?'

'Note?'

'Maria never came back to the base with a note, did she? Who came? Owens himself! How did he know *you* were there?'

Silence.

Winter could imagine him nervously grinding his fist into his palm. Thinking. Wondering what to say.

'How did he know?' Winter asked again.

'Not him . . . Williams. The CIA guy. I was at a place called Puerto Carreno in Colombia working on one of my planes; he appeared one morning out of nowhere. He said you had a valuable cargo of theirs and that they needed to find you . . . Told me I was going to help them. I told them to go to hell . . . Then he said he had the names of my kids in Australia . . . If I wanted them to remain in good health I'd do what he was asking . . . Jesus, man, what was I supposed to do?'

'And Maria? What was her involvement?'

'Nothing. She was hiring the pilots for you. I explained what had happened . . . As much as I knew, at least. She suggested we both should go to Nam, try and persuade you to hand back whatever it was you had.'

'So what was the deal? No, let me guess. You lead them to the uranium consignment and everyone gets to walk away completely unharmed. No comebacks . . . Except you didn't know, because I made sure I told nobody. So what happened next?'

'Owens came out to the base yesterday afternoon. He was with a Vietnamese woman from the British Consulate. He wanted me to show him the aircraft . . . That's all. Then the consulate woman started talking to Corporal Tri – you know, the mechanic guy. He told her he'd helped you change one of the drop tanks. Owens got me to look at it. That's when I noticed the filler cap was welded on.'

'So Owens persuaded you to change it for one of the normal tanks . . . What happened to the one that was on there? Did he try and open it?'

'Shit, no. Said they'd need safety equipment. Reckoned the tank was lead-lined or whatever . . . The woman got Corporal Tri to borrow a truck. They took it off the base . . . to the consulate, maybe. I don't know.'

'And Owens told you where and when to go and collect me.'

'Yes.'

'With the same assurances that Williams gave you, is that right?'

'They've got what they bloody want . . . End of story. They just don't want some lunatic like Saddam getting his hands on fissionable material.'

'And you believed them?'

Ragged breathing over the ICS. The seconds ticked by. 'Why not?'

'How about he's already got plenty of the damned stuff, that's why not. What do you think the UN inspectors are running themselves ragged for? Chemical weapons? Any smart high-school kid can produce chemical or biological weapons . . . Most countries still do. If they have a problem with that they should turn to China and North Korea and a few other places. No, the UN team are looking for material to build atomic weapons . . . tons of which have been sold off by the Russian *Mafiya* and a few thousand ex-Soviet military operators who got in on the act.'

Stevens's voice lifted. 'So the UN is looking for atomic weapons, or at least the bits and pieces to make them: what's wrong with that? Saddam's crazy enough to let them off . . . You realize what you're doing by furnishing him with bloody uranium?'

The same thing Henry did when he sacked the abbeys and the monasteries. Murdering the holy men from Rome. For what? Venal reasons? 'No different than leaving it in the hands of the Western Powers. They're disposing of highly toxic waste in the oceans of the world . . . out of sight, out of mind. Sort of a long-term nuclear war. Contaminating the food chain. Either way, we all get to mutate and die. Sad that the West's leaders should possess the high-flown rhetoric of archangels and the base morals of crooks and tarts. Even sadder that no one really cares enough about the future generations. Forget Saddam. The West's interest in the Middle East lies with oil. Once that runs out, or someone comes up with an alternative energy source, the West will go back to calling the Arabs unpleasant names and having no interest in them or their countries. Saddam Hussein is no worse than the old Soviets, no more devious than Franklin Delano Roosevelt who conned the American people for years by lying about his medical condition, or Tony Blair, a left-wing conservative who took learn-to-love-the-camera lessons from his actor father-in-law and then hoodwinked the British workers by calling his party New Labour, when it's really just a continuation of *most* of the Thatcher/Major policies that have run successfully for years. No, give Saddam time and he'll hang himself with his own rope. They all do in the end. What Saddam's looking for now is protection. If a few hundred kilograms of uranium make the difference in educating western society to the fact that their leaders are equally evil and corrupt, all well and good. If not, they deserve the future. Whatever it holds.'

'Except he's not getting those few hundred kilos now.'

Winter said nothing. Wiped his brow with the back of his gloved hand. Grimaced at the pain that surged through his body. Glanced down more than eight miles of sky towards the Iranian coast. A small island. A spit of land. A bay. They were already passing Chah Bahar. Something flickered in the moonlight. Held his attention for a moment.

'It never was in the drop tank, was it?' Stevens asked, reading the silence.

'No, Red. It never was.'

'What the fuck was all that about, then? What's the purpose in going to Iraq? Why not Bahrain as planned?'

'Why do you think? Like you said in the Soup Shop that night in Saigon, once the word gets out every thief and their dog will be after us . . . The trick is, look for the downside. Patch up all the holes. And if they do find you, make sure they're following your rules of engagement. Iraq is the stepping-stone back to the world. New passports. No unfriendly elements to track you from a place like that.'

'So where is it?'

'Doesn't really matter . . . Your radar working in the back?'

'Yeah, why'd you ask?'

'Couple of minutes ago I picked up two canopy flashes in my two o'clock low. Fighters, at a guess.'

'I'm not getting anything . . .'

Winter pictured a nuclear-powered aircraft carrier making about thirty-five knots into the wind . . . Eight pressurized water-cooled Westinghouse A2W reactors supplying steam to four sets of geared turbines delivering 280,000 shp to four shafts . . . Crew complement in excess of 5,000 . . . Eighty aircraft . . . Three Mk 57 launchers for RIM-7 NATO Sea Sparrow surface-to-air missiles . . . A grey eighty-five-thousand-ton mass scything through the choppy waters . . . Quite deadly . . .

Their refuge in the night sky, the comforting shush of slipstream, the warm red glow of instruments – turned suddenly hostile. The disputed barricade that all soldiers face sooner or later.

'What do you reckon? . . . The USS *Enterprise* on her way to the Gulf . . . Pair of F-14 Tomcats, or something similar, just launched?'

'They couldn't do that . . . We're on a civilian

377

registration . . . On a legitimate flight plan, for Christ's sake.' Panic in the voice now. 'I'll squawk 7500 . . . Distress . . . That we're being subjected to unlawful interference . . . Anybody starts shooting after that . . .'

'Except no one's going to pick up secondary out here . . . And even if Karachi could, TC knocked it out, remember? Which leaves primary radar only, and we're out of range of that.'

'Why don't we go to afterburners and make a run for the coast . . . into Iran?'

'Too late, Red. They're inside of us. They've got all the angles covered . . . I imagine they asked you about our flight planning as well, uh? ETA for Chah Bahar? Flight level?'

Stevens mumbled, 'Something like that.'

Winter tried to work his body into a more comfortable position in the Martin Baker ejector seat, trying to ease the pain. It didn't work. If anything, it got worse.

'Fifty miles . . . In our six o'clock . . . Closing fast.' Stevens's voice was full of disbelief.

The low warbling in their earphones from their RWR (Radar Warning Receiver) confirmed there were other radars up here, sweeping the sky. Hughes AN/AWG-9 weapon-control system with radar able to detect targets in excess of 315 kilometres, track twenty-four simultaneously, and attack six at varying altitudes at the same time. Unbeatable odds.

Winter looked up briefly, taking a bearing on the stars. Their disinterested hard energy somehow transforming before his eyes. Becoming pale magnets, drawing him closer. Peaceful imagery. A contradiction to the hollow emptiness he felt in the pit of his stomach . . . The dry-mouth taste of brass.

The low burbling rose to a shrill beep. Someone had gone to search mode and locked on.

Winter rapped the stick against his right leg, pulling hard. They came through nearly one hundred and eighty degrees before he rolled level, then eased the nose slightly down, and went to afterburners.

Time expanded . . . And he thought about Charlie Riker's warning: 'Flying fighters . . . it's a young man's game' . . . And Maria clattering along on her high heels, clinging to his arm: the big dark flashing eyes, the thrown shoes, she made him smile . . . His late wife, Julia, the way she would lie in his arms at night and ask about his day, she more than anyone, for the best years of his life . . . His grandfather's farm, the barns smelling of paraffin and old apples and hay, specks of dust rising in the sunlight; the innocence and expectations of a ten-year-old boy who dreamed of flying an aeroplane . . .

Moonlight glinted off a canopy. How far away, it was impossible to tell . . . Moments later, two brilliant white flashes . . . Sidewinder fire-and-forget missiles, twelve feet long with fins and carrying a 20-pound high-explosive warhead. Used at close range, homing on target at supersonic speed . . . $100,000-per-copy fireworks trailing their message across the heavens.

Winter took a deep breath and went on to meet them.

Debriefing

In the days that followed, the American Press gave minimal coverage to Senator Joseph Whitethorne (an ex-USAF fighter pilot) who had discovered a mass burial site of more than 100 American MIA's in a North Vietnamese zinc mine.

Time, it seemed, had finally moved on. Few people cared about the first war that the United States of America had lost.

No aircraft was reported shot down and destroyed over the Arabian Sea (near Chah Bahar) on the night of 9/10 October. A ferry flight from Bien Hoa, Vietnam, to Bahrain was, however, reported as missing by the Bahrain Air Traffic Control Authorities when the aircraft became overdue.

As no SAR (Search and Rescue) facilities exist in the Arabian Sea area in question, no wreckage or bodies have been found.

On that same night Iraqi Military Air Traffic, with a coded instruction of 'Nineveh Confirmed', waited in vain for a military jet (Iraqi call sign: 'Babylon Six') to report crossing their border a little way south-east of Badrah. Even so (and on direct orders from Baghdad) they extended the jet's border-crossing ETA window by thirty minutes.

After that time all military commanders in the area resumed normal operational readiness.

The second fax that Yuri Alexsandr Becker sent from Moscow on that fateful Friday night went to an agent of the Dnepre Pipe Company in Diyarbakir, Eastern Turkey. (The agent was another of Sasha's cousins.) The agent contacted a group of young men (via cell phone) who were waiting near the Turkish border. That night they crossed into Iraq not far from Iraq's most northern town – Zakho – following the River Tigris south. The young men travelled only by night, manhandling a 300-kilogram cargo along stretches of barely navigable river on a small carbon-fibre raft. Their final destination was on the outskirts of Mosul on the east bank of the Tigris: the ancient city of Nineveh. At this place is a long-forgotten tunnel that passes under the Shamash gate (so named after an Assyrian god, as were each of the other fourteen original gates to Nineveh) just beyond the Al-Shamal bus garage. The tunnel is a top-secret military storage facility.

Iraqi commandos at the end of the Gulf War established the route down the Tigris to a city that was the centre of the civilized world seven hundred years before the birth of Christ.

On the fourth day of November, Maria Espinosa received written confirmation that one million dollars was being held for her in a numbered account at a small private bank, Bordier et Cie, in Geneva. (Along with that notification were three sealed and addressed envelopes with detailed mailing instructions. She also received a handwritten note from John Winter, written weeks earlier – she called it a love letter. In a stumbling, soldierly way, perhaps it was.) The written confirmation came from a Liechtenstein attorney administering the estate of William Durack. The same attorney also placed half a million dollars in a Trust for the family of Red Stevens, as well as making a transfer of $950,000 to Sergei Grishin – a man who had once been the Director of the nuclear plant in Tbilisi. John Winter's cousin, Sasha – the owner of the Dnepre Pipe Company whose head office was in Dnepre-petrovsk, Ukraine – received $500,000. The ferry pilots, Camille 'Cam' Frenette and Harry 'Hod' Priest, were each paid $25,000 plus expenses (which was about five times the going rate for the job).

The balance of the Durack estate is held in Trust and makes small interest payments periodically to the widows and orphans of the soldiers who fought alongside John Winter in past years.

Maria Espinosa gave up flying after receiving her inheritance. This coincided with the discovery that she was pregnant with John Winter's child. She now owns a house (her first) called Papillon du Rouge in Saint Lucia, where she has taken up painting in oils. She travelled to La Paz, Bolivia, in early December and took early morning coffee (and cheese pastries) at the Café Le Paz on the corner of Ayacucho and Camacho. A pilgrimage of sorts (Winter had told her about it in his letter). A glimpse of what might have been. A place where they should have grown old together. Before she left the city-above-the-clouds she mailed the three envelopes – John Winter's final instruction.

*She has decided that if the baby is a girl she will
name it Caravelle. If it is a boy – John Sibelius.*

No one ever knew about the untimely death of Yuri
Alexsandr Becker, aka Yuri the Yid and briefly Ronald
Melvin, New Zealand national, outside Sheremetyevo
II Airport, Moscow.

*His $15 million still sits in a numbered account in a
private bank in Zurich. Accruing interest.*

One week after their departure from Bien Hoa, Colonel
Vin and his nephew arrived in Paris. They were met
by the colonel's wife. The following day all three left
in a chartered Falcon-20 jet from Le Bourget airport.
The plane dropped them off at Biarritz, where a
chauffeur-driven Mercedes S600 was waiting.

*The black Mercedes with heavily tinted windows
was last seen heading south towards Spain.*

The Ilyushin-38 never made it to the air museum at
Coventry. It still sits at Karachi International Airport,
waiting for a replacement engine. The authorities have
been unable to contact the owner – William Durack –
concerning the unpaid parking fees, which are
mounting daily.

*It is likely that the aircraft will be seized and sold off
at public auction.*

TC is back at his home on La Brea (the Hollywood
Hills end), Los Angeles, with his brother. He never
mentions what really happened on his one and only
visit to South-East Asia.

The fading cuts and bruises were passed off as the result of a mugging in Ho Chi Minh City.

Meanwhile, Tanner Williams and Edeyrn Owens had slipped quietly back into retirement. This followed the opening of the 'dummy fuel tank' in Vietnam two days after the F-4 Phantom had departed – the earliest date that technicians equipped with safety clothing and Geiger counters, among other things, could be flown in by the US Naval Air Force Pacific [NAVAIRPAC] from NAS Atsugi, Japan – and the discovery that it was loaded with lead ballast. It was on the fourteenth of December that Williams and Owens received identical Christmas cards showing Claude Monet's *The Magpie*. The message, at odds with the subject of the picture, was brief:

Who really won?

It was signed 'Sibelius'. The postmark: La Paz, Bolivia. Williams and Owens passed their suspicions to their former bosses at the CIA and the SIS:
That the 300-kilogram consignment of Uranium-235 could now be considered to be in Iraq.

Two days later – December the sixteenth – the American President William Jefferson Clinton, supported by the British Prime Minister Tony Blair, renewed the air war against Iraq. The operation was code-named *Desert Fox*.
The four-day bombing campaign did little to resolve the matter of Iraq's banning of UN Weapons Inspectors (UNSCOM).

Saigon Express

*

Timothy Jaggers was one of the few at Century House who advocated handing over the dummy fuel tank to the American Embassy in Ho Chi Minh City. Giving them all the glory, as it were. Once again, his judgement proved flawless.

He never mentioned that he had been merely acknowledging one of Edeyrn Owens's 'gut feelings' – that Winter might be a frightening chess player.

The last envelope that Maria mailed from the high-altitude city of La Paz went to Richard Richardson – a political reporter on the staff of the *Washington Post.* In his early days Richardson had been a stringer for the *New York Times* in Central America, and was known to be something of an authority on Panama's geography and its political and banking legislation – which was, after all, the key to the country's growth as a peekaboo financial centre. Richardson immediately began investigating allegations (as indicated by the contents of the letter) that the American CIA was somehow involved in a clandestine operation to *supply* weapons of mass destruction to Iraq. Central to his enquiries was information concerning a multi-million-dollar payment made by Iraq to a Panamanian company known as 'Seventh Symphony Limited'. The opening enquiries made by Richardson to his Panamanian contacts were quite fruitful. Seventh Symphony Limited had been wound up days earlier and its substantial holdings (cash) transferred to Nassau and a new account at the Ainsworth-Thorne Merchant Bank.

That the bank is known in certain (informed)

quarters to be a proprietary front/working partner of the CIA makes further investigations very difficult. But not impossible.

The chain reaction continues . . .

POCKET
B O O K S

Also by
John Templeton Smith

WHITE LIE

In their renewed battle with the Colombian cocaine
cartels, South American Covert Operations - 'black ops'
wing of the CIA - try one desperate plan. The
northwards flurry of snow – part of a $100 million a
year black economy – is now settling in the Midwest
rather than Florida. They need someone inside the
network to report, then close it down.
Someone tough and dispensable.

A mercenary like John Winter...

But natural born killers aren't as easily duped. Death
beckons them for years, but somehow they keep
slipping the noose. Somehow they keep coming back.
A little older and wiser - and every bit as lethal.

It is the CIA's decision to send John Winter back to
Colombia. But what he's about to do there could be
beyond anybody's control...

PRICE £6.99
ISBN 0 671 01603 2